BEYOND BOUNDARIES

BY BELA KAUL

Copyright © Bela Kaul 2017

All rights including copyrights and rights of translation etc. reserved and vested exclusively with the author. No part of this publication may be reproduced or transmitted in any form or by any means, electronic, mechanical, photocopying, recording or otherwise, or stored in any retrieval system of any nature without the written permission of the author and publisher.

Author: Bela Kaul
Email: bkaulmn@hotmail.com
website: https://belakaul.wordpress.com
Title: Beyond Boundaries
ebook ISBN: 978-0-9988688-2-0
Paperback ISBN: 978-0-9988688-0-6
Category: Literary Fiction

Publisher: Bela Kaul
Cover Design: Shefali Kaul

LIMITS OF LIABILITY / DISCLAIMER OF WARRANTY: The author and publisher of this book have used their best efforts in preparing this material. The author and publisher make no representation or warranties with respect to the accuracy, applicability or completeness of the contents. They disclaim any warranties (expressed or implied), or merchantability for any particular purpose. The author and publisher shall in no event be held liable for any loss or other damages, including but not limited to special, incidental, consequential, or other damages. The information presented in this publication is compiled from sources believed to be accurate, however, the publisher assumes no responsibility for errors or omissions. The information in this publication is not intended to replace or substitute professional advice. The author and publisher specifically disclaim any liability, loss, or risk that is incurred as a consequence, directly or indirectly, of the use and application of any of the contents of this work.

QUOTE

In all cultures, the family imprints its members with selfhood. Human experience of identity has two elements; a sense of belonging and a sense of being separate. The laboratory in which these ingredients are mixed and dispensed is the family, the matrix of identity.

By
(Salvador Minuchin (20th century), U.S. child psychiatrist, family therapist. Families and Family Therapy, ch. 3 (1974).)

ACKNOWLEDGMENTS

This journey began at the turn of the century when my grandmother, Janki Devi Khanna passed away. Unable to accept this ending of such a grand lady, I decided to bring her back to life. In her fictional form, she has been a living, breathing person, always by my side. Thank you, Ammaji for the substance of your legacy.

Before Janki's legacy could take the shape of a full-length story, my father-in-law, Mohan Kishen Kaul planted the seed, and remained a consistent supporter throughout the writing process, providing constant encouragement. Understanding the region, the people, and their history could not have been possible without long conversations with my father, Vijay Khanna. Through anecdotes, family stories, nostalgic memories, I travelled to the era, smelled the flowers of the landscape, and tasted the fruits of the region that is Baluchistan. My humble gratitude to both my Papas.

The writing process could not have progressed without the intelligent advice from Swati Kaushal, a fabulous writer and a true friend. My deep gratitude to Daniel Slager of Milkweed Publishing for his invaluable guidance and taking time out from his very busy schedule to help me in my efforts in the literary arena. Thank you, my literary friends.

Humble appreciation to my friends Jamshaid Hassan, Sahba Shere, Nargis Saber, Karilyn Jons and Karyn Spaeth for the painful readings of early drafts and useful insights. At different stages of the writing process, I subjected various family members and friends to listen to excerpts of the story. Among them were my mother - Sarla Khanna, my brother and sister-in-law, Rohit and Chetna Khanna and my friend, Abha Bhow. Thanks for listening and helping me think out loud. Thanks to Ragini Bhow for her depth, creative inputs and making time to help with the cover design.

The most frequent victims to my earliest draft readings were my husband, Sanjay Kaul and daughter, Shefali Kaul. As a family, we shed tears with my characters, laughed with them and travelled together to lands beyond our boundaries. Their patience, guidance, support and candid feedback have been invaluable.

I thank all my friends and family for their encouragement and believing in me. And finally, my gratitude to Janki Devi Khanna and all the amazing women in my family, of generations past and those who carry the torch of fortitude forward.

This is a work of fiction inspired by real events from Janki's life

PROLOGUE

A mouse peeps its head out of a hole, looking up and down the deserted alley. Sensing no danger, it scurries off in its hunt for food. Suddenly, a large shadow appears on the wall by the garbage cans. Within moments a black cat pounces, crushing the mouse to pieces. A squeak and the street is silent once again. A haze of smoke blankets the sky. From afar, sounds of mock disdain travel with cries of agony.

The year is 1949. The place is Quetta in the newly created Islamic nation of Pakistan. A young Hindu man walks down an alley, his dark eyes gleaming beneath bushy eyebrows. Thin straight lips tucked under a thick moustache show themselves when he curves them to form soft whistles. His face masked by a thick dark beard under majestically protruding nose and small ears, that turn toward the sounds of mobs. Disturbed he lengthens his stride but confident that the turbulent junta will not advance to this part of town, he slows down. He has a mission. He must see his childhood friends and wish them well before moving to the land of opportunity - America.

Here, he knows he is among friends. He grew up with these men, running in and out of their homes. The strife between

Hindus and Muslims has moved to the outer skirts of the city. Rajendra is happy contemplating the turn of events and envisioning his future. Just before the creation of Pakistan, his family had to abandon their construction business in Quetta as they fled to Kandhar, Afghanistan. There, Rajendra toiled with his father on an American project building the Kandhar airport. Rajendra's American bosses complimented him on his skills and offered him a scholarship for an engineering degree in the U.S.A. First-born of a family of 12 children, Rajendra was the gift his parents worked hard to receive. His mother, Janki, endured fasts, walks on pilgrimages, and the discomfort of necklaces and rings she wore as talismans. Rajendra's father, Ram Lal never missed a quiet moment to be with his eldest son. His parents had high aspirations for him.

Rajendra realizes that not only can their struggle to survive end, but dreams of a comfortable life can now be achieved. Rajendra's entry into U.S.A can open doors for his siblings and his father can retire at last. He will take care of his family so his mother can stop worrying about the children's future.

Rajendra snaps out of his thoughts as he hears footsteps at the far end of the alley. He sees a silhouette of a stout young man walking toward him. *Could he be a fundamentalist scouting the alleys for victims?* Rajendra dismisses the thought, takes a deep breath and keeps his pace. As the man gets closer, Rajendra recognizes him. He is Ali, Halif's brother. Halif had been with the family for as long as Rajendra could remember. He had managed their construction business in Quetta during its flourishing days and now, after the partition, he took care of their abandoned house.

Rajendra stops. He starts to say something to Ali but hears footsteps behind him. Before he can turn, he feels a blow to his head and falls over. He stands up and swings his arms blindly in the darkness. There is a scuffle, he sees something shiny, and before he can react a dagger jabs into his belly, below his ribs. The last thing Rajendra remembers is the vicious look in his slayer's eyes. The street is silent once again.

Several hours later, Rajendra opens his eyes to see a pool of blood all around him. He feels weak and knows he has only moments before his life will end. The alley is once again deserted. Rajendra tries to visualize his bright future in America but only blurred images of his family's sad faces appear. He takes his last breath, calling out "Amma... Bauji, sorry I could not make it to America...."

BELA KAUL

CHAPTER 1

1986

Taara hopped off the long, yellow bus onto the icy path skidding toward the white stucco rambler to its 2-car garage. Above its red brick façade, the red, white, and blue fluttered in the icy wind, waving to empty sidewalks. A dead leaf rolled out of the open garage, ready to brave the elements. A patch of black ice silently waited, hoping to send unsuspecting passerby on a whirlwind skating spree and then down with a thud.

Taara jumped off the path, her boots sinking into the 2-feet of snow packed on the lawns, ice crunching under her determined steps, engulfing her feet into a deep hole. She trudged forward leaving perfect foot prints behind, her backpack slung uncomfortably over her down jacket, her mittens hung dolefully from its sleeves.

She ran in through the garage, stomped her boots at the doorstep, and burst into the mud room. She threw her jacket on the floor of the tiny room, struggled with the wet boots as she tried to keep the outdoors from being dragged in. Jumping over the puddle of melted snow, she ran in to find her mother.

The aroma of basmati rice, frying onions, cumin and lentil greeted her and the pressure cooker whistled her in. Blinding rays glared at her from the south window, she blinked, saw her mother's silhouetted profile and moved to a warm, sun-bathed spot behind the breakfast counter, where she dropped her backpack and stood watching her mother's back.

Dimple stood in front of the gas stove, ladle in hand, her thick shoulder-length hair neatly pulled together with a black clip as always to rest at the nape of her neck. An orange and green *kurti* shirt peeked from beneath the *pashmina* she had draped over her shoulders. Her long legs appeared longer in the straight fit blue denims, with two gold bangles jingling on her wrist as she stirred the onion and tomato mixture. She leaned into the pan to test the aroma of her spices, inhaling through her button nose. Her dark eyes blinked from the steam and she pulled back, guiding a dark runaway strand neatly behind her small ear. Satisfied with the smell and texture of her creation, she turned off the stove, put the lid on the pan, and turned around. Noticing Taara standing quietly, she smiled and walked toward her daughter.

Taara stood in the center of a flood of sunlight as if on stage under a spotlight. Tiny apples danced on her favorite turtle-neck, petite, red, fuzzy feet peeked from underneath the navy-blue snow pants. Dimple attempted to help her out of the thick pants, but Taara took a step back and shook her head, two high pony tails swaying over her dark head.

Taara stepped out of the heavy pants on her own, and stood rooted in her blue jeans. Voices from MPR invaded her space while the exhaust fan over the stove blared, sucking spicy aromas out into the neighborhood.

With chocolate chip cookies and a cup of warm milk on the breakfast counter, Taara sat on the high stool, legs dangling as she enjoyed dipping, chomping, licking and sipping.

The doorbell chimed. Taara dashed out the kitchen, sporting a milk moustache and half-eaten cookie in hand, "Abby!"

Dimple helped Taara with the door.

Beyond Boundaries

As the girls got ready to go outside, Jenny, Abby's mom followed Dimple.

"I'll put the water on for tea." Dimple told Jenny, then turning to Taara, she instructed, "Make sure you have your mittens and hat on. If you need help with the snowsuit and boots, come get me."

Jenny walked in to the family room and settled at the large, pistachio green couch. She watched the girls waddle off to the back yard. Dimple joined her with a bowl of cashews and hot samosas to accompany their tea.

"Can you believe the amount of snow we got this last storm?" Jenny said.

"I don't know how you all do it...driving in this weather." Dimple replied as she walked back to the kitchen.

"It's not that bad." Jenny followed her.

Dimple crushed two cardamom pods, grated some ginger and added them to the boiling water. Jenny watched over her shoulder, as she had done every week for the past year. Dimple added loose black tea leaves and let the blackish water dance and splatter into a vigorous rolling boil. The final touch of sugar and whole milk, a quick boil, and the tea was ready. The two women sat on the sofa sipping their tea, and caught up on the neighborhood gossip.

Outside in the winter wonderland, Taara and Abby tried to decide what to do with repeated 'What ifs'.

"What if we make a huge mountain out of the snow?" Taara suggested, her eyes opening as big as the mountain she was envisioning.

"We already have so many mountains, silly!" Abby pointed to the neighborhood yards with piled up snow. "What if we dig tunnels through them?"

Excitedly the two dived into the laborious task that would only last a few minutes.

"This is too much work." Abby was the first one to admit.

"What if we make a fort? We can hide in it when those boys next door try to catch us."

Tired of this new endeavor, the two settled on a game to look for buried treasure under piles of fresh snow. After not finding anything exciting, they decided to play avalanche by submerging themselves in the white stuff.

A light flurry began to fall, and a delicate flake landed softly on Taara's nose. She stuck out her tongue, tried to lick the cool softness only to feel it vanish into a droplet. She looked up to the sky, jaws opened wide to welcome each unique flake into the confines of her mouth. Her eyes opened to marvel at the wonder of snow falling from so far above her, only to close her eyes again blinking away the wet, fluffy miracle. A voice floated into her dreamland from far beyond.

"Taara *beta*, come on in now. It's too cold for you to be out there so long." Taara's mother always called her in too quickly.

"Uhhhh...! Mummmmie! Just one more minute."

A few minutes later, Taara and Abby walked in through the sliding door from the deck, sniffling and chattering.

Dimple, huddled up in her *pashmina* shawl by the door, was not happy, "Taara, look at your mittens, they are soaking wet. Everything is drenched, no wonder your fingers are so cold. Give me the wet clothes, you too Abby, I'll put them in the dryer. Now go sit by the fireplace."

"Sorry mummy." Taara scowled, but soon her eyes lit up, "It was so cool though. I buried Abby in the snow and then I rescued her. She did the same to me as if we were in an avalanche. We had so much fun. We even found a twig and used Abby's scarf to make a flag to put on the avalanche."

Dimple frowned, "That can be dangerous. Don't play that game again. Now, do you two want some hot chocolate?"

Taara and Abby nodded in quick succession as they made their way to the mudroom. Later they brought their mugs to where their mothers sat by the fireplace. Jenny sat on the edge of the sofa, her back straight. Taara observed her friend's mother. Her face reminded Taara of her princess Barbie. Her short blond hair was stiff and curly. Abby had the same blond curls, but hers were bouncy and soft. Taara took a gulp of her hot chocolate and sat up to listen to the mothers talk.

"So, is that lady still dumping garbage in your yard?" Jenny asked.

"Not this past week." Dimple responded.

"What do you think her problem is? Could it be drugs or maybe…" Jenny leaned closer, "she's a closet drinker."

"She's probably just lonely. She needs love in her life." Dimple stated.

Abby and Taara giggled.

"Who would marry such a crazy woman?" Jenny ignored the girls.

Dimple spoke softly, "Everyone has someone made for them. They just need to find each other, sometimes with help."

"So how did you find Raman?"

Taara's ears perked at her father's name. She ignored Abby's playful pinching.

"I didn't. My grandmother did." Dimple looked down.

"What do you mean?" Jenny's green eyes widened.

"Arranged marriage."

Taara forgot about the now cold chocolate and leaned forward. Abby excused herself to go to the bathroom as her mother was asking Dimple, "You mean you didn't date?" Jenny turned her body to face Dimple, bending one knee to rest on the sofa while her other leg dangled.

"Well, we met once before we agreed to marry." Dimple replied.

Jenny stared at her friend in awe as she swallowed the sweet, creamy tea, and burned her tongue. Flabbergasted, she blurted, "Weren't you scared moving all the way from India to Minnesota with a stranger? Where exactly is your family from?"

Taara raised her hand and blurted, as if in a classroom. "I know, I know. They're from D…Dehra Dun. It's a valley, in the Himalayas." She finished proudly.

"Really?" Jenny then turned to Dimple. "How did you feel

about moving so far?"

"I adapted."

The women didn't notice Taara and Abby as they slipped away to play in the basement.

Dimple got up to refill their empty mugs.

Jenny followed her, "So how does this arrangement work?"

They returned to the sofa. Dimple reached for a samosa and before biting into its spicy filling, she said, "Oh, it's simple."

Jenny sat down slowly, her tea cup in hand. She spoke tentatively, "You must miss your family."

"Very much. Especially my grandmother."

"And your parents?" Jenny suggested.

Dimple slowly shook her head, her gaze fixed on the table.

Jenny sat back and took a sip.

Dimple blinked and softly spoke, "My sister, Ruhi lives in California now, but I missed her the most when I first moved here."

Jenny put a hand on her friend's shoulder and gave it a gentle squeeze. Dimple smiled at her friend and quickly got up to clear away the table.

After Jenny and Abby left, Taara sat on the family room area rug. Head bent over her sketch pad, pencil in hand, tongue twisted out to the side of her mouth, she drew lines, erased, and redrew. Glow from the fireplace cast shadows around her.

Dimple sat on the sofa and stared into the fire. Her thoughts traveled to her valley, the place of her birth, her home of 18 years. Ammaji sat her down one afternoon. An old friend, Kalavati from Kandhar days, was coming for tea with her nephew. She had brought him up like her son as he was orphaned at a young age. Ammaji picked out Dimple's emerald green *salwar kameez* shirt pant with white thread embroidery. A chiffon *chunni* scarf was draped shoulder to shoulder over her breasts. Balancing a tea tray, she walked into the drawing room, her eye lids lowered, her steps measured. Kalavati invited her to sit next to her on the wicker sofa.

Dimple felt his presence in the wicker chair adjacent to her.

From the corner of her eyes, between stolen glances, she noticed his thick, dark hair and bushy eyebrows over intense eyes. He sat with a polite smile pasted under a full moustache, and listened to the old women reminiscence. She poured *elaichi* cardamom tea which he quietly sipped. She offered *pista* biscuits and he took one from the plate as he looked into her eyes and thanked her. She could feel his gaze follow her as she moved to the other side of the table to offer the biscuits to Ammaji and her friend. Dimple took her cup, found her seat and sipped the fragrant, creamy tea. The chatter of the older women continued as a background chorus to the melody in her head. She stole a glance in his direction from the corner of her eyes, but his look held her there, and she felt hypnotized.

Ammaji and Kalavati slipped out of the room taking their musical refrain with them. Her grandfather's clock ticked away loudly from its place on the corner table, each staccato note at a time. He cleared his throat and leaned forward, empty cup in hand. She reached for the teapot but he held up a hand and placed his cup onto the table.

He cleared his throat again and said, "What does religion mean to you?"

Teapot still in hand she set it back with a louder thud than she had intended. She sat back at the edge of her seat, kept her back straight and placed her hands on her lap. Keeping her gaze on her hands, she spoke softly, "Family."

From the corner of her eyes she saw a smile appear on his face. She looked up and noticed a biscuit crumb on the dark hairs of his moustache. She smiled with him and had the urge to reach out and brush the crumb away.

"Mummy."

Dimple slowly traveled back to her cozy home in the Minnesotan suburbs, her gaze fixed on the flames in the fireplace.

"Mummy." Taara repeated.

"Hmmm...?" Dimple said dreamily, a smile pasted on her lips.

"What are those flowers called?" Taara pointed with her pencil.

Dimple looked toward the sun-bathed corner of their family dining room. The glass of the sliding double doors welcomed the warm rays inside leaving the snowy chill outside. A large pot sat by the window balancing a trellis. Ivy of green leaves crept over and around it. This tropical plant had rooted itself firmly into the new soil. It flourished and even bloomed in the winter, flaunting its heart shaped purplish flowers with a hidden tiny white flower within. "Bougainvillea." She told her daughter and went back to staring into the fire.

CHAPTER 2

1913

Jeevani put one tiny foot after another, carefully, deliberately, pointing her big toe. She balanced a *diya* clay lamp on the palm of her right hand, shielding its flame with the cup of her other hand as her steps made the air around her move. The pink chiffon *chunni* scarf over her shoulders fanned the row of flames on the ground. Dark pink reflected from her new silk *salwar kameez* pant shirt onto her round cheeks, making them appear blushed. She reached the doorway and slowly bent down to place the *diya* by the entrance. The cotton wick in it floated in the greasy fuel, its tail sinking and absorbing life for the flame. Its head peered out of the pointy corner of the round *diya*, holding the flame high and spread out wide like a cobra's head. She had spent the morning with her mother making the wicks together as they plucked pieces from fluffy cotton balls, rolled them between the heels of their palms until they had a thin strand 2-3 inches long.

Jeevani stood up and threw her long, dark pigtails with matching pink ribbons, back away from the flickering flames.

Nibbling a strand of loose hair, she stood at the entrance and admired her handy work. Two rows of light guided her path into the house illuminated with several *diyas*. She walked slowly down the bright path while tiny bells in her silver anklets jingled. Her steps picked up speed, running through the *angan* courtyard toward the tiny room in the corner of the house. Her nose had brought her toward the sweet aromas of syrupy *jalebis* and *gulab jamuns*.

She called out in her powerful voice, "Amma."

Her mother stepped out of the kitchen, one hand laced with sticky, yellow dough, another clutching a sieved ladle. "Don't come into the kitchen. Your new clothes will get oil stains."

Jeevani noticed oil spots around her mother's round belly on her cotton *kameez* shirt, "Amma, I want some *mithai*." She demanded.

"Not until Laxmi *puja* prayer."

"But I already placed the *diyas* so Laxmi will find her way into our house."

Amma walked back into the kitchen to continue her frying.

Twirling her pigtails, Jeevani stood in the *angan* courtyard. Sounds of fireworks reached her ears and she called out to her mother again, "Amma, can I go out to light the *patake* with my friends?"

"After the *puja*. Go call your father." Her mother commanded.

Jeevani turned and skipped toward the far end of the house. She opened the door of the small room and found her father in the corner at his desk. A beam of light snuck in from a small window into the otherwise dark room, landing on the chair where her father sat. As she expected, he was bent over his large ledger, making sense of the numbers *muneemji* accountant had entered. He was dressed in his new starched white *salwar kameez* with the embroidered, sleeveless jacket over it.

"Bauji, Amma is calling for the *puja*." She announced.

Her father looked up and extended his arm to motion her to come in. Wrapping his arm around her shoulders, he smiled and kissed her forehead. His thick moustache tickled her delicate skin and she suppressed a giggle. He patted her and said, "I'll be right out, *puttar* son."

Jeevani walked back to the kitchen and found her mother gone. She noticed the silver *thali* plate on the table outside the kitchen. It contained a handful of uncooked rice grains, few saffron strands mixed in with the red vermillion powder, a few silver coins, red and orange thread strings, some cashews and pistachios and almonds. There was also a white blob next to a match stick. Next to the plate sat a silver, baby glass half-full with milk. Just as she was about to bring a finger to prod on the white blob, her mother stepped out of the large room that was their bedroom, and hurried toward the *thali*. She had changed into her new, peacock blue silk *salwar kameez* with matching chiffon *chunni* scarf. She motioned Jeevani toward the *puja* room, next to the kitchen.

As she sat in the puja room eyeing the sweets and the nuts in the *thali*, Amma motioned her to hold her palms together in a steeple, close to her heart. Bauji remained focused on the mantras he was reciting while his hands performed the rituals to honor Laxmi, the goddess of wealth. Jeevani watched him light a match and set the white blob to fire from which dark smoke rose up toward the ceiling. Her eyes followed its twirling path above them until she felt Amma nudging her back to the ground. Bauji mixed the rice grains with the vermillion and saffron strands, added some milk to it and with his finger applied it on the goddess's statue. After he made a *swastika* in the plate with the same mixture, he then applied it on Amma's and her forehead. Jeevani's forehead felt sticky and as her hand was reaching to touch the red dot with orange saffron strands and white rice grains, her mother shot her a warning glare. Bauji then took the red and orange thread rolled up in a ball, tore off a string and tied it as a bracelet to her left wrist, repeating the process for Amma. After the ritualistic offering to the goddess, her parents allowed her to sample the sweets and nuts as they gave her their blessings.

By next week, the household fell back into routine. Bauji left early for the bazaar to meet other traders after the Diwali festivities, while Amma's list of chores remained never ending. If she was not pickling mangoes or removing pebbles from rice or *daal*, she was cooking meals or frying snacks. Then there was the knitting in the winters or sewing and mending all year round. Jeevani did not escape from these lists and as she turned eight her mother assigned her even more tasks.

One clear day, as the sun started its journey toward the western sky, Jeevani spiraled down the steps into the verandah. Twirling her long pigtails, she called out to her mother, "Amma, I finished sweeping the *angan* courtyard and even took down the clothes from the line and folded them. Can I go out to play now?"

Her mother looked up from her needlework, "Make sure you are back soon. The groom's family will be here by sunset to see you."

Jeevani walked out of the gate of her *mohalla* neighborhood. *What did Amma mean by groom?* Jeevani dismissed the thought and skipped off to her friend Sakhi in the next *mohalla*. She looked at the thick rails and the large padlock that came together every night as protection from *dacoits* robbers. Her walk took her through fields on the slim muddy path that divided the plots. As if on a beam, she extended her hands outward like a bird in flight and balanced her way through. She reached an opening and stood on solid ground, flat as all the land around her. Hands still extended she moved first in circles then twirled faster. She went round and round until the blue sky above her spun, the luscious earth around her whirled and she fell to the ground dizzy. The tickle in her tummy gurgled out into free-spirit laughter. Sitting on the edge of the empty field, Jeevani surveyed the landscape around her, watching the golden wheat sway for miles. She observed a family of mice scurrying about in the green fields of mustard and carrots, and noticed a group of farmers walking toward the shade of a tree. They sat next to each other with their legs folded under them, knees bent and palms facing up. Every so often, their bodies moved forward and their foreheads touched the ground. Jeevani listened to the gushing sound of the Jhelum River not far from the fields. Its sweet water gave the town its name, *Khushab* and made the soil all around her rich and its vegetables juicy.

Skipping away, her pigtails bobbing, Jeevani reached Sakhi's neighborhood. She made a quick stop at the community well of her friend's *mohalla*, having forgotten to stop at the one in her own. Jeevani's stop was not for the sweet nourishing water of the well, but a rose from the underbrush surrounding each well. Its syrupy aroma welcomed her as she bent to pick one that would adorn her hair, just like she had seen her mother wear on special occasions.

She remembered the colorful garland Amma had bought on their trip to the bazaar the previous day for the *puja* room and her eyes lit up at the recollection of all the beautiful wares. Empty baskets in hand ready to fill with exotic goods from lands faraway, they marched every week to the bazaar where traders competed at the top of their lungs. Jeevani's favorite stop was the trinket shop with its colorful ornaments. She loved the glass bangles displayed colorfully as arcs of a rainbow, she always ran her hand through the display of hanging anklets to hear the sound of the tiny bells and their chhumm chhumm in unison under her touch. Amma always stopped at the cloth shop looking for yards of material in cotton, silk, or chiffon. She also bought vibrant beads and gold or silver threads. Amma was always working on sewing projects – clothes, tablecloths, bed covers and would stitch, embroider, or string beads for hours. Jeevani had seen Amma nicely pack away each completed project wrapped in a muslin cloth. When Jeevani had asked why she was not using these beautifully tailored clothes and linen, Amma had replied, "These are for your trousseau. When your groom will come for you, then you can have them all."

Groom. Jeevani ran to Sakhi's house trying to run away from the imaginary character that kept following her. She wanted to forget about what waited her at home and play her favorite game of *staapu* hopscotch. Jeevani waited patiently at Sakhi's doorstep while the other eight-year old finished her chores. Jeevani made a face as she waited - if it was not the cleaning or the laundry, the girls had to bring the coals down from storage and light the *angithi* stove for the evening meals. Then there was mealtime when she usually rolled out the *rotis* as Amma served while Bauji ate. Jeevani knew she was luckier since her family could afford to buy coal. Most girls had to collect cow dung, cake them to dry in the sun so their parents could use them for fuel. Jeevani also felt fortunate that her father would sit with her every night, teaching her to read and write, unlike most girls her age.

Bauji never missed their special time together. They sat every night by the light of an oil lamp reading or sharing tales. He told her stories of cities beyond their borders. He showed her maps pointing out where she lived and what was around her. She loved to hear about the tribesmen he met on his journeys where he traded treasures of Khushab. He brought back yarns of silk and other beautiful goods in exchange for juicy vegetables or coal.

Amma was happiest on those days, wrapping the soft shiny material around her, humming a lively tune. She spent days, cutting, threading, or sewing. She hugged Jeevani frequently, staring at her, straightening her hair, running her hand over her cheek, but sometimes Jeevani noticed a hint of dampness in her mother's eyes. Amma always pretended nothing was wrong when asked, blinking her eyes in rapid movements.

"Ow!" Jeevani watched Sakhi trip over the threshold crying out in pain.

"Are you okay?" Jeevani jumped to grab her friend from falling over.

"I...I think I hurt my ankle."

"Why did you do that? Now we can't play *staapu*."

"I didn't mean to." Sakhi hopped while grabbing onto the bad ankle.

"Can you walk?" Jeevani asked.

"I think so." Sakhi replied uncertainly.

Just as they were trying to decide on a game, Simran and Shirin joined them. Simran suggested *gitte* so they all set about looking for stones for the game of jacks. The four girls sat down and started their game, taking turns by throwing one stone in the air, picking one of the four from the floor in time to catch the one they had thrown. The game progressed with picking the stones on the floor two at a time, then three, and so on until somebody did not catch the stone in time. Then the next girl got a turn.

Shirin caught the stones in her expert, but calloused hands. Wheat harvesting was around the corner and the other girls would be seeing less of Shirin in the coming months, even less than they saw her during *Ramzaan*. The other girls shared their excitement over the beautiful wares their trader fathers had brought back from their latest journeys after the Diwali festivities. All the girls chatted in the same *Punjabi* dialect about events of the day, their neighbors, and the boys from the neighborhood who played rowdy games like *pitthu* and *gulli dunda*. Sakhi complained that her brother was not asked to do as many chores as she was, *"It's to teach you so you will impress your in-laws."* Sakhi imitated her mother. Then she asked, "Who are in-laws, anyway?"

Jeevani snuck in quickly, "What is a groom?"

Simrin looked up and said, "My parents had always called that man who took my sister away, 'the groom'." She thought about her 11-year old sister who had moved to her husband's house after the *bidai* sendoff, "Why do you ask Jeevani?"

Jeevani's face fell. She dropped her stones and ran back to her house.

Amma looked up from her needlework, "What happened? Why are you crying?"

Jeevani barged into the room she shared with her parents and sat on the bed. *Amma* tiptoed in and sat beside her only child. She stroked her hair, running her hand all the way down to the tip of her ribboned braid. "The groom's family will be here soon." She said, "go wash up. I'll help you with your hair after you have the *suit* on." Jeevani sat there unmoving, listening to her mother rattling away nervously, "now remember greet the elders with respect in a clear voice. *Namaste*! Like this." Her mother put her palms together in a steeple in front of her chest and bent a little to demonstrate. "Keep your eyes lowered and your head covered. Are you listening?"

Jeevani nodded numbly.

Amma got up from the bed and kneeled down on the floor in front of her daughter. She cupped Jeevani's face in her soft but labored hands and looked right into her eyes. "Jeevani, today is a very important day. If the groom's family likes you, they will promise their son for you. It is a matter of our family honor. Do you understand?"

Jeevani saw a flicker of tears in *Amma's* eyes but her face was stern. "*Amma*, is the groom a man who will take me away?"

Amma gave in to her tears, "All girls are guests in their parents' home. Until the lucky boy who will be your groom comes to take you away, you will be on loan to us."

"Why *Amma*?"

"That's how it is." Amma threw her hands in the air and continued, "We are all bound by our duties. My duty is to teach you all the household chores so you can make a good wife and daughter-in-law. Bauji has to earn enough for your dowry and you, my dear have to uphold the family honor."

"What do you mean family honor, Amma?" Jeevani asked.

"It's like this *beti*." Amma sat back on the bed beside her daughter, "A woman is a vessel." She looked at her daughter's innocent face and continued, "It is a woman who holds the family together with her compassion, love, and most of all her strength."

Jeevani shook her head and said, "But what does that have to do with me?"

Her mother sighed and holding her daughter's young hands she explained, "When you get married, you need to do your duties."

"But *Amma*, I don't want to live with some strange boy and his family." Jeevani stuck her lower lip out and whimpered, "I don't want to leave you and *Bauji*."

"Girls cannot stay with their parents. It's not their destiny." Amma said without meeting Jeevani's eyes.

"But…I want to live with you and bauji forever and ever…." Tears started to gush down her cheeks.

Amma held her close, gently rocking her back and forth until, a voice sliced into their private moment through the small window facing the *angan* courtyard. "Jeevani's mother, where are you? The guests will be here soon."

Amma stood up quickly, "There's *Bauji*." She cleared her throat and called out in a shrill voice, "I'll be right out." She dabbed Jeevani's eyes, wiping off the stains from her cheeks, "Now go, wash up and wear your beautiful new *salwar kameez*." With a swift squeeze she left Jeevani and made her way to the kitchen.

Later, all adorned in her finest clothes, Jeevani sat alone in her parents' room. She fingered the red threads of the embroidered flower on the bedspread she sat on, while gazing into the beam of light that radiated down from the *roshan daan* egress. She stared at the dust particles performing their erratic dance and wondered if this new family would let her go to Sakhi's *mohalla* or play with her friends. Behind the sun beam, deep in the shadow, Jeevani spotted her crocheted rag doll, old and dirty, forgotten in the corner. She stared at it wanting to go pick it up, hug it, but she was afraid. She kept her gaze fixed at the abandoned toy, feeling tears well in the corners of her eyes. Blinking and letting them trickle down her soft round cheeks, she looked away, out toward the *angan*.

Through the small window, Jeevani heard the main door open. She listened to the tip tap of a walking stick, exchange of greetings, loud and rambunctious laughter from the men and muted *namastes* of the women. She heard the creek of the *manji* bed as the rope from its ends stretched under somebody's weight. Jeevani could make out the dragging of the extra *mooddas* to add seating for the unexpected number of visitors. She thought she heard a child's laughter and footsteps close to her room, but was not sure. Curious to get a glimpse, she walked over to the window and saw only adults assembled in the center of their courtyard.

Before she could observe the visitors, *Amma* walked over toward her room and called for her to come out. Jeevani noticed the beam on her mother's face and wished her Amma smiled more often. Staggering her steps, Jeevani approached the group. She could feel the sharp stares from everyone, piercing through her covered head and face, absorbing her every move. Her chiffon *chunni* could not veil her blushing cheeks and the pained expression. Despite her angst, Jeevani's stomach rumbled when she caught a whiff of the *pakoras* fritters Amma had fried. Her mother indicated the spot on the *manji* for her to sit, directing her to keep those eyes lowered to the ground in modesty and Jeevani obliged respectfully.

The adults talked in a formal manner with *Amma* listing out all the skills Jeevani possessed, "*Pahji*, our Jeevani is very docile, and has never given us a reason to be upset with her. She can handle any task without hesitation. We are very proud of her."

Jeevani's father smiled and shifted in his seat. Jeevani could see him wiggling his big toe impatiently as he always did during *Amma's* long discourses. She recognized the familiar smile, which appeared when he was embarrassed by his wife's hyperboles. As for her, she squirmed in her uncomfortable, silky garb, feeling an itch in her ankle, but unable to bend down to scratch it. She blushed with her mother's stories, wanting to show these guests her true self by pulling up the *salwar* pants to her knees, leaving her legs bare and running off to her friends to play.

Amma continued, "My Jeevani has even mastered the art of straight and purl and can make scarves and blankets all by herself with fine wool. I have taught her to embroider and her *rotis*, why they are even better than mine. Don't you think so, *Ji*?" *Amma* stopped for *Bauji* to respond.

He complied. "Yes, definitely, she makes very good round *rotis*."

One of the elders sitting next to Jeevani brushed his hand on her head in blessing. Jeevani stole some glances through the veil of her *chunni*, careful not to stare. Later she learned that he was Wazir Chand Khatri, the groom's father. The elderly man was a stoic, formidable figure with large eyes and a long mustache. He wore a

Kula cap with pride wrapped in a long cotton turban, the end of which hung over his left shoulder. He also boasted a finely carved cane under his palm even in his seated position. Jeevani was a little frightened until she saw the woman sitting next to him. She immediately took a liking to the petite woman with a kind face and later learned that she was Ameerni Devi, the groom's mother.

A middle-aged woman in a white saree had also accompanied the party. Jeevani found herself looking into the big, sad eyes of a lanky woman with slouched shoulders. Her dark hair contrasted the fair complexion and the white saree. Later Jeevani would hear of the misfortune of this young widow, destined to depend on her parents and brother forever. Here in Jeevani's parents' home, the young woman in the white garb flashed a big smile and walked over to Jeevani to give her a hug. "I'm proud to have such a beautiful and talented girl marry my brother. What do you think *Amma*?"

Ameerni Devi walked over and cupped Jeevani's chin in her hand. Tilting her chin slightly, Jeevani looked into soft, black eyes. Without moving her gaze, the older woman said, "Yes, she is beautiful. But I can't have both my daughters named Jeevani." Ameerni Devi wrapped an intricately woven shawl around Jeevani, spreading it over her shoulders as she said, "For my Ram, you will be his Janki."

CHAPTER 3

1986

The evening was bright with a full moon, an expanse of stars sparkling above the snow- covered roof. Their light bounced off the whiteness of the ground illuminating the chilly Minnesotan neighborhood. Inside the house, Taara sat in the center of the large, soft green sofa, nestled between her parents. They shared a long, woolen shawl embroidered with orange and green threads. The soft glow of the fireplace reflected in the tiny mirrors embroidered into the shawl.

The sitting room was the perfect size for the Gupta family. On either side of the sofa sat a matching love seat and an ottoman engulfing an oak coffee table in the center. Mango yellow walls displayed traditional Indian art captured in muted earth tones. The wall above the mantle boasted the face of a village woman from Central India. A saffron saree covered her head, dark silver *jhumkas* dangled from her ears with kohl outlining her eyes, searching, lingering, as if suspended in time and place. A dark shade of terracotta surrounded the border of the print.

Soft rhythms of mountain music echoed through the room,

with *sarod* strings infused with *tabla* beats reverberating in the background. Orange and red hues from the fire and the painting above the mantle fell onto Taara's face, making her glow as she huddled close to her father listening to stories of India. She rested her head on his ample chest as she watched the rise and fall of his potbelly. He was like an immense teddy bear, soft and perfect for a little girl to cuddle in the folds. Raman had just finished with one of the many adventures of young Lord Krishna, affectionately called Kaanha in the village. Behind closed eyelids, Taara pictured the open fields of Gokul where the cowherd Krishna lured the young maidens with the sound of his flute.

Before her mother could announce bedtime, Taara begged for another story. She stuck her legs out of the shawl and climbed onto her father's lap, watching the familiar round face of her father as he unraveled the wrath of mythological characters, like Ravan, from the famous epic Ramayan.

"Ram rescued Sita from the demon king, Ravan, and brought her back to his kingdom. Everybody welcomed them with lights and fireworks and shared sweets." Raman stroked Taara's soft black hair and concluded. "That day is celebrated every year as Diwali."

"In *Bal Vidhya* we learned that Sita had another name. Why did she have two names, Papa?"

"Janki, just like your mummy's *dadi*." Raman replied.

"Yes, and Ammaji's husband's name was also Ram." Dimple answered.

"Are they also prince and princess, like in the Ramayan? That would be so cool to have royal great-grandparents." Taara giggled.

"Sorry to disappoint you *beta*, no royal blood here. But our stock is no less than any nobility." Dimple spoke with pride, "Now off to bed. You better get your sleep if you want to go to the mall tomorrow after *Bal Vidhya*."

"Why do we have to go to Hindu school every Sunday?" Taara protested.

"To learn about your country and religion." Raman declared.

"Nobody else at my school has to so why should I?" Taara demanded.

"They go to their Sunday school or Church. Now off to bed," he commanded.

"But Papa...."

"Stop stalling."

Taara let out a big yawn, "But I'm not tired."

Raman carried Taara to her room. She snuggled into his warm chest and was asleep before they reached her bedroom.

Raman returned to the family room just as Dimple was setting down the tray. She removed the quilted tea cozy from the teapot and poured her special ginger and cardamom tea into two cups, as she had done every night for ten years, no matter how late Raman returned from the restaurant. Husband and wife sipped their late-night tea leisurely.

"What are you working on?" Raman asked as he pointed to a notebook Dimple had set aside. He had seen her immersed in it all evening, filling out pages with her tiny handwriting.

Dimple set her teacup down and picked up the book. She ran a hand over it feeling its smooth cover and admiring its shimmering saffron silken finish. Intricate cashew shapes embroidered in yellow thread added texture to the front. She opened it to see the familiar words carefully composed by her, "I've started writing about Ammaji."

"What kind of things?" Raman put an arm around his wife and pulled her delicate form closer to his generous frame. With his free hand he took the notebook. Opening it to a page, he asked, "May I?"

She nodded.

January 2nd, 1986

Her greatest gift, the Pashmina shawl I always keep close to me, keeps me close to Ammaji. On the days I miss her most, I disappear in its warm threads. The soft threads made from hairs of a goat of special breeding, of higher land, of hardy nature. The fabric is plain in appearance, even dull, the color of mud. A one-inch border of muted red, green, and yellow embroidery revolves around its edges. This simple cloth may not be much to look at but on many a cold nights it has warmed me. On the long, lonely evenings when my thoughts wander back to my home in the valley with Ammaji, my Pashmina has given me healing comfort. The smells it carries - hint of faraway lands, of spices foreign to this land of lakes, an aroma of Ammaji's youth and a reminder of my time there and here.

Raman took a sip of his tea, notebook still in one hand. He leaned back on the sofa without a word, took a final gulp of the tea, put the cup back on the tray and tugged the string that marked the last written page.

Dimple's eyes cast down.

Raman read aloud.

March 25th, 1986

Today I learned that she might have glaucoma. Her eyesight is getting weaker. One day she might lose it completely. Is that what a journey, such as Ammaji's, climaxes to? Darkness? She carried the torch for us all. She's been our guiding light all her life. And now, in the twilight of her years, she has darkness to look forward to. Life is just not fair.

Raman put down the book and turned to his wife, "Why didn't you tell me you miss her so much?"

Dimple's gaze remained low, her fingers tugging at the corners of her *kurti* shirt, rolling and unrolling it. Her moist eyes looked up and she said, "I know it's not easy to make the trip. You know, the cost, your crazy schedule and Taara's school. Besides, I've kept in touch with her through letters." She attempted a smile, "It was hard when phone calls became difficult, with her hearing and all." She took a deep breath in and looked down again, "And now, she won't even be able to read my letters."

"You must go to her." Raman stood up and rolled up his sleeves. "Go for the whole summer, while Taara's school is out." He suggested.

Dimple smiled between her quiet sniffles. Then, with a wrinkle between her eyebrows, asked, "What about you? You can't get away from the restaurant for so long."

"I'll join you when I can get away, even if it's for a week or so." Raman assured his wife.

"But...can we afford it?" Dimple stammered.

"We'll be fine." He smiled.

Dimple beamed and fell in his arms, "Oh, thank you!"

The next morning started early. Dressed in traditional clothes, all three bolted out to arrive at the Washington Middle School cafeteria 10 minutes late. They had missed the announcements but made it for the singing of the *Shlokas* verses. Children of all ages were lined up horizontally facing the podium, holding their palms together. A 17-year old led the group into the first prayer, his eyes closed, head bent, and palms flat pressing into each other close to his heart. Parents surrounded the periphery in equal immersion, moving their lips audibly to each mantra.

Taara stood in one corner of the children's group dressed in her green and yellow *ghaghra*. The cotton skirt flowed full-length to her feet while the *choli* shirt hung loosely over her thin body. A matching *chunni* scarf rested over her left shoulder, carefully pinned to the shirt. She interlaced her fingers and held her joined hands under her chin. Head bent, eyes tightly shut she moved her lips with the rhythm of the room. A minute into the prayer, she opened one eye and scanned the room. She saw Mehek's dark thick curls matted down her back, its intense smell of coconut oil wafting toward Taara. Wrinkling her nose, she noticed her father on the side in deep meditation. Words poured out like rose petals from each movement of his lips as he submitted to the prayer. She could not see her mother without risking turning her head. All the women were grouped in the back chanting melodically in unison. Taara felt an itch in her ankle and bent down to attack it and the bells in her *payal* anklet jingled as she moved her foot. Her father gave her a stern look and she quickly went back to praying position with eyes tight shut.

After Hindu school, the Gupta family headed out to the mall to find some jeans for Taara. With a tiny waist and long legs, finding the right pair was always a challenge. Raman patiently browsed through rows of slim fits while Dimple did double duty between the dressing room and Raman's finds. After much searching, Taara was finally satisfied with a pair of dark blue denims with an elastic pull carefully hidden in the waistline. Success shining on their faces, all three headed off toward the food-court.

Taara walked dreamily, eyeing the stuffed animals in a shop window. She continued walking without paying any attention. At the corner of a shop window she spotted a dancing doll. She had seen one just like it in Abby's house. *It would be so cool if we both had the same doll,* she thought. Without taking her eyes off the doll, Taara called out, "Mummy."

She looked around and saw people everywhere, but there was no sign of her parents. She called out again, "Mummy, Papa." A sea of faces swam past her but none of them seemed familiar. Tears began to roll down her cheeks. She sniffled and wiped her nose with the end of her jacket sleeve. She walked around aimlessly. All around her she saw long legs in skirts and pants ignorant of her existence. She focused toward the center of the mall and watched the house getting set up for the Easter Bunny. Suddenly she became scared of the Easter Bunny. He seemed to be growing ten heads like Ravan, the demon who kidnapped Sita in the Ramayan stories her father told her. Taara ran to the other corner of the mall hiding behind a pillar. The crowd seemed to be getting bigger and bigger, and Taara kept falling deeper into it. She tried to block out all the noises, the voices of the people, the music from the stores, the buzz from the espresso machine nearby. She felt like an ant, crushed under a swarm of giant feet. She tried to disappear, to become invisible. Another sound came to torment her, she ignored it, covering up her ears. The voice came again, louder.

"Taara."

She looked up and saw her mother's ashen face, the familiar *pashmina* shawl draped around her narrow shoulders. Taara ran up to hug her and burst into tears, "Mummy, I don't like so many people."

Dimple knelt down. She looked into Taara's shining eyes.

"Don't be scared *beta*. Mummy and Papa will always be with you."

"Promise?" sobbed Taara.

Raman picked up Taara and set her on his wide shoulders, "We promise to never leave you alone." He led his two girls toward the blended smells of fries and cinnamon rolls. A large red-haired clown with bright yellow clothes smiled at them from the food court.

CHAPTER 4

1916

Jeevani was alone. She sat in her bridal corner shedding silent tears under a long veil. She whimpered, "Amma... Bauji..." her body shaking against the rocking motion of the noisy train. A buzz of festivity surrounded her. Women old and young of the wedding party sat huddled on seats or luggage, their bodies swaying in rhythm. Their voices rose in unison above the train's whistle with lyrics of traditional folk songs. Beats from the *duphlie* drummed as the sole accompaniment to the singing.

Under the veil, tears strolled down Jeevani's cheeks. Behind closed eyelids, she saw *Amma* at the doorstep, anguish clearly painted on her face, and *Bauji* standing next to her without expression, his entire body leaning against the door for support. This last image of her parents is what Jeevani carried with her for the journey to her new home in Quetta, after the fleeting three years of her engagement. Between sobs she inhaled the clean and fresh desert air wafting in from the open windows. Sensing a hint of an aromatic breeze she looked out into the wild landscape catching glimpses of red and yellow tulips. Leaning back in her seat, she sighed as the train chugged up to the plateau leaving her flat land behind. It snaked through rough terrain toward the three craggy mountains that loomed over the gracious city of Quetta. All the mountains formed a ring around it like a *Kuwatta* protecting the valley city as a fort.

Jeevani wondered what this new home would be like for her. *Bauji* had set her down weeks before the wedding. Sitting on her usual seat of honor, her father's lap, Jeevani had listened.

"*Puttar,* your new home is the capital of Balochistan. See here on this map," he traced his finger across the spreadout sheet, "this province spreads out into Afghanistan and Iran."

"O ma! It's so big. I'll get lost there." She exclaimed.

Her father smiled as the map sat sprawled on his large desk in front of them. He pointed to a spot on it, "Look here, this is the Bolan Pass. In spring, after all the snow has melted away, visitors of different tribes herd their sheep and goats and come into Quetta through here. To them there is no Afghanistan or India or Iran, just one big Balochi Land."

Jeevani leaned over to take a closer look.

Bauji continued, "These tribal people don't live in one place. When the Pass is clear and safe, they trudge through the mountains. It is very rugged there and these nomads carry handicrafts to trade like mirror-work embroidery, carpets…"

"Does Quetta have bazaars? Like the one we do here?" Jeevani jumped in with excitement.

"Just as colorful as we do, but they are more fun in spring." Her father responded.

"What happens in winter?" Jeevani asked.

Her father looked up with a faraway gaze, "Beautiful. Those copper red and russet rocks, the crests of the mountains powdered with snow. I can never forget such a charming city." A shadow then crossed his face, "I also remember very well becoming stuck there for days after a blizzard."

Jeevani shivered in her seat and huddled close to Bauji to rest her head on his chest. She could hear the slow thump of his heart beneath the white cotton shirt.

"Jeevani, dinner time," Amma called out from the kitchen. Jeevani tore away from her father's story-time to help with dinner preparation. She had to learn to make good food for her new family. Amma advised her on the regional delicacies of Quetta made from sheep and goats.

"Amma, what are we making today?" Jeevani skipped in.

"*Kababs* and tomorrow will be *mutton pulao*."

"Yum, I love *Kababs*." Jeevani licked her lips.

"Your mother-in-law will teach you the more ethnic dishes," Amma assured.

"What are those?" Jeevani asked.

"*Sajji* is the leg of lamb and *landhi* is a whole lamb dried preserved for those long winters." Amma explained.

"Amma, why can't you come with me to Quetta? I like to learn from you."

Hugging her daughter, she said, "Ameerni will make a good teacher and mother."

Back in her corner in the slow-moving train, Jeevani sniffled. Holding back tears, she realized that *Amma* and *Bauji* will not be with her for guidance. She will have to quench her thirst for knowledge from someone else. Jeevani aspired to understand the local culture and was intrigued by the tribal people. She later came to realize that she was not alone in this fascination. It was the arrival of these tribes from enigmatic lands that made the city dwellers endure anything Mother Nature had in store. The imminent scorching temperatures, the icy chills of the winter or even major disasters like strong earthquakes were forgotten in spring. The season was a time to welcome the visitors, the blooms, the delicacies, and other items from lands beyond the boundaries. It was a festive time.

Jeevani for now was less cheerful than the season and was unable to appreciate the beauty outside. She tried to absorb her new land through the long veil of her red silk *chunni* laden with gold *zari* border. The gold jewelry adorned her person with a collar necklace, and a long *kundan* set hanging down to her chest. Thick gold bangles covered her wrists, silver anklets and toe rings shone from her feet, and a small gold and ruby *tikka* hung down her forehead matching the dot on her nose ring. She felt the burden, the gold weighing her down as much as the heaviness she felt in her heart. She had left the only home and family she had ever known. She missed her parents.

Jeevani recalled the countless shopping trips to the bazaar over the three years of her engagement. They were not as much fun since she could not play with her friends anymore and Amma made her try on countless outfits. Her parents' room shone with all the gold, clothes laden with *zari* or sequins, laid out for the grooms' family for viewing before the wedding.

Over the waiting years the two families met often as her new family lived only a few *mohallas* down. During their visits Jeevani was sent indoors, but she tried to peek through the small window of her parents' room. It was usually the two women – the mother, Ameerni Devi and the sister in the white garb, the other Jeevani. Amma filled them on their future daughter-in-law's progress plugging the gaps with exaggerations. Little Jeevani hoped the groom would visit too, but he never did. She did, however, hear the women talk about him sometimes. She learned that he had left Khushab to study in Rawalpindi. In another meeting she heard that he was planning to move to Quetta to join his cousin in the construction business and the whole family was moving with him.

Jeevani, in her lonely corner of the train, recalled seeing this groom only once. It was the previous day at the wedding ceremony, and that too with his face covered in garlands and hers veiled by the *chunni*. He was a tall boy and when she heard him speak to his parents, he sounded like a man.

Jeevani's new home had a lot more people than she was used to. It was a joint family of her husband, his parents, and his widowed sister. A cousin and his family of three children also lived with them. Jeevani had overheard Amma inquiring about this cousin.

Amma sat crossed legged on the *manji* bed one late afternoon unraveling yarn. She rolled the wool into a neat ball while Jeevani held the yarn between her hands sitting beside her.

Biba, the town crier waddled in as the sun was hanging low overhead. Grabbing the *mooda*, she forced her large behind onto the small seat.

"Biba, just the woman I wanted to see." Amma cried.

"So glad to be welcomed." She looked at Jeevani, "So grown up."

Amma leaned forward and asked, "Who is this cousin at Jeevani's in-laws'?"

"Who knows what the truth is?" Biba dismissed at first.

Amma continued with her wool rolling, as a faint smile formed on her face. She had planted the seed and everyone knew Biba wouldn't stay quiet for long.

Jeevani had watched the game of words and silence over her stretched hands as the yarn slowly unraveled around fingers.

"I heard..." Biba's voice dropped conspiratorially.

Jeevani leaned closer on the *manji* bed trying not to look too interested.

"This cousin was orphaned as an infant. Ameerni fed him her own milk."

Amma gasped, "How is that possible? Was she flowing?"

"Your son-in-law was a month old. This infant was three months." Biba shared.

"*Hai rabba.*" Amma stopped rolling. "So where is he now?"

"Quetta. Some uncle from his mother's side took him when he was ten."

Amma slowly nodded, "So that's why the family is moving to Quetta." She looked at Jeevani and ran a hand on her head, "Taking my daughter far away from me."

As the train rocked her body back and forth, Jeevani recalled Amma's face from that afternoon. She remembered the wrinkles around those sad eyes, the crooked frown from a curve in one corner of her mouth and specks of white in the thick dark hair.

Renewed tears started their journey. Jeevani suddenly realized that she never learned the cousin's name, and will have to call him *Pahji*, elder brother. Relaxing back, she recalled her husband's name that she had learned at the wedding ceremony. Her mother had reminded her of the age-old custom of never letting his name escape her lips – Ram Lal. She also understood now the reason for her own new name. Ram was the name of the legendary warrior king who had defeated the powerful Ravan for abducting his wife, Sita, in the great epic, Ramayan. Jeevani remembered now that Ram's wife was also called Janaki.

According to tradition, her mother had explained that a woman starts a new life when she gets married. It was natural for Ram Lal's wife to be named Janaki but somewhere in the *Punjabi* dialect, an 'a' dropped off. Jeevani Kapur became Janki Khatri. In her corner in the train, Jeevani realized that not only was she losing her home, her town, her family and friends, she also had to lose the one thing she had that was her own – her name. Her new life had to start from a clean slate.

The train screeched to a tired halt after a laborious trek through the mountains. It pulled into Quetta station with a sigh and a shudder. An explosion of movement erupted around her. Women searched for their luggage or called for the *coolie* to lug the baggage out. At some point a voice called out to Jeevani. She stood up and, partially blinded by the veil, tried to keep up with her escort.

Out on the platform Jeevani found herself standing next to the tall man who was the groom. Her head ached from all the crying, the weight she carried in gold and the commotion around her. She did not even try to look at his face. Just as her mother had drilled into her, Jeevani kept her head lowered without making a sound. Back at the house another ceremony awaited the new bride. It was past midnight by the time each visitor had seen the bride's face and paid the bride viewing price, as was custom.

Finally, the time came for Janki, no longer Jeevani, to meet her husband. She was left alone in a room decorated with flowers where she sat in the middle of the bed. Her mother had tried to explain about this moment, her voice echoing in Janki's ears, *sit quietly with your head covered keeping the* chunni *hanging down low enough to cover your face. Keep your head bent and fix your gaze on to your feet. Act reticent and humble.*

Janki suddenly felt a cool breeze, even though it was stifling hot in the room under her heavy adornments. Ram Lal entered the room without a sound, closing the door behind him. Janki's heart skipped a beat as she heard him walk toward her. The bed creaked under his weight when he sat down on the edge. Janki could not stop shaking. Ram Lal put a hand on her shoulder to steady her and articulated his first words. His voice was kind. "There's nothing to be afraid of. I am your husband now and I will take care of you."

Janki did not move but relaxed a little. Ram Lal moved up closer and gently lifted the veil to see her face.

"Beautiful. Just like my sister said you were."

Janki kept her gaze focused down as he stroked her hand lightly with his forefinger. She slowly raised her eyelids and for the first time looked at her husband. His geometric features with a square face, a large triangular nose, and a flat chin gave him a stern look. The thick, dark mustache extending out to his cheeks added nobility while the large, round eyes below his bushy eyebrows could be scary to a little girl. He was a grown man, in his twenties, at least ten years older than her. Janki was shocked at first, but then remembering his kind voice and gentle manner, she relaxed. She took comfort in the warmth of his eyes and the easy smile to match the gentle voice.

When the initial shock of discovering her husband's presumed age wore off, Janki smiled in her timid way. Ram Lal smiled back and continued to stare at her. He was admiring this fair-skinned, shy girl who had just become his wife. He admired her perfect round face with pronounced rotund cheeks and timid, genuine smile. White, even teeth shone between thick, shapely lips for a fleeting moment until his hand moved from her slight chin to her arm and further down. He noted the ampleness of the face did not reflect the slenderness of her undeveloped figure. He admired the way her big brown eyes looked at him with the curiosity of a child and quickly looking down as if remembering her manners. She was so young and innocent and so beautiful.

He helped her shed the heavy, golden load from her person, carefully wrapping the jewelry in a cloth. Still wearing their silken garb, he held her. His touch was gentle but curious and the sensation she felt was unlike any other. He combed his fingers through the length of her hair, tickling the back of her neck, sparking a giggle out of her. At this he left her and turned out the light. In the dark, he gently pulled her down on the bed next to him. With his strong arms encircled around her, she felt safe. Her heavy eyelids could stay open no longer and Janki fell into a peaceful slumber.

CHAPTER 5

1916

The morning sun seeped through the window grille, forming intricate patterns on the bed. Janki opened her tired eyes and found herself staring at fiery brightness splashed onto the ceiling. A crochet of golden patterns laced intricately against the whitewash, as if interconnecting several hearts. She studied the knitted ceiling but when she moved her hand the pattern dispersed. Realizing it was the reflection of her gold bracelet of tiny hearts that had remained on her wrist from the previous night, she played with it and watched the reflected designs change. A dog barked on the street outside the window, bringing her back to the empty room.

She turned to her side and remembered that she had not been alone the night before. Then she heard the sound of water from the bathroom and quickly sat up. She was not sure what was expected of her so she made the bed, dusting off the garlands that had been used to decorate the bridal chamber. Ram Lal appeared with a towel around his waist, showered and shaved. Janki dropped her eyes to the ground, muttered a response to his greeting and ran into the solace of the bathroom, her face pomegranate red. Ram

Lal grinned and moved on with his morning routine of praying and getting ready for the day.

When the couple was ready, they made their way to his parents' bedroom. Janki wore her new, pink silk *salwar kameez* with silver *zari* in its borders. Her hands and feet still boasted the intricate patterns from the henna that had been applied two days before the wedding. Her hair parting shone with red *sindhur* powder freshly applied on top of the vermilion her husband had put in her hair at the wedding ceremony. She also wore the black-gold *mangal sutr* placed around her neck by her husband at the ceremony. Janki would display these two symbols of a bride along with bangles around her delicate wrists for as long as her husband would be alive.

In the parents' bedroom, she covered her head with the *chunni* and the newlyweds touched each parent's feet for their blessings. Ameerni Devi kissed Janki on the forehead and reached for a bundle of keys from under her pillow. She unlocked a drawer in her wardrobe and took out a red pouch. From the pouch, she removed a heavy gold choker with matching earrings and ring and motioned Janki to put them on. From the same pouch, she removed a long necklace, also of gold but this one was heavily laden with precious stones. Janki's eyes shone with excitement and glittered from the precious jewels.

From the same wardrobe, Ameerni Devi brought out a soft, light material with delicately embroidered patterns around its borders. She unfolded the warm fabric and spread it over her daughter-in-law's shoulders. Janki disappeared in its cocoon absorbing the wooly aroma, and in its simplicity and the dull shade, she found a home. The modest but austere fabric of the *pashmina* shawl became her second skin. It healed her, comforted her, shielded her and even would love her through generations.

Later that morning Ram Lal's sister, Jeevani, formally introduced Janki to the wedding guests still camped in the Khatri household. Jeevani directed Janki to touch all the elders' feet and to sit with them while they touched her head in blessing. The guests then proceeded to feel her silken clothes and closely examined her new jewelry. Janki shriveled under their touch feeling as if under attack by an octopus. She sent a desperate look toward Jeevani, tears welling in her eyes. Her sister-in-law stood up and invited all the guests to the dining hall, giving Janki her escape from the liberal clutches.

Janki slowly followed the group and tried to determine what was expected of her. She saw all the men and the elders lined against the walls with plates in front of them. They sat on the floor on thin mattresses covered in white sheets. Round pillows sat in corners or behind them for support. She observed her sister-in-law and quickly fell into step with her serving breakfast, just as she had done in her own home. But this was her own home now and she had to train herself not to think otherwise. What she left behind was her *maika,* her mother's home.

Over the days, as the wedding guests trickled out and the household approached some normalcy, Janki's role began to fall into place. She shadowed her sister-in-law, Jeevani, only eight years her senior, and observed how the Khatri household ran. The chores here were no different from what she was used to in her *maika,* but her mother wasn't here to assign her the easier tasks. The clothes were washed just as she was used to, and beaten with a bat in the cold water, but her mother's gentle touch was not here afterward to warm her shivering hands in the winter. She was used to hauling the coal from the storage room to prepare the *angithi* stove, but her father wasn't here to help with the heavy load.

Jeevani and Ameerni were kind to her and did their fair share of the never-ending work, but they were not her mother. Janki was also used to a smaller family while the Khatri household had many, including little children. The cousin's wife, bed-ridden with an unknown disease, was not able to take care of her children or do any chores. Although Janki missed skipping out to play with her friends in the *mohalla,* she was able find an excuse to play with the cousin's three children who, in turn, welcomed her attention.

Winter arrived with passion and Janki saw her first snow fall.

Enveloped in her warm *pashmina* shawl she stared up into the sky to watch the flakes fall and tried to catch a few on her tongue. It was a sensation as unfamiliar to her as this new land that was her home. It was as sweet as the kind eyes of her husband but as unpleasant as the pain of separation from her parents. Many snowflakes melted in her mouth over several winters and she absorbed them all with a smile.

Tired from the day's labor Janki retired into her room late one evening. Ram Lal had returned from a trip to Afghanistan just across the border. He had been working on a project in Kandhar and was gone several weeks every month. Janki waited anxiously for his returns and looked forward to listening to the stories he brought back from the foreign land. She asked him to bring books, newspapers and pictures from his excursions, which she absorbed hungrily while he was gone. He patiently showed her the routes and sites on a map and enjoyed having a listening ear for his frustrating moments of the construction sites.

He prepared for bed as he related his adventure of the day. She sat on their bed, eyes wide open even though her body ached from lifting the heavy coal. At some point her thoughts traveled to her father and the stories he used to share of his travels. Her head dropped and a scowl appeared on her face as she realized that she hadn't seen her parents for two years. She wrote to them regularly and got all the news of home from her father but…

"What's wrong? Ram Lal asked

Janki sat, solemn-faced, sniffling.

Ram Lal sat next to her on the bed, tucked a finger under her chin and tilted her face up to look into her damp eyes. He put an arm around her and pulled her close to him. "What is upsetting you?" He asked.

"When can I see Amma and Bauji?" The tear sitting on the edge of her eye gave in and slid down her cheek.

He wiped the tear off and said, "As soon as this project is done, I'll take you."

Her eyes lit up, "Promise?" She looked up at him cheerfully.

He nodded. Nestling her in his arms, he spoke softly in her ear, "Your Amma….did she tell you what it means to be husband and wife?"

She replied, "A wife needs to take care of her husband by meeting all his needs."

"What are his needs?" he teased.

"Make sure clean and well-ironed clothes are ready when he comes out of his bath, prepare good food and know all his favorite dishes. Also have fresh flowers ready for his *puja*…"

Ram Lal threw his head back and laughed.

Janki looked up perplexed.

He squeezed her shoulder and spoke in a soft tone. "You are special."

For several months Ram Lal educated his 13 year old bride in the matters of the bedroom. While he was a gentle and a patient teacher, she in turn was a good student. She felt safe and at home with him. The only other happy moments of the day were when she spent time with the cousin's children.

The cousin's first wife had passed away soon after Janki's arrival and it had not taken long for the cousin to acquire a new wife. Within the year of their marriage, this second wife gave birth to a bubbly little girl. Janki transformed from a playmate to the caregiver of the first wife's children.

One afternoon, Ameerni sat with her daughter, Jeevani, in the courtyard, sieving pebbles from rice and lentils. Janki sat at the bottom of the stairs that lead to the terrace, singing while feeding the cousin's children.

Ameerni leaned over to her daughter and whispered. "Janki is 14 now but no child yet."

"She's still young Amma, don't worry," Jeevani replied.

Before Amma could respond, Janki walked toward them and stood in front of them, her face filled with fear.

"Amma…" She changed her mind and turned to Jeevani, "*Didi*, sister… I think I'm going to die," she whimpered.

The two women abandoned the grains they were cleaning and

stood up together.

"What's wrong *puttar*?" Ameerni grabbed her daughter-in-law's arm.

"I have…I have…blood." She managed.

"Where? Did you hurt yourself?" Jeevani asked her sister-in-law.

Janki looked from one face to the other, "It's down there."

Ameerni gasped, "You were expecting and you didn't even tell us…and now you've lost…"

"Amma, calm down." Jeevani cut her off, turning to Janki she smiled, "Do you hurt?"

"A little."

Jeevani proceeded to diagnose. "Have you had blood there before?"

"Never." Janki responded quivering.

Jeevani put an arm around her and led her indoors while Ameerni stayed back, relieved. *There was nothing wrong with her daughter-in-law. How could she get pregnant if she did not even bleed yet?* She pondered.

Two more years went by and Janki and Ram Lal had no children. This time Ameerni was sure something was wrong with her daughter in-law. In her greed for grandchildren, she tried to convince Ram Lal to remarry.

"*Puttar*, you're the only son." Ameerni pressed.

"So what?" Ram Lal said.

"What about the Khatri name?"

"For that you suggest I discard her like a torn shirt?" Ram Lal glared at his mother.

"That's in her stars, just like it is to be barren," Ameerni explained.

"Chhee! How can you even suggest such a thing Amma?" Ram Lal marched out of the room.

Tears of relief rolled down Janki's cheeks as she stood still outside Ameerni's bedroom window out in the alley, having overheard the exchange between mother and son. Her trip to the neighbor's and the empty milk pitcher in her hand were forgotten. Janki recited every *shloka* and *mantra* she had ever learnt silently moving her lips to the rhythm. She prayed to have a child so her mother-in-law would be happy, she prayed for a child so her husband would be hers alone, she prayed for a son who would carry on the family name. Most of all she prayed to be a mother.

The cousin's new wife had already had two children adding to the three from the previous one. In addition to a fertile womb, this new wife also possessed a razorsharp tongue. Every word that came out of her bit like a knife cutting through flesh. Janki was the constant subject of it since she gave special attention to the cousin's first three children. Ameerni for her part subjected Janki to various *fakirs* and *gurus* who concocted unusual syrups for Janki to drink or blessed amulets for Janki to wear around her neck so she would bear fruit.

Oneday Ameerni approached Janki as she was sitting down to knead the dough for the evening meal, "Come with me."

Janki washed her hands, covered her head with the *chunni* and followed her mother-in-law. All the way down the street, she stole glances at Ameerni to guess what this mystery walk was about. Without a word, they moved on through the narrow alleys, turned corners, tripped over neighborhood children, jumped over gutters until, they arrived outside a big white house. The doorway was open and they walked into a large room. It was full of women seated on the floor around the perimeter on colorful, hand woven rugs. Nobody looked up as the two entered. Janki followed their gaze and noticed an ancient man seated on a raised platform with cushions and round pillows.

Ameerni directed Janki to an empty corner and whispered in her ear, "This guru will make our dreams come true. His blessing makes all wishes come true."

Janki nodded, "*Ji Maati*. Yes mother."

After an hour, their turn finally arrived. The two made their way to the center of the room and Ameerni poured out her grievance even before they sat down.

The ancient man turned his gaze over to Janki, his long white beard moving with him. He observed his subject intently and turned to his assistant, a beautiful young woman on his right.

He extended his hand to her and said, "*Annar.*"

Taking the large, ripe, pomegranate he turned to Janki, "*Beti*, the *annar* represents abundance. In its womb reside many jewels, may your womb be like this special fruit."

Whether it was the visit to the *guru* or the praying or that her body was ready, oneday Ameerni discovered Janki with her hand in the big yellow vat full of mango pickle. She beamed with pleasure and announced that Janki was finally expecting.

CHAPTER 6

1992

The long yellow bus ejected its passengers under the shade of vibrant foliage. The Maple and Ash proudly stood at attention on each lawn, to witness the parade of children. A kaleidoscope of leaves in crisp red, bright yellow and faded green showered down as if to welcome them home. Dry leaves cluttered the paths, offering a satisfying crunch under casual steps of dog-walkers or the swift stomp of an occasional jogger. A mosaic of fallen leaves blanketed entire lawns assorted in varying hues. Nudged by the cool breeze, the crisper leaves sprang to life. They danced in circles under the splash of golden rays.

Inside the kitchen, Dimple waited for the water to boil. As tiny bubbles started their journey up from the bottom of the pan, she added crushed cardamom to the water. She listened for the door slam, but none came. Turning off the stove, she walked to her teen's room and stood by the door.

The colorful wall faced her from behind the single bed. A mural of green fields ran all over it with speckles of yellow, purple, and white. Daisies, Taara had called them. A dark golden shape stood within the fields in one corner. My puppy, her daughter had proudly announced in her 8-year old voice. Raman had helped her climb up the ladder to draw a perfect circle with her pencil. She had stretched further to make squiggly rays emanating from the orb. Dimple had patiently watched from below, her hand on her heart. Later, finally on firm ground, Taara had directed the painting of her hand-picked bright orange, to stay within the line, in diagonal strokes back and forth. Raman had been a good student. He followed every command, delicately placing each brush stroke to make the rays bright and avoid any smudges. For the other three walls, Taara had picked the color of the sky. All three had painted them together. Taara took charge of the lower levels, Dimple fine-tuned and delicately handled the edges while Raman painted high up.

Mural in the background, Dimple now saw her teenager crouched on the edge of her bed. White clouds floated on the blue bedspread. A one-eyed white teddy sat up straight by the upright pillow, just as Dimple had placed it that morning while making the beds. She noticed the folded clothes in the laundry basket. Interrupted earlier by a phone call, she had forgotten to put them away. She moved toward them now but decided to sit next to her daughter instead.

Taara's body was slouched, her face bent down. A baseball cap covered her hair and cast a shadow over her face, her fists clenched, as if holding something in. Dimple ran her hand down Taara's spine and felt it stiffen. She reached out to her hands, to her closed fists and held them. Taara's grip loosened and a ball of white tissue peeked out. Dimple looked at it and noticed purple blotches. She looked toward her daughter's face, hidden under the cap, gently placed a hand under her chin, and moved it toward her. Traces of purple stained Taara's cheeks. Dimple's eyes widened and her forehead crinkled as Taara looked away.

Dimple reached for the cap and slowly pulled it off her daughter's head. Soft, dark hair unraveled down to her shoulders. But it was not her daughter's hair, with blond streaks emerging haphazardly. They were everywhere, crawling down, trying to escape as if even the golden strands knew they didn't belong on that head. Dimple stroked her daughter's hair, took a handful between her fingers grasping both colors. She stared at them unsure, then let go and stood up.

Her arms crossed in front of her, Dimple stood tall in front of Taara and demanded, "What's all this?"

"Nothing." Taara mumbled, her head bent down.

"Look at me." Dimple commanded.

Taara tilted her head up and unfolded her eye lids to meet her mother's glare. Familiar spicy aromas mingled with floral perfume reached Taara's nose. She saw her mother wrapped like a present in her *Pashmina*, arms crossed over it like a bow. Tiny yellow, green and red flowers bordered the dull colored shawl. She wanted to reach for it, and feel its soft threads. Instead, she kept her fists clenched, close to her seated body.

"Well?" Dimple tapped one foot up and down. "I'm waiting."

Taara focused her gaze at her mother's forehead, above the pencil thin eyebrows threaded to a shapely perfection, and replied, "I told you, it's nothing."

"Taara Gupta." Dimple's cheeks flared, "I demand an explanation."

"Mummy." Taara stood up to her mother's height. "Why're you making such a big deal? My friends and I were just having some fun."

Dimple reached out and held her daughter's hand. The two sat back down on the bed, facing each other. "Beta, what possessed you to mess up your hair like this and… and… these horrid colors on your face?"

"I didn't choose the colors," Taara shot back.

"Regardless."

"Mummy, you don't know what it's like."

"Why do you say that? I was 14 once," Dimple retorted.

"But…." Taara started as she looked at her mother's angry but kind face. Not a spot on her perfect skin, her glare still held a touch of the innocent twinkle that usually accompanied her dimples when she smiled. Taara looked away and finished, "Never mind."

But why, *beta?*" Dimple asked stroking her daughter's head.

"I... I... don't know." Taara whimpered throwing her head into Dimple's lap.

"Promise me you won't do something stupid like this again," Dimple demanded.

Taara nodded, her face buried in her mother's lap. In a muffled voice between sobs she lamented, "I wish Abby was still here."

"Yes, I know. But she is settled in Bangkok with Jenny and her new dad," Dimple stood up and said, "As soon as I finish up in the kitchen, I'll come help you wash that... thing off your hair."

Taara sat up and nodded absently. Her thoughts traveled back to the girls' bathroom at school. The giggling, the laughter, the fear. Taara had enjoyed the secrecy, the indulgence, even the transformation. After Emma and Grace had admired their handiwork and run off to meet up with some other friends, Taara had stuck around a while. She had noticed her reflection in the mirror and become scared by the stranger staring back at her.

The sound of the pressure cooker whistle brought Taara back to the problem at hand. *How was she going to explain this to Papa?* She went to her bathroom and started to wash her face, scrubbing hard to scrape off the mask the other girls had painted on her. The blond streaks in her hair, was another matter.

At the dinner table Taara sat with her head lowered, a baseball cap shading her from the world around. Even after ten shampoo washes, the blond highlights faded but did not go away. Dimple helped scrub and even applied coconut oil, but the golden color was too stubborn to disappear. From under the shade of her cap now, Taara looked at the palette of artistic display spread before them at the dining table. Dimple had added bright red peppers and shiny green beans with square chunks of pinkish red onions in the spicy yellow Thai curry. Mixed with fragrant jasmine rice, Taara enjoyed the tingling on her tongue as the exotic flavors melted in her mouth. She ate quietly, but hurried her bites to retreat to the privacy of her bedroom.

Thankfully, Raman was occupied with a magazine article that he read and then discussed at length with Dimple throughout the meal. Taara had no idea what the article was about but she heard words like "obesity", "fructose syrup", and "organic" fly around over the dinner table. Just when Taara stood up with her empty plate and asked permission to leave, Raman seemed to have noticed her. She had almost succeeded in trying to be invisible but the very thing she was using to shield herself is what brought his attention to her.

"What's with the cap?" He asked.

At first, she pretended not to hear him and continued to walk toward the sink. He repeated, louder. She took a deep breath and turned around. She gave a sideways glance to her mother.

Dimple said, "I put oil in her hair."

Raman looked at Taara again. She noticed his eyes narrow slightly, just for a fleeting moment, or perhaps she imagined it. But soon he smiled and returned to the food in front of him. Taara started for her room but her father called out again.

"After dinner I'll tell you a new story today."

Taara turned around and almost whispered, "That's okay Papa. I have lots of homework. Maybe another day."

"I'm leaving tomorrow for a week. I promise to keep it short."

Taara nodded and walked to her room.

In the family room later, Taara sat across from her parents in an armchair. She had kept the cap on and changed into her long pajamas. As a young child she used to love wearing shorts or half nighties to bed. Soon after she turned 12, her parents had put a stop to the short clothes. Her legs and shoulders needed to be covered. On the armchair she brought her knees to her chest and rested her chin on them, waiting for her father to begin.

Raman sat sprawled on the green couch next to Dimple in

one corner. He ceremoniously tweaked his bushy moustache, hand combing the hairs to perfect alignment. Clearing his throat, he began, "The greatest epic tale ever told, a literary masterpiece with ingenious characters is none other than the *Mahabharata*."

"Is that the one in the *Geeta*?" Taara asked.

Raman nodded and continued, "It's written in verse just like the Iliad and the Odyssey and is also a story of a great battle fought in ancient times."

Taara shifted in her seat, hugging her legs tighter.

"It was a battle between cousins - the five Pandav brothers, sons of Kunti, against Duryodhan and his followers. But my story today is not about these princes, but of a warrior as great as any prince who fought in that battle."

"Who's that, Papa?" Taara asked wide-eyed.

"The most dynamic and tragic character of all times – Karan. He was of divine birth, son of *Surya* solar deity and Kunti before she was married. He was brought up by foster parents of a lower cast, but grew up to be a great archer who could challenge Arjun, one of the Pandav brothers. Since he could not prove his true lineage, he was denied training in the art of fighting by the great gurus and was even insulted by the masters at various stages in his life."

"How did he become a great warrior then?"

"He learned and practiced with dedication but he studied the art through deceit. He lied about his lineage to a renowned guru and when discovered, he suffered the consequences. His teacher put a spell that when he most needed it, his learned art will fail him."

"How awful for him." Taara exclaimed.

Raman continued, "Carrying his newly learned skills and a curse from his guru, Karan went to the grounds where the Pandav brothers' skills were to be demonstrated in a tournament. He tried to take part in the royal challenge, but the Pandavs' *guru* objected that only princes can participate."

"Then what did he do?" Taara moved to the edge of her seat,

feet flat on the ground.

"Duryodhan, cousin and nemesis of the Pandavs, stepped in and offered Karan a hand of friendship along with a kingdom."

"Why?" Taara asked.

"Duryodhan knew that the Pandav brothers were strong and very skillful. While he himself was no less, he could use another mighty warrior by his side. To Karan this hand of friendship marked the direction of his years ahead." Raman stood up, crossed his hands behind his back, and paced as he continued, "Throughout his lifetime he had struggled between his allegiance to his friend and to follow his heart. His life became one tragedy after another."

Raman stopped his pacing and stood big and tall in front of Taara. He looked down as he spoke, "He knew the path he followed with his friends was not right, which his conscience continuously reminded him. He was constantly at war with himself."

"What happened to him?" Taara looked up at her father.

"He died in the great battle, the *Mahabharat*, fighting for the wrong side," Raman declared as he went back to sit on the sofa, "his skills and art failing him as he was cursed they would."

"Sad." Taara spoke softly leaning back.

Dimple added from her corner, "Yes, very tragic indeed. I remember when my grandmother used to tell me stories from the *Mahabharat*, I always felt sorry for Karan the most. He was unhappy all his life trying to find himself."

They sat silent lost in their own thoughts. Taara knew there was a purpose to this story. Her father's stories were always didactic but she was too afraid to ask this time. Instead, she tried to imagine the big battlefield with great warriors, armed with bows and arrows on their grand chariots. She tried to imagine an open field in India now and her thoughts went to Dehra Dun and the trip there last summer with her mother. The streets had become so crowded and busy. She thought of Ammaji, aging by the years, close to losing her eyesight, doomed to live in darkness for the rest of her days. She will never again see the flickering flames of the *diyas* lined up in a row at Diwali or the twinkling sparks of the sparklers Taara enjoyed twirling on her driveway every year. Taara could not imagine a life devoid of color or light.

Kissing her parents goodnight, she sauntered to her room to snuggle into her bed. Leaving her bedside light on, she slipped into a restless slumber tormented by arrows flying in open fields, a great warrior splitting into two and fighting on opposite sides. In the dream she saw a trembling flame riding high above the arrows, its spark slowly dimming until it finally diminished to shroud the vast field into darkness.

CHAPTER 7

1922

Diwali was a celebration for all the Hindus but the Muslim neighbors took equal pleasure in the celebration. The entire neighborhood blazed with sparks from the firecrackers, flickering flames of the rows of *diyas* that outlined the boundary walls, and from the brightly lit lamps in every room.

The Khatri house shone the brightest as they rejoiced in a double celebration. Neighbors, friends, relatives arrived with sweets and presents to welcome the arrival of not just the legendary prince Ram from exile but also of Janki's little prince, Rajendra.

She lay on her bed recovering from the long exhaustive labor, but her eyes sparkled like the *diya* flames as she watched her baby sleep. She admired his delicate, fair skin, the tiny ears barely visible, and forehead mostly hidden under soft, dark hair. He was tightly swaddled in a sheet of muslin, his face peaceful and heavenly. Noticing a wrinkle form on his little forehead, she put her hand on his chest. His little body curved and stretched as if to free himself from the restraints of the sheet, but with her touch he straightened and was back into the land of his serene dreams. Janki left her hand on him and closed her eyes.

Ram Lal walked in to find mother and son sleeping, their faces at peace in each other's comfortable presence. He stood over them watching, admiring, and awed by the tiny wonder. He wanted to reach out and touch the soft, delicate skin and pick up his little son, but was afraid. He feared he might crush him with the overwhelming joy he suffered from, so he sighed and drank back tears that had started to well up in his eyes.

As Rajendra grew, so did Ram Lal's attachment to his son. Times the two spent together were sacred to both, whether it was playing a finger game or story time or answering an endless array of questions from the little inquisitive mind. Ram Lal hated to be away from his son for too long, but more and more, circumstances called for their separation.

The construction business in Quetta began to slow down and it became challenging to feed two growing families from the single income source. While the cousin continued to pursue contracts to keep his business afloat, Ram Lal ventured into a new business. He invested in a truck and pioneered it across the borders into Kandhar transporting goods to Afghanistan. This meant he had to be gone for weeks.

Janki fell into the family life feigning contentment in her husband's frequent absences. Her days started with the cries of the babies, feeding the children, morning chores, and ended with kitchen work surrounded by all the children listening to stories she weaved. She gave equal attention to all the children to keep harmony in the family, cultivating an atmosphere of love and respect, so the cousin's children never felt the loss of their mother. In her effort to hold the fort, Janki had little time to spend with her son, but she never thought of Rajendra as her only child.

As their condition began to deteriorate, Ameerni had to ration the meals, and soon the women started to skip meals. Amidst the arduous times, a freak accident took a Khatri family member. The roof of the outhouse in the back of the house caved in and the cousin's second wife happened to be using it. She was buried alive.

The cousin was again left without a wife and with even more children.

Rajendra grew to be strong and cheerful, playing with the cousin's five children. By the time Janki's second and third children were born, girls named Sita and Durgi, the cousin had remarried for the third time. This new wife was very lazy and condescending, causing squabbles every day among the women over chores and duties. With her fourth child still growing in the womb, Janki's joint family decided to split. The bickering had gotten out of hand and there was no peace for anyone in the house.

Ram Lal decided to take Janki and their children to Kandhar, across the border into Afghanistan. The Khatri family had ancestral property in Kandhar, and Ram Lal had already added to his fleet of trucks for the lucrative transportation business between the two bordering countries. His parents, too old to relocate to a new place, decided to move back to Khushab with their daughter, Jeevani, to take care of them.

Janki raised objections to this fragmentation. Multitudes of questions ran through her mind. *How can they survive without an elder's hand over their head? How can they move to a foreign land alone with no one to guide them? What will happen to the cousin's children?* Her heart wanted to stay or even move back to Khushab. She wanted to remain part of a family, the one she had lived with for the past 11 years, and grown into a young woman. She did not want to say goodbye to yet another set of parents.

Ram Lal sat her down and gently explained to her their circumstances. He rationalized that one cannot always think just from the heart, and logic dictated that this separation was the only amicable solution. He emphasized to her that he could not do this alone and that he needed her, until finally she agreed, and promised to support him with both her heart and her mind.

One blustery morning as a thick fog shrouded the mountaintops, Ram Lal guided his pregnant wife and their three children out to the street. Rajendra and Sita gave tearful hugs and kisses as the grandparents blessed them, rubbing weary hands over their little heads. Janki bent down to touch her in-laws' feet as Ameerni handed her the fresh food packed for the journey. Janki nestled her children close to her and climbed onto the horse drawn carriage that was to take them to the train station.

Ram Lal climbed up in the front next to the horseman, while the family sat in the back, facing what they were leaving behind. Janki held the baby in the nook of her arm and put a protective hand over her slightly puffy belly, covering them with her special shawl. Waving the other hand, she watched her extended family through blurred vision until their images became too small to see.

It did not take long to reach the station and soon the Khatri family settled into their seats in the train heading toward the border city of Chaman. Janki sat by the window, watching the rustic mountains speckled with snow at their peaks, as the train carried its load over them to cross to the next valley. The rocking motion lulled the baby and the children, but she continued to stare out toward the climb. It dawned on her again that from now on she had no elder by her side. She turned inward to look at her sleeping children, and smiled at her husband through glistening eyes. Soon the mountainous trek was over and the train sped down toward a straight track. In just another day, they would be traversing a different mountain in a new country. Soon they would face a foreign culture with a different language and dialects. Janki rested her head back, closed her eyes and sighed. Her hand reached to stroke her children's heads before she rested it on her husband's arm. She realized that this journey was not hers alone. Her eyes opened to look straight ahead and ready to face the new land as a wife, a mother and a young woman of 22.

CHAPTER 8

1997

A shawl of snow covered the campus. Taara stepped out of her apartment and screamed. She used her powerful lungs to reach the highest octave her vocal chords would take her. She screamed that it was April and instead of seeing colorful flowers, she saw white snow. She screamed because she had an exam in her Calculus class. She hated Math.

Trudging through the six inches of snow in her long boots, Taara ran to the bus stop as fast as her long legs could carry her. She pulled her gray winter jacket closer to her body and stuffed her hands into its pockets as a long strand escaped her dark ponytail. She tried to shake it away from her face unsuccessfully. The icy chill smashed against her, settling on the tips of her tiny ears and perfect nose. Spotting the bus turning the corner she waved to Nata, signaling her to make the driver wait as she hurried to the stop toward her friend.

Nata had been her roommate freshman year and the first time they had met was on move-in day. Taara had arrived with her parents while Nata's family had come and gone. The dorm room was compact with twin beds elevated with space underneath. In addition to the desk already there, Taara's side housed a tiny refrigerator with a microwave plopped over it. At the foot of the bed, barely missing the door, Dimple placed a plastic chest of drawers. In the center of the room, between the beds below a window, sat a large comfy bean bag that Nata had contributed to their room. In the space left, Raman filled up half by just being there, while Dimple took over the rest running from one corner to another in her obsession to prepare her daughter for every contingency. Nata had excused herself after brief introductions and disappeared for several hours while the Guptas settled their only child in her new home.

Surrounded by all the stuff her mother insisted she needed, in the midst of the squashed dwelling, unsure of the stranger she'll be sharing her room with, witnessing her mother's flustered state, even her father's cool manner, Taara looked around, and felt the walls closing in on her, crushing her. She dropped what she was holding, let her clothes pile around her feet, and burst into tears. It didn't take long for Dimple to join in while Raman took them in his arms and consoled. Shrieks of laughter traveled in from the hallways, and sounds of happy students echoed throughout the dorm building. The Gupta family collected themselves, wiped their tears, and returned to the task at hand.

When it was time for the parents to leave, Raman peeled Dimple and Taara away from each other. After a long cuddly hug, Raman ran his hand on Taara's head in blessing. He handed her his tattered copy of the *Geeta* and departed with the words, "May this holy book guide you in your journey ahead."

Later that evening, her cheeks caked with dried tear stains, Taara sat huddled in the corner of her bed. She leafed through some college materials and an art book she had received as a graduation present. The sun had disappeared outside but their room was flooded with light and sound. Music from rooms next door wafted into her corner, mingled with offensive laughter from the hallways where groups of students had gathered. Nata walked in with her cheery smile and blue twinkling eyes. She went to her desk and turned on her portable TV to watch a rebroadcast of *Friends*. Taara tried to ignore the disturbance, the crude jokes, and the loud laughter from the show and from Nata. She tried to disappear deeper into the darkest corner of her elevated bed. Stiff from staying still, she switched sides and her bed creaked. Nata looked up and her smile widened, extending out to her chubby cheeks.

"I didn't know you were here. I thought you had gone out. I'm sorry if the television disturbed you. I want you to tell me if anything bothers you. We're roommates now and need to be able tell each other, I mean, it would be a pretty crappy year if we didn't become friends…. Look at me babbling away, not even giving you a chance to talk."

Taara attempted a smile as she looked down toward her roommate and her cheerfulness.

Nata stood staring up, blue eyes twinkling despite the lateness of the hour. She then asked, "Where are you from?"

"Edina."

"I'm from Milwaukee. You have any siblings?"

Taara shook her head, "None."

"I have four older brothers, all working, two are married and they both have kids. It's fun being an aunt. I made a lot of money babysitting my nieces and nephews. What's your major? I'm doing business, maybe marketing or finance, I haven't decided yet. What about you?" Nata asked.

"Liberal Arts."

Nata looked at Taara, pondered for a moment and then asked, "Are you going to the Sorority Rush tomorrow? I want to get into Chi Alpha. I hear it's a great community, the Greeks I mean."

A rush of tears suddenly overwhelmed Taara. She mumbled an excuse and disappeared back under her covers.

The next morning Taara awoke to complete silence. She maneuvered through the new surroundings and quietly rummaged through her side of the tiny closet. Clothes in hand, she made her way to the bathroom down the hall. Showered and fresh, she returned to find Nata sitting on the bean bag watching the news.

"Morning." Nata said cheerfully.

Taara smiled and tried to sound just as lively, "I'm sorry about yesterday...."

Nata waived a hand in the air, "Don't worry about it. I understand. I miss my family too and it's a nice size one too. There's always somebody coming or going, never a dull moment. I love being around people that's why I'm going to try to be part of the Greek community."

"Good for you." Taara replied. She turned around to put her toiletries and towel away. Nata got up and started toward the door. Taara called out and asked, "Are you going down for breakfast?"

"Are you on the meal plan too? Sure, I'll wait, and after that we can go to the Rush open house together."

The year flew by with classes and Nata's vivacious energy. At first Taara found it hard to stay off the phone with her mother. Nata cheerfully talked Taara into stealing some time away from the phone and going to dorm parties. In time, a new world had started to open up for Taara.

One day, just before Spring Break, Nata gave her an early birthday present. It was a little angel in a glass case with the most exquisite wings. When the case moved, the delicate wings gently flapped. In the dark, the wings glowed, and appeared bigger in the shadow of the miniature angel. Taara placed it on her desk and stared at it for hours every day. Something called her to it as if it was a present she had been searching for in every shop window.

Late into the night, their half-written essays or unsolved math problems sprawled in front of them, the two friends solved world problems, talked of dreams, laughed and cried together over things big and small. By the end of the year, Nata had also accumulated a collection of friends from all over the campus. Her social life took a new spin, a path away from the one-on-one time that Taara enjoyed. It was natural that Taara and Nata would eventually find different living arrangements, one for hosting wild social affairs and the other for serene comfort. Their friendship, however, remained intact.

Hopping onto the campus commuter, Taara walked down the aisle hugging her body to control the shiver. Nata led the way to the rear of the bus. Seating herself comfortably by the window, Nata looked up as she guided her blond bangs out of her blue eyes, finger combing through the rest of her hair.

"So, you made it. What did you do, put your watch an hour ahead or something?"

Taara noticed that her friend was wearing her spring jacket. Looking past her into the dark window, Taara saw her own long thin face contrasted next to the round moon face of her friend. Returning back inside the crowded bus, she turned to Nata and smirked, "Very funny. I'm not always late. Anyways, looks like you have your clocks messed up." She pointed through the front windows as the bus moaned its way through salty streets, "Look outside."

"It's supposed to be spring, besides, I don't shiver like your bony self." Nata shot back.

Taara pinched her friend on her arm and they both started to giggle. "Oh stop it, Taara. Wait, hey listen, what are you doing later?"

"Nothing," Taara said.

"Want to come celebrate with us?" Nata chirped.

"Celebrate what?" Taara asked.

"It's Friday. Do we need any other reason?" Nata grabbed hold of her friend's arm. "Come to the Union with me. I'm meeting some of the sisters from my sorority and some frat guys too."

Taara faced the front of the bus. "Nata, I still have to finish my paper for the History of Religion class. Besides, I don't know if I feel like hanging out with your fashionable, know-it-all sisters."

The bus stopped in front of Wesley Hall. The two girls trekked to the building as Nata shivered in the cold wind and drifting snow. Taara smiled watching her friend in her thin jacket but her own thoughts were of sunny California where she would be going next month. Nata nudged her. "So, will you come to the Union?"

"I don't know. I was planning to catch up on some reading...."

"You're always doing things by yourself. How will you meet guys?" Nata complained.

"I'm not always alone. I hang out with you," Taara countered.

"Me? Your dear and only friend Nata? Big deal."

"Besides, I just don't belong with that group," Taara muttered

They walked through the double doors where a blast of warm air ushered them in.

Inside the building, Nata started her jog down the corridor toward her class. She waved to Taara shouting, "I'll see you at the Union. We'll be in the cafe."

The Union cafe was bustling with energy. Huddled comfortably on the sunken-in couch, a cup of Earl Grey encircled in her palms, Taara looked around the great room. Its vaulted ceilings and fireplace dominated the center. She watched fellow students sipping lattés and sharing stories. Everyone was talking and no one seemed to be listening. She observed the scene as if an audience in the theatre. Nata and her friends were discussing their plans for the summer.

"I'm Europe-hopping all summer," a short redhead with round cheeks was saying. "Four whole months with not a care in the world!" she added for emphasis.

"I'm going down under for some outback adventure," a tall blond with an upturned nose and a forbidding stare exclaimed. "Sydney, Melbourne, Perth, you name it. I might even hop over to New Zealand to see some *hobbits*." She said it as if she might actually come upon some of the tiny, fictitious creatures.

Taara wondered what she was doing with this group. Then the fraternity boys showed up, fashionably late. Like two extreme poles, the two groups magnetically drew closer blending into one. The boys wore charm on their faces while the girls hovered and purred. Taara rolled her eyes and looked away.

Just as she was contemplating deserting the pack, she noticed a lone young man by the fireplace. She saw him rise up from the cozy chair only to set himself down again. He sat on the edge of the big chair. She noticed him trying to steady his right knee from bobbing while his gaze traveled around him uncertainly. He looked like a majestic yacht lost at sea.

She focused all her attention on studying him. She guessed him to be at least six feet tall. Even though he looked adrift in this crowd, he appeared quite together in his neatly creased Dockers and starched yellow Polo shirt. His dark curly hair, combed all the way back, complemented his precise, neatly trimmed mustache. Taara detected a flicker of a twinkle in his eyes, as if privy to some knowledge about the world. Then, for an instant, their eyes met. Taara did not know what hit her but certainly a jolt of some kind. She snapped out of it, embarrassed.

In the chair next to Taara, Nata was saying something. "Roger was found under the dining table the next morning."

Everyone laughed. This was an old story. Roger was always found under a table the morning after a party, with a swollen headache.

From the corner of her eyes, Taara sensed the mystery man stand up from his warm seat.

In the seat across from Taara, Stacy, the redhead, was saying, "This time it was different. He was all there minus his clothes."

Laughter broke out again.

Taara turned toward the fireplace. The chair sat there empty. Taara sank into her couch feeling a touch of disappointment. She brought her warm mug to her lips, inhaling the steamy aroma of her tea. The buzz of activity continued around her. She quietly placed her tea on the table and walked out through the main doors to the snow-ridden path.

Half a mile later, she walked through the double doors of the history library into an empty foyer. Passing the sole librarian behind the counter, Taara found herself surrounded by empty tables and chairs. She snaked her way through the aisles inhaling the rustic smell of yellowing paper all around her. Reaching the section of her choice, tucked away in the back, Taara perused the spines for the titles she was seeking. The aisle was lined with books, boards, and atlases full of maps. Time and space came together here in the maps of every era, every region, and every historic event.

Finding one possible resource, Taara spread it out on the floor of the aisle. Her nose buried somewhere between ancient Iraq and Eastern Europe, she was oblivious to the movement around her. Her map was blocking the passageway into the modern maps section.

"Excuse me." His voice was strong and deep.

She looked up to meet the familiar twinkling eyes. They smiled.

She smiled back and folded the map over to let him pass. He did not move, instead, he crouched down in front of her. Placing his forefinger somewhere near the Northwest region of the Indian subcontinent he remarked, "Beautiful area."

Taara stared at his finger, then at him. "Isn't it also dangerous?"

"It's risky to visit but not impossible."

"Have you been there?" Taara asked.

"Yes, and I'm heading out again in a couple of weeks," he said.

"Do you have family in Quetta?" Taara asked.

"How do you know that's Quetta? It says Shalkot here." He looked impressed.

"You first," Taara challenged.

"My grandmother lives there." He then extended his hand, "I'm Omar."

Taara offered her soft hands into his strong grasp. "I'm Taara and my great-grandmother is from Quetta."

"Is she not there anymore?"

"All the Hindus had to flee after the partition…," Taara

started.

"An unfortunate period." Omar cut in. "My grandmother has told me so many stories…" He stood up, "But I don't want to bore you with them."

Taara stood up as well. "Please go on. I'm interested."

The librarian cleared her throat as she passed by. They put the map away and walked out together toward the foyer.

Her mind on her companion, Taara did not see the half step leading into the foyer. Losing her balance, Taara headed toward a fall, face first. In a swift motion, Omar's arm reached out, pulling her back. Recovering from the shock, Taara flushed in embarrassment. She managed, "Thanks."

"Glad I was there to catch you." Omar smiled.

A few seconds passed in silence as Taara tried to avoid his gaze. Blinking, she finally straightened and asked, "Do you go here?"

"Thinking about it. Visiting for now."

"Where from?"

"California."

"Are you crazy? You want to leave sunny California for this?" Taara exclaimed pointing at the snow mounds outside the windows.

Omar gave a short laugh.

"Is that where you grew up?" she asked.

"In Ventura County, Southern California. Have you been there?" he asked.

"My aunt and uncle live in Newport Beach." Her eyes lit up with the sudden realization, "I'm going there this summer. On an internship."

"I'll be back there this summer too, after Pakistan." Omar shared in the excitement.

"Tell me about Quetta." Taara set her elbows on the table cradling her chin on her hands.

"It's like paradise on Earth." His eyes shined as he continued, "Its fort-like mountains are majestic, the lakes are clearest of the blue, fruit-laden trees line the streets." As if waking up from a dream, Omar blinked, "Of course, recently there's been more ugliness with the tribal unrest and terrorist haven and all that." He let out a long sigh.

"It must be upsetting," Taara stated. "I wish I could see the beautiful landscape."

"I can bring back some pictures for you if you like," Omar offered.

Taara beamed, "I'd love that."

The sound of a cellphone echoed through the hall. Omar excused himself to answer it, but his exchange on the phone was brief. He then stood up, tucked the device back into his pocket and smiled, "I've really enjoyed talking to you Taara."

"Me too." Taara stood up as well and smiled back, "All the best on your trip."

He stood in his place, opened his mouth but shut it back without saying anything. He then turned and left.

"Mystery man." She said to herself as she stared after him.

Taara decided to walk to her apartment just across the river. Strolling on the sidewalk of the bridge, she gazed toward the endless lines of bridges that connected the Twin Cities. They sparkled, each boasting its strings of lights running down its length in waves. Beams of light glared from the headlights of slow-moving commuters. Whether the sun had completely set, Taara could not tell. A hint of purple hung with the clouds, and the darkness of night had not completely descended. Taara stood on the bridge between the two cities and admired the show as if in an art gallery.

The great Mississippi below showed movement from the gradual thaw. Big blocks of ice broke off from its edges, starting the flow down to the southern States. She imagined other rivers, great and small, flowing aimlessly or toward something, unaware of the twists and turns or the barriers thrown in their path. She thought of the multitude of bridges world over that connected banks, drawing attention to the flowing rivers to admire their beauty.

Beyond Boundaries

An icy breeze took a bite out of Taara's cheeks. Enveloping her freezing ears in her scrunched shoulders, she stuffed her hands in the bulky jacket and hurried off to the apartment.

CHAPTER 9

1997

A stream of sunlight poured into Taara's bedroom, flooding her full-size bed. Tiny paisleys danced on her soft comforter, matching with the dark red sheets. A black turtleneck and blue jeans sat discarded by the bed on the brown carpet. Stacks of books and leaves of papers lay scattered on the floor. Bleary-eyed, Taara emerged from the covers and took a long stretch. She had set the alarm for 10am and it rang right on target as she sat up.

She saw the mess on the floor and breathed a sigh of relief. She was done with her paper and had sent it off to the professor, even though it had caused her to stay up to that placid hour which is neither night nor day. Her mission for the day was to clean her apartment and restock her fridge and pantry. Before she could tackle the groceries and all that, she needed energy. She packed her running shoes and a swimsuit, swallowed a glass of orange juice, grabbed a power bar and walked out of the apartment.

All dressed in her black bike shorts, a white racer back shirt, her hair pulled back, Taara made her way to the stationary bikes, her thick jacket in hand. She plopped the headphones in her ears and turned to the classical station on her miniature radio.

Two symphonies and ten miles later, Taara slowed down. Lost in Vivaldi's 'Four Seasons', Taara raised her gaze away from the speedometer. Across the fitness room by the entrance, she spotted him, just as she had at the Union cafe, a majestic yacht lost at sea. Only this time Taara also noticed biceps - finely sculpted, partially hidden beneath the short sleeves of a gray t-shirt. The message on his chest stated "Defy Limitations" in bold red.

She turned off the radio, removed the headphones and watched him from her seat on the bike. A full minute passed before he noticed her from across the floor and started to walk in her direction. Instinctively, her hand went up to her hair, straightening it, smoothing away the flyways. She slid her towel down from her neck to wipe her face, taking care not to smudge her mascara. As she lowered her towel, she found him standing next to her, a big smile lighting up his face.

"Nice to see a familiar face," he said.

Taara slid off the bike but feeling her knees shaking, she put one hand on the handle bar to steady herself. Regaining her balance, she managed a smile and said, "Nice to see you too."

They stood there for a full 20 seconds without saying anything, as familiar twinkling eyes smiled at her. Then they both spoke at once, "Are you lost?" she asked. "Are you following me?" he teased.

Laughing they shook their heads.

"So how is this place laid out?" he asked.

"Well, on this level are the machines - weights, cardio, strength...," she started.

"Are there any running tracks?" he asked.

"They're on the upper level by the studios. I was heading there myself."

"Mind if I join you?" He asked.

"I'd love the company." Taara smiled.

They jogged in silence as Taara listened to his breathing, feeling the pound of his steps on the ground echo in her heart. She noticed his strides were long and clean, as of a seasoned runner. She struggled to keep up with him, running faster, working harder. Beads of sweat sprinkled on her forehead soon started their own jog down to the tip of her nose, over her eyelids down to her chin. Just as they finished their second lap, Omar increased his pace. Apparently, he had just been warming up. She kept up for another lap then slowed to a trot. He sprinted and was off. When he came around again after the lap, he matched his speed to hers.

Out of breath she asked, "So what are you thinking of studying?"

He looked at her while staying in his lane, "MBA."

"Business major." she commented.

His eyes then looked beyond her, as if thinking of the right response. He looked back at her and said, "Law actually."

Taara looked at him puzzled. "Why MBA then?" she asked.

It's…" Before he could continue, as if changing his mind, he said, "I wanted a business degree too." He looked ahead and said, almost to himself, "And so did my dad."

Taara stared at him as they jogged together.

"So what's your story?" he asked a few seconds later.

"Born, bred Minnesotan, parents from India, single child, sophomore, art major." Taara summed up.

"What kind of art?" he inquired.

"Visual mostly." Taara put a hand up and stepped out into an opening off the track.

Omar followed.

Out of breath she finished, "I'm done." She bent down to tie her shoelaces.

He waited, holding the corners of the little towel around his neck. Clearing his throat, he looked at the track, and the stretching area around him, and finally rested his gaze on Taara's dark hair, her sweat-ridden shoulders, her perfectly crouched figure…. He looked away and licked his salty lips.

"Water?" Taara asked standing up pointing to the water fountain in the corner.

"I'm okay, thanks." He took a step forward. "I'd like to take you out for dinner."

Taara blushed as she took in a mouthful of water.

"Tonight, if you're free." Omar said.

She stood staring at him and then started to say something, to come up with an excuse, to say yes, to say no. As soon as she opened her mouth, water dribbled down her chin. She had forgotten to swallow. Embarrassed she dabbed her towel on her face and chest. She looked up to see Omar standing, still waiting for her response, wearing a warm smile.

"I... I... don't know." she stammered, but then said, "I'd love to but I have a lot to do today."

"You can call me when you get done," he suggested.

"I suppose I can do that." She spoke almost to herself. She looked up at Omar and smiled. "What's your number?"

Outside the aerobic studio, by the whiteboard, they found a black marker and Omar asked Taara for her hand. Holding her fingers in his palm, he bent his head. His hold was gentle but the grasp was strong, and she could feel his warm breath on her fingertips causing a tickling sensation. He wrote his phone number in an awkward motion holding the pen firmly between the thumb and fingers of his left hand.

Taara skipped the swimming she had planned and went straight to the showers. She flashed through the grocery store for the bare necessities, scurried around her apartment picking up, organizing, cleaning, and vacuuming. Finally, she stood back and admired her pristine little cottage-like abode with satisfaction. The light in her room had started to dull and she turned on her lamp. As soon as she sat down on her neatly made up bed, she rummaged through her gym bag searching for the scratch paper on which she had scribbled Omar's number before the ink on her hand was washed away in the shower. Finding it at last, she wasted no time in making the call.

He knocked on her door promptly at seven, dressed in a starched, lime green shirt and jeans. A black leather jacket and combed-back hair gave him a sleek look. Taara stood aside in her elegant black slacks and a fitted white shirt. Curled tips hung carelessly above her shoulders at the end of straight hair.

Omar let out a low whistle as he entered her cottage-like apartment while she walked to the dining chair to grab her maroon coat. On her way back to the door, she did a quick scan in the full-length mirror by the dining room wall. Omar moved forward and looked into her eyes in the reflection. They stood there for a moment admiring each other as Taara's cheeks turned redder than the blush she had applied.

The drive to the Tapas bar was short and quiet. They walked into the small restaurant where a live band, accompanied by a male singer, greeted the guests. Omar and Taara settled into a corner table and joined in the clapping and cheering as the Flamenco dancers moved to the rhythm. As the beat became faster, the momentum grew higher and the cheering became louder. Taara's body swayed and her shoulders twirled. Suddenly conscious, she looked toward Omar and gave him a shy smile. He smiled back, obviously enjoying the double show.

"Anything to drink?" A young girl in a black shirt and a hoop ring in her eyebrow stood holding a notebook and pen.

"Non-alcoholic Sangria, please," Taara ordered.

"I'll have the same," Omar added.

Taara wondered if he was being polite or if he was a practicing Muslim. She was, in any case, flattered. Placing a hand on her taut belly, she suddenly realized that the butterflies in her stomach were not from hunger, even though she had forgotten to eat lunch.

As the band finished up, Omar and Taara perused the menu. They selected a variety of Spanish dishes - the fried shrimp, sautéed mushrooms, a platter of cheeses and another of olives.

"This place is wonderful," Taara noted.

Omar smiled, his eyes twinkling as he relaxed back in his chair, his hands stretched in front of him on to the table. He straightened the knife and fork aligning them in equal parallel lines, neatly folded the napkin in half and rested it on his lap.

"Have you been here before?" Taara asked.

"A friend recommended it. I'm glad you are enjoying yourself as much as I am."

It was Taara's turn to smile. "This friend, is that who you were waiting for at the Union?" she asked.

"The very same." Omar offered.

"But he didn't show up yesterday."

"Yeah. Apparently, she had forgotten about our date. Never mind about her." He turned the interest to his current date. "So, you're an artist."

Taara wondered if this girl was an ex-girlfriend. She dismissed the thought and turned her attention to the man in front of her. She noticed that his ears were rather large for his face, as if he was always all ears. His lips were moving, "Do you have plans?"

She perked up her own tiny ears, guiding her hair behind them with a finger. Having caught just his last word, she repeated it. "Plans?"

"As an artist," Omar said.

"I want to do many things. Just not sure which one."

"Like what?" Omar brought both arms up to rest them on the table.

"I have this vision of multiple series. I want to sketch doors, minarets, children's faces." Taara leaned forward allowing Omar to see the sparkle in her eyes. "I can see these images decorating the walls of my room, sketched by me. Imagine all the vibrant colors captured from all over the world."

"That's quite a list." Omar blew out a soft whistle.

"And I also want to teach. An art studio for children, perhaps."

"And?" Omar teased.

The aroma of berries and peaches from their drinks teased their senses while quiet dinner room conversation buzzed around them. From hidden speakers came the lyrical sound of guitar strings."

Their eyes met and her gaze dropped to his hands on the table. They appeared strong, yet soft. She rested her arms on the table, their hands just inches apart. She looked up from his hands to his eyes and asked, "Why Minnesota?"

"Well, it's simple." He leaned back, taking his hands with him. "It's not California."

Taara cocked her head to the right with a furrowed brow.

He smiled, "I'm also considering the east coast." He brought one hand back up on the table to straighten the fork on his plate and said, "But it helps that I have friends here."

Taara smiled and said, "I'm glad."

The server came to clear their empty plates.

In the parking lot of her apartment, the two sat in the car. Neither wished the evening to end.

"Dinner was nice. Thank you," Taara said.

"Can I call you sometime?" he asked.

"I'd like that." She stepped out of the car, "Good night."

He waited until she was inside the cottage before backing out of the driveway.

After spending all of Sunday with her parents, by Monday morning Taara had trouble concentrating. Numbers danced in air above her books in math class. Her gaze stayed fixed on one color of the multi-color art piece she had been laboring over for weeks. She walked back to her apartment after a day of classes, her fingers itching to call Omar. She knew it was too soon, that it might make her sound desperate. Besides, he said he will call her. All logic went out the window when she charged toward the phone. Before she could pick up the receiver, the machine buzzed at her. She answered suspiciously.

"Is that Taara?"

Her legs became weak. She sat down and spoke, "Hi Omar."

"How was your day?" he asked.

"Same old boring routine. Classes, homework, papers. Yours?" she asked.

"Not as great as yours." Sound of hesitation came through the wires, then, "Taara, I was wondering if you are interested in a game of racquetball today?"

"I'm not very good."

"Neither am I. When can you come?"

"Now is good. See you at the gym." Taara rang off, excited. She quickly changed and was at the gym entrance in 15 minutes.

The game moved at a slow pace with frequent interruptions of conversation, laughter, and distraction. Finally, both gave up the pretext of racquetball and went to the cafe.

Later in the evening, back in their respective rooms, neither remembered what they had talked about for three hours. They vaguely remembered the swish of the espresso machine and buzz of the blenders whipping up protein shakes. Each recalled the other's sensation, voice, shy or a flirtatious look, her forehead crinkle when she listened intently, his raising of one eyebrow in admiration of her stories, the almost touching of hands, the accidental stepping of her foot on his under the table. What each did remember was the promise to meet again, soon.

Taara and Nata had planned to go for the Friday night show of "The Saint". Mid-week Nata informed Taara that a few of her friends were joining them so on impulse Taara invited Omar. At first, she feared Omar would get bored among the immature sophomores, but as the evening progressed, it turned out to be better than Taara had expected.

Under the cover of the dark theatre, Taara and Omar found their seats next to each other. She was more aware of the man beside her than the equally handsome character of Simon Templar on the big screen in front of her. She crossed her arms, scrunched her shoulders and snuggled in her seat. He whispered in her ear to ask if she was cold, she nodded and he offered his jacket. Her left elbow rested on the armrest while his arm rested on his leg. Nata, sitting on her right, was completely absorbed in her popcorn and the action and drama unfolding on the big screen. Taara felt a soft touch on her left hand as it rested on the empty cup holder. She let the strong fingers interlace her delicate ones, turned to look at him, studying the glow from the screen cast light and shadows on his face. She gave a shy smile, turned to the picture show and leaned a little closer to his seat, their arms entwined into each other on the armrest they shared between them.

CHAPTER 10

1927

The engine pulling into the station at Chaman spurted a cloud of steam, as coolies bombarded into the cars picking up luggage and forcing their services. In the commotion, Ram Lal hired a coolie, while Janki took charge of the children. Balancing the baby on her waist, she held onto Sita's sweaty palm with her other hand. She commanded Rajendra to keep his roaming eyes focused on her and to hold onto her *dupatta* scarf. Amidst the chaos and under the scorching sun they found a horse drawn carriage to take them to the house of Ram Lal's friend, Nandu. Janki covered the children and her own face with her scarf as they rode through the dry, dusty roads. Smeared with soot from the engine, she looked at her children's blackened faces and hands.

Riding through a street lined with shops, their carriage stopped in front of a structure stocked with fresh and dried fruits. The family followed Ram Lal toward the side of the store, through a narrow corridor, into a spacious house. Ram Lal walked in as if he had come to his own home and called out for his friend. He had told Janki about Nandu and how his friend was helping his mother care for his five young siblings. Their father had relinquished his duties when the youngest was two and had dedicated the rest of his years in service of God. Dadanji, as Nandu's mother was addressed by everyone, was severe but kind, and always welcomed Ram Lal as her own, during his frequent stop overs, as he traveled between Quetta and Kandhar.

Dadanji invited them into the sitting room and gave her blessings as Ram Lal and Janki touched her feet. The children huddled close to Janki on the mattress set on the ground against a wall, their eyes uncertain and curious. Rajendra fidgeted with the tassels that dangled from the corners of the round pillows, while Sita clung to her brother in a tight grip until he yelped and pulled back his arm. Janki tried to settle the fussing baby and scolded the older two to behave. She asked Dadanji if they could wash up and was directed to the back of the house.

Out from the back porch, Janki saw that all the houses were lined up close to each other behind their shops, and from each house's back porch a few steps ran down to a flowing river. Each house had a platform where women washed dishes or clothes or filled their buckets to bring water indoors. Carefully, Janki stepped onto the platform and helped her children wash off the soot and dust from their journey.

Feeling refreshed, Janki walked back indoors, her brood behind her in a line as ducklings in a strange pond. Entering the sitting room, they were greeted by the sweet aroma of melons and grapes and the musky whiff of the pomegranate. In the center of the room among all the luscious fruits, she was enticed by the succulent plums, red, ripe and ready to sink her teeth into. As they sat enjoying the juicy treats, she listened to Nandu and Ram Lal talk of mutual friends and the current business climate. Janki learned that Chaman, the name of this border town meant garden, but she couldn't recall seeing any flowers on their way. Fresh fruits and many products were abundant in its bazaars but she learned that nothing was produced there. Instead, it was a place where traders from two different countries converged, transacted, and developed relationships. Her husband had been one such trader and he had an added advantage of trucks that carted the products over treacherous terrain into Kandhar and back into British India.

After a late meal of chicken biryani, Janki retired to a quiet room. She watched her three children sleep peacefully as she fanned them with a newspaper, and laid a hand on her stomach as if to pat the one inside her to rest too. Ram Lal had insisted that they all get plenty of rest before he stepped out with Nandu to make arrangements for the next leg of the journey.

Before the first ray of the sun next day, the Khatri family arrived at an open ground crowded with people, camels, and mules. Rajendra's feet and hands itched to go touch the animals while Sita covered up her nose and cowered behind her mother every time she heard a snort, bleat, or bray. Even the calm baby babbled and squealed in delight almost ready to jump off into the pandemonium, and Janki had to keep a tight grip on all the children. Ram Lal directed them toward a collection of mules and they noticed that their luggage had already been loaded and secured on one of the shoddy animals. Sita kicked and screamed when she learned that she had to ride on one of these creatures, and it took all of Janki and Ram Lal's patience to convince her to sit onto its back. Rajendra eagerly climbed on his mule, instantly named it Raju, and promised his parents that he will hold onto his sister through the journey ahead. Janki sat sideways onto another mule with the fidgety baby on her lap while Ram Lal climbed onto a third one.

After much fussing and shouting, the caravan of around two hundred people started moving, as the sun behind them began to nibble around the edge of the dark sky. They crossed the border into Afghanistan, led by camels and trailed by the mules, each carrying its load. Rajendra complained to his father why he could not ride on the tall, majestic animals, to which Ram Lal said that one day, hopefully, they will be able to afford the more regal ride.

Dust rose up into clouds behind them, ahead of them, around them and settled on their faces, in their hair, covering their clothes and body like a shawl. Their lips cracked from dryness and their throats needed constant clearing despite frequent water sips. The animals trekked straight ahead in single file with a steady climb up and down and around orange, rustic hills. Leaving behind the Afghani border town of Spin Balduk, Janki began noticing small clusters of mud huts along the way. Ram Lal informed her that these settlements were called *Kalays* and were spread out along the foothills of the various mountains. The sun had reached its peak when the caravan stopped by the Dori River for a much needed rest and nourishment for both the travelers and the animals.

Janki held the baby with one hand and her low back with the other as she walked to a clearing, to spread a sheet and unpack their lunch. Dadanji had packed *Kupri* unleavened bread with pickles that could stay well for the journey. As soon as the children and Ram Lal were done eating and the baby finished her feeding, Janki devoured her share. Putting everything away, she limped over to the river, splashed water on her face after a long refreshing drink, and returned to lie beside her family to rest her aching body under the sweltering sun. She woke to the sound of groans and grunts from men, women, children and even the animals. The sun was still high in the sky and the leader of the caravan was pressing everyone to make haste. The treacherous part of the track had to be crossed before dark. Ram Lal helped load the luggage and the family back onto their mules.

As they rode ahead, Janki looked back at the camp site they had left behind. A small fire still burned where some families had cooked their meals. She noticed a red blanket fly off into the mountain, as if a 'gift' to the land where people had rested a while. She watched her children ahead of her, Rajendra tired but excited about all the unknowns that lay ahead, while Sita clung to him for support, her right thumb in her mouth. Ram Lal behind her looked straight ahead, past her, out into the horizon. Sandy hills and mountains with jagged edges stared down at her from one side, while a treacherous drop on the other side reminded her to get a tighter grip on the baby and the reins of the mule. She spotted the occasional oak or ash and the prickly gooseberry shrubs scattered at various altitudes and breathed in deeply, inhaling the aromatic honeysuckle. Sita shrieked every time she spied a wild goat or a herd of the long-horned ibex, and Janki observed Rajendra marvel at the single-horned *markhor*, and jumped up and down with excitement on his tired mule at the sight of the *urial* and *argali* parading the ground with their prized horns. She shifted her weight to find a comfortable seat and finally, as they arrived at an opening, she decided to defy decorum. Ram Lal held the baby while she reseated on the mule, facing forward with her legs dangling, one on each side.

After a long night full of discomfort and fear, the caravan packed up early the next day and continued its journey. Janki had stayed up most of the night, staring up into the night sky. Celestial specks had stared down back at her, some even offering an occasional wink, as if to say all will be well. She heard the periodic pounding of the sticks by men who took turns to stay up on guard against potential attack by *dacoits* or robbers. Each pound echoed in her fluttering heart, and she looked over to her children, blissfully asleep.

The rest of the journey continued slowly through flat, semi-desert countryside, with fatigue prominent on each face of man, woman, child and animal. Rustic mountains or hills that looked like camels' humps rose up high, far into the horizon on all sides. Suddenly, a buzz rose up from the riders up front and made its way back through the caravan like a wave. Rajendra was the first in the family to spot it - the thick and tall mud wall spread around the city to keep out wildlife and robbers. As they drew closer, an arched gate welcomed them into one of the four streets that led to city center, *CharSuq*. Ram Lal pointed out the Arghandab River running next to the city that helped irrigate this oasis in the middle of the desert, while Janki noticed a stream flowing right through the settlement boasting green foliage all around. The caravan rode into the center of the commercial capital of Afghanistan, Kandhar, where Ram Lal already had arranged for a carriage to take his family to their new home.

From *Charsuq* they took the second of the four streets lined with shops, but these were not like the bazaars Janki had seen in Quetta or Khushab. Most of the shops either sold weapons and arms, or books and writing material. She made a mental note to be sure to visit the literary shops to help feed her curiosity, and absorb all that this new land had to offer.

The carriage came to a halt in front of a high blank wall with a small opening. The simplicity of the entrance to her new home intrigued Janki, and she stepped inside to find courtyards, walkways, open spaces, gardens, and smaller single-level buildings. A city within a city, she learned later, was a sub-division of communities where families shared a lot more than just common spaces. Soon Janki and Ram Lal sat holding their cups of sweet green tea while the children gulped down fresh goat's milk. Their new neighbors also offered the sweet *karvann* and wholesome *roghni naan* bread which they all tasted with delight. As she observed her new surroundings, Janki realized the emphasis was on the family within, not on the public façade. A calm smile appeared on her face as she gathered her children and began to make a home in this foreign land.

CHAPTER 11

1997

Taara stepped out of her modest cottage early Saturday afternoon to be greeted by an orchestra of chirping birds. She looked up to an open sky, canvassed soft blue, with speckles of white puffy clouds. As she made her way to the bus stop, her body bathed in the golden rays that blanketed the Minnesotan landscape, soft whistling sounds escaped her lips. She walked with a bounce in her step into her parents' home in Edina, singing her own tune. With a dreamy look and a big smile, she greeted her mother.

Melting into her embrace, Taara stayed a while longer into the tender hug. She took in the spicy aromas and stole some comfort in the familiarity of everything - her home, her mother, her mother's *pashmina*. All smelled the same as always, but everything seemed different all of a sudden.

She noticed her mother's eyes sparkling with excitement, sending to background the tiny crinkles that webbed out like a fan on each side of her eyes. Her once dark hair showed white roots near the parting and extra lines appeared like parentheses on each side of her mouth when she smiled. The two walked, hand in hand to the kitchen and sat down to a simple meal of *Kaddhi Chawal* yellow curry rice.

Taara took her bites slowly, staring into blankness at length. Dimple rattled off her list of things that needed to be done before the weekend was over. She had places to go, things to pick up, people to see before Monday. Taara nodded and agreed at intervals before becoming lost again into her private thoughts.

"I have the hair appointment in an hour, still need to finish the laundry before I can pack...." Dimple was saying, "...and the ironing, do you think they'll have an iron on the ship?"

"Mom, why're you so worked up? It's just the Pacific you'll be cruising around, not outer space."

"I know...I've never been away from you for so long." She sighed, "I can't believe we'll be on that ship for a whole month."

"You deserve it mom. I'm so proud of Papa for surprising you with this gift for your anniversary."

"It was sweet of him, wasn't it?" Dimple blushed.

Taara smiled, "Just relax and enjoy your romantic getaway. I'll be fine." She put a hand on her mother's shoulder and looked into her eyes, "Really."

Dimple sat back and watched her daughter. Taara's hair, longer now, came together neatly at the nape of her neck, with a clip she had borrowed from her. In that profile, Dimple for a moment saw a familiar image, as if she was looking into a mirror.

Taara dropped her gaze and Dimple smiled back, noticing a new look, something she had never seen before. Taara had always been an open book to her, with one look Dimple used to be able to tell all that was hidden behind those eyes. It wasn't so easy anymore. Was she becoming too old to read her own daughter, or was her daughter drifting away? Behind the curtain of those eyelids, she knew there was something new. All the veins in this mother's body could sense something had changed.

She reached out and held her daughter's closed fists, cupped them with her hands, and then decided to just hold on to them, as is. Taara looked happy and that's all that mattered, then she looked up and Dimple smiled with a slight nod.

At first, she had felt hurt with the realization that her daughter didn't need her anymore. Then Dimple remembered that at 19, she herself had already been married and become an expectant mother. Daughters grew up but they didn't stop being daughters, just like she will never stop being her mother. But her daughter was also a young woman now. Dimple sighed, suddenly feeling lighter. Her daughter was all grown up and Dimple could go away without any anxiety for her.

She stood up and picked up her *pashmina* from the chair, the same taupe shawl Ammaji had given to her before her wedding 25 years ago. She draped it over Taara's shoulders and engulfed her in it. Bending down to kiss her forehead, and before tears could form, she moved to the sink to put the lunch dishes away. The two finished cleaning up the kitchen and went on to the business of packing.

While her mother was at her hair appointment, Taara sat in the family room. She had in her hand the list her mother had handed her of things left to do before their trip. Abandoning it midway, her gaze turned outside to the snow-covered backyard. She watched the squirrels scurry about, hopping from branch to branch showering snow from the branches onto the ground. Two robins flew in to balance on the tallest branch of a fir, observing the yards together. Through an open window, Taara could hear the distinct song of the cardinal as if it was throwing a teasing whistle at another bird. She noticed the bare apple blossom, showing no sign of its pink blooms or green leaves. Tracks of little creatures active after a long hibernation were visible everywhere. Looking toward the hedges by the deck, she hoped to get a glimpse of some shoots of the red and yellow tulips she had helped plant many falls ago. Birds chirped noisily all around the house, crowding around the feeder, as a squirrel chased another up a tree. Courting season was in full swing, and creatures all around her were finding love.

Her thoughts traveled to Omar and a smile appeared on her face.

The weekend passed in a flurry of activities. Taara left her parents with never-ending embraces, several lists of to do's and don'ts, multitudes of advice, and a folder full of contact information of friends and relatives all over the world. She returned to the vast campus, to her cold cottage that greeted her with the smell of emptiness. She arrived armed with food for the week, clean laundry and her mother's *pashmina*. The previous week with Omar and the weekend with her parents, she had started to fall behind in her assignments. She spent all of Monday in classes or in the library, and didn't get Omar's message until late that night.

"Hi there." His clear voice rang from the answering machine. "I... it's me, Omar." A short pause and then, "Call me." Followed by an abrupt click.

Ignoring the lateness of the hour, she picked up the phone and called. A hoarse voice answered.

"I'm sorry to call so late," she said.

His voice became alive and clear as he said, "So good to hear your voice."

Taara remained silent and smiled to herself.

Omar hesitated before speaking again, "I'm leaving this week."

Taara's face fell. She gripped the receiver tight to her ear and asked, "When?"

"Friday."

"Oh," was all that came out through her lips.

"Can I see you?" he asked.

"Tomorrow I have a class in the morning. How about lunch at the Union café," she suggested.

In the cafeteria, the two sat at the quietest corner they could find. Their small table leaned against a glass wall, with a view of the snow blanketing the lawn outside. It had a virginal appearance, untouched beauty with velvety and frosty softness. No one had ventured in this part of the land, far removed from roads and the heavy foot traffic of students. Omar and Taara sat face to face, lunch trays in front of them untouched, their hands held tight, oblivious to the crowd of noisy students around them.

Taara told Omar about her weekend and her goodbyes to her parents. He squeezed her hand when her voice cracked.

"I'm happy for them. Believe me, they really deserve this vacation." Taara explained. "I know it's selfish to say this, but I wish they didn't choose to go for so long."

Omar said nothing but listened, nodded, smiled, or squeezed her hand as needed.

"It was, after all, their dream," she concluded, then stole her right hand from his clasp and took a sip of the chicken wild rice soup.

As his saucy stir-fry sat on his plate, turning dry and cold, Omar looked at Taara and asked, "What about you? What's your dream?"

Taking a big swallow of her soup, she shook her head and said, "First, you tell me."

He pushed his plate to the side and leaned forward, setting his elbows onto the table. He looked straight into her dark eyes and declared, "To be free."

Taara pushed her bowl aside and set her elbows on the table, resting her chin on both knuckles, "Are you in chains?"

Omar shook his head smiling, as he took her hands into his, their elbows standing as pillars. Their heads almost touching and fingers entangled, he asked, "So, do you have the same dual role setup as the other *desis* I've met?"

"What do you mean?" Taara stammered, almost knocking her glass off the table as she withdrew her hands.

"You know a *desi* at home, American with your friends."

Taara slowly picked up her ice water and took a luxurious sip. She stared right back at the man with the deepest eyes she had ever seen and said, "I'm not sure. I don't really think about it."

"So, your parents are cool about... dating, for instance?" Omar put down his drink and looked at her with those knowing eyes.

She shook her head and smiled, "You know, if my dad knew I have been out with you alone, he'd kill me. I am so afraid they will arrange my marriage someday."

Omar was nodding, "I know my parents will find a match for my sister."

"How old is she?" Taara inquired.

"She's 16 now, but in the next few years the word will get out in the community that my family is looking for prospects."

"That's awful. I hope my parents don't do that. I'll run away, I swear."

"You would?" Omar was amused.

"Why is that so hard to believe?" Taara countered.

"I thought you were open with your parents."

Taara cupped her glass cooling her sweaty palms, "Open communication, not open mindedness. I do have boundaries," she smirked.

Omar took a sip of his soda and remarked. "We all do. We just need to figure out how to manage them."

"How do you manage yours?" Taara inquired.

Omar smiled, "I just do whatever I want. As long as I do well in school and am not arrested for anything, all's cool."

"So, you've been a good boy always?" Taara challenged.

"I've done my share of mischief, had some good times." Omar countered with a wink, "The trick is not getting caught."

Taara smiled with amusement, "So, what's the most daring thing you've ever done, something you could get arrested for?"

Omar looked around him and lowered his voice. "Sophomore year, high school." He pulled his chair further up and leaned forward, "A friend got hold of some pot."

Taara leaned forward too.

"A bunch of us met at his house one weekend while his parents were out of town." Omar grinned, "It's the best time I had in all my school years."

"Didn't your parents suspect, I mean you must have come home all high and goofy?" Taara asked wide eyed.

"I was lucky, my father had left for one of his trips earlier that day." Omar laughed.

"What about your mother?"

"She was always busy with friends or doing her *namaaz* praying session."

Taara lowered her gaze unsure whether to feel sorry for him or intrigued.

"What about you? What was your daring feat?" Omar asked.

"I'm pretty boring compared to you," she dismissed.

"Come on, don't be so modest."

"Freshman year, college." Taara began, "Nata took me to one of her parties. There was enough booze to fill Lake Calhoun."

Omar set his elbows on the table and cradled his chin on his hands.

Taara continued, "I had my first taste with beer bongs, tequila shots, rum and coke, and whatever else was in the bright red punch." She leaned closer and brought her voice down, "I don't know this for sure but I am told that I was the life of the party."

Omar's left eyebrow arched up, "So, what did you allegedly do?"

"Oh, I don't know, dance maybe and…," blushing she continued, "on the table, with guys, girls I didn't know and…," she added, "apparently I'm a pretty good singer too. They just didn't understand what I was singing."

"Wow, I wish I was there. Next time Nata throws a party like that, call me."

"Sure, but don't count on me being there." Taara assured, "You can't imagine how miserable I felt the next day."

"Yes, I can," he laughed.

"That was the first weekend I did not go home." Taara confessed. "I felt so guilty but I couldn't let my parents see me in that state."

"Were they suspicious?"

"That was the worst of it. I told them I had too much homework and group study sessions and they took it. No questions."

"It sounds like you're balancing things quite well," Omar stated.

Taara gave a weak smile as they sat there. Omar held her hands into his, gently massaging them with his thumbs. They left the cafeteria to walk around the campus entering stores, strolling through large lecture halls, wandering into the Art and Design school exhibition. He walked her home under the brightness of sparkling stars, after treating her to a *juicy lucy* burger, and a chocolate malt shake. At the door, he kissed her gently. After he left she put her hand on her still warm cheek and walked into her empty cottage.

The light from the moon illuminated her bed as Taara drifted into a restless slumber. Her body shifted under the covers and tossed in all directions until it curled into a ball. Under fluttering eyelids, she saw a vast lake, as big as the ocean and as blue as peace. She spotted a magnificent yacht, flaunting expansive sails gliding majestically over the water, taking each wave in stride, bowing to their energy. Images floated in the sky of the ten-headed Ravan, the demon king from Ramayan, along with the cowherd Krishna, with his flute and dancing *gopis* maidens surrounding him. Off to the side, in the water, she saw a girl with black hair, tiny ears, and tiny glowing wings fluttering in the breeze. As if an image out of Dali's painting, the girl towered over the yacht, her head almost in the clouds, trying to reach up to the godly personas above. Her feet bobbed over the water, each firmly planted in two small boats. Her body swayed as she balanced. Then the wind picked up speed, the water turned choppy, and her balance wavered. The girl saw a loud splash and Taara's eyelids flapped open in a pool of wetness on her pillow.

Taara slipped out of her bed only to sit down on the floor. She stared at the bright moon outside her window, searching. The next morning, she couldn't recall when she had drifted off on the floor, curled up by her slippers. One look in the mirror, and she noticed her disheveled hair, while her fingers reached up to the dried stains on her cheeks. She recalled being wet and wondered if she had sleepwalked into the shower, but her clothes were dry. Feeling disoriented, she stepped into the shower to wash off the confusion.

CHAPTER 12

1997

Omar saw things lucidly. In the next few days, she spent every waking moment with him, seeing her own city through his eyes. They walked in the Ridgedale and Southdale Malls, ate at fast food places, and even drifted through an art museum, hand in hand. She admired the iconic Spoon and Cherry in the outdoor sculpture garden, noticing its larger than life dimensions. He pointed out the ghost-like image of the Minnehaha falls that she had never noticed on her family trips. Even the lakes and rivers looked different at this time of transition, unfrozen but holding on to lingering segments of ice. She was inspired to come back and sketch the falls and the lakes. Her senses awoke to colors and smells she had not felt without Omar by her side.

Over the days she became more aware of his presence, and began to notice the way he meticulously planned each day or showed up at her doorstep at the exact time he had promised. He patiently waited while she hastened to get ready. Finding not a wrinkle on any of his clothes, she asked him if he ironed them every day. She meant it as a joke but was surprised to hear that he actually did. She found his habits quite intriguing.

Friday came too soon. With a heavy heart they said their goodbyes. Taara held on to his lingering touch, the sweet smell of his Gautier, the soft feel of his lips, the gentle sound of his voice. But as reality then stared her in the face, she dived into her school work catching up, preparing for finals, and finishing her art piece. She also embarked on a new project she had been thinking about for months. Soliciting help from two of her mother's friends, Taara started planning a surprise party for her parents on the day of their arrival.

Exams out of the way, sophomore year behind her, Taara had two days to put the party together. Response to the invitations was unanimous and it was promising to be a jubilant affair. Taara was sure about that.

The morning of the party radiated into Taara's old room in her parent's home, accompanied by persistent ringing. Groggily, she put the receiver to her ear, one eye opening for a peek at the clock. Maya aunty's voice roused her and she jolted out of bed. "Oh mygosh, I overslept. Aunty, can you come over to help me?"

"Sure *beta*. I'll see you in an hour."

Taara hung up and ran to the bathroom. Soon she was busy cutting vegetables and salads, creating a racket in the kitchen. Aunty Maya arrived just as Taara was adding the final touch to the *alu gobi* dish.

Taara knew that if there was one friend of her mother's she could count on, it was sweet, demure Maya aunty. Her mellow way of slipping into helping mode made her a welcome addition to the circle of friends Taara's parents maintained. A recent immigrant and craving all things Indian, she prized the company of her new friends.

"Vot else are you planning to make, Taara *beti*?" Maya asked.

"The cauliflower *alu gobi* is all done. I cut up and marinated the chicken yesterday… yes, we need the *masala* gravy for it. Then there's the cheese, the *panir,* in the freezer. We need to defrost it and make the sauce."

"Is the *panir* fried?" Maya asked in calm reverence.

"Yes, cut up in cubes, fried, and... and... oh yes, the *daal.* Aunty, I am deathly afraid of the pressure cooker. Can you help me with the lentils?"

Maya smiled, threw her long braid back to her spine, and rolled up the sleeves of her *kurti* shirt. She pulled out a stool and started bringing down large cooking pots from the overhead cabinets.

"Start chopping a lot of onions." Maya commanded.

Taara hugged her, "Aunty, thank you so much for helping me, I couldn't have done without you. I hope mummy and papa enjoy it."

"I'm sure they will." Maya smiled as she patted Taara's hand, "Now get to work."

Aunty delegated and Taara performed, accomplishing each task meticulously. Sniffling and wiping away tears, Taara chopped away at the onions, followed by tomatoes, hot peppers, cilantro, ginger, garlic and the works. By midday, Maya was wiping off the counters, announcing, "That's it. All your dishes are ready and the kitchen is clean. I'll head on home now. What will you do?"

"I'll go to the campus to get my stuff. I didn't think we'd be done so soon."

"See you in the evening *hanh?*" Maya bobbed her head side to side as she patted Taara on her head.

"Six sharp. Mummy and Papa's flight lands around that time." Taara confirmed.

The campus was almost deserted and very mucky. With the sudden rise in temperature, the snow had turned into slush, creating a complete mess of the walkways. Everyone was dragging in muddy, wet shoes into the buildings. Taara stomped her boots and wiped her feet at the door. Entering her cozy little, cottage apartment, she pressed the blinking light on the answering machine, "Hey Taara. I'm at Kennedy airport, off to Pakistan. Will send you a postcard, as promised. Miss you." Omar's gentle voice echoed. The machine beeped and moved on to the next message, "Taara *beti*. We are at the airport in L.A. The cruise was wonderful. Our plane should be leaving in the next hour. Hope to see you for dinner tonight. We love you," her father's clear voice rolled.

Back at her parents' home, Taara unpacked and laid out her black silk *ghaghra* for the evening. Sitting back with Earl Grey, Taara's thoughts traveled to Omar, *he must be in Europe by now, she calculated.*

Empty mug safely back in the dish washer, Taara walked in a daze to her room, moving in a robotic fashion. She donned her silken, flowing *ghaghra* and silver jewelry and straightened her dark hair to perfect smoothness. Staring at her reflection in the wall length mirror of her parents' bathroom, Taara saw Omar beside her, smiling. The sound of the doorbell shook her out of her reverie.

Aunty Shamma walked in promptly at six, her chubby hand laden with a skillfully crafted three-layer chocolate cake adorned with a bride, a groom, and anniversary flair. The uncles and aunties arrived in succession, helping themselves to drinks and appetizers laid out by Taara and some aunties. Soon the house was filled with a cacophony of loud chatter, vibrant music, and clinking glasses. The aunties came all decked out in their dazzling *sarees* while the uncles wore a mix of western and traditional attire. The notoriously late couple, Uncle Parag and Aunty Lalita, joined the gang well past the surprise hour, but the guests of honor were nowhere in sight.

Uncle Parag suggested a traffic delay since he had heard about an accident on 494 on the radio on his way over. "They'll be here soon."

Another hour came and went. Taara called the airline and learned the flight had landed ahead of schedule. She walked over to Uncle Parag, "The flight landed early. Where was this accident you heard about?" Her lips quivered.

"Taara dear, don't worry. I'll call the airline if they took that flight."

"But uncle, they did. They called me from the airport before getting on it."

Parag patted Taara on her head without meeting her eyes, "I'll find out what's keeping those two. Don't worry."

Aunty Maya held Taara's hand and the others sat quietly with her. The music continued its jangle, luring dancers to the floor. Someone walked over and turned it off while somebody turned on the TV in the family room. Taara sauntered over to watch. The anchor of the evening announced the events of the day – a shooting in North Minneapolis, a house set ablaze by a neglected cigarette, a car crushed under a 14-wheeler. The newscaster at the scene was saying, "… the truck driver escaped unharmed and is in custody. The taxi driver and the two passengers did not survive. From what we have been able to gather, the driver of the 14-wheeler had been driving for 24 hours and was on pain medication. He fell asleep behind the wheel and drove over the taxi in front of him." Taara dropped the remote and limped out of the room. Uncle Parag came to her. His look confirmed her worst fear.

She pushed him away and walked to her room like a zombie. Her eyes remained dry. She sat down on her bed, as she had done in her childhood during time-outs.

Aunties came in, some held her hands, while others massaged her back. They pushed away straggling hair from her face, or just sat close to her. Taara heard sniffles and muffled cries. Somebody helped her change and tried to lay her down. The uncles had gone to the hospital to identify the bodies and had just called home to confirm.

Taara saw all the aunties' faces without recognizing them. She closed her eyes to get away from the crowd around her. Her hands automatically came up to her ears to block out the quiet voices. Her fists clenched and eyes shut tight, she brought her knees close to her chest. A familiar voice from years ago came to her, "Taara… Taara…." She ignored it sinking deeper into her solitude. The voice became louder, "Taara *beti*."

When she looked up, aunty Maya was sitting next to her,

wrapping Dimple's *pashmina* around Taara's shoulders, "Taara *beti*, you need to cry. Let go. *Beti*, your mummy and papa are no longer with us. They have passed on. You need to grieve."

Taara just stared, dry-eyed, cradling into the warmth of the shawl imbued with her mother's unique smell of floral perfume intermingled with fried onions and cumin seeds.

Suddenly, Taara felt a sharp pain on her right cheek. An aunty had slapped her. Another on the left cheek. Her face burned. The aunties shook her and slapped her to get her out of her trance, to bring her back to reality.

Taara let out a sharp wail echoing down the street. A deluge of tears gushed down her soft, ashen cheeks. Her whole body shook with exhaustion and the realization that she was now an orphan. She cried all night, screaming and whimpering, "mummy... papa... mummy... papa...."

CHAPTER 13

1927

"**A**mma... Amma..." Sounds of children reverberated from the *angan*, as Janki bustled from one task to another. Kandhar was unlike any community Janki had been part of. Settling in without an elder to guide her hosted a fresh set of challenges, as minor as setting up the kitchen, or as major as nursing a baby whose body, for three nights, felt as hot as the *angithi* stove. Neighbors of the community poured in with warm food, fresh fruits and medicine for the suffering baby. Janki graciously accepted their welcome, shared her joy of her baby's recovery, and soon began to feel a part of a whole.

Having exhausted their nominal savings, Ram Lal was on the road within few weeks of their arrival, driving his monstrous truck across the border transporting goods while Janki fell into a routine of managing her new home. She was able to find time to get to know her neighbors as her children made new friends. She found her extended family, and soon she began to understand the reason for the elevated respect her family received from the *biradri* community.

Ram Lal, she learned, was a living legend in this town, and Janki heard various tales of his daring feats during his numerous trips. As it turned out, a decade earlier, Ram Lal was the first person to bring a motorized vehicle to this city. He had arrived in the middle of the night, driving his surreal truck through the gates of this walled city and all the inhabitants had come out to observe this phenomenon, awed by the monstrous rumble that one man alone could tame. Powered by coke, a byproduct of coal, wheels resembling cartwheels, the grotesque vehicle was led by a man holding a kerosene lamp in front of the truck while it was in motion over the treacherous route. Janki knew that Ram Lal had gone on to acquire several such trucks, and now that she had seen firsthand the harsh terrain, she shuddered at the thought of her husband negotiating it so frequently. She was shocked at the courage of the poor man who held the kerosene lamp in front of the vehicle, and said a quiet prayer for his wellbeing.

Another dramatic tale Janki heard about her husband came from her new friend, Kalavati. A wholesome woman all around, Kalavati emanated strength of character despite simplicity of mind. Where her large bulk set itself down, stories were endless. Nothing went on in the *biradri* that she was not privy to first. Janki began to enjoy Kalavati's company even though some of her stories were at the expense of others in the community. Janki saw beyond the unsightly mole on her friend's cheek or the miniscule dots set close together as eyes on her plump face. Gossiping and domineering aside, Kalavati was one Janki could always rely on. Not only was she quick to give advice on all matters of life, she never dawdled when it came to giving her time and help to anyone in need. For now, Janki rejoiced in the company of her new friend and the first of many stories she related.

"Unusual sounds used to come from this cave every night," Kalavati related conspiratorially, "Many brave souls ventured in, never to return."

Janki and her children listened wide-eyed. Sita quietly sucked her thumb while Rajendra clung to his mother's *chunni* scarf.

"After Ram Lal *Pahji* came many times to our town with that rumbling monster, one day he had to travel in the direction of the cave outside of the city." Kalavati continued, "We stopped him and told him the cave was haunted, take a different route. He said there were no such things as ghosts and he will prove it to us. We told him about the fate of all those who had gone before him. Stubborn as he is...," Janki smiled knowingly as Kalavati carried on, "he grabbed this big long tool that makes a loud noise and marched right in."

The children held on to Janki's hands and she tightened her grip on them. "Was it his gun?"

"Yes, that's what he called it. As he went in the cave, the whole town was outside, listening and waiting. We heard thunderous roars echoing in the mountain's belly. It was close to sunset when we saw the most amazing sight."

"What? What did you see?" Rajendra blurted.

"*Pahji* walked out into the brightness, gleaming, covered in jewels, and waving his gun in the air." Kalavati finished triumphantly.

Janki was confused, "Jewels? What would a ghost want with jewelry?"

Kalavati laughed, "It was not a ghost, silly. There was a tiger living in that cave and the *dacoits* used that cave as their hideout. They took their loot every night and fresh meat for their "pet" tiger. The *dacoits* haven't been seen in our town ever since."

Rajendra clapped as Sita cheered, momentarily removing her thumb from her mouth. Janki smiled with pride as Kalavati added, "He then distributed the jewels to everybody who he said were the rightful owners." She then put a plump hand on Janki's lap, leaned closer and said, "You are really lucky to be married to such a brave and generous man."

Janki blushed, lowering her eyelids.

In due course, Janki ventured into the bazaars with her long scarf casually resting on her head. Navigating through the little book stores, inhaling the aroma of old books, and listening to the rustle of delicate leaves of yellowed paper, her curiosity about her adoptive city reached new heights. She discovered that Kandhar was the chief commercial center of the country where fruits, grain, tobacco, silk, cotton, and wool were in abundance, while several textile mills, fruit processing and canning plants also flourished. She was not surprised to learn that the majority of the Hindus and Sikhs of Afghanistan lived in Kandhar, growing into a unique community of the *Kandhari Biradri*.

On another day of her venture, she dug into the history of her new home, and read that the city derived its name, *Iskandahar* from its founder, Alexander the Great. In newspapers and articles on current events, she learned that the sitting King Amanullah and his Queen Soroya had just returned from their world tour. The article went on to relate that while on this tour, they had enjoyed lavish banquets. The queen was even said to have discarded her veil while wearing a shoulder-less gown. The royal couple returned with a Rolls Royce and a new determination to modernize Afghanistan.

Several days later, Janki read that King Amanullah issued a directive for the tribal leaders to shave off their beards and insisted they wear top hats instead of the traditional turbans and *Karikuli* Cap. His next proclamation, she read, aggravated the traditionalists even more - a plan to make education compulsory for women. Janki absorbed all the news, and when she discussed her concerns with Ram Lal during his short visits, they fell on deaf ears. He was engrossed in his vision of growing his business.

As Rajendra and Sita made many friends and baby Durgi took her first steps, Janki plodded along managing her home with a growing belly. On a day like any other, she sat blowing on the coal to start a fire in her *angithee* stove in the courtyard in the late afternoon. Durgi napped on the *manji* bed under the shade of the willow, with flies buzzing around in a lazy hum. Janki extended her hand over to the sleeping baby to fan away the pests. A leopard gecko suddenly plummeted from the branch onto the *manji*, nearly touching the baby's head, as it scurried off down to the ground. Janki noticed its violet red stump of a tail before it took off and her hand went to her thumping heart. Enough stories and folklores had reached her ears about the bad omen these reptiles brought to those they dropped on.

Before she could recover from the unfortunate encounter, from the corner of her eye she saw Rajendra running toward her. Soon she heard his scream. Carrying her heavy load she ran toward him, almost colliding into his frail body. Her hands brushed over his tear-streaked cheeks as she screened his head, face, and body for any injuries finally grabbing his shoulders.

Between heaves and sobs he said, "Sita."

Shaking him she yelled, "Where is she?"

When they arrived, puffing and panting at the opening where the children played every day by the stream, she saw her beautiful Sita, sprawled on the banks. Janki lowered her massive body down on the rugged, dusty shore and set Sita's head on her lap. She looked so peaceful with her two, thick, black braids neatly tied with red ribbons on each end, dripping with water. There was a red dot on the corner of her forehead with a small bruise around it. Her clothes clung to her skin as if swaddling her into a cocoon. Janki looked up at the crowd of children surrounding her until her dry-eyed gaze fell on her son. It remained there frozen, searching.

Rajendra was still panting as he stood over them, and ran a sleeve over his dripping nose. Gathering up air between sobs, his 6-year old voice broke as he asked, "Amma, why isn't she waking up?"

Janki was about to answer her son when she felt a sharp pain in her belly. Kalavati and several assembled neighbors carried Sita and supported Janki as she struggled home. `A doctor rushed from the next neighborhood and helped Janki bring a new life to this world. Nobody knew whether to rejoice or mourn as the whimpering cries of the newborn boy echoed in the house, and an unseasonal downpour drenched the muddy streets.

CHAPTER 14

1997

The view from the tightly shut window blurred Taara's vision, as torrents of rain splattered around the glass, the wing, the runway, and the entire plane. The sky was crying for Taara, for she had exhausted her own tears. This was the rain in Minnesota that was supposed to make the grass green and the flowers bloom, but all Taara could see was despair. It was still too hard to accept that her parents were no longer with her in the flesh.

Aunty Maya had placed the call to California to Dimple's sister, Ruhi. She and her husband, Raj, had flown the same night, catching the red-eye. The days had passed in a blur, with plenty of comings and goings, but Taara had shut everyone out. She had locked herself in her room, even on the day of the final ceremony, when the house bustled with well-wishers, servers from the restaurant, the priest and his helpers, and close friends of her parents. Smells of saffron rice mingled with various vegetarian delicacies wafted through the cracks under her door. The familiar aroma nauseated her, and she was thankful for the attached bathroom.

After concluding the twelfth-day ceremony, the *Purohit* and other believers were satisfied that Dimple's, and Raman's souls were respectfully sent off on their next journey. Once the house was quiet again, Taara listened for familiar footsteps of her father walking right through her door. She found uncle Raj stepping in. He spoke to her in his calm, gentle voice advising her of next steps. He held her hand and helped her shed the unending tears, shedding a few with her. He walked her out of her room into the kitchen, holding her hand all the while and coaxed her to get some food. Finally, he convinced her to make the journey to California with them.

She looked out the oval window of the plane into the whiteness of the clouds. The captain's voice came over the speakers to advise the flight attendants to prepare for landing. The scene at the Orange County Airport appeared equally gloomy. Sunny California had no sunshine and the world seemed to move in slow motion. Taara floated through the airport to baggage claim and to the taxi that was to take them home - her uncle and aunt's home in Newport Beach.

As Ruhi paid the cab driver and Raj unloaded the luggage, Taara stood in a daze. Uncle Raj unlocked the front door and the arch-like doorway beckoned Taara inside. She stepped onto white marble floors splashed with Persian rugs. A crystal chandelier hung from the ceiling in the foyer, casting light onto the colorful, abstract art that decorated the pastel walls. Taara walked to the center of the great room and looked up at the 3-story high vaulted ceiling. She looked to the south wall, all glass, through which was the clear blueness of the sky and the sea. Sun had found its way back over the Pacific. Taara slid open the glass door and looked out at the vast ocean with its boisterous, white-tipped waves. She took in the sweet, salty smell as she sauntered down to the carpet of soft sand. It was like a house her parents had always dreamt to have one day. For now, all its beauty was lost on Taara as she harbored the regret of unfulfilled dreams.

Over the next few days, Ruhi returned to her small-time modeling assignments, and Raj went back to spending his hours on the highways of California between customer visits. Taara usually woke to a bright sun, high in the sky, and drifted into the kitchen. There she helped herself to a glass of juice or milk, whatever her hand landed on, a bite of a cookie or cracker, and headed right back to the comfort of her bed. She tried to block the light out by closing all the blinds, but streaks of sunshine always found their way in to torment her. She would dive deep into the comforter and stay there until Raj or Ruhi came home. Whenever he could, Raj worked from home, and at dinner he insisted Taara eat at the table with them. Most dinnertimes Taara rearranged the food on her plate, while some days she rewarded her uncle and aunt with monosyllabic replies.

One evening, Taara found herself studying Ruhi over the chicken pot roast. She noticed hints of Dimple - the same button nose, tiny ears and heart-shaped face. Taara blinked and recognized nothing of her mother. All she saw was a woman with a striking auburn mane with brown highlights, blunt-cut to her ears. Her head was held up high as she glided through life, as if posing for invisible cameras. Her sense of style, her flattering curves, and even the attitude in the way she flipped her hair back from her face, was deliberate. She boasted a trendy, giant handbag wherever she went, slung over her shoulder, along with the chip she housed on that same shoulder. Taara thought it was because of her height. If only Ruhi had been a little taller, she could have been a runway model.

Taara looked at uncle Raj, his gaze fixed on his wife. He saw Ruhi beyond her flaws. He was medium-built with his right arm more muscular than the left due to extensive Squash sessions. His ruffled hair was too stubborn to obey his casual combing, and he always wore pants that were too long for him. Somehow, he appeared put-together quite charmingly, especially when dressed up in suit and tie for an important business meeting. He even sported a small dark tuft of hair below his bottom lip that moved up and down with each word formation, an all-too-frequent event. He was a successful marketing executive and loved everything around him, especially Taara, whom he took under his wing as a daughter. His easygoing manner made life with Ruhi possible, and helped Taara through her current hardship.

As soon as dinner ended, Raj rushed to his den for a conference call with a customer in Asia and Taara stayed to help Ruhi clear away the dishes. The silence hung heavier than the crockpot Taara was trying to scrub. Then the dishes began to clang, the refrigerator door slammed, and the silverware clinked.

Just as Taara was placing the last plate in the dishwasher, Ruhi asked, "So who's Omar?"

Taara looked up in surprise. She had completely forgotten about him, their magical date, their passionate conversations, their intimate moments, and her secret from her parents.... Taara gasped and another flood of tears threatened to flow.

Ruhi waited with her arms crossed.

"*Masi*, how do you know about him?" Taara finally asked.

"A postcard arrived today from him, redirected from Minnesota." She found the card in the neat stack of the day's mail on the kitchen counter and handed it to her. "Also, there was a message on your answering machine at the cottage."

"Why didn't you tell me?" Taara accused as she took the colorful postcard. A beautiful picture of Henna Lake splashed on one side and a short message from Omar scribbled on the back side, 'As promised'.

Narrowing her mascara-clad eyes, Ruhi responded, "I tried. You weren't interested."

Taara walked over to Ruhi and wrapped her arms around her. She dropped her head on her shoulder and said, "I'm sorry *Masi*, I was being selfish I suppose..." she sobbed, "...but I miss them. I miss them so much."

Unpeeling her niece from her silk blouse, Ruhi brushed away the wrinkles Taara had created on her linen skirt. Through pursed lips she mumbled, "I know you miss them. We all do."

"Thank you for... everything," Taara sniffled.

Ruhi was much too eager to move along. "Now tell me about this guy who's sending you postcards and leaving phone messages."

Taara seemed surprised, "I thought you said there was only one message?"

"Yes honey, in Minnesota. He called here today."

Taara stood wordless.

Clearing her throat, Ruhi honed in on her point. Looking straight into her niece's eyes, she began in her flat tone. "Taara, listen to me. Raj and I cannot replace your parents. But, since *Masi* means 'just like mother', I suppose that's what I'll have to be."

Taara grabbed her aunt's hand. Holding back tears, she whimpered, "I know you will."

Ruhi continued, "Yes, but there is one thing I need you to know. You cannot go moping around like this for the rest of your life. Taara, they are gone." Looking at her niece, Ruhi grabbed her shoulders. "Listen honey, you need to return to life. You're only going to get deeper into that black hole you've dug for yourself. It's been six weeks and...."

Ruhi choked on her words and fell to the chair. Taara stood there, gazing. Neither noticed the sun disappear, leaving the room in darkness. Sounds of neighborhood children playing outside entered the somber room.

From the seated position, a feeble voice tried to sound strong. "I miss my sister too. She was more like my mother until...."

Taara knelt down on the floor, next to the chair, and put her hand on Ruhi's arm.

Ruhi looked down, "I know what it's like to lose your parents. Twice."

In a child's voice Taara said, "Don't cry, *Masi*."

Silence hung over them until the creek of the den door reached their ears. Raj was done with his call. Ruhi sat up straight and reaching for a fresh Kleenex, she wiped her eyes, stood up to her full height, chest out, shoulders back.

"Taara, I have a friend, a set designer prop-master, whatever they call themselves." She bent down to switch on the table lamp, flooding the room with a soft yellow glow. She stood up and continued. "Anyway, she is short-handed for a production that's coming up soon. I told her you'll be there tomorrow morning to help with the artwork."

"What? I can't go. I need some time to think about this." Taara cried.

"You've had time, dear. You can't dwell in your cocoon forever."

"No!" Taara marched into her room and shut the door, leaving an enraged aunt behind in the dim light.

Inside Taara threw herself on the bed and let the tears flow. From the open window flowed in warm, sea breeze. The wind rustled the leaves, summoning more neighborhood sounds – an opening garage door, incessant chatter of crickets, and children shrieking. Taara grabbed a pillow to cover her ears, diving deeper into her darkness, floating alone. She was surrounded by all the sounds of life, but life was too burdensome for her. She called out, "mummy... mummy...." This time no reassuring voice came, no one to comfort or rescue her. She fell deeper in the crowd of living and breathing things, sinking, sinking, as if she had fallen in quicksand.

She woke with a start, the heaviness in her head reminding her of her fear. Her tongue felt dry and her cheeks felt sticky. She groped for support as she made her way to the bathroom in the darkness. Turning on the light she found the glass. Taara spied her image in the mirror and knew nothing was the same. Dark shadows replaced the sunshine in her eyes and the perpetual flush on her cheeks had adopted the color of milk. Gone were the days of recurring sparks of vibrant smiles. The image talked back to Taara, challenging her, *will you ever find the happiness you once had?* Taara blinked away the ever-present tears threatening to flow and stared into the eyes of her ghost.

Returning back to bed, Taara reached for her mother's shawl. Wrapping it around her shoulders, she leaned back, feeling the comfort from its warmth and absorbing the hint of its familiar aroma. A string of escaped thread tickled her neck, reminding her of its age and the multiple owners of this blanket of legacy. A voice from a long time ago echoed in her ears, *"Don't be scared beta."*

She burrowed into the shawl and inhaled, feeling her mother's presence. She remembered her father's stories and all the mythological characters he presented so magnificently to her. Their nurturing and wisdom was so bountiful, she recognized, and then realized, her parents also had dreams for her. Dreams they will never see fulfilled. How can she pick up the shattered pieces of their dreams? The crash was too harsh, the pieces were tiny and she didn't have the strength to put the pieces together alone.

But I have to try. Taara found herself thinking, *I cannot mope around like this forever. How long can Masi and Raj uncle put up with me? I can just paint and stay out of people's way.*

CHAPTER 15

1928

Janki's life lay shattered into a thousand pieces as her household fell into a disarray. Frequent cries of discomfort echoed through the house, followed by unsettling wheezes. Narendra, a frail boy born before his time, gained enough strength to survive, but developed lifelong breathlessness and susceptibility to ailments. Shrouded by his mother's desultory manner, the baby screamed endlessly. His arms waved about in the air as if to grab hold of a lifeline. He found Kalavati's plump fingers to grasp, her warm touch for comfort, and her full breasts for nourishment, that he had to share with her own six month old.

Kalavati also fostered the toddler, Durgi, shielding her from the tragic events her family struggled to come to terms with. Rajendra walked around aimlessly with shock frozen on his little face, lost in his own home. Janki floated under a dark cloud, disassociated from all things living. She stayed in her dark room, on the bed she had given birth in, drained of body and spirit.

Ram Lal arrived four days later in a state of disarray. His shirt and pants had become almost black from the multiple layers of dust and soot he had acquired from the agonizing journey. His thick hair appeared matted down with wind and earth, while his bloodshot eyes stared without focus. Arriving home in such a state and then to find his surviving children in disarray, and wife withdrawn from all that mattered, Ram Lal went into a fit. Anger took over all other emotions and he lashed out with words. His first victim was God, the one Ram Lal prayed to every morning and still He let this tragedy happen. God was supposed to watch over his family in his absence, but the Almighty was negligent.

Ram Lal walked away, outside the compound, outside the walls of the city abandoning his suffering family. He walked in anger, his tears blinding his direction or destination. A couple of miles later he found himself south of the city, having walked up on top of a hill toward the Baba Wali shrine. There he stood and stared back into the Aranghabad valley, watched the glistening water of the river peacefully flowing, and calmly observed the fortified city that was his home. He watched the natural cycle of life around him continue with its motions, as scant clouds floated above playing hide and seek with the sun. The river sparkled under the glaring rays, or fell in shadows when the sun winked. Through light and dark, it will continue its journey toward its destiny meandering through the desert, rising in the central Hindu Kush, to ultimately marry into the Helmand River.

Ram Lal drank in a gulp of air, looked up to the heavens apologetically, and started his descent toward his family. He found Janki pasted to her bed like a molten zombie, detached and despaired. He saw Rajendra crouched by his mother's bed, engulfed in darkness. His head slumped like dead weight into his hands, his hair disheveled, and shirt crinkled and filthy. He picked up his *puttar* son and walked out into the bright courtyard. Under the tree he sat on the *manji* bed and set his son on his lap, wiping the tear stains from his cheeks.

Rajendra looked at his father, thousands of questions

swimming in his eyes. Ram Lal put his arm around his son's shoulder, took in a deep breath and explained, "Your sister has gone away to God." Rajendra blinked innocently and listened as his father continued, "It was a very brave thing you did to call Amma. We are very proud of you *puttar*."

Rajendra looked down at his father's shoes noticing the tear at their seams. He crinkled his nose at the odor that radiated from his father, but then took comfort in the familiarity of stale sweat and smell of the earth. He put his arms around the older man, resting his head against his large beating heart. He then jumped off his father's lap, gave his little-man nod, and walked toward his friend's house.

Ram Lal watched his son walk away and allowed himself a smile. He puffed up his chest, standing up with pride, and walked toward his home.

In their room he saw Janki slumped on the bed, eyes closed, and a white sheet partially covering her body. The baby lay sleeping peacefully next to her, tightly swaddled in a muslin cloth. He walked over to the bed, picked up his fourth child and carefully brought its forehead to his lips. The baby stirred in his confined space within the cloth, passed a fleeting smile and settled back into his father's arms. Ram Lal's eyes melted like wax from a burning candle as he watched the delicate creature. He carefully set his young son back by his mother, turned around and walked out to cleanse the dirt and grime off his body and clothes.

Janki's head turned toward the door as she opened her eyes, and watched the silhouette of her husband's back in the doorframe. Bright light from outside emanated around him as a mystical warmth. Sensing the baby stir next to her, she slowly pulled herself up.

Ram Lal walked back into their room, sparkling and fresh. He saw Janki slumped on the ground, her gaze fixed on a dark corner of the room. Her head leaned over the infant in her arms as it suckled on her breast. He paced, cleared his throat and paced some more, before walking over to his wife. He sat on the bed, his feet helplessly dangling next to his wife's sitting form. He shifted his seat moving to the edge of the bed and cautiously rested his hand on her head. He stroked her hair as tears freely flowed from both their eyes, down their cheeks, dropping down to the ground to melt with the earth.

The twelfth-day mourning ceremony came and went with customary offerings and rituals. Ram Lal returned to his rounds to lands beyond, while Janki picked up the shattered pieces of their lives and resumed her duties. Eventually, she tried to find her tracks back to the one place she had found solace in this foreign land – the bookstores.

As she walked through the bazaar, her head covered with the scarf partially veiling her face, she felt stares darting in her direction. Discreetly looking around, she noticed that she was the only woman in the crowded street. Inside the shop she often visited, she asked the kind elderly man who owned the little store what was going on. He handed her a few newspapers and magazine articles and encouraged her to take them home, read them, and not return unescorted. He promised to send his grandson with updates and the latest publications.

Confused, she held the papers to her chest, wrapped her *chunni* scarf around her body and hurried home. Papers sprawled in front of her, she absorbed all that had transpired in the past months. Sitting back and comprehending, her initial anxiety of the politics of the country resurfaced. She read about the uprising in the north of the capital, led by some Tajik tribesman robber, Bacha-i-Saqao, and it concerned her. She was not surprised to see that the King's modernization program had gone too far for the fundamentalists. She sat back and worried that turmoil from the capital, Kabul, which was already spreading to the countryside, was sure to reach such an important city like Kandhar.

Early next morning, as the first rays of the sun were peeking through the branches of the willow, Janki sat on her front porch, sheaves of paper in her hand that the bookseller's grandson had dropped off. Her tea sitting by her began to gather a layer of cream on its surface as her eyes poured into the state of affairs in her adopted country. She looked out through the small door of her house into the bleak morning's snow that had welcomed the New Year. Later that day, Janki heard the news that Amanullah was seen fleeing in his Rolls Royce, just barely keeping ahead of the Bacha's cavalry on the snowy road.

More news streamed in as the new government established its capital in the eastern rocky plateau of Ghazni. Soon after, she read that the new regime had labeled all the dwellers of Kandhar loyalists of the king and the British government. Janki worried for Ram Lal that he might come under scrutiny with his constant border crossing. One cold February evening, on the day before his next departure, Janki sat in her little kitchen rolling out dough for the *roti* breads. She heard a loud bang in a corner and turned to look. A steel plate was rolling on the ground, having fallen from a higher shelf. She looked up at the cause of its fall and spotted the culprit – a black cat. Abandoning the unrolled *roti*, rolling pin in hand, she stood up to shoo this symbol of bad omen away, her heart pounding. When the next day Ram Lal prepared to leave, Janki was restless. She begged him to delay his journey, stay a little longer, finally confessing to the warning she had received in the form of a black cat. He acquiesced.

A few days later, as the family prepared their beds for the cold night, a group of men barged into their abode. Their faces were hidden behind long beards, and their heads were covered under bulky turbans. Fire from their bulging eyes seemed to raise the temperature of the room. They grabbed Ram Lal by the collar and dragged him out as Janki and the children stood in shock. Finding her legs in time, she ran out begging for the men to let go of her husband, and fell to their feet pleading. They kicked her away and she fell back, hitting her head against a *manji* bed in the courtyard. She felt the earth spin around her, stars flashing everywhere and somewhere from another world she heard shouts and screams. Rajendra's voice echoed in her ears repeating, "Leave my *Bauji* alone." She saw faces in the crowd gathered, fear masked on them, as they stood bearing witness to the scene. Then the world went dark and she fell to the ground.

She woke later to find Rajendra positioned by the door, crouched on the frame watching out into the horizon. The moon transitioned through its phases from non-existence to its full brilliance back to its dark nothingness. Rumors trickled in like flurries from the sky, of a prison camp up high in the new capital. Janki remained imprisoned in her own home, unable as a woman to venture out in search of her husband. She read all she could, grasping at any bit of news that could give a clue of her husband's whereabouts, or even to know if he was alive.

Another cycle of the moon completed, her rations slowly depleting, she struggled to keep her household afloat. With the glimmer of hope slowly fading with the darkening moon, she made a decision that she hoped would bring normalcy to her children and help them survive. She resolved to abandon her husband and return to Khushab to be with his parents and sister.

CHAPTER 16

1997

Abandoning her fear, Taara ventured to her new job early, but the commute was worse than she had expected. She had written down directions of all the back roads from Newport Beach to Irvine, avoiding the highways at all cost. That did not save her much time at all. The signal was out at one junction and one-lane traffic crawled on another leg. Taara missed the Twin Cities and its less busy roads.

The studio was a small corner facility in a shopping plaza. At first Taara thought she had come to the wrong place, for there was no prominent sign. Soon she learned that her employer was a one-woman shop with contracts from low-budget community theatres. Taara's boss, Nancy, was a petite, genteel, and soft-spoken woman with a prolific talent for creating massive objet d'art despite her height of five feet. By looking at her, Taara would not have guessed that she had a 13-year old grandson. Eddie was a chubby and a cheerful boy, helping his grandmother on an as-needed basis.

The studio had wall-to-wall canvasses splashed with grand scapes for land, sea, or sky for backdrops of many scenes. In one corner sat a large fountain sculpture and in another, a massive statue of the Hindu God, Ganesh. These were all works in progress for a theatrical production starting in July.

Though hesitant at first, Taara soon dived into her project. Her job was to illustrate earthly creatures on bright colored panels of cloth or cardboard. She became so absorbed in the colors, the shapes, the movement of her brush strokes, and before long, the sky outside started to match the colors on the canvasses – shades of blue, purple, red, orange and yellow.

She donned her faded blue jeans and solid colored T's every morning and came home covered in rainbow colors every evening. Occasionally, Taara joined her aunt in a nice, long dip in their pool in the evening. In a short amount of time, this became her daily ritual. Taara started to feel refreshed and rejuvenated after a few laps.

On infrequent evenings when Taara found herself alone in the large house, she would succumb to her emotions, re-living her life with her parents. One such evening as Taara was deep within her grief, the phone echoed around the great room. She ignored it. After a momentary silence, it rang again. Thinking it could be Raj, Taara reached for the cordless. "You have won a free trip to Orlando, Florida…," came the sound of the recorded message on the other end.

Taara snapped on the OFF button with frustration. Almost immediately, the phone rang again. Taara jumped from her armchair, almost yelling into the mouthpiece, "Hello!"

"Is that Taara?" A familiar husky voice echoed from the other end.

"Who's this?" Taara snapped.

"Omar. Remember me?"

She practically dropped the cordless from her shaking hands. Gathering herself she responded, "Of course I do."

"I'm so sorry to hear about your parents." He paused for a

response. When none came he continued, "If there's anything I can do, I'm here for you." Omar waited patiently.

Fresh tears trickled down Taara's cheeks. She grasped the phone in her quivering hands, "Omar, they are gone. Oh Omar, I miss them so much!"

"I am so sorry." Omar's voice became stronger as he continued, "I never got a chance to meet them, but I feel like I knew them so well."

Taara gripped the phone to her ear, absorbing the warmth in his voice. Wiping her tears she croaked, "Thank you Omar, that's so sweet." She sniffled and continued, "I'm sorry I didn't call you back."

"You don't need to apologize. I'm in California for the summer if you want to talk or meet."

Taara jotted down his number and promised to call. She returned to her emptiness but realized that the deep melancholy had receded and decided to take a dip in the pool.

The next day brought sunshine and a more cheerful mood, and Raj was happy to notice a smile on Taara. Just a month of working at the studio had helped her spirits. Raj thought of this as an opportune moment to bring up the topic he had been pondering, "Taara dear, what are your plans for the fall semester?"

"What do you mean?" Taara was half-listening.

Raj pressed on, "Don't you want to finish your college?"

"Oh that, I don't know. I... uncle... I don't know, I can't see past today and the thought of going back there...."

"I'm sure you'll have no problem getting admission at the U here and you'll be able to transfer your credits."

"Uncle, can we not talk about this please. Besides, there's still two whole months before the fall semester."

Raj tried again, "But you need to start thinking about it at least."

"Don't you have to get to the 4th of July parade?" Taara asked.

Raj looked at his watch, dropping his wrist instantly, "Oh no, Arjun and Bharti must be waiting."

"It's in Huntington Beach, isn't it? There could be traffic." Taara offered.

Raj called out to Ruhi, "Stop dabbing all that make-up and hurry along." When Raj turned back to Taara, she was long gone.

The studio was in a buzz of activity the last week before the deadline. New faces appeared to add finishing touches to the art pieces or to take them to the production site. Taara left early and got home just in time to crawl into her bed to be up again at the crack of dawn and out the door. She didn't see her aunt or uncle for days. It was not until the crazy schedule was over that she received Omar's message.

"Taara dear, who is this Omar?" Raj walked into the kitchen, joining Taara at the table as she ate her cucumber sandwich.

Taara rolled her eyes, "He's a friend I met at college."

"He called twice this week." Raj reached for the freshly squeezed orange juice and poured it into a glass.

"Oh, what'd he say?" Taara bit into her sandwich trying to sound impassive.

"He wanted to know if you were alright." Raj swallowed the juice down in one gulp, "And he wanted to talk to you."

"Oh yah, I was supposed to call him." Taara kept her voice flat.

"So?" Raj asked, "Who is he?"

"Oh uncle, he's a friend I met at the U. His family is from Quetta and you know about Ammaji being from there and all." She took a sip of her juice and continued, "Anyways, we got to talking and... and... oh yea, he's from here. Is Calabasas far?"

"Just an hour and a half or so, in the mountains." Raj then suggested, "Why don't you invite him over some evening? We'd love to meet him."

"I'd like that. Are you home tomorrow?"

Raj smiled and nodded.

"Perfect!" She stood up and gave Raj a hug and ran out to call Omar.

The evening was perfect. All the stars sparkled alongside a

sliver of a moon, up high under a clear sky. Omar arrived right on time, dressed in khaki Dockers and a black polo.

After a hearty meal of chicken lasagna, spring salad of greens and berries with warm baguette rolls, four of them sat by the pool with dessert plates and coffee.

"Omar, how did you get my phone number here?" Taara wondered out loud.

"Oh, I contacted Nata." He relaxed into the rattan chair, his dark polo contrasting with the red cushioned backing of the furniture.

"I hear your family is from Quetta. Have you been there?" Raj inquired.

"I went to visit my grandmother there last month." He turned to Ruhi and politely stated, "Taara tells me your family is from Quetta."

"My father was born there." Ruhi responded.

"I understand it's heavenly." Raj said.

"It's paradise." Omar continued with a twinkle in his eyes, "The view of the rustic mountains and the crystal-clear water of Henna Lake…."

The ripples from the water in the pool and the songs of the crickets in the bushes offered background music to the party.

"Does your grandmother live alone?" Raj asked.

"Yes, in our ancestral home, but her two daughters and their families live nearby."

"How old is she?" Raj asked.

"Must be in her 70's. She's been in that house since her wedding, even through the Partition era." Omar leaned forward to place his empty plate on the table and continued, "The stories she has to share are astounding. It's a wonder she survived those terrible times." He stared out into the blackness as if he could see his grandmother right there.

Taara floated into her own world, of another grandmother in a different valley. Wheels were turning in her head. Suddenly she was interested in Janki, Dimple and Ruhi's grandmother. She wanted to know about her life and hear more stories about her life in Quetta and the partition, like the ones her mother had shared.

Raj turned to his wife, "Ruhi, I wonder if Omar's grandmother knew yours."

"I don't think so," she said.

Before Raj could say anything, Taara stood up, startling everyone.

"What's wrong?" Omar and Raj spoke together.

"Nothing." She sat down again and turned to Omar, "It must be nice to hear stories from your grandmother."

"I always have more appreciation for things after I've spent time with her." he responded.

Raj noticed Ruhi staring out into the darkness, lips pursed stiffly together. He stood up, "Well, I don't know about you all but I'm done letting these bugs feast on my blood any longer. I'm going indoors."

Omar stood up as well and turned to Raj and Ruhi, "Thank you very much for a wonderful dinner. I really enjoyed meeting you both."

Taara walked Omar to the door, "Thank you for coming and…" she looked down to her hands, her fingers tangled in knots, "and… for everything."

"Can I see you again?" he asked taking a step forward as they faced each other on the porch.

"I'd like that." She looked up into his eyes, "Can I call you?"

"Only if you promise to and not forget like last time," Omar teased.

Taara shook her head, smiled and said, "I Promise."

They both laughed then fell silent, searching in each other's eyes. He finally took her hands, untangled them and kissed each one. Taara's cheeks flushed but she didn't pull away. With a wink and a smile, Omar swiftly turned and left.

"Taara," Ruhi called from behind the kitchen counter as soon as she heard the door close.

Taara collected herself and calmly replied, "*Ji masi?*"

"May I talk to you please?" Ruhi's tone was solemn. After they were seated she began, "How serious are you about this guy?"

"We're just friends," Taara said, still feeling warm on her cheeks.

"Keeping this relationship at the friendship level is fine. I would not recommend beyond that," Ruhi demanded.

"Why?"

"He's not Hindu."

"What?" Taara retorted.

"Hindus and Muslims shouldn't intermarry." Ruhi remained cool.

"What do you mean?" Taara demanded.

"I know from experience," Ruhi said.

"What?" Taara exclaimed.

"A Hindu friend of mine married a Muslim man a few years ago, here in California. Both families disapproved but they married anyway. Both said religion was not an issue."

"They were in love?" Taara interrupted.

Ruhi went on, "Within a year, my friend was not allowed to put pictures on the walls. Then he forbade her to go to the temple. Soon after, he started to screen her clothing and disapproved of anything that showed her arms or legs. It wasn't long before he went as far as enforcing the *hijab*, the head scarf, on her."

Taara sat down slowly, her mouth agape.

Ruhi went on. "Slowly, she lost her freedom, and was asked to officially convert to Islam. He even moved back in with his parents."

"Where is she now?" Taara asked.

"I haven't heard from her in over a year, soon after the birth of her son."

"This is a really sad story *Masi*," Taara said.

"So my point is that you better be careful. These Muslim boys are not to be trusted," Ruhi emphasized.

"Not all Muslim boys are the same." Taara shook her head, "How can you stereotype?"

"Even your parents wouldn't have approved," Ruhi added.

"I am not even thinking marriage. And don't you dare bring my parents into this!" she added with disgust.

"Watch your tone with me, young lady."

"Sorry, *Masi* but I cannot take this stone-age thinking sitting down." Taara stood up and continued, "Not that I am planning or anything, but I have no qualms about marrying a Muslim or a Christian or a Sikh if it's the right person." She started to walk toward her room.

Ruhi stalled her with a hand on her arm, her blood red nail polish glistening on shapely fingers, "If you do marry a Muslim, remember this." Taara turned to look into a venomous stare, "You are no niece of mine."

Taara pushed the perfectly manicured hand off her arm in disgust and walked away, almost knocking Raj off the stairs as she made her way to her room. She threw herself onto the lime-green bedspread and buried her face into it before succumbing to sleep.

CHAPTER 17

1997

The Sunday crowd was bustling at Newport Beach. Omar was already waiting at the ice cream parlor tryst, even though Taara was early. She observed him from across the street. He looked so handsome in his clean, lime-green polo and light denim shorts, as always, perfectly ironed and neatly tucked in. Taara walked up to him and smiled her brightest, her shoulder-length dark hair battling the salty wind.

They bought ice cream cones and the two strolled in silence down the promenade, licking their mint chocolate scoops. Omar caught a melting runaway drop with his tongue and said, "It was nice to meet your uncle and aunt yesterday."

Taara dabbed her lips with a napkin to wipe off the sticky cream and answered, "I'm sorry about Ruhi aunty. I hope you weren't offended by her silence."

Omar shook his head as he gobbled down a large bite of the

last of his cone.

"She's not as cold as she may come across," Taara explained, "It's just that… well, I'm not really sure." A crease formed between her eyebrows.

"It must be hard for her, too, losing her sister and staying strong for you," Omar offered, as he cleansed his hands with a wet nap he removed from his pocket.

"I suppose," Taara said, finishing off her cone.

Omar nudged Taara over to a rock where they sat and watched the sun descend across the emerald green ocean. Omar took her hand into his and together they sat admiring the backdrop of deep orange as it transformed into a crimson sky. The last rays reflected off Taara's 22-carat gold bracelet, radiating intricate patterns. Her mother had presented her with the bracelet on her 18th birthday. She sat down on the sand and watched the designs change as she moved her wrist sideways. The tiny hearts from the bracelet became bigger or smaller depending on which side she twisted her wrist. Omar sat next to her and watched her admire her heirloom, while their bodies cast longer shadows on the sand.

Soon the show was over and all that was left was a deep, blue sky tinged with soft orange and pink hues on the horizon. Watching the incandescent pattern had taken Taara to Quetta, although she had never been there. She felt a splash of warmth bathe her as she hugged herself tight.

Omar put an arm around her and she nestled into his warmth.

"Have you thought about returning to Minnesota to finish your college?" Omar probed delicately.

"I don't think I can go there again. I can't face it alone with all those memories."

"What about your studies? Your future?"

"You too, Omar? Uncle Raj has been after me about this already." Taara looked up at him.

"I'm sorry." He snuggled her back into his arms.

They fell silent for a moment.

Omar fidgeted about. Then, shaking his head, decided to dive back in, "Isn't it the memories that should make you want to go back there? That's how you can keep them alive, by re-living your memories with them in the same, familiar surroundings."

"I know what you're trying to do, Omar. Just the thought of going to that house, the same parks, restaurants, library, movie theatres, the malls…. I can't take it. Not alone. I can't."

"Who said you'd have to do this alone?" Omar spoke softly.

"Aunty and uncle have a life here, and all my other relatives are scattered across the world. I don't even know any of my cousins very well." Taara looked at Omar and said, "Yes, I am alone."

"I'm here." He spoke softly.

Taara opened her mouth then closed it. She watched him with misty eyes, smiled and planted a gentle kiss on his cheek.

"That means a lot to me, Omar." Standing up, she said, "But I'm not ready. I can't go to Minnesota yet."

They stood in silence together and watched the beachcombers pack up, carrying their sunbaked bodies back to their cars.

"I'm going to India," Taara finally confessed.

"What? When?" Omar looked at her in surprise.

"Tuesday."

He ran a hand through his hair and said, "That soon?"

Taara started to walk and Omar followed, a cool ocean breeze strolling along with them. Wrapping her arms around her shoulders, she missed her comforting shawl.

"When did you decide this?" Omar asked.

"Not sure, but all that talk about your grandmother and Quetta got me thinking." She stopped walking and looked at him, "I decided to visit my great-grandmother, Ammaji."

Omar stopped as well, and watched her with amusement.

She looked into his eyes and said, "I think before I can move forward, I need to go back." She looked down at her twisting fingers.

A teenager on a skateboard rolled past them swerving around foot traffic.

Omar put his hands on Taara's shoulders and said, "I understand."

"But, whenever I'm ready...", she looked back up into his eyes, "I know I can't move forward alone."

He enveloped her in his arms. "You won't be alone, I promise." The two stood as one in the middle of the promenade while walkers, skaters, and bikers skirted around them.

The sky became a deeper blue above them and they continued to walk to the parking lot, hand in hand. Omar asked, "Where in India does your great-grandmother live?"

"Dehra Dun, but I'll fly into Delhi and stay with uncle Raj's parents first."

Stopping in front of her car Omar said, "I hope you find what you're looking for."

"Me too." She attempted a smile.

He leaned forward and kissed her and she felt the warmth run through her body like an electric current. Her knees became weak and she melted into his embrace. With difficulty, each pulled apart, and she stepped into Raj's champagne Acura sedan.

The drive back home brought the view of the far-off mountains in front of her. Taara's thoughts wandered to the stories her parents told her of Janki as a little girl, playing in the yard, doing her chores, running around. Mountains loomed over and around her, enclosing her in protection from whatever lay beyond. Taara pictured Omar in that backdrop of the vast landscape of the Quetta plateau. She sensed a glimmer of a smile and touched her still-wet lips. Soon moisture welled up on the edges of her eyes. As she pulled in through the community gate, she heaved a remorseful sigh, "You would have liked him. I wish you had met him Mummy Papa."

Sleep that night was restless. Taara tossed and turned, got up to get a drink of water, and tried to sleep again, unsuccessfully. She opened the windows and invited the fresh ocean air in to keep her company. The soothing breeze swayed her into sleep.

Under closed, fluttering eyelids, Taara found herself alone, in a vast field surrounded by darkness. She twirled in the middle of the field in hopes of spotting another soul. A metallic sound came from her body. Looking down she discovered that her body was encased in a suit of armor, ready for battle. Even her head lay hidden under a heavy metal helmet, shielding her from all that may drop from the sky. She felt like a trapped turtle unable to escape its shell. Suddenly she felt her father's presence, as if he was behind her. She turned around facing east and saw a glimmer of light on the horizon. She heard movement, hooves dusting the ground, a haze rising far off, and she felt the earth shake. The sky slowly grew brighter as the pounding on the ground drew nearer. Suddenly, all was silent. Then, just as the sun rose up to completely flood the field with its light she heard the sound of a conch. The call to battle, she recalled her father telling her in his stories of the Mahabharat. She remembered the tragic character he had told her about, Karan. Somehow, she was now Karan. Armies of each side were ready. Kurukshetra was ready to receive them, the battle was about to begin and she was trapped in the middle.

CHAPTER 18

1929

Fertile, open fields of Khushab greeted Janki with open arms.

After recovering from the long journey, she sat in the verandah looking out at the large *angan* courtyard. A crow cawed from its place in a branch, hidden by the lush leaves of the *neem*. She looked up at the tree that stood sturdy in its quiet corner as it offered reassuring bird calls, cool shade from the scorching heat and a promise for healing. Jeevani, Ram Lal's sister, came to sit by her, and gently put her hand on Janki's shoulder. Her eyes appeared red, but a calm smile remained pasted on her face, which had started to acquire thin lines around the mouth and forehead. Ram Lal's parents had melted into the darkness of their prayer rooms, unable to face life as it was presented to them.

More news of further atrocities under the new regime trickled in from Afghanistan, glorified for maximum effect for a juicy tale, the storyteller insensitive to the effect these hailed on the family. Hope grew fainter with each yarn until it weaved into a bleak cloud that fogged up every eye. Janki, however, refused to take off her bridal symbols of the *mangal sutr* necklace and the red *sindhur* powder from her hair. She continued to light a candle in the courtyard every evening, never allowing the flame to flicker or fade. Its glow reflected in her eyes, aspired her to keep feeding her inner spark, and illuminated the courtyard becoming the guiding light to answer a knock on the door in the middle of one dark night.

The knock was faint. Wazir Chand, Ram Lal's father, hobbled toward the sound while the women huddled under the shadow of the Neem tree. Wazir Chand skeptically opened the door, its hinges creaking as his bones did with his stressed movements. A hairy man covered in dirt and grime stumbled through the opened door onto the dusty ground of the courtyard. Wazir Chand warily leaned over the stranger, his cane staggering under his weight, and asked, "Who are you *puttar* son?"

The stranger cowered into a fetal position and a feeble voice escaped from behind the hairy mess, "Your *puttar*, Ram Lal."

As Wazir Chand struggled to hear, Janki ran from her safe shadow toward her husband. She looked into fierce eyes as if an animal ready to pounce but he sank back as though he was trapped in a cage. She helped him walk up to the *manji* and ordered her sister-in-law to fetch hot water and towels. Ram Lal's mother brought a pitcher of cool water to his lips which he guzzled eagerly. She helped peel off his sole-less shoes and Janki tore off his thread bare shirt. Dipping the towels in hot water, Janki gently cleansed her husband, taking care to put less pressure on his various sores and wounds. After she was finished, she sat on the ground by the *manji* and watched him sleep, insisting that everyone else go back to bed.

Flies buzzed in swarms around the *manji* as soon as the sun darted its sharp rays toward her eyes. Janki woke to find her husband still fast asleep, undisturbed by the bright light or the buzzing noise. Her nose crinkled at the stench that still lingered around him despite her thorough cleaning of his blackened body. She washed up and made tea for the family, bringing it back to the courtyard by her husband. He stirred, waved his hands in the air as if to push his demons away, and was still again. She set the tea aside on a low table and walked up to him.

Ram Lal's parents and sister joined them in the courtyard as Janki tried to wake him. He moaned, shaking his head behind closed eyes, until suddenly his eyelids shot open and he sat up with a start. This sudden movement seemed to send a sharp pain and he winced, grabbing his waist. Janki brought a bowl with a pasty concoction that she had prepared from the various parts of the Neem tree and gently applied it to his wounds. He quietly drank his tea and went back to sleep.

As Ram Lal's recovery progressed, the stench from his body and now shaven hair disintegrated, and as the wounds on his body also began to fade, Janki allowed herself to relax. Rajendra never left his father's side, pestering him for stories of his escape or time in prison. Ram Lal just stared right through him as if unsure of who this little boy was. Dejected, Rajendra took to sitting quietly beside him sometimes taking the large hand into his tiny one. Eventually, Ram Lal reintegrated into his family, taking part in simple conversations or going out for walks with his father, but whenever anyone asked him about his time in captivity, a glassy vacant look came over his eyes and they would lose him.

In her habitual reading of regional news, Janki came across an article of the events in Afghanistan that led to the release of her husband. She learned that Nadir Shah, a Durrani royal cousin, with the help of the Afghan army and tribal units from the Northwest Frontier region, had overthrown the Bacha and his illiterate lieutenants. After hanging the robber king and his supporters, Nadir Shah led the country toward modernizing reforms, though less aggressively than his predecessor, Amanullah. Unable to ask her husband, and judging by the physical state he had arrived in, Janki speculated that he must have walked or hitched rides all the way from Kandhar to Khushab. She sat back in thought, amazed that he survived the journey, let alone the captivity, and quietly chanted a prayer of thanks. Her eyes opened to see the mid-morning sun piercing through the south window, flooding the center of the room. Her husband was bent down beside her, his head tilted as he read the article sprawled in front of her. She sat in the light straining to see his face hidden in the shadow.

When he was finished, he stood up and walked toward the window through which light was peering in.

"It was no vacation," he whispered.

Janki strained to listen.

"There was hardly any food or water." He went on, "We smuggled in grass to survive. Disease. Rats. Dead bodies." He turned around to look at her as his low guttural voice sliced through the beam of dust, "It was a hell hole."

Janki got up to stand by him. The line of dust naked under the brightness danced in confusion before settling into a harmonious pattern within the beam of light. She put a strong hand on his arm but could not meet his eyes as she said, "I left you there. I'm so sorry."

"You did what you had to," he replied.

They stood in silence looking out into brightness.

"It's all behind you now," she finally said, "You are here, with us, alive and well." She felt the muscles in his arm relax and he continued to stare out. Changing the topic, she asked, "*Ji*, have you thought about what next?"

Ram Lal turned his face to look at his wife. There was surprise with a hint of the familiar warmth in those eyes. His smile returned extending his long moustache out further.

"I have contacted my cousin. He wants me to join him in Quetta in the construction business."

"What about us?" Janki wondered aloud.

"You and the children are coming with me. His third wife is no more and he needs help with the children."

It was Janki's turn to look up in surprise.

Once again, Janki gathered her brood of three and followed her husband to Quetta amidst tearful goodbyes. Reunion with the cousin's children was bittersweet and Janki soon adjusted to yet another new life. Within the year, as the cousin remarried for the fourth time, Janki and Ram Lal had their fifth child, Bhaga.

Janki finally felt settled, involved in the house and watching her children grow. Construction business was slow and there were many mouths to feed but the blended family managed to stay afloat. By the time her first-born was 12 and her youngest a toddler, Janki was delivering another girl she named Bibo. Rejoicing for this newcomer was short-lived as the earth shook.

The 1935 quake that flattened Quetta and swallowed up thousands proved to be a blessing to the Khatri family. While millions dug their way out of this devastation, Ram Lal and his cousin were safely away on a contract across the mountain and were stranded behind blocked roads and broken bridges. As thousands pounded their chest at the loss of loved ones, Janki, with the cousin's wife and all the children, managed to survive huddled under caved-in rooms and broken walls. Eventually, digging their way out, the women helped the children nurse their wounds, quench their thirst and hunger, and find safe and firm ground amidst aftershocks. Leaving the children under the cousin's wife's supervision, Janki leaped over the crumbled boundary wall out into the neighborhood. Finding wreckage everywhere, she began to notice an unfamiliar stench that had started to hover over the city. She helped move some small boulders or a wooden door to find the mangled body of a mother with a whimpering baby under it. Scooping the baby in her arms she tore it away from the corpse that was once its mother. Over several days, Janki found many such tragic endings, some included distorted forms of children, their faces frozen in shocked confusion.

By the time the men broke through their barrier, Janki's household had increased by several additional children. Ram Lal and his cousin brought out their tools and helped clear away large boulders. They found ways to replenish depleting rations and built a simple shelter for the large family. Slowly things returned to normal as relatives of orphaned children came to take them away, the milkman resumed his deliveries, and walls began to go back up between neighbors, one brick at a time.

In an effort to reconstruct after the massive quake, Ram Lal and the cousin had no shortage of contracts as the entire city had to be rebuilt. To help them manage their growing business they hired Halif Kakkar, an industrious young man with vision and ambition, whose loyalty and efficiency helped bring the business to new heights.

In the next couple of years, Janki had two more children. The girl named Shaku was born exactly a year before a son, Virendra. Including the cousin's children, Khatri household was a constant flurry of activity. There were mouths to feed, noses to wipe, babies to cuddle, clothes to wash or mend, scrapes and cuts to nurse. It was a busy household and a flourishing one. Janki's favorite time with the children was at day's end when the entire brood gathered around her in a circle and her wide-eyed audience became captivated by the stories she weaved. They listened to her unravel yarns of tales about a family of mice or recount the adventures of Krishna, the flute-playing cowherd, or relate the wrath of the demon king, Ravan, who abducted Sita, wife of the legendary king Ram. Sometimes Janki even noticed young faces in her circle that did not belong to her household and she smiled with a warm welcome.

With the flourishing construction business and expertise of Halif's efficient management, there was plenty of comfort, security and joy to go around. Cousin began to enjoy a drink or two with friends as celebrations. When his fourth wife died while giving birth to a stillborn child, cousin found the bottle to drown his sorrows. His moods fluctuated from somber to rage and the children burrowed under Janki's protective arms, fear in their eyes. Oneday Ram Lal returned early from the construction site, his face red with fury. Janki rushed to him, and after he swallowed a full glass of cold water, he sat down. Janki waited patiently but he sat, holding his head in his hands, dejected.

"Cousin's beyond help now," he finally said. "I can't tell what's wrong with him." He walked up toward a peg in the wall, took off his *karikuli* hat and unbuttoned his dust-ridden shirt.

Janki walked quietly behind him and waited for him to continue.

"He kicked me out. Just like that." Ram Lal kicked a toy out of his path as if to demonstrate.

"But... what does that mean?" Janki stuttered.

He continued to shake his head and walked back to the bed, abandoning his hat and shirt on the peg. A baby cried in a neighbor's house. Another neighbor was listening to *ghazals* classical poetry by the renowned K.L.Saigal. Janki felt the beat of her heart match the rhythm of the *ghazal*, calm and serene building up to a climax of rapid vibrations.

His hands rested on the side of the bed as he sat on its edge, leaning his body forward. After a deep drawn-out breath, he said, "I don't know what I'm going to do."

Janki sat next to him, and as she pulled her *chunni* scarf over her head she said, "Maybe it's time to have our own business. Just like you did in Kandhar."

Ram Lal looked into her eyes and held them there. Placing a hand on her cheek he smiled and gave a slight nod. She placed her own hand on top of his and smiled back.

"Before things get any worse, we'll move out." He said as he rested his arm on her shoulder.

"What do you mean move out?" Janki pulled away, "I merely suggested starting your own business."

"Janki Devi, in order to split up from the business, we also need to leave this house," he said standing up.

"But what about the children? They have no mother."

"Don't worry about them, before you know it, cousin will have married again. He has done it four times already," Ram Lal stated.

By the time Janki, Ram Lal, and their brood moved out into a quiet neighborhood on London Street, the cousin had found himself a handsome and smart wife. She was the superintendent of education in all of Baluchistan province and a staunch Sikh. This one was here to stay. Soon after the marriage, having adopted all of her new husband's children from previous marriages, she reorganized the household. All the boys had to grow their hair and wear turbans and when the girls were married, they went to good Sikh homes.

CHAPTER 19

1997

A handsome young Sikh man, boasting a red turban, helped Taara unload her carry-on from the overhead storage in the plane. The flight landed as scheduled at the Indira Gandhi International Airport in New Delhi, in the small hours of a hot, summer night. Taara breezed through immigration, but stood waiting at the baggage claim for what seemed like hours. She stuffed her *pashmina* in her backpack, having served its purpose in the air-conditioned cabin 35,000 feet in the air. Finally, her suitcase arrived and she wheeled it over to customs.

As soon as Taara passed through the doors to the open air, her nose took in the fusion of car exhaust, human sweat, and stale spices. Darkness of the night receded in the background, behind welcoming florescent light. She quickly scanned the sea of people for familiar faces and spotted Uncle Raj's mother, engulfed in the crowd. *Dadi* was a tall woman with a full head of dark curls. She wore a plain burgundy chiffon *saree* with the *pallu* neatly pleated over her left shoulder. Right behind *Dadi*, Taara saw the tall lean man in his sixties who was Raj's father. *Dada* still had a full head of his soft, gray hair and a salt and pepper beard covering his chin. Taara ran to the older couple and hugged each one as she would have her own grandparents, if either one was still alive.

Dada quickly ushered them out of the crowded exit toward the waiting car. The driver, Ramesh, brought his hands together in a steeple for his greeting to Taara, and she responded by asking him of his and his family's wellbeing. Taara had met this driver on all of her trips, played with his children in the corridors of the apartment building, and worked alongside his wife in the kitchen learning how to roll the *rotis*. He put the luggage in the trunk while the women made themselves comfortable in the back seat of the sedan. *Dada* slid beside the driver in the front seat.

The car breezed through empty streets as Taara gazed out of the window. She enjoyed the city scenes while the country slept. Just as *Dada* was inquiring about Taara's college courses, to her amazement, out by the side of the highway, she spotted something that until now she had thought was a stereotype. Even her not-so-well traveled friends in Minnesota would find this scene unbelievable. There was an elephant all dressed up in red and gold, tattered silk on its back and trunk. It was dragging its immense body through the roadside following a lean man. When she pointed this out to her companions in the car, they were equally surprised. This truly was an unexpected site – elephants normally do not roam the streets of Delhi. *Dada* offered that the beast was probably returning from a wedding where a rich groom must have requested an elephant rather than the traditional horse to sit on in the *baraat* procession.

Soon after the minor excitement, their car pulled over outside an apartment building in a gated complex. Ramesh helped lug the suitcase up the four-flight of stairs while the rest rode the elevator. In the four-bedroom facility, Raj's parents reveled in the luxury of Lladros figurines and Lalique vases. Silk rugs blanketed the rooms in tones of red and yellow under the sofa set upholstered in royal blue and tiny yellow flowers. A plethora of miniature silk cushions decked the sofa.

Taara sidestepped the rugs and walked to the guest bedroom, the same room she had shared with her parents on previous visits, and slept on the pullout couch by the alcove. She sat on the king bed that majestically filled the center of the room. The same bed her parents had occupied. She ran a hand over the soft, intricate lace that spread over the bed. Looking around, she realized that she had never noticed how everything in the room was white – the walls, the built-in wardrobes, all the wooden furniture. Even the print in a large, black frame on the wall, above the bed, was an outline of a woman in black ink on white paper. Suddenly she felt a chill and realized how cold this room was. Where was her parents' warmth that had brightened this place up? From the window behind white curtains, she could detect a faint hint of daybreak. She walked toward the glow and sat on the familiar window seat. Drawing her knees close to her chest, she rested her chin on them. Soon she felt wet drops on her feet. Defiant tears spilled like pearl drops.

After a full day of rest and unpacking, Taara watched Gurgaon city from the balcony. She stood among the lush houseplants and colorful flower pots of jasmine and hibiscus that *Dadi* tended with much care. A vine of bougainvillea decorated with tiny purple flowers snaked around the railing. It reminded her of her mother.

Taara took in a deep breath and looked out at the skyline of shiny glass buildings that etched the horizon. She peeked into the glass walls of some of the nearer ones, into their compartmentalized rooms flooded with white light. In one room she saw a heavyset man in a white shirt and tie, slouched behind a large desk. Several computer monitors stared at him as he banged one forefinger after another on the board on his desk, looking up after each strike. In the spacious office next door to him, several young executives sat in close proximity, staring into computer screens and talking to their headsets. Taara recalled just a few years ago she stood out on the same balcony to watch the cows graze in the fields. Back then, countless times she had woken up to the sound of donkeys braying and witnessed meddlesome monkeys sneak in through open windows to steal bananas from the fruit bowl. Did serenity follow the monkeys into the diminishing forests, leaving behind car honks and the persistent buzzing of jackhammers? She looked out at a haze of smog and dust hanging over the skyline, smothering the once-sweet village with its new heights. This progress suffocated the village with influx of suits, their upper middleclass families into brand new high rises, and their newly migrated maids and chauffeurs settled in the slums at the feet of the tall towers.

Taara leaned over the balcony to peek at the children playing four stories below on the sidewalk. A mother's voice called from the apartment below for her daughter to come home. Playtime was over. Taara got a familiar whiff from an apartment in one of the buildings adjacent to hers. It was *daal* brewing under the pressure of a cooker on the verge of whistling out its steam. The neighborhood spewed out sizzling smells of cumin and frying onions intermingled with aromas of incense. The mother below continued to call her daughter to come home.

Taara wondered where her own home was. What about *Ammaji*, which of the three countries did she call home? She instinctively reached for her *pashmina,* but it was safely packed away in her bag.

"How are you coping, dear?" *Dadi* stepped out into the balcony. She put her hand on Taara's shoulder and stood next to her.

Taara jumped in fright unsure of what *Dadi* referred to, "Just watching the sun set. It's beautiful." She smiled and asked, "Where's *Dada?*"

"He's making his drink. Do you want some *Thumbs Up* soda? We also have fresh lemonade," *Dadi* inquired.

Taara shook her head. Just then, *Dada* walked out with a glass of scotch and soda in one hand and a gin and tonic for *Dadi* in the other hand. The maidservant brought out some freshly fried fritters and a bowl of potato chip sticks. As the three lounged in the open terrace, *Dadi* asked again, "How are you, honey? With your parents gone?"

Taara swallowed a lump in her throat and replied, "I'm fine. Thank you."

Dada spoke before *Dadi* made the situation even more awkward, "*Beti*, we are very sorry for your loss. Your parents were one of the few wonderful people we knew."

Taara attempted a smile.

"Since the time Ruhi and Raj got married all those years ago, we got to know your parents." *Dada* sipped his scotch and drifted in his reverie, "Dimple had a great head on her shoulders. How she mothered Ruhi! Your father, what an interesting man he was. Whatever he did, it was with passion. Whether it was cooking, or eating, or religion..."

"Remember the time he dragged us all to *Veshnu Devi* up in the mountains on a helicopter?" *Dadi* interrupted.

"Yes, he was a flying visitor, always in a hurry." *Dada* turned to Taara again. "What an admirable couple they were," he finished.

Taara remained quiet, tears wedged in her eyes.

Dadi felt the need to put in the last words, "Yes, your parents were wonderful, but Taara, you know that we are always here for you."

"Thank you," Taara mouthed, not trusting her voice.

After a short silence, *Dada* sipped his scotch and decided to change the topic. They talked about Taara's plans in India, how much the country had changed since her last visit two years before, and mused over Taara's childhood visit, when *Dadi* lamented, "I had always hoped to have Ruhi and Raj's children come visit us like this." She sighed and continued, "She has her career. It's hard for models to make the time for children."

"That's not true and you know it," *Dada* interjected.

Dadi ignored him, "You know it's not time, but her figure she is worried about. My Raj loves children, but Ruhi, I tell you, she does not have a woman's heart."

"Stop this now, you have it all wrong." *Dada* scolded, "they can't have any kids, even the doctors in America cannot help them…"

Taara stared at the *pakoras*, leaned forward to pick one, and took her time nibbling on the fritter. She stared up at the sky and tried to find the early moon hidden behind the haze.

"Besides, you are making poor Taara uncomfortable," *Dada* finished.

Sounds of children from a nearby playground filled the air around them. A dog barked from the building across the street.

Dadi's muffled voice came between sniffles, "Dimple and Ruhi, of same blood, but poles apart." She cleared her throat and looked straight at Taara, "*Beti*, your mother was so warm and loving, don't ever let anyone forget her."

Taara nodded and continued to look across to the empty balcony of another building. They sat there quietly not realizing the passing of time, not even noticing that night had descended upon them as if the city had wrapped itself in a black shawl. Taara found herself slapping her arms and legs, discovering the buzz of mosquitoes constantly ringing in her ears. *Dadi* suggested they move indoors.

"There's no light. Seems like the whole neighborhood is out." *Dada* declared as he fiddled with the switch, "We'll just have to do with the reserve light till the community generator gets turned on." He explained.

The couple sat with their grandniece in the TV room while the maidservant brought in their dinner, balancing a candle surrounded by food, in the center of the tray. Under the dim buzz of a battery-charged glow Taara suddenly felt eerie in the small room. Large shadows appeared on one wall made by the tiny mosquitoes hovering around the lone light, while a constant hum of the little insects hovered around them. Taara ate quickly and battled the bugs she could not see.

A sudden gush of radiance flooded the room and the television set became alive spewing out loud, colorful clatter. The generator had kicked in. Sometime during the night, when Taara was struggling to fall asleep, the ceiling fan started to move faster and she heard the air condition unit fire back up, its icy air cooling the room rapidly. The electricity in the neighborhood had returned and the loud hum of the nearby generator faded away. Surrounded by cool comfortable air, she fell into a blissful sleep.

CHAPTER 20

1939

The entire house was lit up with little colorful bulbs, twinkling from endless strings up and around the terrace, boundary walls and pillars. "The *baraat* is here! The *baraat* is here!" eight-year old Bhaga, with Bibo and Shaku in tow, ran down the stairs from the rooftop. They barged into the crowded bedroom where the bride sat heavily-laden in glittering gold and shiny silks. The girls admired their 13-year old sister, Durgi, and shrieked with delight as they described her groom.

"His face is hidden behind flowers, like a veil," Bhaga reported.

"And… and… he's riding a white horsey." Five-year-old Bibo contributed.

"Everybody is dancing on the street," Bhaga added.

"I wanna dance," little Shaku complained.

Bibo turned to the three-year-old, "We are from the girl's side, silly. We can't dance with the groom's party."

Durgi smiled under her red and gold *chunni* veil.

The sound of the wedding party grew louder as an army of band masters, dancers, and lamp carriers guided the groom's horse toward the bride's home. The women of the house stood at the entrance, with prayer *thaali* plates and garlands, to welcome the groom's party. After the ceremonial hugging, hand shaking, exchanging of garlands, and waving off the evil spirits, the wedding party walked into the decorated courtyard.

The wedding celebration had started days before the auspicious day. Multitudes of guests that had been camped at Janki and Ram Lal's house, helped create the wedding atmosphere, while hired cooks planted their massive pots on the wood burning stoves in the back of the house. They remained busy for no less than ten days creating delicacies of the region, including lamb and goat meats and a variety of sweetmeats. Every night, neighbors and local friends joined in the celebration at the wedding house, singing and doing the *attan* circle dance around the *duphli*. The drum's beat crescendoed to a rhythm with which only the young ones could keep pace.

Janki was everywhere, taking care of all the guests' needs, supervising the cooks, watching over the children and even joining in with the folk songs. On *mehndi* day, Durgi dressed in an old outfit and sat on a cushion with her feet and hands extended out while a young woman created intricate patterns on the tops of her feet and her palms with henna.

Janki sat with her daughter, her hands *mehndi*-clad, feeding her, as she recalled the first time she had fed her daughter as a baby. Mother and daughter tuned out the drumbeats, the singing women, and the shrieks of the children. Janki smoothed back her daughter's hair, while Durgi melted in her motherly embrace. Taking care not to smudge the intricate henna patterns on her hands and feet, Durgi rested her head on her mother's shoulder, as they enjoyed the comfort of pillows and soft mattress on the floor. Janki circled her arm around and patted her daughter's head as a soft lullaby escaped her lips. Half way through the song, this private moment was over with sharp cries from the kitchen, and Janki was on her feet and back to duty.

"You tried to poison me." A visiting relative, Rabbi, was screaming at the cook.

"Get out of my kitchen." The cook in charge of all the food arrangements for the wedding stood red faced, temples pulsing, sweat dribbling from his forehead.

"What's going on here?" Janki asked in a calm voice.

Between Rabbi and the cook's distorted versions, Janki determined the cause of the problem, and as she had suspected, Rabbi had started it. This 30-year old spinster found faults in everything and everybody and Janki knew that to keep Rabbi out of trouble she had to find her a task. Her bigger problem was to keep the cook happy.

"I refuse to work like this. I quit." The cook proceeded to pick up his things.

"*Pahji*, you can't leave now. We have to feed the *baraat*." Janki pleaded.

"Find someone else."

"In such short notice where will I find someone as good as you?"

The cook swiped his sweat from the forehead with one motion and splashed it on the ground.

"Only your special dishes will please the guests." Janki continued, "Without your touch the food is just plain. I'm counting on you."

He stroked his chin and turned to Janki. "You think I'm that good?"

"The best." Janki smiled.

"What about this woman?" He pointed to Rabbi smirking in the corner.

"Don't worry about her." Janki walked over to the relative and looked straight at her. She turned to the cook and said, "She won't come to the kitchen anymore."

The cook pulled his loose pajamas up to his knees and sat

down to tend to the gravy in the massive pot. The helpers around him kept their heads down and focused on their tasks. Janki grabbed Rabbi by her arm and led her out of the kitchen.

Out in the courtyard she turned to the troublemaker, "I have a job for you."

"But, what about the poison in my food?" Rabbi asked.

"There was no such thing and you know it as much as I do. Now, do you think you can handle this task?"

"What is it?" Rabbi took a small step back.

"There are fresh flowers delivered in the front room. You can find needles and plenty of thread in the sewing box in my room. I want you to make garlands."

"That's a big job. How can I do all that alone?"

"Get some children or anyone else who can help you."

One crisis resolved, Janki went to look for her husband and found him engrossed in deep discussion with an aged relative. Leaving him there, she went to check on the comforts of the guests.

The wedding day arrived before Janki could catch a breath. After the *baraat* guests were duly fed and entertained and the wedding rituals completed, the *dohli* ceremoniously departed. The groom and his family took the first of the Khatri daughters to her new home amidst tears and jubilation. The drone of sad folk songs mingled with celebratory drum beats.

And then it was all over. After the last of the wedding guests left, Janki and Ram Lal were able to breathe. Returning to household duties, Janki had no time to feel the emptiness Durgi left behind. Mahendra, born seven months later, further filled the void.

Her day started before the sun with cries of the baby. Cleaned, fed, and comforted he went back to sleep, and Janki treasured the hour she had to herself before the rest of the household woke. She luxuriated over a quiet cup of tea and the day-old newspaper, learning of events of far off lands and developments closer to her home. A mad man in Germany was raging war in Europe while

Mahatma Gandhi's peace movement was moving to new heights. Janki closely followed Gandhiji's development in his and the country's efforts to throw out the British.

One morning Janki read a line in the news about the success of the movement - India's independence was imminent. She read on to learn that the 200-year struggle for this independence would come at a severe cost with rumors of splitting up the nation. Muslims wanted their own country. Janki sipped her warm tea and thought of how this could affect her family. They were a minority wherever they lived. If they chose to stay in the Muslim-dominated Quetta, soon there would be even fewer Hindus than before. If they chose to move to greater India among the Hindus, they would be far from home. If they crossed the border into Afghanistan to their ancestral property, they would live there as foreigners. Janki pondered this for a while. Was she an Indian, or a Hindu, or a daughter of this Balochi land? As an Indian, could she identify herself with India - the vast land that was unfamiliar to her?

A cry from the toddler brought her back home. She folded up the newspaper, gobbled down the last of her tea, and walked indoors to the call of duty. The rest of the household stirred and soon the day was bustling with activity. Janki melted into the routine of her life within the boundary walls of her home on London Street, in Quetta, capital of Baluchistan, in British India, on the border of Afghanistan. She had married off one daughter and lost one early in Kandhar. Rajendra, her eldest at 17, was helping his father in the construction business while keeping up with his studies. Narendra, Bhaga, Bibo, Virendra, Shaku, and now Mahendra completed the circle of her life. Ram Lal and Rajendra, with the help of the manager, Halif, worked on enough contracts to keep the household running. In another year, Laaji, another daughter, joined the family.

Unfortunately, Ram Lal's business started to take a turn, with uncertainty looming over the future of the country. Janki read one day that the war in Europe was getting intense, learning that the British government had started to send Indian *sepoys* to the front.

This meant there were fewer funds for any construction efforts. Her suspicions were confirmed when Ram Lal noted one day that no new contracts were coming their way. Janki realized that what happened in Central India did affect her and her family. They were isolated geographically, but not immune to the effects of the decisions made so far away.

She started to notice the changes around her. With talk of independence and rumors of a new Muslim nation, the corner shop where she always bought her groceries refused her credit one day. Times were hard for everyone, but Janki was not poor, yet. She learned that her neighbor had no problem buying her groceries on credit from the same store. The neighbor was Muslim. Divisions among Hindus and Muslims were starting to emerge close to home. Janki brushed small incidents aside, keeping her focus on her children and home, still feeling safe in Quetta among friends. Everyone knew her, and her army of children ran in and out of Hindu, Muslim, and even Parsi homes. Neighborhood children continued to come to Janki every evening to listen to her stories. Sometimes the children were so scattered that mothers could not keep track of who they fed, their own or the neighbors'. Religion was not an issue in Janki's area or among the people she lived close to, or so she thought.

Oneday Narendra came home crying. Frail as he was since his premature birth, his 13-year old body quivered. He had been playing outside in an alley where a group of teenage boys had cornered him. They slapped him around and pushed him against the wall, causing cuts and bruises. They then pushed his tear-stained face into the gutter, burying his nose into the smelly water, leaving him there with words of warning, "Get out you Hindu bastard! Quetta is for Muslims in our new nation of Pakistan."

After this incident, and hearing reports of random outbreak of riots and killings on the streets, Janki and Ram Lal considered their options.

"But the violence is all over British India." He sat mulling over their finances.

"How about our house in Kandhar? There's no British control there." Janki suggested.

Ram Lal thought for a moment and then turned to Janki, "Are you ready to face Kandhar again? After… Sita and…?"

Janki put on a brave face, "For our children."

Within a week, Janki and Ram Lal packed up their brood and were off on to their journey through the mountains into Afghanistan. They left their house in Quetta in the hands of their trusted Muslim manager, Halif Kakkar.

The journey was easier this time in the back of a motorized carriage from Chaman, and even though Kandhar reunited old friends, it also opened up old wounds. Reconnected with the *biradri*, Ram Lal learned of the Kandhar airport construction. He took his sons, Rajendra and Narendra, and marched off to the offices of the American firm managing the project and within days, the three Khatri men had jobs.

While Narendra was just feeling his chin for the stubble barely visible at 15, Rajendra had entered the world of young men at 21. His light brown eyes, reserved mannerism, and long swift strides as he walked to work brought the neighborhood girls out to catch a glimpse. As he caught sight of covered heads disappearing behind their doors or curtains, he would purposefully stroke his prolific moustache, or run a hand through his thick, dark brown hair. He arrived early to the site daily, putting his knowledge of English and Pashto to good use by helping interpret for engineers and workers.

In the backdrop, news of atrocities beyond their borders trickled in. Janki was devastated one day, when she heard Ram Lal's friend, Ram Chand, a regular visitor for a game of chess, casually remarked, "the bloodshed is just beginning in our part of the world, Ram Lal."

"It's the British policy of 'divide and rule'." Ram Lal commented.

"It's at its peak and people are agitated." Ram Chand reported, "I heard that in our Quetta even, Muslims are killing cows. But the Hindus there, they are no less, they are putting dead pigs at doorsteps of their Muslim neighbors."

Ram Lal shook his head, "*Chhii Chhii Chhii. Hey bhagwaan* O God, what has become of this world?"

Finally, the news reached the Khatri's that the British had agreed to 'Quit India', and it was confirmed that India was to be divided. East and West Pakistan were created for the Muslims as a new Nation, while India acquired new border lines around its Hindu majority. News of Quetta becoming part of West Pakistan, and then updates on bloodshed across the border, reached Janki's ears. She heard of the mayhem of the largest migration in human history, that left one million dead in a single year, as Hindus, Muslims, and Sikhs fled their ancestral homes. She heard implausible stories, and could not believe that human beings were capable of such carnage.

"Trains filled with Muslims going to Pakistan are stopped by Hindu or Sikh fanatics," Kalavati, her old friend reported, "These men are raping the women and cutting off their breasts. They are torturing the men and killing everyone in sight."

"But why?" Janki was barely audible.

"Can you imagine when the relatives of these migrants find the train carriages filled with dead bodies of their loved ones, covered with flies and that awful stench of death?" Kalavati leaned back, "They want revenge."

"Then what?" Janki was aghast.

"Same thing. Hindus and Sikhs leaving Pakistan for India face the same fate under the swords of the Muslim fanatics."

"Kalavati, how can you be so calm about all this?" Janki remarked.

"I'm safe here in Kandhar, far from the clutches of those fundamentalists."

Janki shook her head unable to understand her friend, but was thankful to be away from it all as well, her family safely tucked away in the mountains of Afghanistan.

Ram Lal and Janki tried to shelter their children from the heart-wrenching stories from their homeland, but what they called home was not theirs anymore. They were the wrong religion for the land they were grounded to and their roots were disappearing. They had transplanted to a foreign land. It was as if the lush, colorful bougainvillea of the tropics was uprooted from its tropical abode and moved to a place in an arid desert, forced to find a way to survive and bloom.

Ram Lal, Rajendra and Narendra worked with dedication as employees of the American company. Janki tried to keep a sense of normalcy in the day-to-day routine, teaching her children to be strong and hardworking. Her Durgi, married into a Hindu household, was safe in the Punjab Province in India. Like the bougainvillea, Janki had to replant and establish roots deep enough in the arid land to find nourishment and the fortitude to survive.

CHAPTER 21

1997

Morning was cool and hazy, with speckles of dew drops resting blissfully on the petals of the pink bougainvillea that covered the boundary wall. Taara waved to *Dada* and *Dadi* as the car pulled out of the complex before sitting back to breathe in the fresh, pre-dawn air. Under Ramesh's expert hands, the silver Maruti sped through clear roads before the population woke and flooded them. Their journey was not long through the mountains, into the valley where Ammaji lived. But after crossing the *Jamuna* River, they drove through several small crowded towns, abandoned road constructions, villages with slow-moving bullock carts on the highways, or speeding, honking buses and trucks. The 250km usually stretched to 5 hours, if no diversion slowed them down.

Taara stayed glued to the window, absorbing her motherland's heartbeat. She watched the children in uniform weighed down with their loaded backpacks. They walked in the direction of the town Taara had passed six kilometers back. She saw young men in dress shirt and pants, riding their bikes up dirt roads. Whenever they passed a slow-moving bullock cart, Taara's nostrils tingled with a whiff of something familiar, a stench from the past. She pictured the horses and chicken coop from her YMCA summer camps. Manure smelled the same everywhere.

Soon an undecipherable reek replaced the familiar stench. Sugar cane was everywhere, out on the fields stacked in piles, bundles riding the backs of trucks or tractor trailers. Ram Singh explained that the stench was from an open-air sugar mill where bullocks tied to a long wooden pole went around a pit to extract the sugar which was then cooked at very high heat. His voice drowned in the musical horn of the overtaking truck decked out with colorful, glittery streamers. It zoomed passed them, leaving behind a dust of stale air. Having over-exercised most of her senses, Taara's heavy eyelids started to droop.

When she felt the rocking motion cease, Taara opened her eyes and found herself sprawled in the back seat. The car was parked in a lot next to a flowing river. Ram Singh announced they had reached Cheetal. Taara remembered stopping at this rest area on her previous trips, and ventured toward the cafe for some hot breakfast. When she returned, she found Ram Singh stretched out under the shade of a nearby Banyan tree.

Leaving behind Cheetal, with its free roaming deer, sightings of proudly parading peacocks, fast moving water of the Ganga, and colorful spread of fresh blooms, the Maruti sped on toward the mountains. Roorkie was the last town before the winding roads started, and Taara geared up for the thrilling segment of the journey. The windy ascent peaked at the opening of the tunnel where everyone halted, at the temple of the goddess guarding the mountain. After bowing to the figure, thanking her for their safe journey, and slurping up the holy water of the river Ganga offered by the priest, Taara and Ram Singh drove on.

On their downward spiral into the valley, Taara spotted monkeys on the roadside, sitting atop the milestones. Some daring ones were even going down the treacherous cliff overlooking a ravine a few miles below. Asking Ram Singh to slow down, Taara threw some bread and bananas, observing the 'pecking order' as the big, hefty monkey grabbed the first bite. The littlest ones waited impatiently but fearfully. Ram Singh drove closer to the babies as Taara threw morsels right at them. The car then picked up its pace and Taara relished in the cool breeze blowing through her hair.

Before long, the cool breeze shifted to dense air as they hit city limits in the valley. Ram Singh expertly changed gears shifting between one and two, both his feet at work on the clutch and the brake. Shopkeepers shouted over persistent honks while pedestrians dodged all the passenger carriers – cars, scooters, bicycles, *tongas* horse-drawn carriages. A cow sat in the middle of the street lazily chewing its cud.

Her forehead sprinkled with sweat, Taara watched the show around her, as the car inched its way through the streets of Paltan bazaar toward Ghunta Ghar, the center of the city. A massive clock tower dominated the center square, its pendulum dancing as it swung side to side. Across the street from the tower, a large colorful poster hung at the head of a rundown building that presented itself as a cinema hall. Massive, colorful portraits of Dev Anand and Tina Muneem smiled out at the crowd below. A loudspeaker blared out the songs from the movie, its phonogram supporting a crooked needle, *"Jaisa Des Waisa Bhes Bhes..."* The crowd around the square was unperturbed and went about their mission for the day.

The car approached the bottleneck as it tried to exit the square toward Janki's home in Krishan Nagar. As they plodded along, in the corner of the crossroads, Taara spotted the sweet shop and could almost taste the almond milk she had enjoyed from there. Further along down Chakrata Road, she noticed the two cinema halls on either side of the street facing each other. One used to be below the street level, but it seemed to have risen up with time. The road opened up a bit and they were able to pick up speed. Two-wheelers zoomed by as the Maruti sidestepped the bigger, slower vehicles. Crossing the Bindal Bridge brought back further memories of her parents. Beyond the bridge, in the *mohalla* neighborhood, stood her mother's first home. Taara remembered visiting the Khurbura Mohalla with her parents one Diwali.

Just as they made the last turn onto their street, a blast of music traveled the airwaves from the new record store, sending a flurry of tremors through Taara's nerves. Finally, the car halted on the dirt road outside the pink house – Khatri Niwas.

Looking past the development, Taara admired the majestic mountains of the summer resort Mussourie. She pictured the snowcaps in the winter from which the icy winds howled into the valley. Taara could not wait for the night when all the lights in the boarding schools, homes, and shops at the resort would be lit up, flickering like fireflies as seen from the valley. She took a deep breath, closed her eyes, and just assimilated the sense of being in her mother's home.

The house, painted pink, stood rooted to its single story sporting a short, wrought iron gate. A simple boundary wall, as high as Taara, ran all around the house. She released the latch from the top of the gate and opened it, ignoring the squeak. She walked in, stepping into the courtyard, and stood in front of the small porch. Freshly washed clothes hung on a line hiding the main door. She took the one step up, dodged the dripping saree and the puddle on the ground and reached for the doorbell. Before pressing it, she changed her mind. She got off the porch and walked the length of the courtyard through the side of the house to the back. As she suspected, the door to the dining area by the kitchen was open. She stepped in and walked straight toward Janki's room.

Taara tiptoed into the square room with tiled floors and whitewashed walls. A long ledge lined on the far side, under a row of screened windows, displayed a plethora of personal effects – soap, shampoo, denture cleaners, eye drops, glass half full of water, tiger balm, deep heating rub, medicine bottles with pills or liquids. Taara's eyes drew toward the center of the room where an antique king bed majestically stood, boasting its intricately carved headboard and posts in walnut wood. On the left side of the bed, close to the bathroom door, lay a slight form buried under blankets, despite the summer heat. Taara walked over to see Janki reclined on her back, chest visibly rising and falling with each breath. Her breasts sagged sadly to the sides, just as the extra flesh on her cheeks that had seen more meat in them in days past. Sensing Taara's presence, Janki opened her eyes, revealing all-white sockets.

Taara tried to speak but no words came. She tried again but a mere whisper escaped her lips.

Janki was saying, "Who is it? Is Taara *beti* here yet? Come *puttar*, sit by me."

Taara sat on the side of the bed and held Janki's hand, which felt softer than silk. She stroked them and noticed a labyrinth of blue veins making their way upwards. Taara could not help staring at Janki's lifeless eyes and observing the pale skin hanging loosely like mini-sacs all over her face and neck, silhouetted by soft silver hair. Her chin had a hint of shaggy white hair-growth, and her toothless smile to Taara was as cute as a baby's smile. Taara absently stroked Janki's hands, squeezed them, held them to her cheeks, and finally kissed them.

Janki did not have to hear Taara's voice to feel the intensity of her emotions.

After a moment, Taara cleared her throat, and spoke her loudest so Janki could hear, "Ammaji, how are you?"

"Just the way as you see, *puttar*. My children are taking care of me. I am dependent on them now." Janki laid her free hand down the side of the bed, palm facing up.

"I know they are. Do you hurt anywhere?" Taara asked innocently, fighting back tears.

"These eyes have betrayed me Taara *beti*. It's because of them I have become a burden. I still try to find my way around the house, holding on to the walls and doors, at least to go to the bathroom. It's hard for Rajinder and everyone else."

Taara listened and squeezed Janki's hand. She noticed

granduncle, Rajendra, come into the room, and smiled at him. He smiled back and stood by the foot of the bed, patiently waiting.

"Even walking to the *vaidda* courtyard outside makes me out of breath." Janki was saying, "I can't manage more than one *roti* at meals. Such is life now." She took a deep breath and exhaled slowly before continuing, "Tell me about you. When did you come from Umrica? Where are your parents?"

With horror, Taara looked at her grand uncle, her eyes threatening a downpour.

Granduncle Rajendra spoke in a low tone, "We didn't tell her. She is depressed as is, and probably won't be able to handle the news of their deaths."

Taara was unprepared for this. She sat there looking out the window with misty eyes, Janki's hand in hers. Granduncle walked over to Taara and squeezed her shoulders. He looked at her with pleading eyes, hoping to protect his mother from knowledge that could emotionally rock her.

She looked at Janki, innocent and helpless at 92, who needed to be sheltered from real life. Her will to survive was strong but.... Taara didn't complete that thought and nodded.

She turned back to Janki and said, "Ammaji, they could not come." She pursed her lips and controlled a sniffle, "But I am here, to be with you." Patting her great-grandmother's hand, Taara got up and abruptly added, "You need to rest now. I'll change and later we'll talk."

After lunch and a short nap, Taara ventured into Ammaji's room. She found her lying flat on her back, staring at the ceiling with the blind whiteness of her eyes. Taara climbed onto the bed and asked Janki to tell her the story of the three mice that she told all the children.

"I can't remember it all."

"I'll remind you the parts you forget." Taara insisted.

Janki acquiesced, transporting Taara into her kitchen in Minnesota 15 years ago, listening to the same story her mother had told her countless time. Tears wedged in her eyes until a drop tricked down her cheek.

Janki felt it on the hand Taara held and stopped, "Why are you crying *beti*?"

"Oh, nothing Ammaji. Do you remember any more stories?"

"That was when I was young. Now with my eyes, my ears, my teeth, my legs, even my memory is going. I don't know why I'm still here. Why doesn't God take me so I can stop being a burden on my family?"

"Don't say things like that, Ammaji. We are so glad you are with us. Tell me about when you were young, your life in Quetta?"

"*Puttar*, life then and life now is very different. Then we had large families. Some days were good and comfortable and others were a constant struggle. But we were all a family and we stuck together and survived."

Taara snuggled closer. Her great-grandmother continued, "I remember when we moved into our own house in Quetta, after *Bauji* started his own business. It was right after Virendra, your grandfather, was born." Janki paused and penetrated deeper into her darkness. Taara noticed a lone tear travel down the side of her closed lids, but then a smile crossed Janki's lips, revealing pink gums, "It was also the year Durgi left us to go to her new home. What a wedding. The whole neighborhood talked about it for years. We also had to use up most of our savings, and feeding six children was not easy…."

"Why are you sitting in the dark, Taara?" One of the aunties walked in the room, heading for the light switch.

"Oh, I didn't realize it was this dark. I was listening to Ammaji's stories."

"*Maati*, here's your tea. Would you like some *biscuit* with it?"

"Just half cup, *Puttar*, I can't digest more than that. Go, Taara *beti*, go have your tea with everyone."

"Ammaji, you rest. We'll talk after dinner if you are up to it." Taara went to the living room to socialize with her cousins and uncles and aunts. After tea, a group of them went for a walk around the *mohalla* neighborhood, dodging two-wheelers, vegetable carts, and *mopets*.

After dinner, when all the visiting aunts and uncles had gone home, Taara ventured into Janki's room. She found her cuddled under her thick *razai* quilt, over a warm fleece. Taara wondered how Janki managed in the winters in this valley.

Sensing Taara's presence, Janki called out, "*Puttar*, come sit by me."

"*Ji*, Ammaji."

"Tell me, why are you sad?" Janki asked abruptly.

Taara was speechless. She had been making a conscious effort to be cheerful. With caution she asked, "Why do you say that, Ammaji?"

"I can sense it in your voice. Tell me what's bothering you?"

"Ammaji... I... I lost somebody very close to me." She choked, "I miss them... a lot."

"*Beti*, I understand the pain of loss. I miss my children who are no longer here, and *Bauji*, your great-grandfather. But life, it's not in our hands." She sighed, "I lived without them all these years. I don't know why I'm still here, but it's His will." She raised her eyebrows as if pointing to the sky with her eyes. "I have learned that there's no point in mulling over the lost ones. They can't come back, but they leave you with their memories."

Taara swallowed a sob, "Yes Ammaji."

"Being sad is not good. It will blind you to the good things around you."

"*Ji*, Ammaji."

"Just keep this in mind." Janki closed her eyes, "You are what you make of yourself." She paused to catch a breath, "Go face your demons and be strong, and remember." She turned to face her, "Remember you have the Khatri blood."

Taara ran out of the room and wailed.

Morning started with its normal buzz of pressure cooker whistling from the kitchen and the rattle of steel dishes under the tap in the *angan* courtyard. Puffy eyed, Taara followed the scent of the incense toward Janki's room. She watched the older woman reclined on her back, trickles of tears running down the sides of her blind eyes. She seemed oblivious to grand aunty's hustle of morning chores.

Clearing her throat, holding her head high, Taara grabbed the corner of her scarf and wiped her great-grandmother's tears. Janki held Taara's hand with all the warmth in the hard-worked, wrinkled, but soft hands.

"My first loss was Sita." Janki started, "She was only four, playing by the river and drowned. Just like that. I still haven't forgiven myself." She sniffled, "Then there were the stories about the War and the partition. Millions died. I still cannot forget the images from all the stories we heard." Janki continued as Taara sat in silence. "Then my son, Rajinder...."

Taara interrupted, "But uncle Rajendra is here."

"My firstborn was also Rajinder; murdered. His soul returned to me in my youngest son, so we gave him the same name, but..." She paused to catch her breath, "How can I forget the one who is no more and died at the prime of his youth?" Fresh tears trickled down her side. "I lost two people that day, my son in body and my husband in spirit."

Taara squeezed the hand she was holding and bent down to put her head on Janki's shoulder. She imagined Janki recalling images of loved ones gone as if seeing reruns of the TV show she had been watching all night. Feeling the older woman's arm circle around her body in embrace, Taara joined her in shedding quiet tears and listening to their heaves and sighs. Janki's soft voice ringed in Taara's ears, "I had to choose between my husband and my children. I chose the future." Taara stroked Janki's hair and the older woman took in a deep breath, "Family is foremost, *puttar*. Never forget that."

Both grieved for lost family together. With each shedding tear, Taara let her parents go. With each heavy sigh she felt lighter, realizing she could not hold on to her parents forever, instead carry their legacy forward, just like her great-grandmother had to move on and did.

"Ammaji," Taara finally said, "You are right. I will go back to Minnesota and will make a future."

Temple bells chimed nearby, their music making their way into Janki's room and into Taara's ears, as if in applause to her decision.

CHAPTER 22

1997

Taara recited a short prayer to her parents as she walked out of the plane - a simple chant she had learned from her father, *Om Bhur Bhwa Swaha*.... Omar greeted her as she came down the escalators at the Lindbergh Terminal at the Minneapolis/St. Paul airport.

Homecoming was uneventful. The white stucco house stood as she had left it, boasting its manicured lawn and blooming hydrangeas. She walked in through the garage, expecting a whiff of steaming basmati to greet her. She listened for the loud whistle of the pressure cooker, or the blast of the exhaust fan. She thought she heard voices coming from the kitchen, the familiar voices of her mother's MPR companions, but when she walked toward it, she found it void of everything reassuring. An odd chill ran through her despite the humid air of the locked-up house, and she crossed her arms over her chest, gripping her shoulders.

A warm hand touched her right shoulder and she turned to

find Omar's comforting presence. Inhaling deeply, she touched his hand and gave him a slight nod. Sidestepping the kitchen, she sauntered to her room and froze at the door to stare at the mural on the far wall. Her eyes saw her parents in that room, painting, encouraging, and helping her eight-year-old self. The colors of the other walls had changed several times, but the mural had survived. She shut the door to her childhood, and meandered to her parents' room. Her shoulders hung and her steps grew laborious, while Omar continued to hold her hand and periodically squeezed it, as he walked with her.

The master bedroom displayed a mango yellow bedspread on the king bed in the center, with a mandarin orange ottoman at its foot. A matching armchair sat in a corner, with a footrest at its feet. A tall dresser stood behind the door, balancing an ornamental tree on it. From each branch of the tree hung a fruit with a picture of Janki encased behind a small, round glass. Fruits with pictures of Taara's grandparents, then her parents and finally her, hung from branches below Janki. Taara grabbed the tree and walked out of the house, its fruits dangling delicately. Omar never left her side.

As warmth spread through their hearts, the air outside grew crisp. The maple had turned fiery yellow with shades of red and orange. Mid-term exams came and went with a quiet Thanksgiving ahead of them. Declining Maya aunty's large gathering, Taara invited Omar for a quiet *Tandoori* Turkey dinner.

"It smells delicious." Omar said as he walked into her one-room apartment. He noticed the fold-out had been neatly tucked back into a couch. The dining table had fresh flowers replacing the piles of papers and books he was used to seeing.

"It's my father's recipe." She said as she set plates on the table, "He always made this for us during the holidays."

Omar picked up the napkins and silverware and set them with the plates.

"It was a tradition. Papa always made the turkey wherever the gathering was. I remember last year…" Taara choked, "…the bird was so big and took so long to cook… and…" She sat down on the dining chair and let her head fall.

Omar put his arms around as her head dropped forward and leaned on his chest. While stroking her soft hair he said, "He is still with us. Through his recipe, and their tradition, you are keeping them alive."

She nodded and snuggled closer to his comforting presence. The alarm clock by her sofa-bed ticked away. Her thoughts traveled back to one of the numerous Thanksgiving celebrations at her home. Their house was as always full with her parents' friends and family. The buffet dining boasted elaborate dishes, each family bringing their specialty. The guest of honor, tandoori turkey, was placed at the heart of the arrangement, surrounded by all the fixings of homemade cranberry sauce, colorful pasta salads, quinoa salad, corn and beans salad, spinach salad, baked beans casserole, roasted yams, rosemary potatoes, curried potatoes, *pettha* (pumpkin dish), and desserts of every shape and form - apple pie, blueberry crumble, almond *halwa,* carrot *halwa,* brownies and pistachio cake. The variety of dishes, the fusion of foods, the melding of families - it was a genuine *Desi* Thanksgiving of old, new, and pseudo Minnesotans.

Taara saw her mother's smiling face, happy to be surrounded by so many friends she called her family away from home. Taara's thoughts traveled back to her mother's home, to Janki, and their conversation a few months earlier. *Future,* Ammaji had said. Taara slowly returned to the man holding her. She heard his steady heartbeat, felt the warmth of his strokes on her head, offered thanks to have this pillar to hold her up and help her move forward. She stood up, blinked away her tears and announced, "I decided to use Cornish hen instead of a big turkey. I hope it tastes as good."

Omar smiled and took her in his arms, "Even better, I'm sure."

The refrigerator in the kitchen buzzed away, while the aroma of cinnamon wafted from the candle on the dining table. Omar moved his head closer and found her lips, Taara's hands circled his neck. A full minute went by before their lips parted. They smiled, swam in each other's eyes, licked their lips, smiled some more. He squeezed her as she sank in his embrace, both of them tumbling onto the big couch. Just as Omar was about to lean over, the oven sounded its chime.

"Chicken's done. Now we can have our Thanksgiving meal," Taara announced as she stood up pushing him aside.

Omar mumbled, "I thought I already was."

Taara ignored him and went to the kitchen to remove the cooked bird from the oven. Omar found the packet of *naan* breads and heated them, while she heated *daal makhni,* black creamy lentils and assembled a *cuchumber* mixed, crunchy salad. Finally sitting down, holding hands, Taara and Omar gave thanks by the light of a single candle. They remembered their loved ones and embraced their newfound love.

With the long weekend behind them, both fell back into their routines that revolved around their respective class schedules. Some snow systems moved eastward, dumping a few inches, and once even a foot, to cover the prairies. On one such post-storm day, under the facade of blinding sunshine, Taara trudged through the motions of riding the bus, walking to her class, and bundling herself against the arctic breeze. After suffering through a long lecture on the philosophy of art, Taara rushed to the Union to meet up with Omar and start the weekend.

Seeing him seated on an armchair engaged in conversation, Taara observed her man. He looked so handsome in his black turtleneck and blue jeans. Taara smiled and waved to get his attention. He looked up over the blond head of the woman he was talking to and gestured her to join them. As Taara came closer she took in the citrus scent with floral notes that filled the air around them. His companion stood up and turned around, smiling her hazel eyes under long lashes. Taara noticed how her turtleneck wool dress hugged her at all the right places showing perfect curves.

"I want you to meet Lindsey." Omar put an arm around

Taara, "And here's my Taara." He beamed.

Taara took Lindsey's soft, gentle hands in hers and smiled. As they sat, Taara continued to stare, ignoring Omar who was offering to bring drinks. Lindsey stood up and said she had to get back to the lab. She shook Taara's hand and gave Omar a hug before walking off in her knee-length high heeled boots. Her shapely hips moved from side to side with each determined step.

They made themselves comfortable in a loveseat in the corner, Omar's arm spread over Taara's shoulder. She removed his arm and reached for his coffee, sipping it slowly. He playfully tugged on strands of her hair. She squirmed and asked him to stop as she put the hot cup down on the table.

"What's wrong?" he asked.

"Nothing." she said.

"Come on Taara," he pressed.

"I was just thinking. You never really told me why you chose Minnesota, of all the places."

Omar rolled his eyes and put his arm around her shoulders, "Okay, you've got me."

"It was for her, wasn't it?" She confirmed.

"I'll tell you a secret." His lips leaned closer to her ears, "She's not my girlfriend anymore. You are."

Taara smiled, "I know. I was just curious,"

He drummed his fingers on her neck. She giggled. His fingers moved to her shoulders and to her back.

Taara slapped his hand. "Stop it Omar. You know I am ticklish."

He smiled, enjoying himself. His fingers moved back to her neck but this time to massage it.

"That feels good." Taara closed her eyes.

"Do you have anything going on tonight?" He asked.

"What do you have in mind?" Taara replied, eyes still closed.

"A dinner date."

"Oh? That Tapas place again?" She sat up straight, "But wait… I can't."

"Why? Do you have another date?" He turned toward her.

"Maybe I do."

"Who might that be? Do I know him?" Omar's lips curved downward.

"No, you don't. He's this really cute boy with dark, curly hair...."

"Come on, stop teasing now, Taara."

"Okay, okay, don't get so jealous. I'm supposed to go to Maya aunty's place to babysit her son."

"So, a baby is standing in the way of me and my date." Omar laughed, "How about tomorrow, then?"

"Sure, that'll work."

He knocked on her door promptly at six, dressed in a gray sports jacket and navy dress pants. His shirt was starched white and his hair combed back as usual, with care. The masculine aroma of his signature Gautier filled the room as he entered her living room. Taara wore a dark blue straight dress that ended just above her knees. Her hair hung straight on her bare shoulders.

Omar let out a low whistle as he entered, "You look gorgeous." He interlaced his fingers in hers and gave a soft kiss on her lips. She quickly grabbed her shawl and a coat, and locked in each other's arms, they walked to his car.

Dinner was exquisite at a quaint little Afghani restaurant in St. Paul. They sat on the floor on colorful, embroidered cushions and ate at short tables. Taara had to remove her heels and cover her lap with her shawl to sit comfortably. Mountain music played in the background, complementing the aroma of spices and meats mingled with the essence of rose. Each table displayed a patchwork tablecloth in dark hues, sequins and mirror-work. The tiny mirrors reflected the flame from a red, rose-shaped candle floating in a glass water bowl, placed at the center of each table.

When their dishes arrived, Taara dug into the *Karahi* chicken, pouring its red sauce over the *basmati* rice enhanced with fragrant cardamom, colorful saffron, nutty *kajus* cashews, and sweet, golden *kishmish* raisins. She next devoured the lamb chops, tasting the yoghurt and mint, each chunk of the meat melting in her mouth. Omar watched her break up the corner of the large Afghani *naan* and dip the pieces fervently into the creamy sauce of the *Kofta* meatballs.

"This is a meal fit for a king." She declared between mouthfuls, "I've lived in the Twin Cities all my life, but never even knew of this restaurant's existence."

He smiled and enjoyed watching her savor the delicacies.

"These lamb chops taste just like my mom's." She waved the half-eaten chop in her hand and continued, "In fact, most of these dishes do."

Omar laughed and held up his napkin to dodge any potentially flying lamb meat. Plates empty, dishes cleared, they dipped their saucy fingers in a small silver bowl, slowly rubbing their nails with the slice of lemon floating in the hot water. Taara then stepped away to find the ladies' room.

Fingers cleaned, bowls cleared, Omar stood up only to sit down again. He adjusted his cushion, searched for the most comfortable seat, settling on a cross legged position. He fidgeted with his napkin, folding and unfolding, laying it flat on the table. He looked around the charming room, observing soft glows from the center of each table, until he spotted Taara gliding back toward him, a bright smile on her face. The server placed the sweet *Asabia el Aroos* bride's fingers at their table just as Taara found her place on the cushion. Omar watched the glow of the candle fall on Taara's face, its flame dancing in her eyes, her smile bringing warmth to the table. He smiled and took in a deep breath as he ran his hand through his hair.

Just as the aroma of their nutty, syrupy dessert teased their senses, before Taara could clobber one of the bride's fingers with her fork, Omar took her hands in his and said, "Taara." He swallowed, his Adams apple visibly moving before he said, "Will you marry me?"

His face was so serious that Taara was not sure she heard him right. Finally, as the question sank in, her first reaction was her jaw dropping. She realized she had lost feeling in her tongue, unable to spill any words. She started to cry.

Omar did not know how to react, "I've upset you. How could I be so insensitive? It's too soon after… how stupid to act in such haste. I'm sorry, sweetheart." He squeezed her hand.

Taara was shaking her head, her dark hair swaying. Behind muffled sobs she cried, "Yes, Omar. Yes, I will marry you." Her head moved up and down, laughter and tears all escaping together.

Now it was Omar's turn to be tongue-tied. The two looked at each other and laughed. He slipped the modest opal encrusted gold ring with ease onto her third finger and smiled his widest, his eyes shining. They reached across the table and kissed. When the Afghani server came to refill their tea cups, they blurted out loudly, "We're engaged!"

CHAPTER 23

1948

Transplanted in Afghanistan, Janki reintegrated into the Kandhari *biradri* community and continued with household chores. Life moved slowly, but she dived into learning the intricate, special local delicacies like fragrant rice bakes and tender meaty roasts. Ram Lal, on the other hand, began to take too much notice of minor aches and pains. He cut short his work hours letting his sons do their bit for the family, as he whiled away the hours under the ancient oak with his friend, Ram Chand over endless games of chess.

The children, however, struggled to adapt. The boys walked for miles to get to school, drenched in sweat in the summer, or almost frostbitten in the winter, often trudging through snow-covered, coarse terrain. Eventually they made friends from various ethnic groups, including Hindu, Sikh and Muslim, played *gulli danda* and marbles in the dusty courtyard of the school and, in the absence of toys, made their own playthings with sticks and stones.

At school, they spoke Pashto and had to study Persian, in addition to other subjects. The bigger challenge was for the girls. There were no schools for them and they could leave the house only under a *burkha* veil, and with a male relative. It bothered Janki that her daughters would grow up illiterate in this ancient land, in addition to her frustration of being homebound and unable to go to her favorite bookstore. Over the next five years, some of the children integrated well in this rugged, ancient land, while others continued to face some challenges.

Of all the children, Virendra had the hardest time. He had turned ten the year of the partition and was a shy and gullible boy. He was also the shortest and the thinnest in class, and was constantly victimized by bullies on the long walk to school. One day, Virendra heard about a Hindu boy who could not manage the long walks any longer, so the boy asked his father to buy him a bicycle. His father refused, but one of his Muslim neighbors heard them and approached the boy. He said to the boy that if he converted to Islam, he will buy him a brand new, shiny cycle.

The boy did not hesitate, and the next day he rode to school, showing off. Virendra was impressed when he saw that cycle wheel into the schoolyard and heard the story of how the rider got it.

A few months later, when he found Ram Lal under the oak tree, pondering whether to move his pawn or the knight, Virendra felt resentment rise inside him. By now, Ram Lal had gained the reputation of forgetting his duties, his family, and even his wife when he played chess. Ram Lal had promised to take Virendra to see the legendry cave with jewels and the tiger. He had once again been stood up, another promise had been broken in lieu of a chess game. So, this eighth-born marched up to his father and shouted.

"Bauji, I am going to convert to Islam!"

He succeeded in getting his father's attention, as eyes met and nostrils flared. To the son's surprise, without a word, father marched toward his young boy, grabbed his right ear and dragged him to the house. While Virendra whimpered in the corner of the room, shaking, Bauji rumbled loud enough for the whole courtyard to hear.

"I am sending you to Gurukul where you will learn true Hindu customs and philosophy. We will leave for Hardiwar tomorrow." He marched out.

Virendra sat there with a gaping mouth, massaging his swollen ear. Sure enough, next day the two of them were on a bus to Chaman, Pakistan. From there they took a train to Delhi, India, and then another bus to the holy city of Hardiwar. It was a cold and a mountainous city in the northern region of India, where many Hindu pilgrims went every year to wash off their sins in the *Ganga* River.

Father and son's final destination was Gurukul Kangri, on the banks of the holy river, outside Hardiwar. Virendra was introduced to yet another new way of life and education system - ancient Vedic and Sanskrit literature and philosophy.

Virendra was deposited in the new school where he sulked for days, refusing to talk to anyone. Then he met Ashok, the boy who introduced him to a life outside of self-imposed solitary, inducing him to sneak out after lights out, to bend the rules of the school, or play pranks. Virendra taught himself to swim when the boys crossed the fast-flowing Ganga under the cover of darkness, balancing their clothes on their heads, to catch a movie or a play in town. When caught in the acts, both boys suffered their canings with brave faces. Of the sacrifice, devotion, duty, commitment, endurance, diligence, and perseverance taught by the school, the two out-of-control boys were definitely learning the last three, as they persevered diligently on their rule-breaking excursions and endured their punishments. Within a few months, Virendra found himself absorbed in his new, remote life far away from his family.

Ram Lal returned to Kandhar without incident. Janki was aghast when she saw him alone and blasted at her husband.

"*Ji*, I didn't think you would actually leave our son in a school so far away, in a different country, and during these unruly times."

"It is because of these violent times that Virendra had to be protected within the school. Janki Devi, all this Hindu-Muslim clash was making our Virendra unsure of his identity and drastic action had to be taken. Learning the Hindu way of life in a strict, disciplined setting should help him understand his roots. Trust me."

Janki pondered this question of their true roots. Did their religion alone define them? She could see that Ram Lal had closed the subject, so there would be no discussing her thoughts. Besides, she had other news to share with her husband, so she cast her doubts aside for the moment.

While Ram Lal was on the banks of river Ganga, getting Virendra situated, Rajendra's bosses approached him. Recognizing his talent and diligence, they offered him an opportunity to reach his potential through training in America. Ram Lal rejoiced at this news and arranged a celebration with a grand feast – Afghani style. Friends native to the land performed *Attan*, the national dance of the Pashtuns, and shared in the feast of Afghani bread, rice *pulau* and lamb dishes. The children adorned their colorful, velvety attire – the *ikot chappan*. Women sipped sweet, green tea, while the men blew on their *hukkas* and shared stories about America - fabricated or exaggerated versions of overheard conversations.

Ram Lal boasted proudly of his son's feats as Janki smiled. She wished Virendra was with them to share in their joy, realizing that Rajendra will be gone too, in four short months. She put one hand on her stomach, feeling the movement of her unborn child. With the other hand on her heart, she prayed for all of her children's success and happiness, but feeling a soft flutter, she became uneasy. For a split second, she sensed her heart jump into her throat and hop back in place. Becoming unsteady she tried to find an empty spot on the ground in the women's gathering to sit down. No one noticed this momentary drift while Janki recited quiet prayers.

CHAPTER 24

1998

Taara's heart pounded and fluttered, unsure of how to break the news to her family. As spring-breakers hit the beaches of Florida or Mexico, she headed to California with Omar, her destination Newport Beach while he drove off to Calabasas.

Raj's reaction was not surprising as he picked her up from the waist and twirled her around like a little girl. She slapped his shoulders, laughing hysterically, and shouted, "Put me down uncle. I get it, yes, you're happy."

Ruhi remained silent and walked out of the room.

Raj frowned, walked to the French windows, and stood staring into the vast expanse of the Pacific beyond, his hands in his pant pockets. His body swayed as he shifted his weight from toes to heels, back and forth. Taara followed him and put a hand on his shoulder. They exchanged faint smiles and looked out together, as if the clear blue sky could help them find the amicable solution they sought.

By the end of the day, it was clear that Ruhi avoided Taara and her decision. Raj tried to reason with her, tempers flaring between husband and wife until Raj marched out of the house, slamming the door behind him. Taara watched in shock and fear.

Darkness descending over the neighborhood like a black shawl, Taara sat huddled in a corner of her room, under the comfort of her *pashmina*. She found herself drifting, felt the wind carrying her across lands, over mountains and oceans, finally landing her in the middle of a desert. On firm ground she looked around, staring into dry sand everywhere. She screamed, only to have her voice carried away with the hot wind. She walked, looking for a soul, someone to carry her away from this desertion as the sun peered into her eyes, and she tried to shade it away. From under the awning of her hand she saw the ocean, gleaming and far off into its expanse she spotted a familiar yacht, majestically battling the waves. Behind her a sand storm began to brew, mischievously looming over her. A strong gust suddenly lifted her, carrying her off and depositing her into the raging sea. Blueness surrounded her from the water and the clear sky above. She treaded water, trying to stay afloat, while the yacht stayed its course toward her as it struggled, and she began to swim toward it. She did not want to sink. She wanted to be rescued. The yacht was her only hope in this solitary vastness, and she swam hard as water sprayed onto her eyes from the choppy sea. She woke to find tears gushing down her cheeks, uncontrollably, and she remained there, adrift, while the sun began its descent in Newport Beach.

***

On the edge of the San Fernando Valley, the sun was slowly sinking behind the Kakkar mansion. Haider Khan stood in the center of the great room facing the fireplace. His hand behind him, he rocked back and forth observing the rug that hung above the mantel. Its navy blue woolen weave showed off the delicate golden silk threads that inscribed the 99 names of Allah Pak. He had picked up this rug years ago on his first trip to Pakistan with Omar.

His son was eager to learn the Arabic script and every night the two of them read all 99 names together.

Haider bent his head and walked over to look at the framed calligraphy hung on the wall behind the *takht* divan. He read out loud the short *aayat* Quranic verse beautifully inscribed in *Urdu*. He read it three times so his family will be protected from harm or suffering. Sitting down on the gold and green fabric of the *takht* divan, he rested his elbow on the *gao takkia* round pillow. Its mirror-work reflected the vivid green, yellow and blue threads of the embroidery. He reached over for the green tea his wife had set on the round silver corner table. Next to his teacup, he saw the gold leaf picture frame, from which Omar's face smiled at him. He had graduated from law school that day. Haider remembered how proud he was of his son. One look at his thick, dark hair and that touch of mischief in his eyes brought back memories of his childhood. His favorite time had been when they went to the Masjid together for Friday prayers and during *Ramzaan*. He had taught his son how to prepare for the *namaaz*, and which prayers to perform when.

Finishing his tea, Haider paced in the living room, the sound of his footsteps absorbed by the soft wool of several Balochi rugs sprawled across the cherry wood floor. An elaborate hunting motif in camel brown and terracotta red of one rug contrasted with the repetitive patterns in vivid earth tones of another. Haider's thoughts traveled to the day Omar told him about moving away. He had made so many plans for his son, a job lined up at a prestigious law firm, the perfect match with his cousin's daughter. He had intended to surprise Omar with the news, instead his son had given him the surprise. His decision to leave home didn't make sense, but his choice to move to Minnesota, the icebox of a place baffled him the most.

At least he'll be home soon, and this time Haider hoped to keep him here, in California. He stopped pacing and went to the far corner of the room. Sidestepping the ottoman that sat with its legs crisscrossed, he moved toward the curvaceous vintage chair behind it. The rosewood armchair invited him in the folds of its rich fabric and he majestically obliged, resting his large feet up on the ottoman. The door opened, and Omar walked in.

"*Assallam-o-Aliakum, Abbu.*" Omar greeted.

"*Wallaikum-Assallam,* son," Haider replied from his seat, "At last you're home. Have some tea."

"Ji." Omar left his duffle bag by the door and sat on the edge of the divan, and poured himself a cup.

"How are you, son?" Haider asked, his eyes smiling.

"I'm well, *Abbu*," Omar said and as he sipped his cold tea.

"And the studies?"

"Business school is going well." After a brief pause he added, "I plan to take the Bar exams this summer."

"But you already passed the Bar here. Why again and so far away?"

"We've gone through this before *Abbu…*"

"But your family is here." Haider cut him off, "Besides, Ahmad is getting impatient."

"Who?" Omar asked.

"You do remember your uncle, Ahmad." Haider accused.

"Oh yes, Ahmad *mamu.* What about him?"

Haider took his feet off the ottoman and put them on the ground and said, "His daughter Parveen's hand has been promised since you were children."

"So?"

"So what? Ahmad has been waiting for you to be ready." Haider said.

"People still do that, in this day and age?" Omar asked.

"So what date should I give them for the wedding?" Haider asked.

Omar's eyes grew larger and he stared at his father. Unsure how to respond he bent his head down. He looked into the empty teacup he was holding, as if some magical tea leaves will show him the way. His palms growing clammy and the cup almost slipping from his hands, he clenched his fingers around the tiny ceramic.

Hearing footsteps, he looked up to see his mother walking into the living room. He stood up and walked up to meet her half way, "*Assallam-o-Aliakum, Ammi.*" And bent down to kiss his mother on the shoulder.

"*Hazaro saal jeeo* live a thousand years." Shahnaz said and tapped the side of his head with her hand in blessing.

She followed him to the divan and sat down, her short legs hanging on the side, not touching the floor. Holding the *dupatta* scarf in place on her head, she bent one knee and pulled herself up. Sitting sideways, she looked at her son, her eyes glistening and lips curved into a smile. Omar held her hand.

"Don't you get food in Minnesota?" she accused, "You look so weak."

"*Ammi*, even if I gain ten pounds, you'll think I'm starving." Omar laughed, and then said, "But you are right. They don't have food as good as yours. What is for dinner?"

"All your favorite dishes. As soon as Zahira comes back, I'll set the table." Shahnaz responded.

"Where has that girl gone off to?" Haider asked.

"She's at Shirin's house. She should be here after the *Maghrib ki namaaz* sunset prayer."

Haider nodded and stood up, "It's almost time. I'll go perform *Wudhu.*" He turned to Omar and said, "You should go wash up as well."

Omar nodded and walked up the long winding staircase to his room. He dropped his bag by the door and after washing his hands, face and feet he sauntered toward his prayer rug. Instead of reaching for the rug, he dropped onto the brown beanbag chair by it. A cacophony of thoughts went through his mind. *Who is this Parveen? What about Taara.* He didn't notice as the room grew darker and he sank deeper into his thoughts. *How to break the news to Abbu?* Of one thing he was sure - it was not going to be easy.

"*Lala!*" Zahira ran in through the open door. She switched on the light and gave a big hug to her brother.

Omar stood up and kissed his sister on the forehead, stood

back and looked at her sparkling green eyes and innocent smile, "Where was my favorite sister Zira? And how come she grew so tall in just eight months?" he asked.

"Sorry, *Lala*. Shirin needed help with her homework and I couldn't say no." She spoke excitedly, "Forget all that, you tell me all about Minnesota."

Omar smiled, "It's a beautiful place. You must come visit me this summer."

Zahira looked down twirling the corner of her *dupatta* scarf around her finger. Her smile curved into a smirk as she murmured, "Yah, like that's ever going to happen."

Brother and sister stood silent until Omar put his hand on hers and said, "It will happen."

Zahira suddenly slapped her forehead and exclaimed, "*Hai Allah. Ammi* must be waiting for me." She started to run toward the door but stopped to say, "Come down for dinner *Lala*. *Abbu* will be there in ten minutes." With that she ran down.

A sparkling crystal chandelier hung over the dining table showcasing the lamb *pulao* rice, *aloo gosht* potato and meat in gravy, and the beef and lamb *seekh kababs*. In the center of all the fragrant delicacies dominated the large Afghani *naan*. Haider Khan sat at the head of the table facing the window. Omar took his place on his father's left and ravenously dug into all his favorite dishes. He broke off a sizable piece from the *naan* to moisten it lightly with some gravy before wolfing it down. His fingers worked expertly with the gravy-drenched rice and with prying the *gosht* off the bones. After finishing his third helping, he looked up and saw his father watching him licking his fingers. He leaned back, his food-stained fingers resting at the edge of his empty plate. Shahnaz brought green tea and Zahira helped serve before sitting down. While the men drank their green tea, the two women ate in silence.

"So, you didn't tell me... what should I tell Ahmad?" Haider asked.

Omar looked at his father and started, "Abbu, I... I really don't know." He looked down at his cup before continuing, "I mean I don't even know what type of person this Parveen is that you talk of."

"She comes from a very good family." Haider said.

"But Abbu…"

"No but this but that." Haider's voice rose a decibel or two, "This summer we'll go to Pakistan and finalize everything."

Zahira peeked at her brother from the corner of her green eyes as she quietly nibbled on her *naan*.

"But Abbu, I can't. I have my Bar exams and still have to finish the MBA." Omar pleaded.

"What do you need all that for, *Baché* son? You have a job waiting for you here in a good law firm." Haider downed the last of his tea and said, "It's time you settled down."

Omar ran his clean hand through his thick hair. He swallowed a non-existent lump his throat and said, "Abbu, it's not just that. I…"

"What?" Haider leaned forward.

"I… there's this girl…" Omar murmured. He glanced up at his father just in time to see his round eyes grow larger under his bushy eyebrows. He also noticed a few strands of white in his thick, black moustache that extended out almost to his cheeks. On his reddish-black beard that formed a V under his chin nested a tiny grain of the saffron rice from the *pulao*.

Shahnaz and Zahira witnessed the conversation unfold as they continued to eat quietly.

Haider calmly slid his teacup out of the way and rested his elbows on the table. He asked, "Who? What kind of family is she from?"

"Her family is from Quetta." Omar twirled the empty tea cup with his left hand.

"A Balochi?" Haider asked, "Which family?"

Omar looked at his mother and sister who were intently watching him. He turned to his father and swallowed the frog in his throat. His hand continued to twirl the cup and he focused his attention on it as he spoke, "Abbu, she's… ummm… she's, her name is Taara Gupta."

"What?" Haider growled, "A Hindu?"

Omar continued to keep his head lowered, staring at the teacup. He could feel his heart pounding within the confines of his chest, bursting to explode. He slowly raised his head and looked straight into his father's eyes and said, "Yes and I have decided to marry her."

Haider stood up kicking the chair back with a crash and growled again, "What?"

Omar stood up as well and kept his voice low, "*Abbujan*, we are engaged. In fact, I wanted to invite Taara and her *Khaala* and *Khalu* over this week to meet you all and set a wedding date."

"Who are you to set a wedding date? Six feet tall and you think you've outgrown your father in years as well! I am not going to allow some Hindu girl come into my house."

"*Abba*, she comes from a well-respected family, and as I told you, her family is also from Quetta." Omar turned to his mother, "*Ammi*, explain to him."

Shahnaz *begum* lowered her scarf-covered head, ignoring the gray strands sneaking out from the corners. A low voice came from her diminutive form, "But she is not like us…."

His father interjected, "She is not of our faith. I cannot accept her in my house."

"But *Abbu*…."

"What's wrong with you, my son?" Haider interrupted as he paced the room, his voice rising with each word. "You are not thinking straight. How can you even think of marrying somebody from that faith? They will turn around and stab you in the back just like they did….." Haider broke off and walked to the living room.

"What?" Omar stood waiting.

Some minutes passed before Haider spoke again, barely audible, "You'll never understand, corrupted by these western influences. It's my fault for not sending you all back to Pakistan when you were children."

Omar looked helplessly at his mother, but she offered no

help. His sister, Zahira, made herself invisible behind the large glass of water in her hand.

Haider Khan Kakkar turned around and spoke in a low, guttural voice that could rock the table before him, "I will not give you my permission to marry that Hindu girl as long as I live." He then turned around and walked away to his room.

Omar stood there, staring at the chair toppled on the floor, his hands hung to his sides, fists clenched. He slowly walked toward the main door, ignoring his mother calling out to him, and walked out of the house, slamming the door behind him.

Hours later, after walking endlessly on the cool sand of the Zuma beach, Omar thought of calling Taara but didn't know what to say to her. Disillusioned, he wandered back home in the dark. Hearing his father's bellowing snores from his room upstairs, he walked to the family room in the back corner of the house and found his mother on the *takht* divan in deep prayer. He sat quietly on a rocking chair in the corner and eyed the tray of dry fruits in the center of the round gold-plated wooden table. He reached for a handful of *chilgoze* pine nuts and focused on the process of peeling the small nuts. Putting one tiny, peeled piece on his tongue at a time, he made their milky flavor last longer. Putting the shells into the empty cup on the table, he looked around him. Across from him a floor mattress leaned against the wall with *gao takkias,* round pillows, at each end and tiny cushions in the middle. Gold, blue and green threads with mirror-work dominated all the fabric in the room. Above it a large tapestry his parents had brought back from the Haj hung on the wall. The wall behind him was all glass overlooking his mother's garden, where a variety of colorful flowers were in bloom.

Shahnaz opened her eyes to find her son sitting on the chair in front of her. She smiled and looked up toward the ceiling and gave her thanks, then spoke softly, "Are you hungry, *beta?*"

Omar shook his head and continued to stare up at the tapestry on the wall across from him and asked, "What does *Abbu* have against Hindus?"

Shahnaz folded her *janemaaz* prayer rug and carefully placed it on the side. She crossed her legs and leaned her back to the wall before answering, "He thinks there will be too many problems. In mixed marriages there always are."

"*Ammi*, I know that. But we'll work through them." Omar looked at his mother and smiled, "Wait till you meet her. You'll love her too."

"Will she convert?" Shahnaz asked.

Omar snapped, "How can you ask that, Ammi?"

"*Beta*, your *Abbu* will never give in to this unless she is one of us."

"Why is he against them so much? He has Indian friends, business partners of all faiths. What has any Hindu done to him that is so bad?"

"*Khuda hi jaane*, only God knows what the truth is." Shahnaz picked up a silver box from a table by the divan and opened it. She took a few pieces of pre-cut betel nuts and put them in her mouth. As her teeth became busy grinding the nuts, she stretched her legs on the divan, placing her elbow on the round pillow. Between chews she said, "I guess there's a story from Partition days."

"What story?" Omar asked.

"Your grandfather, Baba had a brother, Ali." Shahnaz shook her head and threw one hand in the air, "There's some story of murder and hanging. Only your grandmother knows the truth."

"So, what is Abbu's hatred for?" Omar asked.

"Omar *Beta*, when you grow up like your Abbu did," Shahnaz swallowed the red betel juice that had started to collect in her mouth before continuing, "Hearing horror stories from the Partition, some involving your own family members…"

Omar leaned forward on his chair, "Ammi, what was so horrific? Did you ever ask *dadi*?"

Shahnaz sighed and shook her head, "She never talked about it. Your Abbu heard the stories from relatives and neighbors."

Omar sat back and absorbed all this as the grandfather clock in the room ticked away into darkness. He got up from his chair, standing tall over the divan, and wondered out loud, "Ammi, all this happened years ago. Why is Abba carrying it around still?"

"All I know is because of a Hindu boy's murder, your father's *chacha* uncle was hanged." Shahnaz shook her head as she absently caressed her silver box and continued, "What happened we don't know. Maybe your Abbu is still looking for answers."

"But this still does not change my decision to marry Taara."

Shahnaz looked up at her son and half smiled, "Beta, both you men are as *ziddi* as a mule. Now go get some sleep and, hopefully, you both will have come around by tomorrow." She reached out and patted the side of her son's head, "Shab Bakhair."

Omar walked to his room and shut the door. As he lay on his bed mulling over his dilemma, he heard a feeble knock on the door.

"*Lala?*" Zahira slipped quietly in, "I... want to say something... if you don't mind." She cracked her knuckles.

"Zira, what is it?" He stood up by the side of his bed.

She tugged between her teeth a corner of the scarf hanging around her neck, which usually covered her dark brown curls in the presence of outside company. She stood slightly stooped, her shoulders slouching, while her chin tilted up to face her brother. Her thick lips pursed together before she cleared her throat and began, "*Lala*, I think it's a very brave thing you are doing." The frog in her throat did not seem to want to go away. She cleared again, "Whatever choice you make, I want to let you know that I'm with you."

Omar reached out and hugged his sister, "Thank you, Zira. This means a lot to me."

Zahira froze, surprised. She had no recollection of ever being hugged by any man, including her father and brother.

"If I can help in any way...." She managed.

"I wish you could. I don't know if I can help myself at this point with Abbu's temper that is sure to stay..."

"He can be rather loud, but he means well. You know that he loves us."

Omar smiled at his sweet little sister.

"Yes, I know he does, but he has a funny way of showing it. Anyway, this time it's different. It's just his own personal vendetta he is harboring."

"What's that?"

"I'll tell you some other time. Now it's late, go get some sleep."

Zahira turned to go when Omar put his hand on her shoulder, "Zira, thank you for your support. No matter what happens now with this whole mess, I want you to know, too, that if ever you need me for anything, this big brother will be there."

"I know that." She hesitated then asked, "Tell me about my *bhabhi*."

"Taara? She is sweet and beautiful. She always finds beauty in everything and is a wonderful artist. I know you will like her."

"I look forward to meeting her someday." She walked to the door, "*Shab Bakhair Lala.*"

He sat up the rest of the night, waiting for the new day to begin. A look around his dimly lit room from the comfort of his bed took him to his school days. He fixed his gaze at the far wall where trophies and plaques lined up on shelves tracked the progression of his life. Soccer in his early years, basketball and swimming as he grew taller and stronger, track and debate team in high school. He remembered his father cheering him on in the early games, when all his little feet did was run around the field and occasionally kick. Omar soon began warming the benches at the big games. He changed sports, and history repeated until his father stopped showing interest. By the time he started high school, his father had started extensive travel for his work. The prizes became meaningless, but his mother insisted on displaying them. He had convinced her to put them in his room rather than the family room.

Omar looked outside into darkness. The wind howled through the mountains and entered the open window by his bed. He caught a whiff of the desert air and breathed in dry heat. As soon as the first rays of the sun peaked through, he reached for the phone.

CHAPTER 25

1949

A sliver of moon, like the tip of a fingernail, edged upward, offering no illumination. Janki struggled to breathe in the dry desert air, as the crescendo of Afghani music matched the beat in her heart, speeding as the evening progressed. While everyone rejoiced in Rajendra's fortune, Janki slipped indoors, seeking silence and solitude. She sat in a dark corner praying for the bad aura to pass as she grasped her swollen stomach for a sign.

Sauntering out to accept the guests' wishes as they left, her trepidation rose and eased with each step. She found Rajendra with his siblings, his eyes sparkling with excitement about his future in America, his laughter heartfelt, promising to share his dream with them. She walked up and watched as her brood shared their joy, muscles in her shoulders relaxing. As she was about to turn, Rajendra called out and informed her of his decision to make a quick trip to Quetta before leaving the subcontinent. Her feet froze and her head shook adamantly.

Stories of occasional rioting continued to reach Janki's ears and she did not want her son crossing that border. It was only a week ago when she had heard of a Hindu woman who had been raped, tortured and abandoned on the streets to die.

"Our house is there." He protested, "I'll stay with Halif *kaka* and his family."

Ram Lal joined the group, standing next to Rajendra. The two men, towering over Janki, played down her fears, and tried to assure her that Halif was there to take care of him. She was outvoted, and the decision was made. She looked away, blinking away tears.

Rajendra walked up, circled his long arms around her, and said, "*Matti*, I promise I'll be back soon."

She patted him and attempted a smile, her heart weighing her down.

A blustery morning greeted them, and under its gray veil, Rajendra waved to his family. He hopped onto the truck of an acquaintance, heading to Chaman.

Finishing his journey on a *tonga* horse-cart from the train station in Quetta, Rajendra, covered in soot and dust, finally reached his childhood home. Halif Kakkar greeted him at the door with his big bear hug and loud welcoming roar, towering over the young man with his turban and ruffled beard.

Inside, Rajendra found Halif's mother, sitting on the *manji* bed in the courtyard. He touched her feet for blessing, the Hindu way. She patted the side of his head, then raised her hands, palms facing up in *dua* for his long life, the Muslim way. His gaze turned toward the sound of an infant cooing in his mother's arms. Rajendra bowed his head to his own raised palms, in greeting to Halif's wife, Jamila. She responded with a slight nod, eyes lowered and head covered with her *dupatta* scarf.

Rajendra freshened up, then walked into the kitchen and inquired of Halif's mother, "*Ammi*, how have you been?" The smoky smell of freshly made *roti* bread, with a hint of fragrant *gosht* curry and familiar spices, floated around him.

"*Beta*, it has not been the same without you all."

Rajendra sat down on a mat next to Halif, an empty plate in front of him.

"At least you were safely away from here." She continued, "*Tobah, Tobah, Tobah*. I still get nightmares from all the screams we used to hear...."

Halif interrupted his mother, "Why are you starting all that. Rajinder has just come."

"You are right, *beta*. We can't change what has already happened."

The men ate their dinner while *Ammi* made fresh *rotis* and Jamila served. Rajendra licked his fingers after each bite, as he did with his mother's cooking. Halif watched the younger man, and smiled until a cool draft entered the cozy kitchen.

"Assallam-o-Aliakum, *Ammijan*." Ali, Halif's younger brother greeted as he walked in. His disheveled hair nested on his head, while similarly bushy moustache extended out to his cheeks into razor-thin points. A small man, he walked in like a large one, puffing up his chest like a pigeon and tweaking a pointy edge of his moustache. He slapped the two men on their backs and sat down with them.

"Wallaikum-Assallam, *beta*. Have you eaten yet?" *Ammi* asked.

Ignoring the women, Ali looked at his brother, one side of his mouth raised into half a smile.

"So, where were you this time?" Halif inquired.

"*Pindi*, working on some roads." Ali then turned toward Rajendra, "So how is Kandhar?"

Rajendra nodded, his mouth stuffed with *biryani*. Ali stared at Rajendra with a silly smile pasted on his face, while Ammi and Jamila started their meal. Halif gazed at his empty plate, absently running his food-stained fingers on its rim. Sounds of chewing, swallowing, and the jangle of Jamila's bangles echoed in the warm kitchen. The baby broke the silence with a yelp from his cozy cradle, and Jamila left to attend to him while Ammi cleared up the dishes. Halif let out a slow breath and stood up and the men walked out to the *angan* courtyard. Comfortably seated on the *manji* beds leaning against big round pillows under the light of an almost full moon, each took turns with a *hooka* pipe.

Rajendra turned toward Halif. "*Kaka*, so was it really as bad as how *Ammi* said?"

He blew the smoke through his nostrils. "What can I tell you?" Passing the pipe to Ali he sighed, "Trains full of death, butchered, even the little babies glued to their mothers' breasts."

"Was it the Sikhs or Hindus who did this?" Rajendra asked.

"What does it matter? God's children all of them...."

"What do you mean God's children?" Ali interjected, "They were not *Musalmaan*."

Halif ignored his brother and continued, "Rajinder, this was a terrible tragedy. Thanks to Allah our families were safe."

Ali shifted in his *manji* and glared at Rajendra. "*Lala*, as if killing was not enough, so many men were tortured, those Hindus touched our women, raping and killing them."

Rajendra squirmed in his seat while Halif remained silent. A dog barked on the street. Baby Haider could be heard fussing in the room as Jamila gently patted him. Halif coughed as if about to speak, but remained quiet. Ali's body moved in agitation, one knee bobbing as the *manji* strings creaked under his shifting weight. Call for prayer broke up the group and the brothers went in for their *namaaz*. Rajendra took a deep breath, feeling the tension in the air releasing.

In his room that night, he lay awake for a long time. Images of screaming women and crying children tugged at him. A crinkled map with lines drawn in blood quivered above him, disoriented but searching for a home. Men with tattered clothing, fingernails missing, seemed to be coming at him, gnawing at his Hindu face. Waking with a start, Rajendra's forehead dripped with sweat. He swallowed a glassful of water set by his bed before lying back down. Sleep finally engulfed him into a tortuous slumber.

Morning brought overcast skies, and a chill in the bones felt only in the deep, winter. Ready for the day, Rajendra was about to step into the courtyard, when he heard Halif and Ali's voices exchanged in anger. So as not to intrude, Rajendra stayed by his door until some unsettling words fell on his ears.

"This is Pakistan, a Muslim nation, and Hindus have no claim here. *Lala*, don't be so naïve..."

Halif interrupted his brother, "I will not entertain any corrupt ideas."

"You're a fool. This house is yours and you should kick him out." Ali nodded in the direction of Rajendra's room and noticed him standing there.

Rajendra entered the conversation, "So you are conspiring against me, Ali *pahji*? What have I done to you?"

"N... nothing." He turned to face Rajendra, "But I think that all Hindus should give up their properties in Pakistan. This house is ours now." Ali replied.

"Did you work for it? This house was built with my father's sweat, but what would you know about hard work?"

"Rajinder, I can lay claim to this house. This is Pakistan." He took a step forward, "If you don't go by yourself I have friends who can help you leave."

"Halif *pahji*, this is your brother so I am restraining myself. Please ask him to leave my house this instant."

Halif tried to calm them down, "Ali, leave now."

"I will remember this insult, Rajinder. You better watch your back from now on." Ali slammed the door behind him.

Halif put his hand on Rajendra's shoulder, who in turn patted it. A knock on the door helped clear the air.

"Oy Rajinder! What are you doing here?" Amir, Rajendra's college friend, cried as he walked in.

Rajendra walked up and slapped his friend's shoulders, "Amir? I was just coming to your house. Let's go get the rest of the gang."

"Don't bother. The others went to Lahore but they'll be back today." Then, as if just remembering Halif's presence he said, "Assallam-o-Aliakum, *Lala*. Here's the medicine you had asked for baby Haider."

"Wallaikum-Assallam. So why didn't you go with your friends?"

"*Ammi* didn't think it was safe. Rajinder, let's have a *mehfil* party at my place tonight. We can sing *ghazals* and *shér* like old times. Hope you haven't forgotten all the poetry."

Rajendra smiled wide and nodded with enthusiasm as he threw his arm across Amir's shoulder.

The sun crossed the sphere and settled in for the night at its allotted time. The unseen moon rose up high in the sky, hiding behind the curtain of dark clouds, refusing to witness the scene below. The evening came and went. Rajendra took his last breath in the dark alley in a pool of blood, one hand outstretched in a final grasp at his family's dream left unfulfilled.

Halif, summoned the next morning by the police, identified the body, and in a note stained with tears he wrote to Ram Lal. His shaking hands scribbled illegibly for his friend to come at once. His apologetic scrawl made no mention of the tragedy only the urgency of his friend's presence. Then he waited in a trance, locked up in his room for two days, praying for forgiveness. On the third day, he stepped out to make arrangements for last rites.

CHAPTER 26

1998

California sun peeked into Taara's room directly onto her eyes. Her lids flickered, seeing shades of yellow, orange, and red with a dark speck of the majestic yacht floating over the waves. She emerged from her nightmare as if from a trance, determined to get on that yacht. Her eyelids flew open as she threw back her shawl and marched out of the room in search of Ruhi.

Bright and early, Taara found her aunt in the spare-room-cum-fitness center. Ruhi's body was bent down with her palms flat on the mat next to her feet. She reverse swan-dived up and took her arms above her head. Her body stood erect, arms reaching for the sky, hands joined together, spine stacked, legs stretched tall, and all the muscles engaged. Taara watched her look like the letter 'I'. Ruhi took in a breath, reached up higher, took a long exhale sliding her arms to her heart center, palms together. She then brought them to her sides, relaxed her body and slowly turned.

They stood staring for a few seconds.

Taara took a step forward and said, "*Masi*, please understand. We love each other."

Silence.

"If it weren't for him, I would never have been able to go back to Minnesota, go back to my studies or my life." Taara continued, "You can say that he saved my life."

"Why would he do that?" Ruhi asked.

"He loves me."

"So you think."

"Of course he does. Why do you find that so hard to believe?"

"What if he's using your emotional state to his benefit?"

Taara stared at her aunt. Finally, she shook her head and said, "What?"

"Does he want you to convert?" Ruhi asked.

"We didn't talk about that. Why should we?"

"Don't be childish, Taara. Remember the story I told you about my friend? The one whose husband changed after the marriage."

"Omar's not like that."

"It's your life, Taara. If you want to throw it down the gutter, it's your business. You know that he can have multiple wives." It was not meant to be a question.

Taara glared, "In America that's illegal, not that Omar's the kind to do such a thing."

Ruhi rolled her eyes, "You will have no freedom. He will tie you down at home to cook, clean and have babies."

"*Masi*, which World do you live in? Whatever happened to your friend does not happen to everyone."

"Your parents wouldn't have approved." Ruhi shot back, a slight smirk appearing in the corners of her mouth.

"Don't you bring mummy papa into this. They may not have liked this mixed marriage thing, but I know they would have shared in my happiness." Taara shot back.

The phone rang. Both turned their gaze and stared at it, until Ruhi walked over and answered. Her face changed colors as she heard the voice on the other end. She blasted into the mouthpiece, "You leave my daughter alone. If you think she's going to be added to your collection of converts, you're mistaken." She banged the cordless down hard into its cradle.

"*Masi*, how could you?" Taara yelled, "Poor Omar," she cried and ran out of the room.

In the San Fernando Valley mansion, Omar sat in his room and stared at the phone. He could not believe that Ruhi had banged the phone down on him. Frustrated, he got out of bed to take a shower. He let the warm water massage his body, water dripping from his hair while his muscles relaxed. As the steam rose, the cloud in his thoughts began to clear. Refreshed, he stepped out and picked up the phone to call again. This time Taara answered.

"Omar, I called your cell but you didn't answer." Taara said.

"I was in the shower..." Omar responded.

"I'm so sorry about *masi*." Taara interrupted.

"Don't worry. Things are not as great at this end either." He reported.

"What's wrong?"

"Listen, when can you meet me?"

"Anytime. Do you know someplace that's half-way?" Taara asked.

"How about around five in Santa Monica?" Omar said.

"Where? You'll need to give me directions."

"There's this little bar called 'Monsoon' on the promenade. Just take the 405 to Santa Monica, get on freeway 10 toward the ocean..." he reeled through the directions.

After setting the phone down, Omar sat on the edge of his bed and smiled. Just hearing her voice had sent a rush of warmth through him. He looked at the clock and charged down to join the family for breakfast. His father sat in his place of honor at the head of the table. His mother sat on his right, ready to kick back her chair and run to the kitchen at a moment's notice. Zahira sat at the far end delicately nibbling on her toast. She was dressed in her modified school uniform wearing loose dark pants under her blue skirt. Around her shoulders, over her long sleeved white blouse, a scarf was draped, poised to go over her head the moment she stepped out.

Omar sat down and greeted everyone. Haider ignored him and continued to read the paper as he sipped his tea. Ammi stood up and began to fuss over her son. She poured him tea, brought him back warm toast from the kitchen, buttered it and placed it next to the boiled egg on his plate. He protested, but she ignored him insisting he eat. She picked up the fruit bowl and set it in front of him. Haider stood up, folded his paper and walked to his room. Zahira glugged her glass of strawberry milk and ran to get her backpack. After they left, Omar finished up his breakfast and helped his mother clean up, despite her protests.

As Omar was considering what to do next, he heard the garage door. His father had returned after dropping off Zahira instead of heading straight for the office. Omar was sitting on the living room divan, pretending to read the newspaper as he braced himself for what was to come. Through the corner of his eye he saw his father walk toward the tapestry above the fireplace. Omar recalled reading from it the 99 names of Allah with his father every night. Everything was simpler then. He didn't question the significance of the rituals or the meanings of the Aayats he had memorized like a parrot. In innocence there was bliss.

He looked up to see his father glaring at him. Folding the paper, neatly, he placed it aside on the table next to his smiling picture, and stood up. He walked toward his father and said, "Abbu..."

Haider looked away and put his palm up like a traffic cop and spoke in a guttural tone, "Don't bother... unless you've decided to..."

"But Abbu... give Taara a chance. At least meet her and her uncle and aunt." Omar pleaded, "You'll see she comes from a good family."

"What do you know about family and honor?" Haider mocked.

Omar stood still.

Haider turned his head toward Omar and said, "I gave my word to Ahmad and now, because of you, my head will be lowered with shame."

Omar shifted his weight from one leg to another and ran his hand through his hair. He then planted both feet firmly on the soft rug with the hunting scene motif. He looked at his father and words tumbled out, "I don't even know these people you talk of and besides, what about my promise to Taara? Why won't you give her a chance?" He sighed before entering his final plea, "Please give us your blessings."

"Never!" His father growled, "You choose to defy your father, your own flesh and blood for that infidel!"

Omar locked eyes with his father and spoke calmly, "I plan to marry the woman who has given me more love and attention in just one year than I ever got in this mansion full of divine greatness." He walked up to his father, "In this mansion, God is the only one loved while the living and breathing people in it are like empty souls. Here the holy book is hugged more than the children ever were." Omar stood straight with both his feet over the horse and rider design, "I am going to marry Taara Gupta with or without your wish or blessings."

With that, Omar marched out of the house leaving two shocked parents behind. His head throbbed as he got into his rental sedan and drove away. A strong gust of dry desert wind blew through the mountains leaving a cloud of dust in its wake. The grand ocean with its majestic waves and unknown depth awaited him as he sped down the Pacific coast highway.

CHAPTER 27

1949

A strong gust of dry desert wind blew, shrouding the rustic mountains in a cloud of dust. Ram Lal rushed at his friend's summons unsuspecting of what misfortune awaited him. As soon as he heard the news, he stared at his friend in disbelief. He grasped Halif's collar in accusation of lying, then his body failed him as he fell to his knees.

"He was going to Umrica to make a future." Ram Lal cried, burying his face in his rough hands, "This can't be happening, he can't be... dead?" His body rocked as he mumbled, "My *puttar*. Why? Why now? Why here? This city, he loved so much." He looked up to the sky to plead, his body rising with his voice, and from deep within his throat, a guttural eruption bellowed, "My puttar Rajinder...."

Halif stood by his friend's side helpless, edging closer to put a hand on his shoulder, squeezing it gently. He noted that the gray had overtaken the dark on his friend's disheveled head. They stood together in the a*ngan* courtyard, motionless, their gazes fixed at the emptiness in front of them. A crow cawed from the large Juniper and suddenly flew off, as if rushing up to a call only it could hear.

Ram Lal sat back on his heels, ironically in the *namaaz* position, and lingered in his blank stare. His chest began to heave, in spasmodic breaths. With bloodshot eyes, he slowly raised his head toward Halif and demanded, "Who did this to my *puttar*?"

Halif shook his downcast head, his eyes fixed on his entangled fingers.

"I should have listened to Janki." Ram Lal cried, "It's my fault." Tears spilled out in a rush of guilt, streaming down his cheeks, losing their way into his salt-and-pepper moustache. He rocked back and forth repeating, "It's my fault."

Halif pulled up his friend by the elbow and gently guided him into the house. Ram Lal had to wash up, to pull himself together. He had his son's funeral to go to. Despite the lack of Hindu *pundits*, Halif had managed to find someone who could perform the last rites, and the cremation was scheduled along with all other Hindu rituals in the newly created Muslim nation.

Halif pushed aside for the moment the questions that had been tormenting him. Why had he let Rajendra go alone that night, or who could have done this and why? He feared the accusation his friend will make, the one he completely deserved. After all, Ram Lal had entrusted his son to him, and it was under his watch the tragedy had taken place.

Late in the evening, after the cremation, Ram Lal sat on the *manji* bed in the courtyard engulfed in darkness. Halif's mother walked over to him with a candle in hand and put her free hand over his head. He slowly looked up toward the light, then let his eyelids fall back down to gaze into the shadows.

Ammi sat down on the *manji* next to him and said, "*Puttar*, Rajinder was a special boy." The ropes in the *manji* stretched under her weight as she adjusted her seat, "He was more like a son to me than my own Ali." She carried on, "I don't know how to say this. Please forgive me…." Her face buried into her *dupatta*, trying to contain her sobs, she drew in a deep breath, and almost in a whisper, she confessed, "I know who did this horrible thing to Rajinder."

Ram Lal looked up from his stupor, slowly readjusting his gaze to the soft light as he turned his body to stare at the old woman.

Taking the edge of her *dupatta*, she wiped her eyes and stammered, "P...*Puttar*... I...I... have given birth to a snake."

Ram Lal's eyebrows furrowed.

"There had been an argument among the three that morning but Halif had sent Ali away." She stared into the flame as if she could see the events of the day unfolding in front of her, "That afternoon, Ali came back when Halif and Rajinder were out." The flame on the candle flickered and was steady again, "This time, Ali had blood in his eyes and a dagger in his hand."

Ram Lal's eyes widened as he clenched his fists.

"I talked to Ali, told him to spit out his anger and tried to calm him down." She put a hand on Ram Lal's arm and said, "He did. Calm down, I mean, and I even kept his dagger. When he left, he said he was better." Ammi's gaze then averted from Ram Lal's as she murmured, "I haven't seen him since and his dagger is gone too."

Ram Lal scrunched his fist until his knuckles turned red. He punched the knotted ropes of the *manji* with all his fury and walked out into the darkness of the night.

When finally Ali was arrested, he boasted, "Pakistan is a Muslim country. It's just a dead Hindu, who can prove that I was involved?"

Eventually at the trial, Ali's mother stood at the witness stand and related the events of the day. With her testimony, Ali Kakkar was sentenced to be hanged for the murder of Rajendra Khatri.

After filing the police complaint, Ram Lal had gone back to Kandhar, to his remaining family, to Janki. He stood facing his wife unable to utter a word while tears liberally gushed down his cheeks. Janki stared, feeling the pound of her heartbeat getting louder. She grabbed his collar and then beat his chest with unsteady fists all the while screaming, demanding.

Ram Lal held her wrists and finally let the words come out, "Janki, our *puttar* is no more."

"Naaahhhhh!" Janki screamed. She then grasped her swollen belly and fell over unconscious.

Ram Lal sat down next to her with a blank stare and began to stroke her head, unaware of her movements. Narendra, now their eldest son walked in. Seeing his mother on the floor and his father mumbling like a mad man, he ran to the neighbors.

While the doctor attended to Janki, Ram Lal sat withdrawn, in a corner. A rosy-cheeked boy with a full head of dark hair arrived kicking and screaming. Ram Lal sat in his corner drowning out all sounds. He ignored Narendra and his pleas to get up. With his head buried in his hands, he sat in that corner all night.

Janki looked at the newborn and saw in his eyes the son she had lost, "My *puttar* Rajinder. You have come back to me."

She gave him the same name, Rajendra. Swallowing the sorrow of her loss with a big gulp, she nestled the newborn and put a protective arm over the rest of her brood.

Ram Lal, in his dark corner, continued to poke at the scar in his heart, picking at the scab over and over, never allowing it to heal. As some form of normalcy appeared in the household, Ram Lal's absence from the scene grew. At first, he stayed out for hours, then he began to skip meals at home, until finally he even stayed out all night.

Janki was used to her husband's absences when he traveled for his work. While the household carried on under her care, she became concerned for her husband's mental state. Whenever she tried to talk he turned his back to her, and walked away.

On the rare occasions he was home, he floated through the house as if in a meditative state, completely detached from all that surrounded him. Neighbors claimed to have seen him in the *Gurdwara* Sikh temple, lost in prayer. He had no concept of time or place, night or day, home or temple, people or divine, the living or the dead.

Janki continued her duty as a mother but became restless as a wife. Her patience had been tested long enough. Even the baby had started to walk by now but Ram Lal had not once taken the child into his arms. One day, she picked up the toddler and stood facing her husband, "Look at him. Your flesh and blood."

Ram Lal looked up impassively. She searched in his eyes for the familiar warmth and love, finding only a glassy stare. Putting the toddler down, she placed her hand on Ram Lal's arm.

He smiled without sentiment and simply said, "Let's go."

Her eyebrows furrowed.

"Just the two of us. To an *Ashram* retreat."

"What about our nine children?" she asked.

"Forget them, all they bring is sorrow." Ram Lal said.

"*Ji*, they are our responsibility and we have to take care of them."

Ram Lal walked out without responding. Janki stood there, eyes wide, mouth agape. The toddler tugged at her *chunni* scarf, she picked him up and went off to the kitchen.

The next day, Bhaga, their neighbor barged into Janki's kitchen. "Save me, save my son. They have taken him away."

Janki looked up from the bread she was rolling, "Who?"

"My precious son, they locked him up." Bhaga lamented.

"Calm down first." Janki put down the rolling pin and gave her a glass of water, "Drink this and then tell me what happened."

Bhaga sat down on the wooden slab in the middle of the kitchen, "As you know, Ajit was at the university in Kabul," Bhaga began, "Yesterday, the government came and took all the students and locked them up."

"What for? Was Ajit involved in the student liberalization?"

"What is that?" Bhaga's hand flew to her chest in fear.

"Narinder was saying something about it the other day. A group called 'the Awakened Youth', university students demanding more freedom ever since the new open-minded parliament came to power."

"What's wrong with that?" Bhaga asked.

"Nothing where you and I stand but with what you say happened in Kabul, the prime-minister seems to think differently." Janki looked toward the fire in her stove and whispered, as if thinking out loud, "This is not good. Cracking down on the youth like this will take this country in reverse."

Bhaga looked at her friend. "Janki, what should I do?"

"Leave." Janki said.

"What?"

Janki looked at her friend and smiled, "I mean, we must leave this country. There is no future for our children here." She held Bhaga's hands, "Narinder will ask around and see what can be done to bring Ajit back."

Later that evening, Janki ventured toward Ram Lal in the *angan*, "Ji, I'm ready to leave."

Ram Lal looked up in disbelief.

"But not to an *Ashram* and not just the two of us." She said.

Hope faded as soon as it had arrived and he looked away.

"To India, for our children's future." She paused.

He continued to stare into a dimension known only to him.

She carried on, "The girls can't go to school here. The boys are being put in jail at the university. We must leave Afghanistan to be among the Hindus."

At the last word, Ram Lal looked at her. He appeared to be thinking for a minute and then nodded, "We'll go to India this summer."

CHAPTER 28

1998

Taara left the house early to beat the traffic. The little bar was not hard to find and she arrived at her tryst on time, breezing through the freeways. Omar walked in just as she was being seated, his hair ruffled from the wind, his T-shirt hung loosely outside his pants and his beach slippers covered with wet sand. Taara ran up to him, but before she could speak, he pulled her close and held her tight for a full minute. Finally sitting in their booth, facing each other across the granite-top table, they held hands in a strong grasp. Lost in each other's eyes, they sat without words, citrusy aroma floating in the air around them. After having stopped at their table several times, their server gave up on them.

"I missed you." Taara broke the silence.

"Me too." Omar replied, his voice almost a whisper. He looked down at her hands, stroking them with his thumbs, then leaned back and took his hands with him. His eyes slowly moved up to meet Taara's as he said, "My parents are refusing to accept you, Taara. But I refuse to let you go."

"Oh Omar. But why? They haven't even met me."

"They don't want to meet you or your family or anyone. I am so ashamed to say this but they only want a Muslim daughter-in-law." Omar could not look into her eyes.

"Aunty Ruhi's the same way, she is refusing to accept you, she thinks the only reason you want to marry me is to convert me."

Their hands together again, squeezed tighter while each smiled to reassure the other.

"I wish there was an easy solution to this." Omar ran one hand through his disheveled hair.

"Maybe they'll come around. We should give them time." Taara offered.

"I know *Abbu* won't. His ego is as inflated as a hot air balloon."

After finishing their iced teas, they walked on the promenade heading for the pier. Hand in hand, they strolled toward the ocean, relishing the cool breeze and the sound of the waves, their sojourn at the edge of the pier. Gazes locked into blueness beyond, they watched the sun high up but felt no warmth from it.

Far off in the Pacific, Omar saw a light flash. It came from a yacht out at sea, its sails fanned out against the wind. The sun reflected off something shiny drawing Omar's attention to the twinkling light. With a smile on his face, he pulled Taara close, his arms protectively around her shoulders. With each spark, his smile widened and he squeezed her shoulder.

"What is it?" Taara asked.

"Will you marry me?" Omar asked excitedly.

"I thought I already answered that question." Taara responded, confused.

"I mean will you marry me tonight?"

"What? How?"

"Vegas. It's only a five-hour drive."

"But what about our families?" she asked.

"We are consenting adults in love. If we keep waiting for everyone else, we'll never get married." Omar made his case.

"But they are our family, Omar. They are not just everyone else."

"Taara." He cupped her face in his palms and looked into her eyes, "Sweetheart, this type of family I can do without, those who impose their beliefs on others. You and I will be family. It will be you and me. If they want to be part of our family, they are welcome, but on our terms, not theirs."

"I don't know, Omar. This doesn't seem right."

"Do you trust me?"

"Of course, I do."

"Then don't worry about my parents. Come, let's be free." Omar then added, "In any case, I think once we are married, they'll come around."

"I can't be gone all night. I have to say something to *masi* and uncle."

"Call them and tell them the truth. We have nothing to hide."

Taara looked out toward the ocean, into the vastness. The vision looked familiar, as if from a dream. The reflection from the far-off yacht continued to blink beckoning a response. With each blink it faded as if the glimmer of hope in this expanse was slowly disappearing. She blinked and suddenly she knew.

Turning to Omar, she squeezed his hand and said, "Okay, let's do it."

He encircled her waist in his arms and lifted her off the ground and swung her around as she laughed. Her feet planted firmly on the ground again, the magnitude of her decision sunk in, only then did she allow herself enthusiasm, but not without a tinge of anxiety.

Back at the Kakkar mansion, Haider Khan sat alone on his *takht* in the vast living room. His hands rested on the edge of the divan as his body leaned slightly forward with scrunched shoulders. His feet crisscrossed underneath, behind the *jhalars* fringes that hung from the daybed. He stared at the gold leaf frame with Omar's smiling face that he had placed on the center table and replayed the conversation between them. His ears turned red as he recalled Omar's audacity to defy him and to put him to shame in front of the *biradri* community. To top it all off he wanted to marry a Hindu. Haider shook his head.

His mind traveled to the stories of the past, from his home in Quetta. His own parents had never spoken of it, but the incident had been the talk of the neighborhood for years. It had happened in the very house he had lived as a child. Patching together bits of information like pieces of a jigsaw puzzle, he had construed there had been a scuffle between his *chachajan*, Ali, and a Hindu boy. The boy had been stabbed in the very house he had claimed to be his, and Uncle Ali had been put on trial and hanged for the murder. It was during the tumultuous time when the stabbing of a Hindu in the newly created Islamic nation was not unheard of. So why was this incident so different? Why was his uncle prosecuted? Haider never understood that but one thing he knew for sure was that it was this incident that had changed his father. Even though he was an infant at the time of the incident, relatives and family friends, everyone talked of times when his father had been happy and social. His father had the utmost respect of the *biradri* community where people seeked his counsel and trusted him with their most intimate situations. That's not the father Haider had grown up with. He grew up with the one who was distant and reserved. He had detached from the family and was completely immersed in religion. His praying sessions were long, strenuous and frequent, as if performed as an act of penance.

It was because of this incident that Haider grew up without the love and guidance of his father. It was because of that Hindu that he never got to exchange more than two words with Abbu. And now there was this Hindu girl and she was taking his son away from him. Haider's face turned red and his nostrils flared. He picked up the frame from the table and placed it next to his heart. In a swift motion, he threw it across the room and heard it smash against the fireplace before it shattered on the ground. Omar's smiling face bled gold from the chipped frame as it lay half-buried in the wool rug. The sun had made its final descent outside leaving Haider on his *takht* in darkness.

Surrounded by desert darkness Taara and Omar followed their headlights toward the beacon of bright lights of Las Vegas.

"I wish we could have been married in India." Taara mused as Omar raced down 15 North, "You could have paraded on an elephant or a white horse, as my knight in shining armor." She continued, "I would have waited for the *baraat* with my marigold garland in hand, all decked out with *mehndi* designs, a beautiful red saree and covered in glittering gold."

Omar gave her a sideways glance, "Are you sure you want to go through with this?"

"I was only remembering a cousin's wedding many years ago. I don't care if it's in a nameless chapel in Vegas or the Taj Mahal as long as you are the groom." She leaned over and gently caressed his cheek with her lips.

"I promise I'll make this up to you someday." Omar circled his free arm around her. She nestled in and rested her head on his shoulder.

They remained silent, watching the headlights guiding them toward their future together as if through a dark tunnel.

The wedding ceremony breezed through uneventfully in a tiny chapel off the strip. Two unknown men dressed in tuxedos signed as witnesses. With the marriage certificate in their hands, Omar took Taara's hand and walked her out in the open desert air. Minutes later they entered Ceasar's Palace and stood in the center of the casino. All around them slot machines chimed, crowds buzzed at the tables, gamblers cheered or moaned, roulette wheels rattled, lights flashed for jackpot winners, women's jewelry glittered under the sharp lights. Hands clasped together, Omar and Taara walked in circles. Finally finding the lobby, they made their way to the counter and checked in for the night.

The next day, Raj welcomed them with open arms soon after

the sun had set. He offered a toast to the occasion and persuaded Ruhi to join in. She escaped into her room right after dinner, feigning a headache but the three enjoyed their dessert of a small wedding cake.

Early next morning, the young couple was ready for their journey to San Fernando Valley. Taara borrowed a *Salwaar Kameez* shirt pant from Ruhi's closet to look the part of a *desi* daughter-in-law. Her only signs of a bride were the hastily bought metal ring shining next to the opal on her third finger. The absence of the *mangal sutra* wedding necklace and *sindhur* vermilion in her hair did not bother Taara. They accepted Raj's blessings and drove hopefully and anxiously toward their next stop.

Parked outside the mansion Omar sat in the car bracing for what awaited him inside. Slowly he started to step out. When Taara opened her door, he put a hand on her shoulder and asked her to wait in the car. She watched him walk in and focused her gaze on the car's digital clock as it slowly changed its minutes. She looked around the driveway and decided to step out. Venturing into a garden on the side of the house, she stopped by a small water fountain. Surrounding it were bushes boasting blush pink rose buds. Tiny leaves sprouted on healthy green stems. A tall banana tree stood as a pillar in one corner fanning its large leaves over the smaller bushes. The garden was small but covered in an assortment of well-tended foliage. She walked toward the front to stand by a large peach tree. Taking in the fresh aroma of spring, she shifted her weight from one leg to the other. She adjusted her long scarf to hang on one shoulder, then back on both shoulders, finally deciding on covering her head with it. Omar had been gone fifteen minutes.

She looked toward the immense entryway and examined the cherry-stained mahogany double doors, admiring the intricate embroidery laced with dark metal at the center of each. Standing in the garden, she felt shut out from her new family. Edges of her scarf held tight, she decided to walk in.

Before she could put her hand on the knob, the door swung

open. Omar's face was redder than the roses in the garden and he was in the process of bolting out. Taara peeked in to catch a glimpse of his parents. Haider Khan's hairy face flamed and his eyes widened as he spotted her. Shahnaz *begum* stood on the far side of the room holding her daughter close. Taara caught a glimmer of smile on her kind face when Shahnaz spotted her. Zahira made a move to come forward, but her mother's hand and father's glare held her back.

Taara made a feeble effort, by raising her palm facing up to touch her bent forehead and she said, "Salaam…"

Zahira responded to the greeting with her hand while her mother did a slight nod of her head. Omar had already gone out and he called for Taara to come too.

"But Omar, I want to meet your family."

"Taara, we are not welcome here. Before there are any insults, we must leave."

"But….Omar…"

"Come Taara. We have to leave right away."

Nobody said anything from inside the house, standing, waiting for the scene to be over.

He grabbed her hand and they walked to the car. Thunder sounded far away and sunny California's sun disappeared behind overcast shadows.

The drive back to Orange County passed in silence with Omar staring straight ahead with pursed lips and stiff hands on the steering wheel. Taara watched her new husband for a reaction, an outburst of some sort, she ran her fingers through his hair as if the gesture would make his thoughts come pouring out. He gave her a stern look and returned to focusing on the road ahead. She retreated into her passenger corner and let him battle his inner tempest on his own for now, watching the raging downpour outside.

Back in Newport Beach, the only one who made an attempt at conversation was Raj. The newlyweds retired early that evening and by mid-morning were at the airport for their return journey. As they sat by their gate waiting to be boarded, Omar's cell phone rang.

A soft voice spoke from it, "Omar? Beta?"

"Ammi?" Omar stood up and walked away from the crowded area.

"Beta... I... you have my blessings. Both of you."

"Ammi, oh Ammi, thank you. This really makes me happy."

"I always pray for your happiness. That's all a mother wants for her children."

"I wish Abbu..."

"Yes, I know. Someday he'll come around. *Insha'Allah*. God willing."

A loud voice of the announcer from the overhead speaker interrupted their conversation. Boarding at their gate was starting.

Shahnaz continued quickly, "Don't forget us and try to forgive your father."

"*Ji*, Ammi."

"And, stay in touch, and give my love to Taara, and call me when you get there."

"I will, Ammijan."

"Zahira sends her love." Her voice cracked, "*Allah Khèr*." She abruptly rang off.

Omar walked back to Taara, his head low. She held him just as he had held her a thousand times, oblivious to the crowd around them. It was her turn to help him overcome the loss of his parents.

"Ammi and Zira send their love and blessings." He murmured in her ear.

Taara smiled. At least he had his mother and his sister. Someday, his father will accept too and she will have parents again. She held his hand and the two walked to the gangway to their plane, to their new life together as husband and wife, to the land of 10,000 lakes.

CHAPTER 29

2000

Taara returned home sweaty and tired after a five-mile jog around Lake Calhoun, "Surprise!" Everyone cheered as she walked into her living room.

"So you finally did it. You're a college graduate." Nata yelled.

"How does it feel?" Ben, Nata's boyfriend asked.

Taara stood at the door motionless, her mouth and nose cupped by her palms. She searched for her husband in the crowd of familiar faces and found him standing in the back corner with a cheeky look. He walked over and kissed her.

"Congratulations."

She waved a finger at him, and smiled, "I should have known you'd do something like this. Now I feel guilty."

"What for?" Omar asked.

"For not doing anything when you finished your MBA and

passed the Bar."

"I don't like surprises. You know that." He reminded her.

Taara felt a tap on her shoulder and turned around to find uncle Raj.

"I can't have my niece be monopolized by her husband all evening."

Taara squealed with delight and hugged her uncle. She did not ask but he answered anyway, "Ruhi is in Europe, on an assignment. She'll be back tomorrow."

Taara nodded. Aunty Maya came up to offer her wishes and the two fell into a warm embrace. Aunty Lalita, uncle Parag and several of her parents' friends congratulated Taara, showered their warm wishes and blessings, and reiterated how proud her parents would have been of her. Taara nodded and smiled and thanked and hugged and kept her tears hidden back, way back into her throat, inside her heart, all the way down into her stomach. Slipping away to wash up, but in seclusion, her tears gave in to momentary release. Hastily she returned to the party, refreshed and dressed for the occasion.

Philip, Omar's colleague and friend, tapped her head from behind and Taara turned. He engulfed Taara in his massiveness. His wife, Julie, gently moved in and grasped Taara's hand.

"Et tu Brutus?" Taara shrieked at Julie.

"Omar made us promise."

"Julie, so tell me how you got Phillip to keep it a secret?" Taara whispered loudly in her ear.

"It was hard. He almost gave it away, several times."

"How long did he have to keep it inside him?" Taara asked.

Julie moved closer and lowered her voice into a conspiratorial tone, "A whole week! Can you believe it? Of course, Omar's been planning it for months."

Philip budged in, "Hey, I can't help it that I'm an honest man. I can't lie."

The two women rolled their eyes at the solid man towering over them.

"Ya. And that's why you became a lawyer." Julie grinned.

Nata and Ben joined the group and Taara introduced them. A few moments later she left them discussing the problems of outsourcing of American jobs overseas. She found Raj engaged in conversation with Uncle Parag so she went in search of Omar, gliding from room to room filling up the flutes with the bubbling champagne. She found Omar in the kitchen replenishing the *kabab* platter. Fresh aromas of tropical fruits, lamb chops, chicken *tikka*, samosas, *panir tikka*, potato cutlets, and vegetable *pakora* fritters mingled and floated in the air.

Amidst laughter, passionate conversations, jazz music from hidden speakers, the shrill ring of the phone permeated.

Uncle Raj excused himself and ran to the bedroom to answer it. "Hello?" Muffled sound of music and conversations seeped into the room. A voice, barely audible was on the line. He strained to listen, "Yes… No but this is Raj here. Who? Oh yes… yes… oh no! When? How? Okay." He put the receiver down slowly and plopped on the bed. Several minutes later he raised his head, stood up, pasted a smile and joined the party.

Food platters empty, all the wine duly consumed, tired music finally turned off, Omar and Taara waved to the last of their guests. They slumped on their black leather sofa completely exhausted.

Raj plodded out of his room with his eyes to the ground. He walked up to Taara, attempted a smile and handed her an envelope. Taara looked up surprised, confused and stood up. She opened the envelope and her jaw dropped. Finally, she found words, "But why? This is too much."

Omar observed the scene from his seated position.

"I should've done this two years ago. Consider this both a wedding and a graduation present." Raj said.

"But I can't accept it. No." Taara shoved the envelope back at him, but he took a step back and shook his head.

Omar stood up, curious, "What is it?" He finally asked.

"It's two tickets for a 7-day cruise in the Caribbean," Taara informed.

"Wow!" He exclaimed, "But Taara is right. We can't accept such an expensive gift."

Raj shook his head and said, "Ruhi and I want to give this present to our daughter and son-in-law." With that he sat down, settling the matter.

Taara asked about his plans. He hesitated and finally said, "I was planning to be here through the weekend but I will change my tickets for tomorrow now."

"Why?" Both Taara and Omar asked together.

"Ruhi will need me. She's back tomorrow."

"But she's used to having you gone for all those business trips. She'll be fine." Taara offered.

Raj shook his head and said, "That's not it."

He looked at his hands. Taara noticed he had been sitting at the edge of the sofa chair, his body tense.

"What's wrong uncle?" She leaned forward.

"There was a phone call earlier… while the party was going on. It was from India, from Dehra Dun." He looked up to meet Taara's eyes, "*Ammaji* is no more."

Taara's hand covered her mouth as she gasped. A muffled cry escaped from her as she tried to hold herself together, her shoulders scrunched up, heaving. She drifted away from the men toward the window and stood motionless, staring out into the night.

Omar and Raj exchanged looks and strolled toward her. Omar put his arm around her shoulder and pulled her close to him, her head falling onto his shoulder as teardrops trickled down her cheeks. Raj stroked her hair and offered her a Kleenex.

"I just wrote to her, last month. She always replies with someone's help." Taara sobbed.

Omar held her, "She is at peace now." He said, "You yourself told me how much she had been suffering."

"She had turned 95 last month." Raj offered, "A long full life."

Taara sighed deeply.

"Did you know that for the past six months, her heart only functioned 60%?" Raj continued, "But her brain was as sharp as ever. She knew exactly how much money she had in her account, down to the last *paisa*."

"What an amazing lady she was." Omar said.

"I had so many questions for her." Taara blew her nose. "It's too soon. I wanted Omar to meet her."

Omar squeezed her shoulder.

"I needed her. Why do they all keep leaving me?" Taara choked.

The room remained silent. They all stood by the window and continued to stare out into darkness.

All night long Taara tossed and turned as unknown demons tormented her soul. She saw her great-grandmother blind, helpless, alone, floating above the clouds. Darkness surrounded her with no one to hold her hand. She reached out for all her loved ones and only grasped air. Somehow Ammaji's face changed into her own. Taara's eyes flew open. She reached out to Omar but found his side empty.

Omar had left to drive Raj to the airport for an early flight. He returned to find Taara still in bed, covered in sweat. Her eyes were open and staring at the white ceiling, watching the fan turn in slow motion. She appeared mesmerized. Suddenly, she jumped out of the bed and ran to the bathroom and Omar heard her getting sick. He went in and ran his hand down her back, held her hair back, and supported her until she could steady herself. All the tears she had been holding back throughout the party, the sadness stuck in her throat, the sorrow buried in her gut, all came pouring out. She finally allowed herself to feel. She had missed her parents when she married, and now, again, at her graduation. Meeting all their friends again reminding her of her losses and now to learn that she was orphaned yet again - the void gnawed at her. She felt her body become numb, her arms hanging limply by her side. Ammaji, Janki Devi Khatri was no more. Her heart screamed for somebody to hold her up, to ground her, to keep her sturdy, to give her strength, to tell her who she was.

After sitting on the bathroom floor for some time, she managed to clean up and stagger back to her bed. Omar brought her some juice and toast and insisted she eat. He then sat with her, holding her hand.

She gave him a weak smile.

"Feel better?" He asked.

She nodded and sipped her juice. Omar rummaged through the house clearing up from the party while she spent the rest of the day in bed, sitting up staring out of her window into a dreary, overcast morning. When the downpour hammered onto the window pane with a vengeance, blurring her vision, she reclined back. Her eyes watched the rough patterns on the white ceiling and the fan hanging still. It had stopped its endless circling. Her eyes closed only to find an image looking back at her from underneath her eyelids. Ammaji stood tall, watching with perfect eyes, in a cotton floral blue *salwar kameez* with white chiffon *chunni* scarf over her head. Her dark long hair draped over her shoulders, she sported a golden purse on her arm. Taara reached out with one hand and grabbed a palmful of air. She called out to her but only the disapproving eyes stared back. She screamed pleading Janki to hold her, to support her, to keep her from falling deep into the abyss of her life. But her scream had no sound. Tears dribbled down to her temples to the pillow beneath her. She opened her eyes to find Omar standing over, his hand on her shoulders as if he had been shaking them. His face wore a worried expression. History was repeating. Dear sweet Omar, always by her side. Her hand reached out and stroked his face. Janki had told her to look to the future.

Taara sat up and walked to the bathroom. She splashed her face with cold water, brushed her teeth and stepped into the shower. When she entered the kitchen, she saw a platter full of the delicacies leftover from the party on the table, warmed up and ready to be eaten. Omar smiled and welcomed her back. They ate in silence by the light of three tall candles and to the sound of soft

Bollywood music in the background.

The next day, while Omar was at work, the phone rang. Taara was in the room looking through her mother's diary and pictures of Ammaji in their album. She ignored it and it went to the voicemail. Soon after that her cell phone buzzed. She picked it on the third ring.

"Taara? Good, I got you." Raj spoke hurriedly.

"What's wrong uncle?"

"It's your aunty Ruhi. She's in the hospital."

"What?" Pictures in her hand fell splaying all over the floor. "What happened? Is she alright?"

"I don't know." She heard him take a deep breath before continuing, "She got back from Europe last night. After we got home I told her... you know, about Ammaji."

"And?" Taara asked.

"And, she seemed to have taken it quite well. We ate and she went to bed early. Jet lag, so I thought. This morning as I was getting ready for work, I saw her standing over the sink for a long time. Then, in the next minute she was flat on the bathroom floor."

"I'll be right there." Taara spoke quickly, her mind racing 100 miles an hour, "I'll catch the first flight I can get. Call you back." As soon as Taara put the phone down, she picked it up again. Omar answered on the first ring.

He drove her to the airport that afternoon. He asked her again, "You're sure you don't want me to come?"

"Sure."

He gave her a sideways glance.

"I know I should've tried harder. She fools everyone with her strong woman act." Taara said more to herself than to Omar, "Paper tiger, that's what she is. It's all my fault, I should've reached out."

"Stop blaming yourself," Omar said, annoyed. "Did uncle Raj say what's wrong with her?"

"Nervous breakdown, he thinks."

Omar pulled his Honda Accord into a spot in the short-term

parking, switched off the engine and turned to Taara, "It's not your fault. If you keep this attitude, uncle will have two women to manage." He reached for her hand, squeezed it tight and asked, "Now tell me, truthfully, are you up for it?"

Taara nodded. She stepped out of the car and grabbed her hastily packed carry-on from the back seat before Omar could get to it. In her straight blue jeans, white polo, fitted short gray jacket and matching sketchers, she held her tightly tied ponytailed head high and rolled her bag toward the terminal.

Taara drove straight to the hospital in a bright red Grand Cherokee, the only rental available at the airport at such short notice. She found Ruhi in her private room, propped up over a heap of pillows, eyes sunken in, hair disheveled, face as pale as the sheets under her. Uncle Raj sat by the window, *Economist* in hand. He stood up as soon as he saw Taara walk in.

"You didn't call. I would have picked you up from the airport." He protested.

"I didn't want you to leave *masi* alone." Taara turned to Ruhi and smiled. She walked over to the bed, held her hand and said, "How are you?"

Ruhi attempted a weak smile and whispered, "Not good, honey. Not good at all." She broke into a sob, tears freely gushing down her sallow cheeks.

Taara sat on the bed beside her and held her heaving body. Tears scrolled down both their cheeks as each held the other for their dear life.

"Who will watch over us now?" Ruhi droned.

"I know *masi*." Taara whimpered, "We are orphans once again."

"We are losing them one by one. I always thought Ammaji would live forever."

Neither noticed Raj quietly step out of the room.

"Tell me about her. What was she like when you were growing up?" Taara asked.

Ruhi sat back melting into her pillows. She closed her eyes

and spoke softly, "Storyteller. It was a ritual almost, every evening after dinner all the children sat around her on that grand bed of hers. During winter, we all sat under the same, warm *razai* cover. I wish I remembered those stories."

"I do. Mummy told them to me."

"Why didn't I spend more time with her, like Dimple *didi*?" Ruhi's eyes opened, "With both of them gone, I know nothing of her."

"*Masi*." Taara looked in her eyes, "Mummy left a journal. It's all about Ammaji."

Ruhi stared at her, "What do you mean?"

"An account of Ammaji's life. Mummy had started to write but it's unfinished." Taara reached into the front pocket of her bag and removed the beautiful book.

Reaching for a wet towel, Ruhi wiped her face and hands before taking Dimple's journal in her hands. She ran her hand over the soft silky cover, her fingers lingering over the cashew shaped embroidery. She opened it to find the familiar handwriting of her beloved sister. Taking the book to her heart she hugged it as if it was Dimple in body and soul. Words spilled, tripping over each other, "Why? Why does she have to leave me? I was so mean to her. She was my mother and I was mean to her. I'm so sorry *didi*, please forgive me. I'm so sorry...," she wailed.

Taara held her and stroked her head. They rocked together, slowly back and forth. Raj cocked his head back in the room and Taara gestured for him to come in. Ruhi reached a hand out to her husband and he took her in his arms as Taara moved away.

"I'm so sorry." Ruhi moaned, "You've been so patient with me."

"Shh… shhh…" He ran his hand up and down her spine, massaging her back.

"I can't even give you children." She complained.

"Quiet now Ruhi. Don't think about all that. I want you back home, healthy and strong." he coaxed.

By that evening Ruhi was deemed healthy enough to go home.

The week flew by as Taara chiseled and sliced, piece by piece, to get to the softer side of her aunt. The wall slowly reduced to rubble and Taara stepped right in. In losing Janki, Taara had found Ruhi. She did not miss the *pashmina* she had forgotten to bring in her haste.

On the last day before returning, Taara sat by the pool nursing her morning tea. She watched the clear sky welcome the rising sun with open arms. The light and warmth added sparkle to the blue water in the swimming pool, put a smile on the yellow roses and red begonias, and raised spirits all around. Taara heard Ruhi humming her way to the poolside, coffee mug and a plateful of Parlé's glucose *biscuits* cookies in hand.

"Yumm! Omar loves these." Taara took one and dipped it delicately into her creamy tea before taking a sweet bite.

They sat in silence listening to the birds chirping. Taara nibbled on her biscuit, taking small pecks as she stared into the cool water. "*Masi?*" she said without moving her gaze, "I am sorry."

Ruhi looked through the steam of her black coffee, her eyebrow furrowed.

"That we didn't see eye to eye about Omar." Taara reminded.

Ruhi shook her head, "I should be the one to apologize, to both of you."

"You know if it wasn't for Omar...."

"I know," Ruhi said, "I realize that now. You needed me and I well..." she stopped mid-sentence.

Taara observed her as she looked away.

Softly Ruhi spoke, "Late into the nights, I used to sneak into the bathroom and cry my heart out. Dimple *didi* was all I had after my parents."

Taara listened, her mug of tea hanging in midair.

"I was her shadow in Dehra Dun." Ruhi continued, "When she got married and left, I never forgave her for abandoning me. Ammaji was there but I rejected her and everyone else." She dabbed her eyes, blew into a tissue and moaned, "What a fool I was."

Taara reached out to squeeze her hand.

Ruhi offered a weak smile in return.

They listened to the chirping birds and sipped their morning beverages. Time traveled in slow motion like the ripples of the water in the pool.

Taara swallowed the last of her tea and probed, "I heard you say something at the hospital." She looked at her aunt, "About children."

"I've gone through multiple miscarriages and fertility treatments. No one can help us." Ruhi lowered her glance avoiding Taara's eyes and spoke, "*Didi* always had everything - Ammaji, friends, the kind of life she wanted, and she had You." She looked up, "I didn't even have the career I wanted."

"It's all in the past." Taara consoled, "Now you're the only mother I have and you better be a damned good one." She challenged.

"It's a mother's promise." Ruhi smiled. A flower from an overhanging tree branch fell into the serene pool, causing ripples of blue water to spread outward in perfect circles.

CHAPTER 30

1951

Time traveled as fast as the raging waters of the Ganga River as it rushed down from its home in the mountains into the unfamiliar valleys. Janki stood in the courtyard and looked around her humble but warm abode. Her thoughts traveled to all the journeys she had made, past the fertile fields of Khushab, over the rustic mountains of Quetta, and through the rugged terrain to Kandhar. With each journey she had carried salty tears, carefully packed precious memories, and snuggled in her heart a piece of each of the lands she had called home. With each hesitant step into a new city or a border crossing, she had wept for the family she will miss and the childhood she never had, following her husband dutifully and her destiny faithfully.

She had felt secure in her home in Kandhar, shielded by the boundary wall that surrounded the courtyard her family shared with the biradri neighbors. In one corner, the willow that had offered its shade all these years stood majestically, strong and grounded. Janki walked over to it to stand under its shade one last time. Running her fingers over the thick, solid trunk she looked up at the branches spread outward and down leaning to kiss the ground, as if weeping or offering thanks. She noticed its branches, each as distinct as her children.

Stepping back, Janki took a moment to take account of her brood. They were her basket of pride and joy. They were her rich jewels just like within the pomegranate, the fruit of abundance. Her children were reminder of the love she and Ram Lal once shared, the chirag light of the family walking on the path to a bright future.

Rajendra was her first, who almost made it to the light at the end of the long tunnel, into the land of dreams. Now lost to her forever, she blinked away tears and stared at another, stunted branch. Sita, her second had been with her a short time and gone so young, the fire in her eyes extinguished forever. Durgi was her oldest living child now, happily married to an engineer in India with two children of her own. In just her last letter she shared her joys of motherhood, writing, maati, when I was younger, I used to resent having to share everything with my brothers and sisters. Now that I have little ones of my own, I can see why you had so many of us. Children are such delightful gifts.

Smiling, Janki thought about her second daughter, Bhaga, also in India as a newlywed. Soon she will be blessed with the gifts of children as well. Bhaga reminded her of herself recalling how she mothered the younger children with a firm hand, entertaining them with stories and keeping them busy. Narendra, the eldest son now, was born the day of Sita's death. He had come earlier than his time and frail, his asthma a constant companion. Despite his delicate health, he was the only earning member of the household since Rajendra's death. Janki knew that now, at 23, he was ready to settle down with a family of his own, but was burdened with heavy responsibilities on his fragile shoulders.

Her next two were the teenage girls – Bibo, the most challenging of all her children with a headstrong determination to get her way. She was ready for college at 17 but Janki could see her shy 15-year old Shaku aspiring for further studies. Her eyes full of wonder reminded Janki of Sita's curiosity. With no schools for girls in Afghanistan, Janki had found ways to feed her daughters with the education they deserved and yearned for. She borrowed books from neighbor boys and spent hours with the girls, never letting their candle for knowledge burn out. Now with the political turmoil in Kabul, proper college education for even the boys was questionable. Janki reminded herself once again that the decision to move to India was a good one where all her children would have the choice and the chance to shine from the brilliance of knowledge.

Her next two were boys, Virendra and Mahendra, just two years apart and inseparable, as if they were twins. Both were naughty and found creative ways to avoid chores. Ever since Ram Lal had dragged Virendra to the Hindu school in Hardiwar, India, Mahendra walked around aimlessly, disinterested in even mischief. She decided to let Mahendra join his brother at Gurukul.

Janki's mind turned to her youngest daughter, Laaji, who at nine was turning out to be the prettiest of all and seemed to know it too. She spent hours in front of the mirror, doing and re-doing her long dark hair. Janki's eyes then turned toward a delicate branch recently sprouted and her thoughts turned to her baby, Rajendra reborn, and his gentle soul gave her the strength to carry on. Despite her heavy heart, she looked ahead into the future of her children in a land where they will have the freedom to choose, move forward, grow and glow.

Looking back at the trunk of the grand tree, her thoughts turned to Ram Lal, her husband, father of all her children. Before she could formulate any thoughts on his state, a cry from inside the house brought her back to the task at hand. Plenty needed to be done and only a month was left before they had to leave.

While the Afghans were out planting trees as is the tradition every spring, Janki gathered her troops to do the annual safedi. Narendra led the gulegutch project in which a white, toxic and messy substance was applied all over the walls with hands and a rag. The younger children eagerly helped with the unpleasant task in anticipation of the juicy fresh fruits they could indulge in as a reward. Eyeing the blush red and yellow apricots and dark red plums piled in baskets in the courtyard, they worked hard and fast longing to sink their teeth into the fruits letting the juices run down to their elbows.

On the eve of their departure on a starry summer night, Janki and Ram Lal walked under the protection of darkness toward the famous cave where Ram Lal had acquired his reputation of valor. They entered through its small opening and went to the center under the protruding ledge from its ceiling. Counting ten steps to the right, then five steps to the left, Ram Lal bent down. Janki handed him a stone with a sharp edge and he started to dig the earth. It was damp, making the ground soft, so in just five minutes he struck something hard. Pulling out four small bundles of red cloth with bulging sides and a large knot, he handed one to his wife and carried the other three burrowed under his pattoo shawl.

Since their marriage, it had become a tradition every Diwali for Ram Lal to buy gold. When his businesses were at their peak, he bought several pieces and even during challenging times he managed to acquire a small coin in the name of tradition. Adding this collection to Janki's wedding jewelry, their life's savings amounted to 100 taels of gold which they carefully lugged hidden under the cover of darkness.

At home they packed the coins and jewelry in various bags and stitched some in their clothing to hide from prying eyes during the journey. Janki rose before the sun on the day of their departure waking the older children to help start the preparations. As light was beginning to split the heaven and earth into two, Ram Lal and the children loaded their luggage onto his bus, the last of the monsters that had survived from the transportation business days. Janki took a final look around the empty house and noticed how it sparkled with the fresh whitewash and no clutter. Blinking her eyes, she realized that without her family in it, it was just four walls. She quickly turned, shut the door and locked it with the heavy padlock. In the courtyard, she walked over to the willow as it wept and touched its sturdy trunk. She stood there a moment hoping for some of its strength to flow into her, so she could also hold her branches as majestically and gently as the tree. After she got on the bus, it coughed and rumbled as Ram Lal blew the musical horn announcing their final farewell to the land of their ancestors.

Unlike her previous journeys Janki was ready to cross this boundary. She looked straight ahead, determined to move forward without sorrow or painful memories, leaving behind all attachments. Janki looked toward the rising sun for a new beginning and a bright new day.

CHAPTER 31

2000

Taara landed in Minnesota greeted by a glorious sunrise. She returned to a new life and soon after, they moved from their uptown condo living into a 3-bedroom twin home in a new development in Eden Prairie.

Taara and Omar stepped onto the maple hardwood floors and walked into their new living room, arm in arm. They stood admiring the wood-burning fireplace with its rustic stone hearth. Their soft cushioned beige sofa set looked right at home with its solid pine coffee table companion. They spread a burgundy wool rug, with blue and yellow repetitive patterns in the Balochi style, in front of the fireplace and placed two *gao takkia* round pillows on each end, as parenthesis. White or tan walls spread throughout the house and Taara set her mind to change the colors. She chose to add a combination of mango yellow and mandarin orange in some rooms or taupe, avocado and wine in other rooms.

Omar's case-load at the law firm picked up with long days, and frequent travels, while Taara continued to make their new dwellings a home. After spending several blustery, solitary days painting, unpacking, organizing, and decorating, Taara reeled outdoors as soon as the sky cleared. Dressed in loose capris, short t-shirt and sketchers, she ventured out to explore her new neighborhood.

Walking down her driveway, she decided to turn right, but after just ten minutes of walking on the clean, newly paved path, she found herself in a cul-de-sac. Before she could complete the circle, she spotted a dirt path leading into the bushes. Feeling adventurous, she decided to follow the sound of the birds inviting her in. She gingerly continued only to find herself onto a paved trail deeper into the wilderness. Her steps sped up, and soon she saw a small lake through an opening where she observed a family of geese lounging on the water. Thick algae floated toward the bank adding greenness and a veil for the lake; she wondered what secrets lurked beneath. Birds around her continued their chatter, undisturbed by the intrusion. Taara watched a cardinal perched on a branch high up a golden ash and admired the bird's bright red majestic air as it clucked and tooted, waving its spiky crown. A red breasted robin flew close to Taara and set about the business of worm digging. Taara was amused by a family of ducks as they made a smooth landing, sliding onto the lake. They splashed and lapped the water as they frolicked in its coolness. A lone loon glided on the far side before it disappeared into the vegetation.

An orchestra of chirps, tweets, quacks and honks surrounded the lush trail. Even a yodel or two reached Taara's ears as the loon asserted his domain. A smile formed on her lips as she hugged herself and breathed it all in. Lost in nature's melody Taara jumped when she felt something touch her leg. She turned to find a little puppy wagging its tail and looking up at her with its big brown eyes. It had very curly golden fur and fuzzy floppy ears. Taara bent down to pet it and the dog jumped off running into the bushes, only to appear again in the clearing, to see if she was following. Its wagging tail ruffled the leaves in the bushes.

"Have you seen a puppy come through here?" a slim athletic woman panted up to the opening.

Taara looked toward the puppy still standing in the bushes, staring at her. She nodded to the woman, "There he is."

The woman smiled, got down to dog level and with a treat in hand called him. The little ball of fur walked tentatively toward them, and took the treat offered. Before he could dash, his leash was back on his collar and he stayed put.

"Thanks. He's quite a handful and full of energy. I don't know what happened, the clasp on his leash must have come loose. He was tugging very hard." The woman chatted away.

Taara watched the young woman, her mouth moving a million miles an hour. Her dark brown hair was neatly pulled back into a ponytail, exposing a broad forehead. Her square shoulders glistening with sweat shone under the warm sun, contrasting red against the white racer shirt she sported. Below a medium chest, Taara noticed a bump on her tummy. The dog sitting next to the woman's feet looked up and whined.

"He's so adorable." Taara commented as she bent down to pet him.

"Don't let those innocent eyes fool you. He's very naughty. Hey, did you just move into this neighborhood, in that brick-front twin?" she asked.

"Yes, I'm Taara." She stood up and extended her hand.

"I'm Lynnette."

"Where does this trail go?" Taara asked.

"Nowhere."

Taara stared at her.

Lynnette laughed, "you want to join me? Oscar and I are doing the circle. It's just a mile around the lake."

As they walked Taara learned that her suspicions were right. Two babies were on the way around Thanksgiving and they were going to be their first. Lynnette chatted along the way as Taara listened. A squirrel crossed their path and Oscar tugged to run off on its chase. He barked at the lost prize as it scurried off up a tree trunk onto a branch.

"We've been here two years. A good neighborhood to start a family, we thought, when we finally decided on the house. Good school district, a walk to the park, safe, and these trails." Lynnette waved her free hand in air. "This lake is so beautiful. I enjoy coming here at all hours, even in the winters." Taara nodded in agreement.

Taara began taking regular walks, several times a day. On many occasions she would bump into Lynnette and Oscar and join them. Mostly, she just strolled leisurely, stopping to admire, to observe, to listen. On those days she would come rushing to her home at the end of the circle, anxious to get to her canvas in the studio she had set up in the basement. She splashed colors, blended hues, created large subtle scapes in unusual blends, adding a dot of a yellow sparrow on a slight branch or a hint of a gray face in a potpourri of clouds. She experimented by layering oils and acrylic to bring out textures.

Immersed in colors and lost in her isolation, Taara formed a connection with her natural surroundings. She began packing a snack for the ducks in the lake, capturing squirrels and birds behind the lenses of her camera that became a fixture in her sling bag. So when Lynnette asked one day if she could dog sit for her, Taara jumped at the chance. She had become quite fond of the little rascal and often brought treats for him when she visited Lynnette at her two-story across the street. At first, she was not sure how Omar would take to having a dog around the house for a week, but after much pleading and reason, he conceded. He agreed that he was gone more often than at home and Oscar would be good company. As it turned out, one of Omar's project was delayed and the two of them ended up taking long walks together with Oscar.

They became quite fond of the curly haired doodle and were sad to see him go back to his family after their return.

Leaves turned color and walks became crisper. The changing season brought new rush of inspiration from nature's colorful palette. Omar returned to his corporate schedule and Taara immersed herself in her work in her underground studio or walks on the trail alone or with Lynnette. Her friend's pace slowed to a waddle with her heavy load. She shared her anxiety over the imminent arrivals, expressing concern over the care they would need for two babies. Her apprehension extended to Oscar. On one particularly cold morning, as the eerie wail of the loon resounded along the trail, and dark clouds ominously loomed overhead threatening to unload snow or icy rain, Lynnette grabbed Taara's arm. In a desperate cry, she asked if Taara could to adopt Oscar.

"But he's your baby," Taara responded.

"I'm not sure I can manage him and them," she complained, pointing to her swollen belly.

"But..."

"You will be a better parent to him than I can be. I know it," Lynnette continued to make her case. "Look, here's the deal. We've already decided to find Oscar a new home. It will be unfair to him with all the commotion there will be in our household. With you he'll be with all the things familiar to him."

Taara nodded but raised her hand before her friend could shriek with delight, "I'll talk it over with Omar and get back to you."

Lynnette shrieked anyway, which was just as well, since Taara called her that same night with the good news. Oscar moved into their home the next day. The little dog appeared confused at first, but soon took to following Taara around the house and kept her company.

Several weeks later, as Taara sat at the kitchen table admiring her humble Thanksgiving feast, Oscar sat at her feet under the table. Omar called to confirm yet another flight reschedule and his disappointment of missing the holiday with her. She packed up the food, uneaten; leashed Oscar, bundled up, and stepped out.

The refreshing breeze welcomed her to the outdoors while the night offered her a comforting cloak. Several houses on her street stood in darkness with their dwellers away, celebrating with their respective families. Approaching the cul-de-sac, Taara skirted around an array of cars parked on the street and on several driveways. She sneaked a peek into one of the well-lit houses through its partially folded blinds. She saw a group congregated around an oval table, which was covered with a variety of delicacies. All the people were absorbed in cheerful conversation, oblivious to the stark cold and solitude of the outside. Taara and Oscar completed their circle and hurried home to huddle in their solace.

The next day, with Oscar at her feet, Taara sat on her bean bag in the basement studio by a low window and paged through some art prints. Snow lay thick on the ground outside covering up the backyard in a shroud of winter. She walked over to the book case to look for a copy of techniques in art and came across her mother's diary. She had left it with Ruhi and it had arrived in the mail the week they were watching Oscar. Since he was known to have nibbled at books, she had hastily put it on a high shelf.

Now with the delicate diary in hand, she sat back down and began to flip through the pages. As she came to the last written page and sat facing blank pages, she felt the need to fill them up. But this was not her blank canvas to paint with her images and stories. This was the story of a lady she knew not enough about. Putting her painting work aside, Taara decided to start a new project. Winter offered the perfect time to delve into history, ponder the past, and pick up where her mother had left off.

One chilly Saturday evening, wine glass in hand, Omar reached his arm over her shoulder as they sat by the fireplace.

Taara rested her head on his chest as she drew patterns on it with her finger. Focused on the task she spoke softly, "I was thinking... perhaps we should take a vacation."

"That's a wonderful idea," Omar responded. "You have any

place in mind?"

"Well, definitely somewhere warmer," she said.

Omar nodded as he swallowed the smooth Cabernet.

Taara lifted her head to face him and suggested, "how about India?"

Omar took back his arm and set his wine glass on the side table. Taara sat back on the sofa and continued to look for a reaction. He slowly turned to her and asked, "for how long were you thinking?"

"Oh, a month or so," she said.

Omar shook his head, "I'm afraid it'll be hard for me to get away for that long. Why not somewhere closer for now, like Mexico?"

Taara's face fell.

Omar took her hand into his and said, "It's not that I don't want to go to India but not for a fleeting visit. And the workload won't let me get away for more than a week."

"I know but… I thought…" She shook her head and said, "never mind."

"In a few more years when I'm made a partner, I'll ease down my hours." Omar pulled her closer, "then we will plan a longer vacation to both India and Pakistan."

Taara remained silent.

Omar pulled her closer and whispered in her ear, "let's go to Puerto Vallarta for a few days."

Taara nodded. She spoke almost to herself, "I suppose I can write to grand uncles and aunts."

"What?" Omar asked picking up his wine glass again.

"For my research," she said.

"What?" Omar asked again.

Taara smiled and explained, "I'm trying to complete what mummy left unfinished."

Omar looked at her quizzically.

"Her journal, it has so many things about Ammaji and her fascinating life and I want to know more."

Omar gazed in amazement.

"So get this." Taara pulled her feet up on the sofa and perked up, "that story your Ammi told you, about a murder in Quetta. Remember?"

"About my grandfather's brother getting hanged for a murder of a Hindu boy."

"Guess what? I found a story similar to it in my mother's book. How freaky is that?" Taara continued excitedly, "mummy wrote that her uncle was the victim."

"Interesting…" Omar relaxed back in thought.

"And my mom has her dad's version," Taara continued excitedly. "So, there could be missing pieces still. Here's what my mom wrote." Taara brought out the journal from the drawer of their coffee table and read…

Virendra, my father, at age 11, had heard about the demise of his brother through the boarding school principal and had stayed in a state of shock for several days. Soon, he had involved himself in his studies and sports and his sad state had passed. However, when the family arrived in Hardiwar, Virendra heard the details of the murder and the whole family cried together, except Ram Lal.

Taara was curious about how the whole family ended up in Hardiwar. She wondered why Ram Lal did not cry and she was also curious about Janki's reaction. Now that she was no more, Taara could not ask her, but she recalled snippets of her exchange with her great-grandmother during the last visit. Janki had said, "murdered… she lost two people that day, her son and her husband… somebody had to take care of the children…"

"Where are you?" Omar nudged her.

She returned to her husband lounging next to her and gave him a distracted smile. Her stomach suddenly felt a little queasy. She wanted to return to her research to find answers to all her questions but felt too tired.

"I don't feel well," she stood up and went to the bedroom, Oscar in tow.

Omar was on his feet in a snap. He helped her get into bed

and tucked her in like a baby. Oscar cuddled at her feet into a ball and began his steady, comforting snores.

Taara met her mother that night. Dimple visited her in her dream, offering her blessings. Taara woke up drenched in tears and cried all the next day without understanding why. She missed her parents all of a sudden. Omar tried to comfort her but he also had a flight to catch. He was torn between leaving his wife alone in such a state and an important client meeting on the East Coast. Taara assured him she would be fine.

"Take a break from your mother's journal," Omar advised.

Taara nodded but her questions were burning a hole inside her. She had to continue to work on it.

After Omar left, Taara took herself to the pharmacy. Back home she agonized over the result. It was the longest three minutes of her life.

Taara slumped into the couch, all five test strips in hand. She laughed and cried all at once, then reached for the phone, dialed Omar's number but hung up before his phone started to ring. She dialed another number, she needed confirmation.

Taara returned from the clinic, still uncertain. They did the test but the results were not immediately available. She paced the length of her kitchen, her knuckles clenched and entangled together. She felt scared, thought of how her mother would have felt if she were alive.

The phone ring interrupted her thoughts. Taara shushed Oscar, who started barking at a squirrel by the window, and walked to the phone. After a few yesses, she slowly set the cordless down, scrunched her fists again and let out a loud scream. Turning back to the phone, she immediately called Omar but got his voicemail. She tried all his numbers without success. Joy was taking over her fears and Taara excitedly paced all over the house. To calm herself down, she decided to bake a cake and celebrate. Just as she was about to place the batter in the oven, licking away at her chocolaty fingers, the phone rang. Taara ran to the phone, placed a hand on her tummy and answered.

"Taara honey, what's wrong? Are you okay?" Yes, it was Omar.

"I'm fine. In fact, fantastic. We're going to have a baby!" She almost screamed.

"What?! When? How? Never mind. I'll be home on the next flight." Omar yelled back.

After the news had sunk in, Taara and Omar decided to share their joy with the family.

"Uncle Raj. Guess what?" Taara suddenly became shy and passed the phone to Omar.

"You're going to be a *Nana*, a grandpa," Omar exclaimed.

"Yoohoo!" Raj shouted over the mouthpiece, "Ruhi, come listen to the good news."

"Is that true?" Ruhi came on the line.

By now both sides were on speaker, all four talking at once. They made plans. Ruhi promised to be by Taara's side just as Dimple would have been, for as long as she needed her.

The next call was not as simple. Omar tried to avoid it, but Taara insisted.

"They deserve to know. Ammi will be happy."

"I know. But Abbu will be home now." Omar was careful to call Ammi at specific times of the day when Abbu was sure to be out. Even though calls were infrequent, they meant a lot to Omar. He had learned of Zahira's engagement, then of the grand wedding in Pakistan. The brother of the bride was not invited and Omar had, however, managed to contact his sister on her wedding day. They had shed joyful tears together. Omar wanted to be sure that his sister was not forced into anything and that she was happy with the *rishta* match. Zahira had sounded happy. She had met her fiancé a few times and had fallen in love. She was also happy to be out of California. Her husband had a business in Karachi. Her only concern was for their mother who would become lonely. Omar made his calls to Ammi more frequently after Zahira's wedding until the calls became a weekly ritual.

He dialed the familiar number and waited.

"Yes," a loud voice answered.

Omar hesitated.

"Who is it?" Haider Khan growled.

"A... a... abbu?"

Omar heard a slight hesitation and intake of breath.

"Omar beta?" Haider finally managed.

"Ji. Salaam Abbu. How are you?"

"Just as you had left us, son."

"Abbu, I have some news." Omar wavered, "Is Ammi there?"

"She's praying. What do you have to say?"

"I... I... You... are going to be *Dada*. Taara and I are having a baby."

Omar could hear the chair creaking on the other end. His father was moving, walking, breathing heavily.

"I don't recognize your marriage." Haider Khan started in an icy cool voice rising to a growl, "I have no son." He slammed the phone down.

The cordless in Omar's hand started to shake. He stared at the phone as if it was going to bite him. His body sat frozen, unable to move, and he felt his ears grow warm. He let Taara take the phone and put her arms around him while he sat rigid staring into nothingness. She embraced him, planted a soft kiss on his forehead and continued to hold him.

CHAPTER 32

1951

Dehra Dun embraced Janki with a kiss of its mountainous air and a refreshing shower of new beginnings. She welcomed the romance and took delight in the feeling of coming home, to a place not unlike another home, another valley of a similar mountain range.

As their taxi wheeled down the winding roads, she reflected on how simple it was to cross the borders, first from Afghanistan into Pakistan and then into India. With each crossing her papers said she was in a different country, but the air she breathed or the warmth she soaked from the clear sky remained same. Even the trees stood just as sturdy and tall in each land offering shade and a home for the birds that knew nothing of boundaries. She saw the same crooked-tooth laughter of little grannies sitting under the shade of the trees weaving tales to the wide-eyed children surrounding them. The rugged peaks looming over rivers that shimmered and snaked through the valleys could belong to any place Janki had called home. After a refreshing rain shower, the wet *mitti* mud emanated a unique fragrance that could only come from the limitless earth. Borders for these countries were non-existent in her mind as she observed the faces and realized she could be related to any one of them.

Peering over the open window of the taxi, she looked down to the ravine below, the curving road, the shrubs and trees, not unlike those in Quetta or Kandhar. Even the jagged edges of the cliffs looked familiar in this new land. She had journeyed long and now, descending the Doon valley with her husband and children, she was finally coming to set up her *dehra*, to settle and put down roots.

The ride in a taxi down through the twists and turns created much excitement among the children, especially when they spotted monkeys squatting on roadside. At the children's pestering, Ram Lal asked the taxi driver to slow down while they threw some leftover bread and bananas out of the window. The car picked up speed as it descended into the valley, and the cool breeze ruffled hair and drooped eyelids. Janki felt herself dozing off, with the sleeping toddler cuddled in her arms.

The persistent honks, sweat rolling down her brow and the crying baby in her arms woke Janki with a start. She looked around and thought they had stopped, but just then the taxi jerked forward and stopped again. In the midst of trying to comfort baby Rajendra, Janki spotted bicyclists, *tonga* horse-drawn carriages, rickshaws and some cars.

Ram Lal had a friend from Quetta who had settled in Dehra Dun soon after the Partition. The Khatri family stayed the first few weeks in the cozy home of this friend, until Ram Lal found a comfortable house in the newly constructed colony of Khurbarra Mohalla. A house with four large rooms, a sizeable courtyard and terrace, attached private bathroom with running water and a separate kitchen - Janki was unsure if so much space was necessary, but went along with Ram Lal's decision.

The first night in her new home, Janki looked up toward Mount Mussourie from her terrace and saw those living in the mountains light their lanterns, which appeared like the dance of fireflies. Several months later, when the icy winds pierced through their skins, Janki snuggled in her *pashmina* while the children bundled in layers of clothing, and climbed up to the terrace to watch nature's spectacular performance. Squeals of delight escaped their shivering lips as they admired the snowflakes pirouette down to the mountain tops as if moving to the cadence of a sonata.

Most winter evenings the family burrowed under the covers after dinner with a coal fire burning in the *angithi* portable stove next to the bed. Janki related tales from the Hindu mythology or stories she crafted to help the cold, dark evenings pass quickly. Before long the bougainvillea in their tiny garden began to sprout lively green leaves, and delicate little buds, until one cheery morning the family woke to find an eruption of purple bursting in their garden.

As the children bustled with excitement, running in and out of neighborhood homes, gearing up to wrap up school activities before the imminent arrival of summer vacation, Ram Lal wandered from one room to another without direction. His mind traveled to the days in Quetta and Kandhar where friends dropped in at odd hours seeking advice. He recalled his fleet of employees who relied on his leadership or when his children looked up to him for guidance and direction. Crossing the threshold from his bedroom to the courtyard to the main door, he continued to walk out of the *mohalla* neighborhood and when he finally lifted his head, he found himself walking through a lush orchard of lychees.

As the weather became lively, Ram Lal began disappearing for hours. Some days he found himself in open wet Basmati fields, other days in a lychee or a mango grove. Maneuvering through the labyrinth of pathways or trackless trails, he ended up miles from home never remembering which route he took. Engulfed in the serenity of these groves, Ram Lal walked endlessly spotting the bright green parrots picking at unripe mangoes or listening to the *koel* koo ooing from the thick branches. Occasionally a loud sound of a man would reverberate, and the birds would instantly flutter their wings in frenzy.

Ram Lal's thoughts always traveled to the days of his past and the land of his ancestors. Nothing in Dehra Dun held him – his friends, his business, his children, and even Janki had moved on, leaving him behind, alone. Only his dead *puttar* son kept him company. Ram Lal found his body moving forward with his family but his spirit refused to take another step, choosing to hold hands with the shadow of his dead son.

On one such walk on a particularly hot afternoon, his feet suddenly became tired, and he stopped under a lychee tree to rest under its shade. The trunk supported his head and back while his eyes disappeared behind the dark curtain of his eyelids. Through the curtain he saw a silhouette, of a young man standing in front him. The man then began to climb up the tree looming high that began to take the shape of rustic mountains. He stared down at Ram Lal through blood shot eyes, his moustache streaked pomegranate red. Ram Lal extended his arm out beckoning. But just before skin touched skin, strong fingers grasped weary ones, the orchard shuddered with flapping and chirping. The man dissolved in the branches high up over the tree, fading away with the light behind the setting sun. Ram Lal's voice rumbled among the trees, bouncing off its trunks, as he howled for his son, Rajendra. His cry roused him and he woke to hear rustle under the pile of dried, fallen leaves. He stood up with a start, avoiding the slithering creature. His legs rushed him home as his heart raced with the excitement of his new resolve. He barged in to find his wife sitting at the corner of their bed.

"Pack your bags," he demanded.

Janki looked up, the crochet needle falling to her lap, mid-stitch. Ram Lal rummaged about in the room, his eyes shifting, widening, and searching. He opened the door to a cupboard, shut it and walked out to another room. He returned with a tattered suitcase in hand, looked at Janki and exclaimed, "Why are you still sitting there?" he rattled on as he sorted through his clothes, "come, we'll go back...."

She observed his disheveled hair and dirty clothes, noticing the mud and dead leaves he had dragged in.

"... We'll go to an *Ashram*..." he carried on as he moved around franticly, oblivious to his scruffy state.

Her head dropped and she gave it a little shake before speaking, "you must be becoming senile, Ji."

He stopped his packing, and for the first time since he'd entered the room, looked at her. With sweat running down the side of his head and his breath uneven, he said, "it's you who has gone crazy, happy playing house with all the little ones."

She looked at him and smirked, "this is not a game but real life. It might do you good to live it."

Ram Lal continued to pack.

Janki stood up, the half-crocheted baby's booty plummeting to the floor as she approached him and put a hand on his shoulder. He pushed her hand away and roared, "you have forsaken the land of our ancestors." He pointed his accusatory finger and snapped. "Even forgotten our son, Rajinder."

Janki stood motionless as tears threatened from the corners of her eyes. Holding the footboard of their bed, she steadied herself. Seconds ticked away on the wall clock while Ram Lal stood facing her, his eyes bulging as if ready to pop out of their sockets. She straightened her trunk planting both her feet firmly on the ground, raised her arms up spread out as if they branched out of her body, and placed her splayed hands on his shoulders. With a deep inhale she looked straight into his eyes and said, "I weep too, but... all of our children are our responsibility."

Ram Lal stood still and glared at her dogged stare. He then took a step back, picked up his suitcase, but just before he could reach the threshold, she grabbed his arm.

"You need to know one more thing," she said as he stood with his back turned to her. "I am with child," she informed in a soft voice.

His shoulders fell back as he sucked in air, then he gently removed her hand from his arm and walked out of the room, the house, her life. She stood on the threshold watching her husband leave, one hand resting on her stomach, the other reaching out as if to stop him.

Before even one tear could escape, before she could realize that her heart weighed as much as the gold they had brought from the land of their ancestors, before her quivering lips called after him by the name she was never to call him, she was called. She was called by her children who ran in from their play or studies or tasks of the day. Duty called and she had to get to the business of feeding them for the day and for the days to come.

Days crawled by layering one after the other. Virendra graduated from *Gurukul*, the Hindu school and she asked Mahendra to return with him and finish his two years in Dehra Dun. The children did not ask of their father and Janki did not offer any details. Instead, she noticed that each child stopped asking her for spending money. She discovered that Narendra had secured an office job with the government while Virendra delved into various businesses, like selling fruits at carnivals, starting a paper route, and even establishing a tea stall. Mahendra worked with his brother after school and the older girls tutored children. Janki watched how her family came together especially when the newest member arrived, a round faced, full-headed girl she simply called Baby. Even though this was the first child of hers to be born in independent India, she sadly recognized that this would be her last.

Janki's main concern was the depleting reserve, but hoped that with discipline, she could make it last. The gold had to get her through not only the basic needs, or the education of each child, but also for dowries and weddings of her daughters.

One morning, while the children were out and Baby sound asleep, Janki sat on the floor in her room by their large metal trunk; its lid wide open, its padlock on the floor, and its contents scattered and exposed. A golden beam streamed in from the door and shone over them. Sweaters and shawls were haphazardly shoved to one corner, piled next to silk sarees that peeked out their purples and pinks from a disturbed muslin wrap. Janki's hands rummaged through the layers searching each corner, in case they had fallen out. She looked in the box in her hand, an intricate piece covered with soft velvet in rich burgundy and lined with a wide gold border. Shiny threads unraveling from the edges showed its wear as she looked at the tiny mirror inside the lid, "they're all gone. We've used them all up," she murmured to her reflection.

"What are gone?" Virendra stood tall at the entrance, his body obstructing the bright sun intruding into the room.

She looked up toward the voice and promptly shut the box, wiped her round cheeks, and shook her head. Watching the silhouette blocking the sun, Ram Lal's image appeared in front of her and she burst into tears. At first, they were angry, flowing like the downpour in a rainstorm. Her eyes were as white as lightning throwing bolts from trunk to box to the silhouette. She clenched the empty box and hurled it in the trunk with a loud clang.

A light touch on her shoulder centered her, but as she looked up at her son leaning over her, a fresh deluge started and she heaved uncontrollably.

"*Maati*," Virendra sat down and wrapped his arms around her in a tight grasp. He ran his fingers over her salty cheeks and repeated, "*Maati*."

"I have nothing left to give," she lamented as her body sagged in his arms, "I'm tired."

He cradled her slumped body and rocked as if consoling a child.

"How can I find good families for Bibo and Shaku?" she repeated, "I have nothing left."

"We'll take care of it," he said.

"But..." She freed from his grasp and looked at him through bleary eyes, "we have used up all the coins," she said.

He looked at her quizzically.

"Gone, used up." She offered, "we bought this house, lived on them for years and now... there's just the jewelry."

Virendra repeated, "we'll take care of everything."

"Promise me you won't tell the others," she pleaded, "I don't want them to worry."

He stood up, pulling his mother up with him and said, "first you promise me that you will not worry."

"How can I not, when I can't even feed my children?" she lamented.

Virendra squeezed her hand and stroked her head as if to a child.

She stole back her hands, wiped her tears and bent down into the trunk. From a box similar to the empty one but larger, she removed a thick gold bangle. Handing it out to her son she said, "pawn this for me."

He ran his finger over its delicate carving, feeling the pure softness of the glittering metal as he took it in his hand. He looked up at her and tilted his head sideways.

"My mother gave this to me when Rajinder was born." She sniffled, "she was so happy..." Janki turned away facing the trunk and said, "what does is matter now? They are both gone."

The baby stirred on the bed. Sound of her sucking her two tiny fingers became louder in the quiet room.

"Someday we can buy this back," Janki murmured, then suddenly turned to her son and nudged him out, "go before I change my mind."

CHAPTER 33

2001

Taara's heart-shaped bracelet glittered in the soft glow of the fire as the whistle of the far off freight train echoed in the living room. Her head rested on Omar's chest listening to his quivering heart while he stared at the phone as if it was going to jump up and bite him. His father's voice still rang in the air. Taara shifted to snuggle in the crook of his arm and began to stroke her belly in slow, circular motions watching the glittering reflection.

"I was sure he would be over it by now," Omar murmured.

"Call Ammi tomorrow and tell her." Taara patted his chest and spoke softly, "also, after talking to Ammi, we'll call up Zahira."

He sighed deeply.

She squeezed his hand again.

The two sat listening to each other's sighs and feeling the emptiness. They heard the sound of the train whistle die down as it reached its destination. Through the window Taara spotted a family of deer trekking through the snow-laden backyard. She noticed the two fawns being nudged toward the thick collection of evergreens where all four sat down on the snow covered ground and lounged.

Taara whispered, "I wonder if we'll have a boy or a girl."

Omar rested his head back on the couch, let out a deep breath and said, "I hope it's a girl."

"I'm scared Omar," she murmured.

"Me too." He turned to look at her and said, "but we'll figure this out together."

"What if she has really hard questions like, like about her grandparents, or religion, or even about family?"

He squeezed her hand and kissed her softly on her lips. Looking into her eyes he said, "you will be a fabulous mother."

Taara attempted a smile.

Omar repositioned himself on the sofa and pulled Taara up closer, "now, let's think of names."

A few thoughtful moments later, Omar's hand danced in the air as if directing an orchestra. He hummed, "Chhumm Chhumm Chhumm... I always liked the melodious sound of the anklets, little girls running around in their bright-colored *sharara* skirts and chiming bells around their ankles."

"You mean the *pajebs*. I liked wearing them too." Taara sat up.

"Yes, but not the Urdu but the Hindi word, *payal* is what I was thinking," Omar said, "I like that name for our little girl."

"Payal." Taara pondered, "like a calm and soothing melody. I like that."

As warmth from the fireplace cast a soft glow on the reclining couple, they drifted into their own dreams. She heard chimes of anklet bells, saw little girls and fawns and shadows of her parents in the background.

Omar saw the pretty face of a little girl in her pink *sharara* skirt and shimmering anklets. He saw her run toward an older couple, her anklets jingling, her melodious voice calling out to them, "Dada, Dadi." They ignored her and kept walking away. The little girl continued to cry out raising her tiny hands to reach out.

The sound of ringing sliced through the living room interrupting their slumber. Omar jerked with a start almost knocking his wife off the sofa. Taara held on to his arm and avoided a fall as she rubbed her eyes and tried to orient herself. The moon was high in the sky casting a silvery glow from the skylight above.

Omar fumbled for the cordless and just as he found it, it had stopped ringing. Swearing under his breath, Omar helped Taara up and the two made their way to the bedroom. After some time with tossing and turning and hearing his wife's steady breathing, Omar decided to give up on sleeping. He reached for the phone to see who had called. In the den he dialed his voicemail, the recorded voice echoed in his ear.

"*Lala,* its Zira. I... I... I guess I'll call you back."

Click.

Omar gaped at the phone. He looked at his watch, doing some mental math. *Must be late morning in Karachi.* He dialed his sister's number and after several rings, a droning voice answered. Omar all but barked into the phone, "Is Zira there?"

"Who?"

"Zira...I mean Zahira."

"Zahira *bibi* is out. Who are you?"

"Her brother from Umrica. Tell her I called."

Omar sat on the edge of the easy chair running his fingers through his thick hair. He stood up and paced around the small room, cracking his knuckles.

"What's wrong Omar?" he hadn't noticed Taara standing by the door.

"I don't know. It's Zira."

"What do you mean?"

He handed her the cordless, "listen to the message."

Clicking the off button, phone still in hand, Taara sat on the chair by the door, "what does it mean?"

"I called her back but some servant woman answered. Zira was not there."

Taara punched some keys on the phone and then looked up, "her home number does not show in the caller ID. She must be calling from a public phone."

"There was something in that voice I did not like," Omar said, "I hope she's okay."

Taara walked over to her husband, "I'm sure it's nothing. You know how connections are on public phones. She's probably having trouble getting through."

Omar nodded, "I suppose."

"Now come back to bed and get some sleep."

Omar dragged himself and followed his wife.

Taara opened her eyes to the sun's rays warming her face but turned to find Omar's side of the bed cold and empty. After a bout of morning sickness, she went to find him. He was sitting in the easy chair in his den, his head dropped to one side, eyes closed. She walked over and gently touched his arm. He shifted then cuddled into his slumber, and she let him rest there, while she had her tea. Reaching for the phone, she dialed the number in Karachi. As the sound waves and electrical signals traveled their distance bringing lyrical ringing tones to her ears, Taara pictured her sister-in-law, in her *salwar kameez* and scarf around her neck under her long, dark hair. Recalling the wedding photographs Zahira had sent them, Taara remembered her looking beautiful, yet timid.

From their conversations over the years, Taara had enjoyed listening to her sweet, lyrical voice that never forgot the ever-respectful '*ji*' at the end of every sentence. Taara thought her sister-in-law was always afraid - of saying the wrong thing, of offending anyone, of acting against etiquette. She was never relaxed. Taara wondered what Zahira was really like, on the inside, if able to chip away at the shield of reserve and fear.

After several rings Zahira answered, but before Taara could ask her about her cryptic phone call, Omar walked in. He grabbed the cordless and bellowed into the mouthpiece in a hoarse voice, demanding an explanation for frightening him in such a way. Accepting that all was well and her call from the *STD* was impromptu, and her shaky voice in the message just the crackle in the line, his voice gradually returned to normal. Zahira spoke cheerfully, shrieked with delight on the news of soon to-be an aunt and promised to call often.

Some commotion in the background interrupted their conversation and Zahira rang off to help break an argument between her mother-in-law and the servant woman.

Omar stood motionless, with the phone in hand hanging down with his arm on his sides. He proceeded to sit, but changed his mind midway and stood facing the window. Taara interrupted his confusion and proclaimed, "see, everything's okay. You get worked up for nothing."

Omar shook his head, still unsure.

"Now let it go and stop being such a worry-monger," Taara said.

He looked at his wife's cheerful face and smiled. Nodding, he planted a kiss on her forehead and grabbed a cup for his espresso.

As Taara's waistline disappeared, Omar's workload gained momentum. There were nights he spent at the office, buried in a case while Taara waited in hope, finally nodding off on the couch cuddled next to Oscar. Outside, the air grew crisper shaming the trees into a dazzling flush. The vibrant and the shriveled leaves danced their way down from the branches to the sidewalks, twirled by the icy breeze and lay down for their burial under the impending snow. Taara waddled to the Lamaze classes every week, completing the full course *sans* partner. She fretted over Omar's health and began to feel anxiety for the baby's condition. On dreary, damp days she wrapped herself in her *pashmina,* disappearing into its familiar aromas and sat by the window in her basement with a mug of decaffeinated coffee and her mother's journal. She reflected over her great-grandmother's life and realized that throughout her life, Janki was never alone. She was always surrounded by people, especially children. Taara stared outside watching the rain on the leaves as they relished in the showering kisses of the water from the sky. She absently stroked Oscar's resting head on her lap and wished she could be showered with as many kisses as the desolate leaves.

Some days when the sun shone brightly through her window, she bundled her large frame, leashed Oscar and headed for her favorite trail. The sound of the honks directed her gaze upward to the blue sky to admire the beautiful formations of the geese as the flock started its journey south. After such walks a sudden rush of inspiration lured her toward her canvas to dab several shades of blue and gray to create a large scape.

On the days she received a letter from a relative, her attitude toward everything changed. Taara had written to several of her family members asking simple questions about their memories, anecdotes or insights they had into Janki's life. When these letters arrived, they helped her move forward with her mother's journal and served as reminders that she was not an only branch but one of several branches of the same tree. This tree, she began to realize, had roots reaching deep into fertile soil. Pouring her thoughts into the journal she became lost in its magnetic pull and as she delved deeper into her own feelings, she became surprised when an actual anecdote about Janki would make its way toward her.

One afternoon she sat down with her mug of aromatic herb tea by the window and sifted through the day's mail. With her bulk she had taken to sitting on the armchair while Oscar found a spot by her feet. She positioned herself to have an uninterrupted view of the backyard with its tall trees, constant activity of squirrels, birds, rabbits, and sometimes even families of deer or turkeys. The late sun glowed in on her as she focused on opening the envelope that bore a stamp of the Ashok Chakra in the corner. One of the granduncles from India had responded to her questions and by the thickness of the envelope, she could tell that it carried a story.

She read through it quickly, took several sips of her tea and went back to read it again more slowly. From the letter she learned of the time when the only son living in Dehra Dun and was taking care of Janki, was transferred to a different city, Janki wanted to stay back. Her other sons were dispersed on their respective assignments across the country. She was in her early 70s, in good health and tried to convince her children she could stay on her own. Her daughters were all married, some living in the same city. Duty and concern for their mother foremost in their minds, her children refused to leave her alone. Now what happened after that Taara found intriguing. The uncle wrote in his account:

As you may know Taara dear in India when a girl is married off, she goes to live with her husband and his family. The girl's parents may visit their daughter but will not partake in any meal or refreshments not even touching water to drink in her home. Going with this premise, when one of Ammaji's daughters, Laaji volunteered to take care of her while the sons were posted elsewhere, our mother refused to move to her daughter's house. In this event, the daughter with her husband and children, moved into her mother's house. However, the daughter's husband was a man of immense pride. To reach a compromise he offered to pay rent while he and his family stayed at the house. That created another dilemma. Anything that was cooked would be in the daughter's kitchen and how could a mother eat her meals coming from her daughter's kitchen? Another compromise was devised. Ammaji set up her own little kitchen by the dining room with her own stove, supplies and a pantry. She cooked her own meals and had her own maid to wash the dishes and run her errands. This setup went on for years until one of the sons returned and relieved the sister and her family from mother duty.

That night Taara lay awake in her bed watching her mountain of a belly rise and fall with each breath. A lovely sensation flowed through her body as she felt a kick. Her hand automatically reached out to Omar's side. As usual, she found it empty, but she knew his sleeping form would occupy it before daybreak. Taara took comfort in this, except during those occasional bouts of uneasiness when her hormones waged war in her growing body. Even Oscar would jump off to his own bed, abandoning Taara's fidgety form. The crescent moon outside climbed higher as Taara lay alone on her side, staring at the white ceiling.

Somewhere before sleep completely engulfed her, Taara saw herself in flight cruising over vast mountainous landscape. She glided high above, spreading her wings over the span. She saw

Janki with her brood in the valley below. She saw Omar with his grandmother in the same valley. Realizing, she was not alone, she turned to see Omar by her side, high in the sky. Soon more faces appeared with bird-bodies – Ruhi and Raj, Omar's parents and sister, her own parents and many other faces she recognized. They glided happily in their flock in a V formation, until the faces started to change. They were unfamiliar and kept increasing in number. The formation broke. Taara felt trapped in the strange crowd. She flapped hard to get away, to be free and be with her own. Her wings gave way and she felt the pull of gravity. Screaming she tumbled down into the valley, the crowd closing in on her. Just before reaching land, a large wing reached out to cushion her. She lost sight of the crowd and looked into warm eyes and a round face with prominent cheeks. Janki was so beautiful without all her wrinkles. Her idyllic smile drew Taara in. Her words were few but enigmatic. Even though Taara did not understand, she found them soothing. Close to the ground Janki drifted away and blended into the background and her image became blurred. Taara called out as she stood suspended.

"Don't leave me," her hand reached out grabbing fistfuls of air. "Come back," she continued to shout, feeling drenched, as if she had been standing in rain for hours.

Her eyes opened to stare back at the white ceiling. She felt wet between her legs and the sheets below her were soaked. Her arm reached out to the snoring body on her side.

"What...?" Omar woke up with a start having just dozed off.

"My water... it broke," Taara managed.

CHAPTER 34

1955

Dark clouds covered mount Mussourie and steadily made their way to the Doon valley. Before the morning was over, heavy showers pelting marble sized hail, teemed to the ground. Virendra darted from one end of his tea stall to another with pans in hand, as he placed them at various stations to collect the water seeping in from the roof. Several people ran into the stall to take cover and enjoy a warm cup of sweet, creamy tea.

    Virendra noticed from among the swarm a young man he knew from Gurukul. As clouds dissipated and the crowd moved on, the two friends caught up on lost years. His friend, from a well-respected and wealthy family mourned the sudden loss of his father from a heart attack, and lamented having to shoulder the responsibility for his 25-year old unwed sister. Virendra listened as he looked out of his little tea stall and spotting a beautiful rainbow, he smiled contentedly and invited his friend home to meet his mother and older brother.

With the agreement of the friend's sister and Narendra and the blessings of the two mothers, Khatri family soon welcomed a beautiful, heavy-set bride into their home, along with the equally heavy-set trunk-load of her trousseau. Within a few months of the wedding, arrangements were made for Bibo's sendoff. Virendra and Narendra suggested that Janki approach the family of a young man who worked in Narendra's office and who they presumed to be a good match for their headstrong sister. The wedding was simple, but with help from the dowry of Narendra's bride and some of Janki's jewelry, the groom's family had no cause for complaint.

The household shape kept changing with the weddings and Mahendra's now-lucrative engineering job in a different city. Virendra's business endeavors went through peaks and valleys and he struggled to see what lay ahead for him. Janki's repeated efforts on stressing education gnawed at him until one day he gave in and decided to enroll into a college.

Soon after his studies started, Janki excitedly approached him with a letter in hand. The white papers with a tiny neat handwriting in black ink contained an invitation, she related - to visit Ram Lal's friend Nandu and his mother Dadanji. Janki reminded him of this family in Chaman where Ram Lal had made frequent stops during border crossings. Dadanji with her family had settled in Amritsar in Independent India after the partition and was now proposing a match for one of her granddaughters with one of Janki's sons.

Virendra looked at her quizzically until it dawned on him that he was the son Janki was proposing for the match. His head began to shake with multitudes of excuses spewing from his mouth - his studies, not the right time, she was too young at 16... but Janki heard nothing. She told him that arrangements were already made, he was taking the train to Amritsar the following week and she will follow him a few days later and with that she walked away.

Virendra stood motionless in the middle of the room he

shared with Mahendra. A desk lamp shed light on his text books as the leaves of the pages flew from the gusts of the ceiling fan. He placed a paperweight on the right page and tried to think of the family he will be visiting, recalling the family's never-ending line of girls so close in age. He thought of the place they had resettled in and when he realized that Amritsar bordered Pakistan, a smile appeared on his face.

Later the same week, Virendra was on a train to Karachi planning to catch the Quetta express from there. He cited a business opportunity and told Janki he had to leave early and take a detour, leaving out further details.

Quetta, scenic and rugged, cold in its temperament but warm in its hospitality, sheltered and accommodated Ram Lal. He sat in the *angan* courtyard of his house sipping black, sugarless tea with only the shadow of his dead son for company. He carefully blew on the hot liquid and envisioned the faces of his family in its reflection. Seeing Janki's severe face he thought, sweet and innocent no more, and bowed to her in admiration of her strength. Countless times he had contemplated returning but fears always kept him away. Will the shadow of his dead son accompany him beyond the boundaries of this home? Ram Lal feared leaving him behind, alone and helpless. He feared forgetting him like Janki and the rest of the family had done. Most of all, he feared himself. He couldn't just return with his head hung low when not one of his children even bothered to get him to return.

The first few weeks of his return to Quetta had been hard but soon he fell into a routine, losing himself into prayers and the service of God. Occasionally, he had visitors, friends new and of the past. Halif stopped by everyday with one pretext or another, but Ram Lal knew his friend was just checking up on him, to see if this lone soul was living or dead. After all, Ram Lal was living in the same infamous house that was the cause of his beloved Rajendra's demise. There were too many demons in the house and Ram Lal faced each and every one of them. He confined himself within its sanctity as it evolved more and more into a *mandir* temple. He became a prisoner in his own home, nestled in his devotion and its rituals. Where the two years faded to Ram Lal had no idea.

One frigid morning, as the sun squinted through the mountains, Ram Lal answered a hesitant knock on the wooden door. A young man mirroring his own image stood before him with a toothbrush moustache and long side burns contouring his longish face. Virendra smiled and greeted the father who had abandoned this son more than once.

The two Khatri men walked to the kitchen and Ram Lal set about making tea. Their awkward exchanges were interrupted only by long silences. Virendra looked around the warm, tiny room before settling his gaze on the older man. Additional folds of skin drooped over his eyes dimming the vibrant alertness they once possessed. His hair and his signature, majestic moustache sat limply, now completely frosted white. An intricate pattern of protruding veins branched out from his wrists to his knuckles, while his hands shook as he poured hot water into the kettle.

Isn't anyone here to help you with that?" Virendra asked.

"Yes, yes, this girl gets in later to clean and cook and things," Ram Lal looked away.

Virendra planted both his feet firmly on the ground, turned his gaze at his fidgeting fingers and said what he had come to say, "*Bauji*, I've come to take you back."

Ram Lal handed his son the teacup, filled to the brim. Its aromatic steam dissipated into the air, while a few spoonful of the milky liquid spilled onto the saucer.

Virendra took the cup and settled down on the floor leaning against a wall. He held the cup in one hand and proceeded to slurp the spill from the saucer. Glancing up with one eye, he noticed his father doing the same and at this realization, for the first time both looked at each other directly. Then a shadow passed over Ram Lal's face and he began to shake his head.

Before he could say anything, Virendra insisted, "we need you." He leaned forward and said, "*Maati* needs you."

"She can manage," Ram Lal looked into his tea. A leaf had escaped the strainer and ended up in his cup and now he hoped it would show him the way.

"Managing and living are two different things," his son said.

The lone leaf swam in its warm pool drifting from one rim to another. From the corner of his eyes he noticed the restless taps his son made with his toes. He felt Virendra's eyes on him, waiting, anticipating, scowling. Both sat in silence, neither wanting to slice through the tension that hung thickly in the air. Birds chirped in the trees outside creating a racket as if at a wedding. A dog barked out in the alley and voices of early risers traveled over the boundary wall and into the kitchen. The world around them was waking up to start a new day.

Ram Lal set his empty cup down and asked his son to follow him. The two men stepped into an almost bare room that contained a naked mattress in one corner, while all the popular Hindu Gods inhabited another corner, within a picture frame or as miniature effigies. The older man covered the mattress with a white sheet he pulled out from under it as he said, "get some rest, we'll talk later."

Leaving his son, Ram Lal walked out to the *angan* courtyard and parked his breathless body into a rattan chair. He looked up at the overhanging branches of the large juniper, where the birds seemed to be busy telling their tales and chattering with purpose. He watched a sparrow break from the flock and fly above the tree just before his eyes closed. Through closed eyelids he saw the image of the bird transform to that of his dead son, flying toward him. The two conversed without words or voice until his eyes released tears down his sagging cheeks. The sun reached higher in the sky, shining on his slumped form. He opened his eyes and stared into brightness.

Two days later, the two Khatri men began their return to India. At the station in Karachi as they waited for the train that would take them across the border, Virendra informed his father of the short detour he planned into Amritsar. Without any details, he updated him on his friend Nandu's family and his formidable mother, Dadanji. Later, in the train, as Ram Lal stared absently at the carpet of golden wheat swaying in the open fields whizzing past them, Virendra informed him of his impending engagement to one of Dadanji's several granddaughters.

Ram Lal looked at his son proudly and smiled, "I have a lot of respect for Dadanji and I'm glad of the match."

"What is she like?" his son asked.

Ram Lal met Virendra's curious eyes and, momentarily animated, he said, "she is one tough lady, raising six children on her own." He shifted in his seat as he shared stories of his visits with the family his son will soon be part of. Lowering his voice conspiratorially he said, "you see, her husband disappeared when their youngest was a few weeks old."

"How sad," Virendra said simply.

"Amazing how she managed on her own when her husband abandoned her," Ram Lal said.

Virendra did not even blink as he responded, "just like Maati."

Ram Lal stared at his son and then looked away, back to the open fields. The sound of the rickety tracks under their carriage and an occasional sharp whistle interrupted their silence, while a thick blob of black smoke spewing from the steam engine left its mark of charcoal dust on their faces.

At Amritsar station Virendra guided his father through crowds of people while the older man struggled to keep pace with the son's long strides and the labyrinth of bridges, stairs, platforms, doors and people. Mothers rushed their children dragging them as they cried, while families tried to keep up with their red-shirted coolies who speed walked while balancing stacks of trunks on their turbaned heads. Platform number 18 was a long walk from the exit of the station. Father and son lugged their bags and bed bundle across several bridges over the railway tracks. In the middle of one of the bridges Ram Lal stood still and looked out to the horizon noticing how the tracks beneath him held the link between two divided countries.

Catching up with his son, Ram Lal reached the front of the station where a mad rush of drivers of *tonga* horse-drawn carriages, rickshaws, and taxis greeted them, each trying to outdo the others with their volume and low price. Virendra and Ram Lal chose one *tongawalla* at random, and haggled over the price for the trip to *Badda Darwaza* before mounting the back of the carriage. The horse pulled their load with a snort and a neigh as the driver whipped and cried for the beast to move faster.

CHAPTER 35

2001-2006

Payal greeted the world with her shattering cries, a full head of dark hair and an unmistakable set of dimples on her cheeks. Taara smiled at the sweet little dents, just like her mother's. Omar ceremoniously participated in cutting the cord while Taara, amidst joyful tears, observed the two people in her life she loved the most. The sun had reached its height when Taara and Omar held their daughter for the first time. Somebody took a picture, which would adorn Taara's bedside table.

Aunty Ruhi and uncle Raj arrived in time to greet Payal into her new home. All four, equally clueless about baby care ran in all directions at the sound of a whimper. Directions, support, and advice poured in from family members from across the world. Raj's mother explained to Ruhi the importance of baby massage before each bath and walked her through the process on the phone. Others suggested the significance of tightly swaddling the baby in a muslin sheet before putting her down. Some even suggested tying the swaddled baby with a string, one suggestion Taara disregarded. While Omar took over bath duties, Raj tried to be helpful in the kitchen or running errands. Soon three generations of mother and daughter began to establish a routine while the men returned to work. Ruhi *masi* delayed her return until Payal turned two months old, just as Dimple would have for Taara. Oscar, the most confused of the lot ran around sniffing everything from the baby oil to the diaper Geni. He was by the baby's side at every cry and next to Taara at feedings. He even accompanied Taara as she paced or rocked while the rest of the house slept and took to sleeping under the crib whenever Payal was in it. Eventually he became used to the new addition to his family and designated himself the official protector of the baby.

While Omar's new cases took over his life once again, Payal took over Taara's. Revolving around her napping and feeding schedule, Taara stole moments to make her journal entries. From a cousin in India she had received an extravagant journal-style baby book. The cover with its pistachio green print of a mother and a baby elephant felt soft to the touch. The two elephants, dressed in royal garb of purple silk with silvery sequence stood huddled together. Jewels sparkled on their forehead while a backdrop of two intricately carved, palatial pillars stood sturdily, as if watching over them. Taara filled this beautiful book's pages with everything Payal.

She started with the facts and statistics, adding summaries of new feats as they happened. These entries gave voice to her hopes and fears, and to wonder about how such a little person had the ability to change so much. She recalled Janki's loss of two of her children and as she shuddered at the thought she watched the peaceful, sleeping face of Payal. The tiny mouth was making sucking motions even as the pacifier lay abandoned beside her on the sheet. Taara smiled at the realization that another branch was added to the tree, and she hoped to keep it sturdy and connected to its roots. Reflecting on this she recognized that Payal's roots included Omar's tree and that connection was just as important for their daughter. But sadly, there was nothing she could do about that.

By the time the mounds of snow outside dissipated, Payal was cooing with the chirping birds. Taara welcomed her favorite season with open arms, lugging her mildly bundled daughter to mommy-and-me classes, baby socializing groups, and to thawed-out parks. She introduced to her baby the vast world, as new blooms and animals emerged before Payal's curious gaze. Taara made new friends with other mothers of babies. She found completion in motherhood, immersing herself entirely in it, and forgiving Omar's frequent absences.

Payal progressed in her determination to capture the world, first by her babbling sounds, then by her crawling fingers, finally by her toddle walks. Parroting Taara and Omar's words, she added to her glossary in dual languages, rapidly working on complete sentences. Soon the proud parents were searching for preschools to start her on her path to a strong education.

"Should we go with Montessori or try the church programs?" Taara brought up one evening looking up from her art magazine as she sat by the window on the den couch, while Omar sat at his desk. Payal had finally succumbed to her tired body and was sleeping soundly in her bed enjoying her thumb, bundled in her mother's special *pashmina*.

"Let's go check some out," Omar responded.

"When Omar?"

"I know, I know. Guilty as charged." He looked up from over piles of files stacked on his desk, "things should slow down after next month as the New Year kicks in."

"About the pre-school…" Taara stopped mid-sentence. Omar had returned to his computer screen. She stood up and went to stand by the door facing him but he didn't notice. She took a deep breath to suck in the anger that was beginning to rise. Calmly, she walked up to him and put a hand on his shoulder. He turned his head for a quick glance and went back to the computer. She squeezed his shoulder and said, "you know, lately I've been having this problem."

"Uh? What is it?" Omar said, his eyes squinting at the screen in front of him.

"Come to think of it, this problem started about three or maybe four years ago."

"What is it?" he continued to hammer away on his keyboard.

"It's just that… I've been talking to myself a lot."

"How come?" he asked, without looking at her.

She swiveled his chair to make him look at her. "Well, there are times when I'm saying something to you and I turn around and see you walking away as if you never heard a word I said to begin with. Or, when we're having a discussion, like today, your eyes are glued to the screen, concentrating on whatever's on it," she accused.

Omar put his arms around her waist and pulled her to him, "I'm sorry but there's so much to do and so little time."

"There's also very little time before Payal will be all grown up," Taara responded. "You'll miss out on her childhood."

"You think I don't feel that?" he defended.

She sat on his lap and circled her arms around his neck.

"From what I see, you eat, sleep, and even dream your cases. I understand you have to invest in your career but…"

He pushed a strand of hair away from her face and smiled, "I agree… with everything."

"Good. So, you'll be happy to hear that I've booked us for a one-week trip to Disney World," she announced.

"All of Us? When?" Omar asked.

"The three of us, second week of January."

"I'll have to check my calendar and talk to Joe at the office and…" Omar began to list his usual excuses.

"All done. Joe has approved and he's agreed to cover for you."

"But…"

"You have no excuse. We are going," Taara dismissed and

stood up.

Omar was about to list another excuse, then paused, looked at his wife and finally, raised his hands in defeat.

Mickey and Minnie Mouse greeted them with open arms. Payal ran to them and posed for the photographer. Waving to the host of this fantasyland, they made their way through the bustling street to Cindrella's castle. Payal walked in a daze, her eyes wide open, mouth shaped as the letter 'O'. She pointed out the horse carriages, the train pulling from the station, colorful candy shops, and all the children carrying oversize stuffed animals. The three darted from one character hug to the mouse ride to the kiddy coaster. Payal's tiny fingers pulled Taara's hand who in turn pulled Omar as their little girl squealed with delight. They acted goofy together putting on Mickey's hat with big round ears. They went crazy trying to outdo each other in the teacup ride and laughed until tears rolled down their cheeks.

Standing in line for 'It's a Small World,' their last ride of their last day, Payal fell asleep on Omar's shoulder. He was tired but insisted on doing the ride. Even Taara did not want the day to end. She stood close to Omar and lightly leaned her head on his free shoulder and he put his arm around her.

"Why didn't we do this sooner?" he asked.

Taara lifted her head and momentarily glared at him.

They walked in sync as the line inched forward.

"Thank you." He kissed her head, "You've been very patient with me."

Taara lifted her head.

He adjusted Payal on his shoulder and turned to Taara, "I promise from now on I will spend more time with my girls."

All through the flight back, Payal did not stop talking about all her favorite characters she met, posed with, shook hands with, or danced with in the parade. She related the fireworks display and laser shows to strangers at the airport.

Amidst excitement and fatigue, the threesome returned home late in the night only to find mountains of fresh snow in the city, an avalanche of mail in their box, and a bombardment of messages on the voicemail. Ignoring everything, they crashed into bed.

Taara woke up to a dazzling day bathed in sunshine. Fresh snow glistened outside, swaddled the branches of the pine trees, and drifted where the wind chose to carry it. Turning the heat up a notch, Taara draped her *pashmina* over her shoulders and sat with her piping hot cup of tea in the kitchen while her family slept. She spent the rest of the morning unpacking, and when Payal tumbled out of bed disoriented and searching for Oscar, Taara helped her get ready while reminding her that he was still at the doggy hotel.

At the time when neighbors were sitting down for lunch, Omar, with ruffled hair, yawns he could not suppress, and a steaming mug of coffee in hand, plopped down at the dining table to attack the pile of mail. Screening out the junk mail, he came across a letter with his name and address scrawled in the familiar handwriting of his sister. He held the unopened envelope in his hand, afraid of what he might find inside. In the age of SMS and electronic mails or instant responses with cell phones, Omar felt a foreboding in the traditional form of this message. Taara noticed the look on his face and the unopened letter in his hand.

"What's wrong?" she approached him, a bowl of oatmeal in her hand as she gestured Payal to sit at the table.

"Why would Zira write me a letter?" Omar mumbled.

"Perhaps opening it will help answer that question," Taara remarked.

"What?" He looked up at his wife and nodded, "Yes, yes of course."

He skimmed through the five sheets written in the delicate hand he knew so well. His expression changed with each page with cheeks flushing more at every turn. After scanning the entire text, he went back to the first page and reread it all. Taara kept a keen eye on Omar's agitated figure while trying to be an attentive audience to Payal's incessant chatter and detailed accounts of all her dreams.

"I knew it!" Omar hurled the letter onto the table and

marched out. Payal stopped mid-sentence. She stared at her father and started to howl. Taara was speechless. She had never seen Omar lose his temper like that. She calmed Payal down and reached over for the discarded letter. She scanned through the first part quickly with all the usual greetings and health wishes. Her eyes opened wide when she got to the gist of the message.

...about four years ago, Khaled's mother tried to get him remarried while I, his wife, remain in the household. Her reason was my barrenness. If you remember, I had left a message for you that you were upset about. I had to call from an STD. By the time we talked, Khaled and his father had resolved the matter. They had talked his Ammi out of the idea. I didn't think I needed to burden you with any of this since the issue had been sorted out. Plus, you had good news to share with me and I didn't want to sour your happiness.

However, Lala *today, four years later, Khaled's Abu is no more and I am still childless. Khaled has succumbed to his mother's nagging and has agreed to bring home another bride.*

The letter went on to describe the circumstances of Khaled's decision and how he was not being a man standing up against his mother. With the sensible father not there to reason with his mother, Khaled was taking the easy way out. Zahira lamented about her parents refusing to interfere. Once given away, she belonged to her husband's family and the parents had no power. Omar was her only hope to save her marriage and in essence, her life.

The letter shook in Taara's trembling hands.

"Why are you crying mummy?"

Taara returned to the kitchen, hastily brushing away tears, "Oh, nothing sweetheart. Are you done with your breakfast?"

"All gone." Payal spread her palms out and flashed a big smile.

"Good job. Now go play with your Legos."

Payal ran off to her room as Taara went to find Omar. He sat in his black leather office chair staring into nothingness. Taara noticed faint white streaks in his hair and the bags under his eyes. He always put a brave face for Taara but she knew that walking out on his parents ate him up inside. Zahira was the only real connection to his family and they had become close.

"Hi," Taara put a hand on his chair.

Omar didn't look up. She stood behind the chair and massaged his shoulders. He reached up to hold her hands and squeezed them.

"Why is this happening to my Zira?" he finally spoke.

Taara put her chin on this head, "she is such a sweet, delicate woman that anyone can walk all over her."

"What should I do? What *can* I do for my sister?"

"First of all, call her."

"What if they don't let her talk?"

"Let's try at least."

"I wish I could be with her," Omar let out a sigh.

"Why don't you go to her then? Maybe you can talk some sense into her husband."

"I'm not sure…" he trailed off lost in thought.

Taara grabbed his hand to pull him up, "come, let's try calling her."

After multiple tries, they were unable to get hold of Zahira. A maidservant always answered, "Zira *bibi* not here." Even her cell phone seemed to have been switched off.

Omar sat on the couch bent over, his head in his hands. Taara watched him crumble and a line from her past spiraled in her head, *"Family is foremost," Ammaji,* her great-grandmother had said to her on their last meeting.

She jumped out of her contemplation and announced, "it's time we went to see your parents."

"What?" Omar gave his wife a curious glance. He then looked out the window, shaking his head in slow motion, "why do you want to put yourself into that drama?" He looked back at her, "Abbu will just insult you and I won't stand for that."

"We must try, for Zira's sake. Besides, we'll take Payal with us. They won't throw their own grandchild out," Taara added.

"Why not? They threw out their own son."

"Don't you know that everyone loves their grandchildren more? Come on, let's try," she pleaded.

Omar got up and walked toward the window. His body bathed in sunlight as he stood there with his hands in the pockets of his sweat pants. He simply stared out at the mountains of snow piles and let Taara make the arrangements.

CHAPTER 36

2006

Leaving behind the pristine, snow-laden landscape of Minnesota, Taara left with her family for California the next day. Landing at LAX they drove straight to Calabasas. Taara thought of the gray day nine years ago on that same road, but now she looked out toward a clear blue radiant sky, filling her with hope.

They pulled into the familiar driveway with the garden on its side, which showed a few green leaves, but without the colorful blooms it sat there in a state of melancholy.

Omar started to say, "stay here…"

"No you don't, not this time," Taara interjected sternly, "we will all go, as a family."

The mahogany double doors with the dark wood trims stood regal and strong, while two large, extravagant flower pots sat empty of life in their corners. Omar rang the bell. Taara looked around and noticed an army of ants marching toward the door disappearing underneath the sill. Payal fidgeted in her spot and tried to shake off Taara's tight grasp. Omar ran his hand through his hair and seemed to be on the verge of turning around when they heard sounds of the handle from the inside. The doors seemed to be jammed, as if no one had walked through them in years. After some struggle, they finally opened. Taara stood looking at the familiar, kind face she had glimpsed on the morning after her wedding. She could not recall if the many wrinkles she saw now or the sadness that had made a home in those eyes had been there before. She noticed the white strands that escaped from her awkwardly covered head. A fearful smile inched its way on Shahnaz begum's lips as she engulfed her son in her arms.

Taara watched the reunion with quiet tears and a restrained smile. She heard a squeal and looked down to Payal, who was trying to pull her hand out of her mother's tight squeeze.

Shahnaz looked down as well.

"Ammi, meet Taara and our daughter Payal," Omar stepped aside formally to introduce his two girls.

Shahnaz gave them both a hug and showered them with kisses. She guided them in and they followed, taking care to keep their pace as slow as that of their unsteady chaperone. Passing through the foyer, the great room and a narrow corridor, they reached a small, simply furnished room. A television screen displayed the faces of two beautiful Pakistani actresses, speaking in crisp and formal Urdu. Taara recognized the famous drama serial she had once watched some episodes of with her mother years ago. Suddenly, she needed to know its name and turned toward Omar's mother who must have read her mind.

"*Dhoop Chhaon*, I must have seen it so many times but it's a good pastime. It takes my mind off things during these long days and nights."

Taara sat down uncomfortably on the edge of the *takht* and Payal jumped onto her lap, while Omar made himself comfortable on the rocking chair across the room. Taara looked around the room, observing a prayer rug with beads and the holy book neatly tucked away in a corner. The view from the large window facing east displayed peach trees and several flowering bushes begging for attention.

Taara turned to Shahnaz sitting beside her and asked, "Ammi, how are you?"

"As you see me, both my children are gone." Shahnaz waved her hand, "now this big house and the pain in my knees are my constant companions."

Taara put a hand on Shahnaz's and looked into the warm eyes, "I'm sorry."

"We had lost him long before," she responded understanding her.

Taara looked down, examining the pattern of the fabric on her seat, "I'm still sorry," she said after a while.

"Mummy, why are you saying sorry to this aunty?" Payal made her presence known.

Omar then spoke, "Payal, this is your *dadi*. She's my mummy." He turned to his mother and asked, "Where's *Abbu*?"

"He'll be back soon," Shahnaz responded.

Payal got up to admire her newfound grandmother. She touched her wrinkled face to see how it felt and showered her with questions. Shahnaz took delight in her three-year old granddaughter and patiently answered and laughed at her silliness. Taara watched them with amusement, noticing a glimmer of happiness return to Shahnaz's eyes. She turned her smiling face to observe Omar and saw his face turn suddenly white. She turned to follow his gaze and saw a large man with bulging eyes, scant white hair and a round belly standing in the doorway. Taara hastily covered her head with the scarf she had draped around her neck. She noticed his stance was slightly drooped as if ready to bow, his cheeks sagged and his eyes had sad little sacs hanging from them. He looked tired.

She slowly stood up and started to walk toward the door. She bent her scarf-covered head and raised the palm of her right hand as she greeted her father-in-law, "Assallam-o-Aliakum, *Abbu*."

He ignored her greeting and continued to observe the scene in the room. As she approached his formidable presence she looked to his feet and bent down to touch them for his blessing. She had no idea if feet touching was done in Pakistan but had observed many cousins, aunts and uncles perform this ritual with elders on her many trips to India. As her fingers touched his toes that peeked from his large leather sandals she said, "*Abbu*, please accept me as your daughter."

Haider Khan took a step back as he looked down. Omar stood up and came to protect his wife from further embarrassment, and found himself staring into his father's eyes.

"Mummy," a whimper sounded from the divan.

Payal walked over to her parents and leaned on Taara who was still crouched by her father in-law's feet. Taara took her in her arms and stood up, "Payal, this is your *dada*."

Haider Khan stood as if frozen, his hands hanging on his side.

"Mummy, what is a *dada*?" Payal asked.

"He is your papa's papa."

Payal looked at her grandfather and studied him head to toe. She reached out and placed her tiny hand on his cheek.

"Mummy, are all *dadas* so big and scary?"

Taara shook her head, "he's not scary. Go to him and see for yourself." She leaned forward toward her father-in-law.

Omar stood, watching the exchange.

A few seconds ticked away. The TV drama ended and the room turned silent. Haider Khan took one hesitant step toward them. He extended his arms to take Payal, immediately swallowing her in his massive body. He smiled and proceeded to shower her with kisses.

Payal giggled, "your *mooch* tickles, just like my papa."

Eyes glistening, Haider looked at Omar and extended his arm, inviting his son into it.

Taara watched the reunion through moist eyes. She put her head down and moved forward and he brushed his hand over her head in blessing. Taara looked at her mother-in-law, still sitting on the divan, and smiled, as tears rolled down her cheeks. Her family was complete.

Later that evening, the whole family sat at the dinner table together. Shehnaz begum hovered and fussed as she served, offered and chastised Taara for being too thin and not eating enough. Taara helped herself to the unique dishes and helped Payal with her food. Omar devoured the familiar *aloo gosht,* potato and meat with gravy and *bhindi keema* okra with ground lamb. He broke off pieces of the Afghani *naan* bread and scooped up the food with each bite. Haider Khan slowly took his bites and observed Payal use her dainty hands to spoon some gravy-covered rice and meticulously place it inside her small mouth. He was impressed at her deliberate movement taking care not to spill a single grain and smiled at the reminder of his son's childhood.

He turned to Omar and asked about his work. Finishing the last morsel of his *naan,* Omar reached for some rice as he dived passionately into the details of his cases. For once, Taara was happy to see her husband absorbed about his work, and she noticed a glint of pride in Haider Khan's eyes. Suddenly, in the middle of the conversation, Omar turned to her and said, "I almost forgot."

Taara looked up and tilted her head, waiting for him to continue.

"Remember when I stopped in at the office this morning? Joe..." He turned to his father and explained, "My boss called me into his office."

Haider Khan nodded and watched him in anticipation. Shehnaz's spoon hung mid-air, a mound of rice and gravy balancing on it.

Omar looked around the table and smiled, "you are looking at the newest partner of my firm."

Taara squealed with delight, jumped up from her chair and hugged Omar. She noticed Haider Khan's glare and Shehnaz's disapproving look and sat back down. She had forgotten that touching Omar in front of them would be inappropriate. His parents showered their blessings and congratulatory wishes on him as well. Confused by the excitement, Payal decided to join in. She stood up on her chair, circled her arms around Omar and blew a raspberry on his cheek.

Shehnaz went to the kitchen to bring back some sweet *mitthai*. Passing the plate around, she said, "thanks to Allah for Omar's success. We must have some sweet."

After dinner the men retreated to the great room while the women cleared away the dishes and cleaned the kitchen. Payal went to sit on the *takht* with the men and listened to them discuss serious matters.

Omar brought up Zahira and his father dismissed it as her family problem.

"But *Abbu*, she's a member of our family and she is suffering."

Haider put a hand on his son's shoulder and said, "once a daughter is given away, she is not ours anymore. This is how our society works."

Omar shook his head and stood up, "she will never stop being my sister and it is my duty to help her."

"What can you do?" his father asked.

"I will go talk to that husband of hers and knock some sense into him," Omar responded.

Haider looked at his hands as they sat on his lap and shook his head, "our interference could make the situation worse."

"How much worse could it get for Zira?" Omar retorted.

Haider raised his hand and said, "do what you must. I can't be a part of this."

"So it's settled," Omar said, "I'll take the first flight out to Karachi."

Taara caught the last sentence as she walked in and asked, "What about us?"

"Your flights for Minnesota are booked later this week. You can stay with Ruhi aunty and go from there."

Next day, Taara, Payal and his parents waved to Omar as he passed through security at the LAX airport. Returning to the

Kakkar mansion, Taara called Ruhi and told her to expect them after breakfast. When she started to pack their things Payal threw a tantrum, refusing to leave her *dadi* and needing to hear all the stories her grandmother had hidden inside her. At bedtime, she insisted on spending the night in her grandparents' room and fell asleep in her *dadi's* arms.

Taara lay alone on Omar's bed that night and allowed her thoughts to travel to the past. She thought of her mother and her journals. She considered the relationship Janki had with Dimple. It was a strong bond the two shared and her mother carried those memories with her across the ocean and passed them on to Taara, through her stories and her journal. It struck her that her insistence on moving to Ruhi's right away and then returning to the Twin Cities was all wrong. She would be getting in the way of a little girl and her grandmother. She had noticed the change in Shahnaz's eyes into pure joy whenever she looked at Payal and that made Taara realize that Shahnaz needed to be with her granddaughter, even more than Payal needed a grandmother.

Next morning, when Taara announced that their stay had extended another week, she was met with squeals of cheer from her daughter and showers of blessings from her mother in-law. She visited her aunt and uncle briefly and spent the rest of her time with her newfound mother. Omar's father usually stayed out or in his room.

That evening, she waited anxiously by the phone to hear if Omar had reached Karachi. His phone call was short, calling soon after reaching Zahira's home in Clifton. Zahira was ecstatic to see her brother after all these years. Taara was happy for them and also for Payal and Shehnaz, who had become inseparable.

One lazy afternoon, their last day in California, while Payal listened to folk tales from her *dadi* in her sitting room, Taara sat huddled over old photo albums admiring Omar's baby pictures. At the back of the shelf behind the TV, she came across a black binder shrouded with dust. She pulled it out and spread it open on the floor, seeing pages of certificates and awards with Omar's pictures sprawled on each sheet. She admired his graduation pictures from Kindergarten through law school, read through cuttings of newspaper articles with Omar's achievements on various contests in science, debate, math, swimming and so on. Taara's eyes poured over each historical event in her husband's school and professional life.

"Omar's Abbu collected all these," Ammi said from the *takht*.

Taara looked up and saw Payal asleep in one corner. She stood up, and carrying the scrapbook she went to sit next to her mother in-law. She flipped through the pages and asked, "did you put all this together?"

Shahnaz shook her head and started to stroke Payal's hair, "Zahira put them in this book after he left." Her voice sounded as if from a distance as she continued, "his Abbu had saved the cuttings and used to boast about Omar's triumphs to all the relatives. He had so many dreams for him."

Taara looked down and ran her hand over Omar, the soccer star's picture, then touched her mother-in-law's hand and gave it a gentle squeeze. Returning to the scrapbook she embraced her discovery of hidden treasure, a chance to peak into her husband's past. Going through the album, listening to his mother, and observing his room, she realized that she really did not know Omar as deeply as she thought she did. He never talked about his past and she never even took the time to ask.

"I guess that's why his Abbu took it so hard. He expected Omar to follow our traditions, our beliefs, and continue to be the high achiever," Shehnaz lamented.

"He still is a high achiever, *Ammi*. He works very hard, how else would he have become partner at a prestigious law firm at such a young age?"

"He also did well when he chose to marry you," Shehnaz said.

Taara blushed and looked to the album in her hand.

Payal with her *dadi's* stories, and Taara armed with Omar's past, returned to Minnesota later that week. Snow mounds still lined the driveways and streets, the air remained razor crisp, the wind howled and whistled like a ghost but the sun shone high and bright. After having spent a couple of weeks at the dog hotel, Oscar returned home, his tail wagging incessantly and his tongue licking Payal's face nonstop, over squeals of her laughter. While trying to keep some normalcy in the house during the day, Taara anxiously waited for Omar's phone calls each night. They spoke briefly every day but it was not until several days later that he was able to update her on the issue at hand.

Taara learned that as the sole male member of the family, Khaled was under tremendous pressure from his mother and the extended family to supply an heir to carry on the family name. Zahira had panicked, believing the rumors that....

Omar told Taara, "living in a joint family, husband and wife don't have much privacy. Khaled and Zira have no chance to clear away their misunderstandings."

"So how did you help resolve this?" she asked.

"Well, first I talked to each one separately," Omar explained, "then, a few days later, all three of us went out for dinner and then a walk on the beach."

"And?" Taara prodded.

"We talked. Actually, they talked and I, well mediated."

"Is that all?" Taara asked.

"It's the first time they openly discussed the issue and realized how each was suffering."

"That's fantastic! So, Zahira is okay, and your work is done." Taara inquired, "when are you coming home?"

"In a few days," Omar promised.

Taara endured his absence while Omar enjoyed getting to know his brother-in-law and spending time with his sister. He observed the changes around him since his last trip nine years ago and shared with Taara over their daily phone exchange.

"The young people are so much more confident," Omar shared one day, "I can see it in the way they walk or discuss world affairs, sit in clusters at coffee shops or fast food places. I can't believe the number of internet cafes that have popped up all over the city." Then his tone lost its enthusiasm, "yet, so much is still the same with traditional, fundamental thought in many households."

"You mean like Khaled's family," Taara offered.

"Oh, I almost forgot," he informed, "I've booked my return for next week after a quick trip to Quetta to visit *dadi*."

"Is it safe to travel there?" Taara asked.

"Relax. My family lives there and I'll blend in."

"Come back soon. Payal misses you."

"Just Payal?" Omar teased.

"Oscar too." Taara teased back and then admitted, "It's been kind of lonely."

"I'll send you a postcard from Quetta," Omar said.

Placing the receiver down dreamily, Taara tried to picture Quetta, the city on a plateau protected by the looming mountains. Someday, she should take herself there, she thought.

That was the last time Taara spoke with Omar.

CHAPTER 37

1956

On the second floor of the three-story building off of *Badda Darwaza*, over an elaborate breakfast, Dadanji filled Janki in on the gossip from Quetta and Kandhar. Amritsar's strategic location as a border city made Dadanji's home a stop-over for family and friends and the frequent visitors not only brought delicacies, but news of the *biradri* community before carrying on to inner India or back to Kandhar.

As Dadanji talked and Janki learned of so-and-so's daughter in trouble or husband beating his wife, or a son who moved away to England or America, she struggled to keep her eyes open after a sleepless overnight journey. The numerous cups of tea she downed did not keep her eyelids from falling until Dadanji finally conceded and directed her to a room to rest.

The bedroom was small, neat and inviting, with its soft bed, sheen fabrics, and pastel hues. She crawled under the crocheted bedspread, woven with delicate pink beads, and gently placed her head down on the cool, white pillow. Melting into the ambience, she was immediately transported into another dimension. She saw Ram Lal standing next to her, tall and strong watching their children with pride as they literally grew in front of their eyes. The loud rumble of his fleet of trucks hummed in the background as a soothing concerto. Suddenly she found herself in a mango grove listening to the loud, flirty whistles of the mynah, followed by an abrupt chatter of many birds as they took to the sky. In the midst of prattling birds Janki heard giggles, as if from little school girls. She tossed and turned finally giving up further attempts at sleep as cackles from the foyer grew louder.

Three young girls stood in the middle of the hallway, crisp clothes cradled in their arms that they had just stripped from the line on the terrace. They brought the bundle closer to their developing chest and inched back with muffled laughter as they saw their grandmother enter. Before Dadanji could reprimand, Nira, the brave one spoke up, "The guests... Devi's fiancé is here. We saw his *tonga* turn into the alley."

"So soon?" the old woman exclaimed. She shouted out orders all at once, "Devi, go change into the saree I gave you and for god's sake, find a way to tame that hair. Nira, help her make a braid. Gita, come with me to the kitchen and... and... where's Sita? Sita! Oh, there you are, send Ramu to get *samosas* and *jalebi* snacks from the H*alwai* shop. Take the money from the *dubba* can in my room and tell him to hurry up. You go start the tea." she commanded.

Right then the big knocker on the door thumped. Dadanji stood still, one hand to her heart. She covered her silver head with the white *chunni*, patted the creases on her shirt and hobbled to the door. The two Khatri men stepped in, each touching Dadanji's feet in turn, for her blessings, and she invited them into the spacious living room.

Ram Lal's voice reached Janki's ears and she slumped back onto the soft bed, puzzled and elated. She quickly smoothed her *kameez* shirt and hair, covered her head with her *chunni* and all but ran to the drawing room, her eyes searching for her husband in the large room. She found him sitting in a large, purple high-backed chair, his back turned to the door listening intently to Dadanji. Virendra walked over from his place on the *divan* pushed back to the wall, touched her feet before fading to the background. Ram Lal turned around and stood up wearing a puzzled expression, but Janki also noticed a hint of delight before he masked it by looking away. She noticed the white strands had won battle in his overgrown, unkempt hair. Feeling her knees weaken within the folds of her *salwar* and suppressing the quiver in her voice, she asked after his health. He nodded without meeting her eyes and walked off to look out the open window.

Dadanji observed the exchange with her keen eyes then politely excused herself, muttering something about tea and the girls.

Virendra invited his mother to sit next to him and asked about her journey. His head bent low, long legs extended out, he sat at the edge of the *divan*. As he listened intently to her response, his eyes diverted to the doorway.

Devi walked in, adorned in a soft peach saree, intricate embroidery in white threads decorated a slim border. She had no makeup to mask her 16-year old face, but the saree *pallu* over her head framed it like a beautiful portrait; soft shadows of peach hues casted on her tanned face accentuating her sharp features. She carried a tray layered with refreshments, keeping her walk straight in the high heels her grandmother had instructed her to wear, the only way to make the 10-inch height difference less noticeable between the soon-to-be engaged couple.

Devi offered tea and snacks to Ram Lal and Janki, keeping her eyelids lowered. When she moved on to Virendra, she sneaked a quick look at the handsome face of the man soon to be her husband. He smiled, but she quickly turned around and left the room. Ram Lal and Dadanji, reminiscing about the good old days in Chaman failed to notice the innocent exchange, but Janki had caught that glimpse and felt her own cheeks flush.

Dadanji was saying, "Nand would have loved to see you but all my sons are spread out all over the world, busy running their business." She put a hand on Virendra's head and said, "he is very happy about his daughter going into your home."

Janki smiled and asked, "The *rishta* match is *pukka* official?"

Dadanji stood up and gave Janki a hug on each shoulder as she said, "we are family now." Still standing, she announced to the men, "you must be tired from your long journey. I'll go check if the room is ready."

"I'll help." Janki followed her out.

Ram Lal walked back to the window to watch the children playing down in the alley. Virendra sat with his teacup in hand and as he sipped thoughtfully, from the corner of his eyes he noticed curious faces of two young, giggly girls peeking out from the doorway. He looked directly at them and as soon as Ram Lal went through a small door into the bathroom, Virendra took that opportunity to confront the two girls.

Before he reached the door, Nira marched right at him and asked, "are you going to be our *jijaji*?"

"Well that depends on who you are," he threw back.

"We are your *saalis* bride sisters."

"Then you will be the *Aadhi Ghar Waalis* half-brides," Virendra flirted.

Nira and Gita blushed and ran out.

After dinner Virendra sneaked up to the terrace for a smoke. He had never lit up in front of the elders out of respect, even though he suspected they knew of his habit. High up on the third level, under the stars, he looked out over the neighborhood. An intricate network of electric wires draped across endless line of terraces, crossed over the alleys, streets and neighborhood boundaries, and spanned out in all directions. At the edge of the boundary wall, he spotted a dark silhouette, her hair as black as the night snaking down her spine all the way to the back of her knees. He took the matches out of his pocket and struck one to light the cigarette hanging loosely on his lips. Acrid smell and the sound rippling through the placid night sparked Devi to turn around, and upon noticing who the offender was, her hand flew over her mouth in surprise. She tried to make her way to the door, but her steps wavered when she heard his voice.

"Do I scare you?" Virendra asked.

Devi shook her head, frozen in place.

"Then why do you run away every time you see me?"

She shrugged, her back still to him. She heard his footsteps come closer until she could feel him near enough for his warm breath to brush her bare neck. He whispered next to her ear, "you are very beautiful."

She felt color and heat rise to her face and as she made a motion to run again, Virendra grabbed hold of her arm.

"Are you happy with this *rishta* match?" he asked.

She nodded slowly.

"I need to hear you say it," he demanded.

"Yes." A squeak escaped Devi's quivering lips.

"I'm glad you are not pressured into this marriage," he moved even closer, "do you realize this is the last time we'll meet before the wedding day?"

"I know," Devi replied as she reclaimed her arm.

"Do you want to ask me anything?"

A passing cloud hid the stars and the dark night wrapped her nervous body like a shawl. She stepped back, disappearing into its shadowy comfort before finding her nerve.

"Can you give up smoking?" she mumbled.

Virendra looked at his unsmoked cigarette, threw it on the ground and stubbed it out. "Done," he declared.

Silence hung heavy between them before Virendra broke it, "anything else?"

"I... I... have something to tell you," Devi managed to say.

"What's that? That you smoke?"

Devi pursed her lips to hide her smile, "no, only that...that I..."

"I what?" Virendra interrupted.

"I'm a vegetarian," Devi blurted before she ran off.

CHAPTER 38

2006

"Umrica! You are from there *saabji*?" the taxi driver asked Omar, a cigarette hanging loosely from his lips, engulfing the car with its acrid smoke. He snaked through crowded Quetta streets from the train station to the Kakkar home, constantly glancing at his rearview mirror to study his passenger.

"*Ji*." Omar replied. He looked out into the hazy streets, his view from the stuffy cab obscured by the drizzle turning into sleet. Street vendors crouched under temporary shelter, shivering from the mountain winds. He spotted men in *karikulii* caps and faux leather jackets over their *salwar kameez* walking with hunched shoulders. A beggar sat huddled in a corner wrapped in a large moth-eaten shawl. Omar gazed up toward the mountains catching glimpses of white between the shifting grim clouds.

He turned to the cab driver and asked, "what's the weather forecast for the next two days?"

"Maybe snow. Maybe not. Only Allah knows," he waved his hand up.

"What is it like in February normally?" Omar tried again.

"Sometime snow, sometime sunny." Then he added, "Sometime both." Changing the topic, the driver suddenly asked, "*Saabji*, how long you be here?"

"Two days."

"I take you back to the *tation*. Tell me when," his head turned to look at his passenger, his ungroomed beard dyed red with henna in full view. A skull cap rested on his head as if he was on his way to the mosque.

"Come at four," Omar said.

"You picked the wrong day Umerica-*walle* Saab. It is Ashurah that day, you know, the tenth day of Muharram?"

"Are you on holiday?" Omar inquired.

"What holiday for us, I work - I eat, wife eats, children eat. I no work, no food. But problem is roadblocks and maybe strike. Everyone worried about safety," his slits that were his eyes looked up at Omar through the mirror.

"Isn't it just a procession of *Shias*?"

"Yes, but we are few of us here, more *Sunnis* here like you. *Saabji* sir, last year two *Sunnis* got a room over the watch shop," he lowered his voice conspiratorially while dodging slow moving motor rickshaws, "they fired with guns and grenades at the procession, killing over 40 people. And then, then their own selves. Bam!" He raised his hand and pointed a finger as if a pistol.

"Wasn't there any security? I thought the military is always alert for these things," Omar asked.

The cabby continued with a touch of pride in his voice in educating an American-returned Pakistani, "yes, yes there is security. This year will be better. But shops may be shut down. You won't find a taxi or rickshaw and if you do, you can get stuck in the procession."

Omar noticed a sly smile from the corner of his driver's face. He leaned back and casually observed the taxi. A crescent moon and star decorated the front and a plaque with 'Allah' written in Urdu leaned on the dashboard. He determined the driver to be an obviously religious man and a *Shi'ite* with dislike for *Sunnis*. Omar felt a sudden distrust of this overly curious fellow. Noticing his obvious stare through the mirror, Omar decided to ask, "how do you know I'm from America? I'm a Balochi like you."

The driver smiled broadly revealing rotten teeth that had seen too much tobacco and betel nuts between them, "it's easy. Fingernails. No matter how smart we dress up and all clean, but those from Umrica have very clean fingernails." Then changing the topic, he asked, "s*aabji*, what's Umrica like?"

"Clean," Omar replied.

"It's really so rich with lots and lots of money and no poor people?"

"We have our share of poverty," Omar remarked.

"My *birader* went there and came back with so many things. Gold watch, music recorder, he even had a...a...compooter."

"Good for your brother," Omar tried to be dismissive.

"One day I'll go to Umrica," the bearded man said in a raised voice.

The cab turned into the narrow road leading to the Kakkar home, in one of the oldest neighborhoods. Access to the house was a maze of twists and turns. Omar's father had wanted to sell this place and put his mother, Jamila, up in a new home higher up in the mountains, closer to his sisters. The air was fresher and the new construction safer, especially in this earthquake-prone zone. Jamila refused, planning to die in the house that carried all her memories.

Omar looked to the west again, toward the mountains shrouded in a fog. He could see the flickers of brightness from peoples' homes as lights and lanterns came on. The taxi honked persistently to alert the playing children and stray dogs on the street. Omar looked ahead and realized that with all the demands of balancing a career and his new family, Omar had lost touch with those from his past. He planned to make up for all the lost time by spending every moment with his grandmother during his stay.

The taxi honked its way to the front door and some of his aunts, uncles, and cousins came out to greet him. Apparently, Zahira had called them despite Omar's insistence on wanting to surprise them. Past the greetings and hugs, he made his way into the large house through the courtyard into Jamila's room.

She was just getting up from her prayer rug, beads in hand, finishing-up her *namaaz*. Her small eyes squinted, then opened wider in amazement as she saw Omar. She straightened her elfin form in anticipation of a hug by her towering grandson, instead he lifted her off her feet and swung her around as she slapped his shoulders and shrieked for him to put her down.

"*Dadi, dadi*, my dear *dadi*," Omar stood strong and kept his hands on her shoulders after he set her down.

Tears rolled down Jamila's eyes as she tried to find steady footing. Leaning against him she said, "Omar beta. It was my wish to see you one more time before I die."

"My *dadi* is so young and beautiful she will live forever," he said cheerfully.

Later, by the cozy fire in the large kitchen-cum-dining room, everyone sat eating and chatting. His uncles inquired about his work while the aunts wanted to know about Taara and Payal. If there was any animosity against him marrying a Hindu, they did not show it. Omar showed his *Dadi* and the rest of the family pictures of Taara and Payal. He proudly shared cute stories about Payal and declared that someday he will bring them to Quetta to meet everyone.

After dinner, he walked with Jamila to her room and helped her get under the heavy, thickly stuffed quilt. Vivid colors, cross-stitched into intricate geometrical patterns appeared haphazard at first glance, but a pattern emerged of a village scene. Fringes of vibrant threads dangled from its three sides. He ignored the lone, straight back wooden chair in the far corner, and sat down beside her on the bed. His head turned toward a whistling sound in the direction of the window, but saw that the shutters were tightly closed. Above the window hung a dark brown *jhalar* valance decorated with bright red beads over a zig zag pattern of green threads. Red thread fringes with green beads dangled and swayed from it. As if reading his confusion, his *dadi* explained how the wind howled and whistled into her room. The house was too old to have every gap or opening closed up. The icy mountain air always found a crack to slip in through, as if looking for a willing ear to whisper its secrets into.

"So *dadi*, have you lived here all your life?" Omar asked.

"Most of the years since I got married," she replied.

He asked her if she recalled an incident involving a Hindu boy.

She contemplated for a moment and sighed deeply before speaking, "Rajinder...yes, very clearly. As if it happened just yesterday." She shook her head, "poor boy, what a tragedy." Jamila looked up at the ceiling as if the scene of that day was replaying high above her eyes. She recalled from that morning —menace in Ali's eyes, fear in those of her husband, Halif. How different the two brothers had been, and how lucky she was to have been married to the righteous one. She couldn't picture Rajendra that morning in the *angan* courtyard as Haider's one-year old hunger cries had called her indoors. Later she heard about the threats showered that morning, much later after her mother-in-law, Ali's own mother, stood up in front of the court and pointed at her son for the murder.

Omar sat, speechless, his head lowered, as Jamila related all she recalled.

Jamila turned sideways to look toward the door, as if looking through an opening into the past. She said, "I can't imagine what Janki *bhabhi* must have gone through..." Omar looked up at her to make sure he had heard her right as she continued, "...but nothing compared to how Ali's mother suffered."

Before she could carry on Omar interrupted, "*dadi*, can you tell me more about Janki...I mean did you know her, her husband's name?"

"I'll tell you...but tomorrow. It's my time for *namaaz*."

Omar pulled his thick jacket in closer and walked out to the courtyard, breathing deeply. The non-existent sun had set and gradually the lights in the high up houses turned off. His uncles and aunts had gone home and he sat alone in the middle of the *angan* on an old wooden chair. He looked around and tried to picture the scene of three young men in 1947 having an argument at the very spot he was now sitting. Sensing their ghostly presence, he felt oddly reassured.

The next morning, he arose well rested to a golden sun. Soon after breakfast, grandmother and grandson spent hours over endless cups of green tea and conversations that flowed from history to family to past connections. Omar poked and Jamila obliged, unraveling facts about the incident or tales of ancestral anecdotes. Jamila took delight in Omar's revelation of his family's connection with Taara's as if their stars had been aligned even before they were a twinkle in their parents' eyes. Their chance meeting in the library over a map of ancient Quetta was by design of their destiny.

On the tenth day of Muharram, he left early for the train station. As the car pulled away from the ancient house on what in early Quetta days used to be London Street, he waved to his *dadi* from the foggy window of the back seat of his uncle's car.

CHAPTER 39

1956

Dehra Dun was the same as Ram Lal had left it, cool evenings with fresh mountain breezes gliding down into the valley, just as it did in Quetta. The *mohalla* bustled as usual with activity as neighbors dropped in unannounced to share a dish they had made or the juicy gossip of the day.

As the celebration of his return and of Virendra's engagement receded, Ram Lal watched his family from the sidelines. His oldest son, Narendra had mapped his daily schedule around his job, his wife and child, while his other two adult sons darted between their studies and work. His unmarried daughters diligently helped their mother with the household chores and the care of their younger siblings, fitting it in between their own studies and tutoring jobs. Each member of his family was either coming from somewhere or going to something as they sidestepped him. He watched this constant whir of activity while his head spun with confusion and hindrance.

Janki was the least still of the members, her fingers moving expertly over a yarn and needles, even as she sat on the *manji* bed in the courtyard, intermittently fanning the sleeping baby. He watched her eyes fidget in every direction, wheels turning in her head, thinking of the next task or watching over their youngest son at play in the alley through the open door. Throughout their stay and journey from Amritsar, she had not spoken a word to him and he had not attempted to reach her either. He arrived into her home as a guest and remained as one. Everyone around him respectfully attended to him, squeezed out few moments of their time to make polite conversations with him, but Janki remained in charge of the household.

She did not notice Ram Lal disappear in the shadows to melt into the background of the *hungama* hustle-bustle. Occasionally, she would spot him in a corner, an orange *tilak* shining on his forehead obviously applied by the priest from the neighborhood temple. At other times she noticed dirt on his *pajama* or a blade of grass in his hair, which she had become accustomed to seeing after his long walks and naps at the lychee or the mango groves.

With Virendra's wedding date set, Janki sat on her *manji*, with half-knit sweater in hand, agonizing over the cost. It was not going to be cheap for the *baraat* groom's party to travel to Amritsar and live up to the high standards of the bride's family – Dadanji's sons had come a long way from their struggling Chaman days. Janki considered swallowing her pride to consult Ram Lal of her dilemma but concluded that nothing would come from this exchange except for more bitterness. Instead, she went to Virendra with another family treasure to pawn.

Weeks leading up to the wedding passed tumultuously as friends, neighbors, and family gathered to sing and dance late into the night with endless cups of tea and midnight delights. Janki ran from kitchen to rooms to dance floor to courtyard, shouting out orders, haggling with the vegetable sellers, joining in the chorus of traditional wedding songs, or cooing the upset baby. Constant music buzzed around them even as they boarded the train to

Amritsar with *dholki* drum and several singing voices as accompaniment.

Wedding ceremonies duly performed and celebrated, in the twilight hours of a cool spring morning and after a long train journey, the Khatris brought home the new bride. Devi and Virendra ceremoniously crossed the front door into the courtyard amidst fiery *diyas* clay lamps, a shower of flowers and a grand welcome by the entire neighborhood. A large trousseau accompanied the bride, and an assortment of its contents were put on display covering each available spot on the furniture, walls and floors of Janki's bedroom for everyone to admire. Janki escorted Devi to the drawing room to sit down to perform the *tilbhare* ceremony. In a corner lay a tray of rice and sesame seeds of which Devi gathered a handful in the cup of her palms. She exchanged the seeds into the cupped hands of another woman who repeated this exchange three times, while a chorus of traditional folk songs reverberated around them. Many women took turns to perform the ritual with Devi and each woman ended her turn by lifting Devi's veil to see her face. In exchange for the bride viewing, each handed her a welcome gift.

Rituals completed, trousseau stored away, decorations removed, the household returned to its normal drone of activity. Devi immersed herself into the routine, making the morning tea with her hennaed hands or washing clothes by the tap and drain in the courtyard, her bridal *choorra*, red-colored ivory bangles, jingling as she beat the garments with a bat. From her place in the courtyard, she could see directly into the room she shared with her husband, nestled between her husband's sisters on one side and the older brother, Narendra, with his family on the other side. Janki's room stood tucked away in the far corner, behind a pillar which she shared with her youngest two children. Ram Lal and his unmarried son slept outdoors in the *manji*, under the stars.

Devi had noticed the awkwardness between her husband's parents back in Amritsar when she had first met them, but had not given it much thought. Now, through her downcast but discerning eyes, she observed the sadness set deep in her father-in-law's gaze and his extended disappearances from the house. Through her keen ears, she also detected a hint of bitterness in Janki's voice when she inquired of her husband's whereabouts from one of the children. Watching the constant movement of all the other members of this loud and hectic household, Devi cowered into her timid shell.

With the approach of the rains and then the chilled mountain breezes, Ram Lal's sleeping arrangement shifted indoors onto the *manji* bed squeezed into a corner in Janki's room. One night, Ram Lal sat on his temporary bed in his wife's room, a prayer book in hand, as the family huddled together in a *razai* quilt in the next room playing a game of *antakshari* of singing songs or sharing stories of their day. He heard explosion of laughter or playful teasing emanating through the walls and he pondered how happy and complete his family was, even without his presence. The next morning, he made his travel arrangements.

As snow fell over Mount Mussourie, Ram Lal prepared to head back to the familiar mountains he called home. Janki stood in the doorway watching him hurl his unfolded clothes into the small suitcase. Her head covered with her shawl, arms crossed over her breasts, she sported a smile as she watched her husband wrestle with the case that was too stubborn to close.

"So, this is it?" She walked in to help.

Ram Lal looked up, then, stepped back.

"When does the train leave?" she asked as she rearranged his clothes.

"Tonight," he mumbled without meeting her eyes.

"It was good while it lasted," Janki said, banging the bag shut.

"Yes."

"Do you remember when we were first married?" Janki turned around to face him, "I was still a child then."

"You were so innocent," he whispered.

"You helped me stand up for myself. Without your support, I would never have survived all those wives of *Pahji*," she let out a sad laugh.

"It is I who has been the weak one, Janki Devi," Ram Lal engulfed his wife in his arms.

Janki melted in his hold, smelling the familiar musky aroma that was her husband. She tried to recall the last time anyone had held her so close as her tears seeped through his *Kurta* shirt.

"I miss you," her voice was broken and muffled.

"Forgive me," he stroked her hair. They stood as one and then Ram Lal let go and stepped back. He abruptly reached for the suitcase and walked out of the room and out of her life. She stood alone engulfed in the warmth of her shawl as tears streamed down her cheeks.

"Yes, I forgive you," she spoke to the walls.

CHAPTER 40

2006

Tears of joy streamed down Taara's cheeks as she drifted into blissful sleep, travelling to places in her comforting dreams. She saw herself in a seat of honor with Omar and Payal on either side. Not only was she a mother and wife, she was finally a daughter again. Haider and Shahnaz stretched their hands out in blessing. Ruhi and Raj stood close by for support. From under her flickering eyelids, Taara saw her parents offering their blessings from their cushion of clouds. Above everyone else, she saw Janki with her angelic smile.

Taara opened one eye, startled out of her bliss, as she reached for the blaring phone.

"Baaji! Baaji!" Zahira screamed into the receiver.

"Zahira? What is it?" she slurred into the mouthpiece.

"It's *Lala*."

Taara sat up fully awake, "what about Omar? What's wrong?"

Zahira broke into uncontrollable sobbing.

"Tell me what's wrong with Omar!" Taara screamed into the phone.

Khaled's controlled voice came through the wires, "this is Zahira's husband. You see, the thing is that, Omar…Omar was supposed to come back today from Quetta."

"Yes, I know, he was supposed to call me when he got back to your home," Taara interrupted.

"Yes, but…you see… his train came… but he did not."

"What do you mean he did not?" Taara screamed again. Collecting herself she spoke softly, "did he stay back in Quetta then?"

"We called there. It was hard to get through…the phone lines were jammed. Anyway, we just spoke to Zahira's uncle there. He said Omar left on time for the station in their car. Well.…"

"Well what?" Taara demanded.

"The car had a flat tire mid-way. While the driver tried to fix the flat, Omar got out of the car. The driver said that they were in Liaquat Bazaar and Omar told him he was going over to a shop across the street."

"Then?" Taara demanded.

"You see, there was a Muharram procession then. It went right through Liaquat road."

"Oh my gosh!" Taara gasped, recalling an article she had read on violence often occurring during this procession in Sunni dominated areas.

"After the car was ready to go, the driver looked around for Omar. The streets were full of people. He went to the store and the *shop-walla* remembered seeing a man of Omar's description, but didn't know where he went after his purchases. The driver searched everywhere, driving through the crowds."

"No, it can't be," Taara wailed.

Khaled continued, "the driver went home and Zahira's uncles went to look for Omar. They talked to people, looked around all night. But no sign. Nowhere." Khaled related, "I don't know what to say."

Taara quietly placed the receiver down not wanting to listen to another word. Before she could ascertain the facts, understand the situation, consider the impact, chart a plan of action, and let it all sink in; Payal came bawling into her room.

"Mummy, I heard a loud cry. I'm scared."

Taara reached out to Payal and held her for her dear life.

"Ouch, mummy, you're *joking* me," Payal coughed and wiggled to get some air.

She loosened her grip keeping a strong hold around her daughter, "I'm sorry honey. I didn't mean to choke you. I just love you a whole lot."

"Me too," Payal put her little arm around her mother's neck.

Taara cuddled her daughter up in the bed with her, stroking her head and lulling her back to sleep. Soon, soft snores escaped little nostrils and Taara remained sitting in her bed going through various scenarios in her head. *Maybe he got lost in the crowd and was trying to find his way home. Oh come on Taara, he's a grown man. Maybe he decided to take a different route to come home. But it's not like Omar to not inform anybody.*

Taara stayed up all night inventing and reinventing the situation, devising action plans, who she could reach out to, any legal route she could take. She kept her head clear and thought through her options. One thing she was sure about was that Omar was somewhere in Pakistan and she was going to find him. By morning, she had decided, she was going to travel to Pakistan.

Her first stop was Newport Beach in California. Aunty Ruhi and uncle Raj were once again there for Taara in her time of need. Ruhi *masi* gladly offered to take care of Payal for as long as it would take. Her next stop was Calabasas, where Omar's parents lived.

It was a bright morning with a clear blue sky. The drive was surprisingly smooth with no traffic delays. She rang the bell and waited, fidgeting with the scarf around her neck. She covered her head with the long scarf, which kept slipping from her silky hair.

As the door opened, Taara looked into the face of an old woman whose eyes were swollen. Her white hair stuck out from under a long scarf that partially covered her head at an awkward angle. Shahnaz *begum* seemed to have aged a lifetime in just a week.

"*Assallam-o-Aliakum, Ammi,*" Taara raised her hand in greeting.

"*Wallaikum-Assallam, Beti.* Come. Come in."

Taara followed the old woman, tottering through the familiar corridor, in an awkward silence. The TV room was the same with the same faces peering from the screen, the same drama turned on.

The two women sat on the divan. After a few awkward moments, Taara reached out and held the older woman's hand.

"Where's *Abbu*?" she asked.

"He left for Pakistan this morning," her head dropped into her free hand through which she mumbled, "I just found my son and he is lost again. Yah Allah, what sins have I done?" she wailed.

Taara put an arm around her as the two rocked, "nothing is going to happen to him." She whispered, "I'm going there. I promise I will find him."

Shahnaz stared at her, "*beti*, what will you do?"

"Find my husband," Taara said.

"The men are already doing that. His father will have all the family out looking for him. You don't even know anyone there," Shahnaz reasoned.

"I can't just sit here and do nothing. I have to go," Taara asserted.

Shahnaz remained quiet. The two women watched the sidekick on the drama serial do practical jokes on a neighbor. Where once this scene evoked peals of laughter, now it seemed to mock the two women.

"Taara *beti*. As a mother, I want to advise you not to go, at least not now."

"*Ammi*. I call you that because I consider myself to be your daughter. I respect your advice but… why?"

"Quetta is not safe for you to go alone. Omar's *Abbu* can't look for my son and protect you. A bad situation could become worse."

"I don't need protection," Taara said.

"It's not like Karachi where women drive around alone and don't need to wear *hijab*," Shahnaz paused but before Taara could say anything, she inquired, "What about Payal? Where is she?"

"She is with my *khaala* aunt."

Shahnaz spoke softly, "can I see her?"

"I can bring her tomorrow," Taara acquiesced.

With a weak smile, Shahnaz reached out to hug her daughter-in-law.

Shahnaz doted over Payal, cuddling her, showering her with gifts. She took joy in feeding Payal with her own hand, spoiling her with bars of chocolates. Payal was glad to be with her *dadi* again and loved the attention, the pampering and all the sugary treats. Haider Khan called from Pakistan but had no news to share.

Taara spent the nights alone in Omar's room, guilt gnawing at her as she ran her hands over his trophies. She regretted suggesting that he go there. Yes, family was important, but she and Payal were his family first. Omar was all she had and without him... she didn't let that thought take form. Instead, she tried to think of what could have happened. Perhaps a kidnapping. But who? Why? It couldn't be Taliban rebels, but the more she fingered that train of thought, the more convinced she became. She realized that Omar's Americanness made him a target in that region. Feeling helpless, sitting oceans away from where Omar disappeared, miles away from her own home in Minnesota, Taara became restless. As the Hindu festival of colors, *Holi,* came and went, Taara made plans to return home. She had to do something from this side of the ocean and Minnesota was where she knew people who could help. Amidst tears and hugs, Taara and Payal said their goodbyes to Shahnaz and drove back to Orange County, where Ruhi and Raj drove them to the airport.

Through all the goodbyes, Payal became inconsolable. She was beginning to feel Omar's absence, and now leaving both her new-found *dadi* and then Ruhi *nani*, she couldn't understand why everyone couldn't stay together. She sensed the anxiety all the adults experienced and didn't know what to make of it. She began to cling to Taara as the only constant in her life and broke down at the littlest things.

Payal's insecurity grew as Taara struggled to balance her own emotional state and her daughter's unsettling behavior. On the Ides of March, Taara and Payal returned to their Eden Prairie suburb facing icy winds. Terrible foreboding gripped Taara's chilled bones as she heard the newscaster on the car radio relay the possibility of a massive weather system moving their way in the next 24 hours. Giving heed to the warning, Taara stocked up on groceries.

With the refrigerator and pantry bursting at their seams, Payal fed and tucked away in peaceful slumber, Taara proceeded to tackle the mail. Bills did not wait for people to be found, advertisers did not care whether their targets were in any condition to filter through their flyers. Taara skimmed through the pile from her mailbox, mechanically sorting the junk from 'to be looked at later' stack. She almost threw it in the junk pile, a small envelope with large stamps of a man in a *topi* hat. *How could she have not recognized the scrawl with their address?* One word escaped her lips, "Omar".

Taara stared at the crumpled envelope for what could have been an hour or just two minutes. She was happy for what it represented – that he was alive. She was afraid what it might say – that he was not coming back. He had left her. She finally tore off an edge and removed three crumbled sheets with blotches of dirt on them and proceeded to read.

Taara Sweetheart,

I have missed you so much, wishing every minute that you were here with me. I bet Payal is keeping you busy. I miss her constant chatter and the warm hugs. Soon I'll be home. I am so glad I came to see dadi. We talked so much and I learned so much about my family and something about your family as well from her. That's why I am writing to you rather than wait to come back and tell you.

Remember about the murder of your grand uncle, Rajendra. It was by my dada's brother, Ali. What weird coincidence. My dadi witnessed the fight that led to the crime. Ali did viciously slay Rajendra for greed, using religion as an excuse. Ali's own mother (my great-grandmother) testified against him, and because of her testimony he was executed.

You see what this means? I know Abbu has reconciled to the fact that we are married. But now I can go to Abbu and tell him all this. He will have no reason to have anything against Hindus. He will be able to welcome you with open arms rather than just accept. I am so happy so had to write all this down to believe it.

I'll be leaving in a few minutes to catch my train to Karachi and then off to see my two favorite girls in the Twin Cities. I'll mail this letter at the railway station but most likely I'll be in your arms before you touch this letter. We might even be reading this together and laugh over the silliness of it.

Loves and hugs to Payal.

Yours always,

Omar

Taara folded the letter and proceeded to insert it in the envelope. Before she could get it all in, she noticed some writing on the back of the pages. It was messy and crooked but Taara noticed the "r's" curved in the same way Omar's did, with an eye. She tried to decipher the squiggles.

Kidnapped. Left in a room. Warehouse? Small window high up - egress. Can hear bazaar, procession. Help!

Taara sat frozen in shock. She sat at her kitchen table staring at the note and started to mumble, *"what do I do? Oh my gosh. What do I do? Who do I call?"* Flustered, she walked from one room to another, tugging at strands of her hair twirling them around her fingers. She opened the phone book skipping through the pages, unsure of what she was searching. Frustrated, she banged it shut. Back in her room, she stopped by her bedside table picking up the picture of the three of them from the hospital. Payal was less than an hour old and Omar was next to them. His body was slumped with fatigue but the spark in his eyes glistened with love and joy. Taara set the picture down, wiped the salty stream off her cheeks and marched toward the phone.

"Khaled *Bhai*?" Taara spoke hastily.

"Taara? Sorry, nothing yet. How are you and Payal?"

"Not so good Khaled *bhai*, but I have something to tell you."

Taara described him the note on the back of the letter she received. He promised to inform Omar's father and keep her posted on any developments. Taara also informed Khaled, "I will be coming there next week. Can I count on you to help me out?"

"Of course."

"I will need to travel to Quetta. Can you arrange that for me please?"

"I'll do better than that. Both Zahira and I will take you there."

"Thank you." She almost rang off then remembered the other item on her list, "oh, one more thing. Have you contacted the American Consulate in Pakistan?"

"That's the first thing Abbu did when he got here."

"Excellent," Taara set the phone down gently.

Her next phone call was to the senior partner at Omar's law firm. Taara hoped the partners could take some time off their corporate lawyering to help her find one of their own. The least they could do was to direct her to the right legal course. As an additional measure, she filed a complaint with the FBI. After informing Shahnaz and then talking to Ruhi about the new developments, Taara tried to make her travel plans. Luckily, she had already taken the visa in person at the Pakistani embassy in LA and getting an outbound from California to Karachi was not going to be hard. The hard part will be saying goodbye to Payal. For now, Taara's concern was getting out of Minnesota.

The flurries outside had increased in intensity, the snowflakes coming down fast and hard. The forecast called for more of the same for the next two days, blanketing the land.

CHAPTER 41

1957

Mount Mussourie and its range stood regally, towering over the Doon valley. Its peaks glistened with snow, and blew icy winds into the city below. Devi stood huddled in a shawl on the terrace atop the large house to take in the full view of the valley in all directions and enjoy a peaceful respite from the daily household duties.

Since the departure of her father-in-law, things were not much different. Janki continued to run the household with a frugal hand, accounting for every *paisa*, every morsel, and every yard. Clothes were mended or patched. Burning coals were used for cooking, for heating the bath water or for keeping a room warm until the last one turned to ash. Even the ash was used, for scrubbing the cooking pots with a mesh. Narendra's wife and Devi helped Janki in the daily chores while the remaining three unmarried daughters of the house were either too young or too busy to help.

Winters in Dehra Dun felt more chilling than Amritsar, the

household more bustling, the members more vocal. Although an expert cook under her *dadi's* guidance, Devi was occasionally scoffed at for the way she prepared certain dishes. If she poured water into the cauliflower as per the generations-old recipe from her grandmother, Laaji would laugh, "*phabi* put the water in the *gobi*. Who makes *gobi* with water?" Devi quietly accepted these outbursts, tucking them away into some deep corner of her heart. In the calm moments, up on the terrace she massaged the collected outbursts or remarks, and washed them away with her tears. Such was the daily routine where hard labor and few pats on the back were the order each day.

Times of greatest joy were when Virendra and Devi rented bicycles and wheel down into wilderness peddling for hours together. Theirs was a quiet romance where words were not foremost. A visual exchange, a direct look or a flutter in the eye; a short smirk or a hearty laugh; hunched shoulders or straight spine communicated copious amounts. Theirs was a language that was their own. During the long rides through the lychee and mango orchards, Devi sacrificed numerous sarees as they shredded or discolored in the spokes of the two-wheeled vehicle. Apart from their biking excursions, Virendra took his bride to cinema halls, billiard rooms, and pubs. He enjoyed showing off his town to his wife, which she soon started to accept as her own. With their weekly outings, the two of them put in miles while the wheels of their bicycles and time kept moving.

In her second year of marriage, Devi managed household tasks with a swollen belly. Amidst their impending joy, the Khatri family received a proposition for Shaku's hand in marriage. Within days of the engagement celebration, Dimple arrived without event and Virendra and Devi welcomed their first-born as the product of their love.

No sooner was Devi well enough to ride her bike, than the couple took off every Sunday again, though on shorter excursions. Every departure started with feeding and bundling up Dimple and handing her over to Janki who watched over the sleeping infant.

On occasions if Dimple let out a cry, Janki held her close and simply put a nipple from her ample breast into the baby's mouth. Pacified, Dimple would peacefully suck away at the empty nipples and nod off.

Soon after Shaku was sent off to her new home, Devi felt another life growing inside her. Sunday outings again had to be limited to cinemas or pubs for soft drinks. She was enjoying Dimple so much that excitement of another baby gushed through Devi's pores. On one dismal day in her third trimester, women in the neighborhood gathered to perform the *godd bharai* ceremony, blessing the mother-to-be. After the tortuous task of sitting in one spot for two hours as each woman recited her own version of mantras and blessings, Devi escaped as soon as the crowd dispersed. She hurried up the terrace for a quick reprieve before getting back to chores and to Dimple.

A fresh shower had left the alleys and the stairs that led to the terrace wet. Devi carefully walked up as she clutched her big belly, held up her saree, and hung on to the end of the *pallu*. Whether it was the wobble in her step, the slippery tread, or the six yards of material she had wrapped around her, something caused her to trip and fall down the ten flights. Lying in the hospital bed later, shedding quiet tears, she recalled the nurse telling her that it had been a boy.

Janki sat by her daughter-in-law, holding her hand while a lone tear slid down Devi's temple, disappearing in her hair.

Janki spoke softly, "did I ever tell you about Sita?" She hesitated, "maybe another time but I'll say one thing. You'll never get over it. No matter what anyone says, a mother never gets over losing a child." She let out a big sigh, "time does not heal, but it helps."

Devi let out a sniffle.

"You have Dimple and you'll have more. Cherish that."

The women sat in silence, each remembering the part of herself she had lost forever.

Getting back to daily life was not hard for Devi with enough chores waiting to be attacked. If it was not cooking or cleaning, there were clothes to mend or new outfits to stitch or sweaters to knit. In anticipation of Laaji's marriage, as soon as a good match was found, preparation for her trousseau had started. The women would spend an afternoon sitting around a saree, each grabbing a corner or an edge to embroider with gold and colorful threads. Many simple clothes became artistic attire and glamorous garbs in just a few afternoons. Devi also took delight in Dimple's developments, the awkward walk with her cloth diaper hanging low under her dress or her parroting everyone having discovered the art of spoken words.

It was two years before Laaji finally got married. It happened around the same time as a proposal was made for Mahendra, and the Khatri family celebrated a dual wedding that summer. In one moment, they were shedding tears during the *doli*, send off, for the daughter of the family, in another moment rejoicing at bringing home a beautiful bride.

Devi and Virendra's biking excursions continued at a more erratic pace. Traffic in the city had grown with motorized vehicles taking over the congested streets, while *tongas*, rickshaws, and bicycles continued to compete for road space. An occasional trip to the movie theatre brought Devi and Virendra together away from the joint family but Virendra also started to loiter on his own in the billiard bars. More than once, under Janki's direction, Devi had to stomp into the pubs unescorted in the twilight hours to bring her husband back home. Hidden in a shroud of shawl, she was ashamed to show her face to his constant companions at the bar. It was during one of those late-night journeys home, their first moment alone after a long time, when Devi shared the good news with Virendra. In just six months, Dimple would have a brother or a sister. Due to the mishap of three years ago, Devi was extra careful with this pregnancy.

Ruhi arrived, kicking and screaming at only five pounds. Devi had refused even vitamins during her pregnancy afraid they might harm her baby. Her paranoia remained even after Ruhi was pronounced healthy and grew robustly. Six-year old Dimple immediately adapted to her new sister, helping in her care giving. As soon as Ruhi treaded her first steps, she tried to keep up with Dimple, following her big sister around like a shadow.

The girls and Narendra's three children circled around Janki every evening listening to *dadi's* stories. They all knew about the mythological figures Ram and Sita, and their 14-year exile - the story of the Ramayan. They learned about Krishna, the cowherd and his flirtatious nature attracting the *gopians* maidens and his favorite Radha with his flute. Then there was the story of the mouse looking for a husband but their favorite of all was the story of the three mice who were sisters. They all repeated the chorus, bobbing their head side to side.

"Oil man, Oil man, walking through the woods,
Oh please, Oh please, if you could;
Give this message to the mouse,
Who lives in the Chakki *in your house;*
That your sister in the sugar cane fields,
Her husband is dead!"

Watching their children laugh or sit quietly in the weaving of a tale, the mothers sometimes joined in the listening. In time, even neighborhood kids started joining in for the story hour and Janki welcomed them all. Occasionally, Devi would notice the faraway look in her mother-in-law's eyes or catch a glimpse of moisture in them. Devi would move closer and hold her hand, remembering the letters locked up in Janki's trunk, the letters Ram Lal had written to Virendra, informing the family of his whereabouts and health.

Ram Lal had decided to sell the house in Quetta and settle down in Kandhar. His long-time friend, Halif, had helped him out by buying the house at a decent rate and Ram Lal used the money to lead a simple life in the company of his friends from the community in Kandhar. He had a lot of respect in the *biradri* many of whom continued to seek Ram Lal's advice on life-changing decisions. Virendra occasionally wrote back, informing Ram Lal of marriages and births, though Ram Lal never offered to visit or help. One blustery day, instead of a letter, the *postman* delivered a telegram postmarked from Afghanistan. Only one sentence appeared, "RAM LAL EXPIRED HEART ATTACK ADVISE LAST RITES".

Janki wore her widow's white at the age of 61. She had already lost her husband when she chose to stay with their children instead of following him to an *ashram*. She had said goodbyes to him so many times. She had lost him in her heart and mind. She had physically lost him past the boundaries of the subcontinent and now she had lost him beyond everything. His broken down, sad soul had departed this world into a new life.

Janki participated in the solemn ceremony at home as well wishers dropped in with their condolences. After all the mourners had gone, Janki sat alone in her room staring at the whitewashed wall, unblinking. Devi walked in to quietly sit by her.

"Finality of the event is more painful than any separation before," Janki spoke softly.

Devi squeezed her hand.

Light began to fade as the day drew to its end. Silence hung heavy in the darkened room where two women sat holding hands.

"My husband was a gentle man," Janki's voice was a whisper and then her body shook as tears escaped unblinking eyes. Devi engulfed her in a strong hold while Janki reconciled to her new state. Her journey had started as a daughter, transitioned to wife and then elevated to mother. Now, as a widow all she had was her children.

Virendra took the next train out to Delhi to catch a plane for Kandhar. A son must perform all the rituals for proper passing of the soul and this son was going to get to Kandhar fast. After the cremation and the fourth day ritual, Virendra decided to sell the house in Kandhar, and having completed all the property transactions and the 12th day ritual, he returned to Dehra Dun. All connection with Kandhar and Quetta broken, Khatri family looked to the future as Indians with no ties outside their boundaries.

The married Khatri sisters returned to their respective homes having mourned the father they never knew well enough to love. While life in Janki's household returned to routine, Dimple and Ruhi, with Narendra's children kept a cheerful atmosphere, bringing smiles to forlorn faces. From her petite days as of a two-year old, Ruhi blossomed into a healthy five-year old, while Dimple matured into docile pre-teen.

One weekend, after a long gap in the couple's excursions, Virendra decided to take his wife on a trip to Mussourie, leaving Dimple and Ruhi in Janki's care. The car trip from the valley into the mountain was just about an hour, but unforeseen obstructions were known to block the paths up the winding roads where monsoons could bring mudslides or flash floods. Summers brought multitudes of buses belching with tourists from the Capital or other hot, dense areas and winters brought families of the various boarding school students for their holidays to crowd in the ice arenas and teahouses.

It was toward the end of the summer that Virendra and Devi drove up in a taxi. With each winding turn, Devi looked away from the sheer drop at the edge of the road. The driver swerved expertly around sharp bends avoiding the flimsy barriers by the edge. Occasionally, a few pebbles rolled down from one side of the mountain, landing close to the vehicle or on top of it, creating a sharp tap. The earth was loose around the cliff with years of erosion and fewer trees as they clambered higher. Just as their car managed a particularly sharp turn, a fast moving van headed straight at them with horns blaring, lights flashing, and Beatles music booming from the tape deck. Devi clung to Virendra as they saw the black Volkswagen jammed with young boys in white shirts, navy sweaters and striped ties loosened around their collars. The Fiat's astute driver steered the vehicle inward to avoid being thrown off the cliff, stopping just before hitting the mountainside.

The two passengers and the driver breathed a sigh of relief as the van passed untouched, continuing on the wrong side of the road. Just as the driver was about to back the car out to get back on the road, a bus filled with tourists and carrying a burden of luggage on its roof cruised down the blind turn. Devi and Virendra's Fiat did not have a chance to move out of the way, never seeing the approaching monster. All they heard was a loud bang, metal against metal, screeching of tires and the slide down the long cliff, racing with the pebbles and rocks, as they made their way into the ravine below. After a few somersaults, the car paused on a thick branch before plunging into a free fall into the river.

That day, the monsoon rain came pelting angrily from the sky bringing with it a raging river gushing into the valley. Janki stood still in the center of the courtyard, drenched under the torrents, her tears melding with the water from the sky, her ears red with rage, her heart throbbing with self-pity. Her insides screamed wanting to lash out at the world - a 64-year old mother is not supposed to mourn for her adult children. A tired old woman, having already shed too many tears, now her fountain was drying up. She watched the orphaned girls, too young to lose their parents, and looked up to the sky into the plummeting water to ask a furious question – why? She knew there would be no answer and she had to take charge, once again. Walking back into her dry room, she put her hands on Dimple and Ruhi's heads as they blissfully slept.

Learning that their parents had passed on into another world, Dimple and Ruhi disappeared into their own world. Dimple took over the role of mother for her little sister while Ruhi, who eventually stopped asking when their parents would return, continued to follow her big sister around like her shadow. Playtime and story time continued with cousins, friends and with Janki, and as Dimple stepped into womanhood, she spent more quiet times alone with Janki. The two talked for hours – Janki about life in Pakistan and Afghanistan, and Dimple sharing her daily activities at school or outside. One day, Dimple reached up to Janki's hand and pointing to the knuckle she asked, "Ammaji, what is this?"

"It is an imprint of 'Om'," Janki responded.

Dimple ran her finger over it. Still looking down closely, she inquired, "is it painted?"

Shaking her head Janki let her hand relax under Dimple's gentle touch, "it's permanent."

"Was it painful to draw?" Dimple asked.

"As if thousands of needles were pinching."

Dimple pondered for a moment, "how old were you?"

"I was a little girl in Khushab, with my parents."

"Who did this?"

"It was at the spring *mela*, in a carnival," Janki looked up with a smile, "at the bazaar in the city where my parents lived."

"Why did you get it if it hurt?"

"My parents wanted me to get this and…" Janki turned her hand over pulling up the sleeve of her shirt to show the inside of her arm, "and also this."

Dimple read the words scripted and asked, "who's Jeevani?"

"Me."

"But isn't your name Janki?" she asked, puzzled.

"In those days when girls got married, they were given new names by their new family. My parents gave me the name Jeevani and my in-laws changed it to Janki."

In this moment of revelation, Janki saw scenes from all the events in her life flash before her. Images of people, of places, of events replayed in front of her eyes. She thought of all the lands she had traversed, the ties she had made and broken, all the tears she had shed. She remembered the sad goodbyes, the abrupt endings, the farewells without words.

Her one driving force through all the trying times was her duty to her children and she reveled in the comfort and joy of her family. She reassured herself that the measure of a parent's success is the happiness of her children, feeling sad that Ram Lal chose not to be a part in this contentment but died alone, unhappy and a broken man.

Running a hand over Dimple, she rejoiced in the solace of being surrounded by the love and affection of her grandchildren, the respect and care from her own children. She knew that by choosing her children, she had chosen the right path.

CHAPTER 42

2006

Taara turned toward the sound of the playing children as she waited for her luggage at Jinnah International airport in Karachi. She recalled the tearful Payal she left behind rolled up in their special shawl. A fleeting regret trailed her strong desire to find her husband. At any cost, and for any length of time, Taara was going to stay in Pakistan. For Omar. Payal was safely away from this chaos with two grandmothers to dote and watch over her. Taara had to focus on finding her husband and made a deliberate decision not to be distracted by maternal pangs.

Zahira and Khaled received her graciously as she exited the terminal. Khaled was taller than what Taara had imagined, towering over his petite wife. He sported a thick beard matching his light brown hair. Dressed in a black *salwar kameez*, he projected a regal image. When he spoke, however, his soft voice undermined that perception. Khaled slid into the front seat next to the driver as the women sat comfortably in the back. The 40-minute drive to the upscale neighborhood of Clifton passed in a haze.

If Taara had looked outside, she would have observed how similar Pakistan and India were. She would have assessed the likeness of the faces with the same dark features and skin shades from milky coffee to caramel to mocha to chocolate. She would have enjoyed noticing the trendy attire coalescing western and *desi* styles in all the colors of the rainbow and beyond. Her concern would have shown if she had seen the sad faces of the street-children running out to clean the car windows at red lights, seemingly insignificant with the enormous high-rises behind them. If she were paying attention, her nose would have caught the familiar whiff of meaty kababs, ocean air, and *desi* sweat. Even the spoken language was analogous. Inside the confines of the Mazda sedan, Taara remained locked in her thoughts and worries, responding only to her immediate company.

After a few silent minutes, Taara turned to her sister-in-law and regarded her diminutive form. She was dressed in a trendy *salwar-kameez*, splashing hues of lime green and yellow. Her hair was fashionably cut with shoulder-length layers, framing an oval face with bright eyes widened with the help of thick mascara. This was the first time Taara had observed Zahira and she realized how similar some of her features were to Omar's. Taara remembered the mouse-like face of a scared girl peeping out from behind her mother on the day when Omar was thrown out of his parents' home. She also recalled the raging face with big eyes of his father and shuddered.

"Where's Abbu?" Taara asked.

"He's in Quetta. We'll see him soon, when we get there." After a short pause, Zahira added, "He has not been himself."

"What do you mean?"

"He has taken it harder than we thought he would; about *bhai*. You know, under the circumstances."

Taara nodded and asked, "what else can you tell me about the investigation on Omar's whereabouts?"

Khaled put his arm on the back of the driver's seat, half-turning to look at the two women, "nothing new."

Taara dug into her handbag removing the letter from Omar. She turned it over and showed it to Khaled and Zahira.

Khaled raised his bushy eyebrows, "so this must be the note you mentioned in your phone call. Abbu is out of his mind about it. He says he needs to see it to believe it."

"How soon can we leave?" Taara asked.

"I have train tickets for the Baluchistan Express for tomorrow evening, we should be in Quetta by 10 the next morning," Khaled related.

"Hope you don't mind the overnight trip. The AC sleeper should be comfortable," Zahira added.

"I'm sorry for causing all this trouble for you both…" Taara started.

"Don't say that *baaji*." Zahira interjected, "It's not just your husband but my brother who is missing… or rather ki…d…napped as this letter says," Zahira choked.

Taara squeezed the younger woman's hand while both stared ahead, each afraid to blink.

The train ride from Karachi to Rohri Junction was unlike any Taara had experienced. The climb up the mountain via the 100km long Bolan Pass, through tunnels and high bridges, she observed the most astounding view. Taara wished her trip had been under different circumstances when Omar and Payal could be with her to enjoy this journey. Still on American time, she struggled to keep her heavy lids from dropping until it was too dark to see outside. It did not take long for the rocking motion to lull her into a deep sleep.

Taara was completely oblivious when at Rohri junction, around midnight, the express jerked to a stop. Passengers disembarked to wait or run for a connection on different lines. Those carrying on to Quetta got off to stretch their legs or savor a midnight snack from the *balti ghosh* or *chai walla* stands. After a half-hour halt, the train chugged its uphill journey through the mountainous terrain.

Quetta station was a mishmash of human bodies, wrapped in blankets or shawls, scurrying from one platform to another.

Taara and Zahira followed Khaled over the footbridges, through the throng of people, dodging the tea vendors with their flowing vats and kettle. Outside the railway station Khaled led them toward their waiting car. It would take them through the crowded bazaars of the capital of Baluchistan, to the old neighborhood in the heart of the city, to Jamila's home. Taara sat fidgeting throughout the ride, recalling her trip into a similar valley in India - Dehra Dun. These memories intensified when she met Omar's *dadi* and tears, under control until then, gushed out in rivulets as Taara hugged the older woman.

"*Beti*, I don't know how this happened. May *Allah* watch over him," Jamila lamented.

"*Dadi*, we'll find him. Don't worry," Taara consoled her.

"Yes, we will," a voice roared from the doorway.

Taara looked up and saw the silhouette of her father-in-law. She walked over to him and raised her hand in greeting, "Assallam-o-Aliakum, Abbu."

"May Allah be with you, *beti*," he responded, "how is Payal?"

Taara gave him a short update on his granddaughter and quickly moved to more urgent matters, "Abbu, I have a letter from Omar."

Khaled brought out the "S.O.S." note from Omar. After reading it three times, Haider carefully folded the note and tucked it in the inner pocket of his *kameez* shirt. As the elder to the family, he slashed out orders to his nephews and cousins to organize another search party. The focus was changing to the search of a victim of kidnapping. He then ordered Khaled to join him at the police station.

After two days of no leads, Taara sat in agitated frustration, in the segregation of the *zanaana* women's quarters, protected from the outside world. Quetta was not a city where women roamed free and unescorted. She had spotted some on their drive from the railway station, specks of *burkha*-clad women on the streets, standing out like lost vessels in a sea of bearded faces. There was no question of Taara stepping out, scouting the streets or the bazaars in quest of her husband. The men of the house assigned to that task investigated while patient women sat, waited, prayed, did household chores, consoled each other, and shed quiet tears.

On one such day of waiting, Taara sat huddled over sheets of paper and a half-written letter to Payal. Feeling a shadow cross over her bent head, she looked up staring right into the bulging eyes of her father-in-law. Setting her letter aside, she sat up urgently making sure her head was covered with the *dupatta* scarf. His gaze turned softer as he handed some folded sheets to her. She glanced down and noticed they were the sheets she had brought with her - Omar's last letter to her.

In his controlled guttural voice Haider said, "*beti*. I think I owe you an apology."

Taara lowered her gaze and mumbled, "abbu, elders don't owe apologies to their children."

"I read Omar's letter and talked to my mother about what happened here, in this very house, almost 60 years ago. My prejudice was without merit."

The two stood facing each other in silence. Taara's lowered gaze followed the movement of her finger coiling around the *dupatta* end.

A few seconds passed before Haider spoke, "I am happy to welcome you into the Kakkar family. The friendship of our forefathers has developed into a family."

Taara's voice cracked as she responded, "I am grateful for your blessings." She sniffled and continued, "I am honored to be part of the Kakkar family and... and... Omar will be so happy to hear that... when we find him." Then she looked up, "we will find him, won't we?"

"Yes, we will. Have faith." He ran his hand over her head as she rejoiced in receiving sincere blessings from Omar's father.

After Haider walked out to tend to search duties, Jamila made herself visible with a glowing expression. She had witnessed the momentous scene between her son and Taara.

"You have done what even his mother couldn't do all these years. You have Janki's formidable blood running in your veins."

Taara looked up, still recovering from the encounter.

As days turned into a week and then two, Taara waited. Khaled made plans to return to his work back in Karachi while Zahira decided to stay back. One day before Khaled's departure, at Zahira's suggestion, Khaled offered to drive the two women to the outskirts of Quetta and to the famous Hanna Lake. Zahira wanted to show Taara the panoramic view of the fruit basket city during the time of blossoms.

Taara sat quietly by the lake nursing her thoughts of Omar. She recalled their first meeting in the Union and his undying support and presence after her parents' demise. A smile crossed her lips remembering their happiest moment together at Payal's birth. Returning to the present, she could not help but admire the greenish blue tint in the horizon. She looked at the far end of the lake marveling at the reflection of brownish, rugged mountains in its crystal-clear water. Golden fish swam right up to the water's edge, as if to admire her.

Leaving the mid-afternoon lake behind, they drove out on the road toward the mountains they had crossed to get into the valley. It was a beautiful, sunny day with a nip in the air blowing fresh aroma from the young tulip blooms. Pomegranate and pistachio trees boasted bold foliage ready to sprout their fruits of abundance. Zahira pointed to an unfamiliar collection of branches and Khaled explained it was the *Garma* tree, getting ready to bear the unique variety of melon. The valley was celebrating the season with its lush, colorful blooms and sprouts. New life was growing all around her, but Taara's heart wept for the one who was not with her.

Throughout the journey out of the city, the three talked about Omar and other avenues they could take in their search effort. As the sun started its descent behind the craggy mountains of Quetta, Khaled turned the car around for the home stretch. They approached the city in a dusky haze down a straight, tree-lined road. Zahira pointed out how the trees stood at attention, as if waiting for their marching orders. A smile escaped Taara's lips with her gaze fixed at the mountain range ahead. They seemed to be flaunting an inferno as the setting sun glided down their folds. The city dwelling extended up the valley plains into the ridged terraces of the mountainside, their lights beginning to sparkle in the distance, like dancing fireflies. Again, Taara reflected on a similar show of Mount Mussourie in India of bright lights or lone, darting flickers.

The last time Taara had visited India was to visit Janki. Realizing her great-grandmother was no longer living, Taara felt a sudden pang of remorse. Back at the house in her sullen state, Taara ventured toward Jamila's room. She made herself comfortable on the only chair while she waited for Omar's grandmother to finish her prayers.

"Did you know *Ammaji* well?" Taara asked as soon as Jamila rose from her prayer mat.

"Janki? No I did not." Jamila sat on her bed as she extricated a silver miniature box from under her pillow, "I have heard a lot of things about her."

"What kind of things?" Taara leaned over in her chair.

"She was one of few women of her time who could read and write and made sure her daughters got a good education." Jamila cracked the betel nut in her palm using the nutcracker as she continued, "Haider's *dadi* always talked about how Janki brought up all those children with a strong hand and everyone we knew had tremendous respect for her."

"Did you ever meet her?" Taara wondered.

"Once at my wedding. Haider's *dadi*, Ammi, was very fond of your family. She always said that Janki was her first daughter-in-law. I was the second." Jamila folded the cracked nut in the betel leaf before stuffing her mouth with it.

Taara pondered for a while before approaching the delicate subject, "it must have been hard on Abbu's *dadi* when... when the...

murder..."

Jamila shifted the stuffed betel leaf to one corner of her mouth and spoke in a muffled voice, "Ammi was devastated. She considered Rajinder as if he were her own grandson. Ali, well no matter how he was, he was still her flesh and blood. Holding that heavy heart of hers she told the truth." Jamila looked at Taara, "What mother does that? Send her son to his death."

Taara suddenly felt a pang of guilt for having suggested that Omar visit Pakistan. She sunk back in her chair.

Jamila continued, "Ammi didn't live very long after that, Allah rest her soul. She did what was right." Jamila leaned forward, "I see a lot of her righteousness and devotion in Omar."

Taara half smiled, "let's hope that also helps him get out of whatever he is in now."

After Khaled's departure, another week passed without development. Omar's father went in and out of the house meeting men of questionable trades, high and low-ranking officials, street vendors – anyone to supply a lead. He left no rock unturned, no avenue unexplored, no person unquestioned. The distress and realization of accepting defeat showed in his wrinkled form and haggard body. His quiet manner was foreign to even Zahira. Taara observed her father-in-law to be at war with himself. It was a battle he had to fight alone in order to come to terms with his past decisions and present circumstances.

Taara, on the other hand, had to deal with her own frustrations of being stuck in the house, feeling helpless, weak, and even ill. She missed Payal and Omar, and was deathly afraid for him. So she decided to take a bold step.

Despite the unwritten rule of the society, Taara one day sneaked out of the house toward the bazaar. Just the fact that she was a woman walking on the streets of Quetta, unescorted, dressed in respectable clothes, she stood out like a baby bird without her flock. No amount of veiling would hide her from prying eyes. Asking beggars or vendors, she found her way to the Kandhari

Bazaar, where she decided to find the shop close to which Omar's car had stopped. She, as a lone woman, was looking for a penny lost in sand, surrounded by hyenas and wolves.

Scanning the busy street for gift shops with Baluchi products, her only clue, Taara avoided the ogling gazes. Wherever she turned, there were shops exhibiting traditional wares, with their mirror-work embroidery and useless trinkets. The stalls were decorated with lights and metallic streamers. She caught the whiff of fresh Afghani *kababs*, saw groups of men in *salwar-kameez* and red embroidered caps huddled around a corner tea stall, sipping sweet tea over grave conversation. Moving from shop to shop in hopes of finding a sign, any indication, or inkling that Omar was there, Taara prodded along. His note had said he could still hear street sounds.

She crossed the street running from one shop to the other, dodging cyclists, mobile vendors, compact Suzukis. Amid crossing, out of nowhere a quiet procession of sorts passed through the bazaar. Hordes of people poured into the street in some kind of celebration. The men from the tea stall joined in, even the other shoppers became part of the procession. The crowd moved in a trancelike state, and Taara found herself caught in the middle.

A lone woman in a crowd of men, surrounded by so many people, set off the age-old fear of being lost in the crowd. Instinctively, she shut her eyes and froze in the middle of the thoroughfare. She covered her ears drowning out the sounds. Oblivious to her whereabouts, Taara felt her legs moving with the group walking toward the *muezzin's* sobbing call to prayer. Surrounded by chants, her inner voice drowned out. A whimper escaped her lips, "Omar... Omar... Omar." An image appeared in front of her, striding backwards in tune with her step. She knew this form, had seen this face. Taara concentrated, exerting to recognize the blurred vision. A young voice emerged from a wrinkled face, the whiteness of its eyes staring at Taara. The familiar *Khushabi* accent projected from the wise one, "Taara *puttar.*" Ammaji's voice resonated, drowning out everything. Taara lifted her hand to touch, grabbing only thin air.

She called out, "Ammaji. Help me. My husband is lost."

"*Puttar.* Go back home. Go to your children. They need you."

"But my husband. I can't leave without Omar."

"Your child is lost without you. You can't help one lost love, but you can help the other. Remember, you are a mother."

"But how can I go knowing he is out here, suffering."

"So are your children. Payal is suffering without her father and her mother. She needs you more now than ever. It is your duty as mother and woman to keep the family together. Go home."

The voice faded as the image disappeared. Taara called desperately, "Ammaji... Ammaji".

She stood alone on the cross junction of two Bazaars - Kandhari and Liaquat. She turned around to look down Iqbal Road, the one she had traversed. She then looked to the sides, down Liaquat road. Unsure of the path to go down, Taara remained irresolute at the crossing. The procession had reached its destination for the quiet prayers for respects to the Prophet's birth and death anniversary.

She looked forward, down the length of Iqbal road she had not covered. A little girl in rags, Payal's age, ran across the street without purpose. Taara noted the deep-set pain in the child's eyes, the familiar loneliness in her manner. A shopkeeper yelled at the child to clean the entrance to his stall. The child grabbed a sweeper bigger than her, and set to work. Taara walked toward the girl, a single thought taking over. *Payal needs me.* Other thoughts crowded in her mind. *I need Omar.* She picked up her pace, unmindful of the attentive stares. The voice in her head became louder and she felt her head would explode. *Payal needs me.* She brought her hands to her ears but the voice carried on. *I can't live without Omar.* Her legs felt fluid. The little girl sweeping was gone. Taara felt a hand on her shoulder just as the world around began to twirl. She felt her body collapse into strong arms.

Taara opened her eyes to a white ceiling and recognized the floral curtains waving in the breeze from the open windows. Her eyes turned toward the doorway where a silhouette blocked the bright light from the courtyard into the darkened room. She called out, "Omar."

The figure entered the room looming over her. She looked up with mild disappointment at the grim face of her father-in-law. Taara noticed some movement around the far side of the room. Turning to look down the length of her legs, she saw Zahira sitting on a rug. Her *dupatta* covered her head, tugged behind her ears, hands cupped in praying position.

Haider Khan was the first one to speak, "how are you feeling *beti?*"

Shame-faced Taara replied, "I'm sorry for causing all this trouble."

"I'm just glad you're safe. If something had happened to you, I don't know how we would have shown our face to our granddaughter."

Taara let a tear slide down her temple.

Zahira came around to sit on the bed and held Taara's hand. Taara turned to her, "my heart tells me that Omar is still here." She reached for the end of her *dupatta* to dab her eyes.

Zahira looked up to her father, shifting her gaze back to Taara, "I know *bhabhi*. Inshah-Allah, we will find *Lala*. God willing, he will be with us soon."

"Wherever Omar is, Taara *beti*, your presence here will do no good," everyone turned toward the door watching the owner of the voice shuffle up the two steps to enter the room. Jamila gripped the doorframe tight before walking over the threshold. Haider stepped aside to help his mother but she shooed him away out of the room. Jamila directed even Zahira to leave.

When they were alone, Taara watched Omar's grandmother settle her weathered form down on the side of the bed. As she slid up to sit, making room for Jamila to sit comfortably, Taara mumbled, "*dadi*, I will feel so helpless so far away."

"You can do more for him in Umrica than you can over here. Payal is not only far from her father but also her mother, the two people who have been the center of her universe."

Guilty tears slid down Taara's cheeks as she sat up on the bed, recalling Janki's image in the bazaar.

"Then there is the one yet to come. You have to be cheerful to stay healthy for your baby."

Taara stared at Jamila. "What one yet to come?" she finally managed.

"Didn't Zahira tell you? B*eti*, you are with child."

"I thought I was feeling queasy and tired from missing Omar and traveling. It all makes sense now," she spoke as if to herself.

Jamila smiled and Taara smiled back with mixed emotions.

Long after the bright sun had set, her room lay in darkness. Sounds of barking dogs and the night guard's sporadic whistles entered the open window. A fresh breeze danced upon the floral curtain. Taara stared into space, one hand resting on her belly. Her heart was leaping with joy on the news of her pregnancy but her eyes sank in sadness. She wanted to be happy but was afraid to allow herself the thrill of joy. The thought that part of Omar was growing inside her exhilarated her, but at the same time left a hollow feeling in her gut. Taara wanted to share this joy with Omar. Instead, she had to carry this burden of happiness alone. Laughter and tears intermingled on her face with no one to comfort her. She had lost all her pillars.

Taara sat up on her bed looking out of the window into the overcast sky. Misty eyes looked upon her belly and spoke to her unborn child, "nothing has really changed. Both my feet are still on two separate boats on the same lake." She sighed and stood up from her bed, walking toward the window, "only the lake is not serene anymore."

Taara stood for a long time. Her hair, teased by the wind, vexed her ears. Her tear-stained cheeks reddened from the cool mountain air. She wrapped her shawl around her shoulders to absorb its warmth and to feel the familiar comfort. "I am afraid that my children will fall in the water with me," she told her baby yet-to-be-born.

As the wind swept the clouds away, Taara glimpsed a few twinkling stars. Suddenly, she found herself bathed in a flood of light. A full moon had emerged high in the Quetta sky. She looked out of the window, holding her head up. Soon her eyes widened. Taara held her belly again and proclaimed, "I am the mother ship now and it is my duty to keep my fleet from drifting apart." She stood up straight, "I cannot fall in the water. I will not fall into the water no matter how choppy it gets. I am, after all, Janki's great-granddaughter."

EPILOGUE

A dog crosses the street scanning for moving vehicles, his nose guiding him to the butcher shop. Suddenly, a large shadow appears on the road before him. He looks up to find a horse drawing a carriage coming his way, and he straggles to avoid getting trampled, his stride becoming erratic. In confusion, he scurries hither and thither getting nowhere. The horse avoids him but the carriage passes over him, large cartwheels missing him by an inch. Luck has been on his side. Kababs forgotten, the dog heads back to the street he calls home just as a large procession of humans takes over the street.

The year is 2005, the day of Ashura. A young, Muslim man walks across the street, whistling softly, while the driver changes a flat tire. A mild delay to his journey out of Quetta but he is confident he will catch the train in time. There is no sign of the Muharram celebration other than the choppy presence of official-looking armed men, ready to react at any sign of disturbance. The previous year the Shi'ite procession was attacked by a handful of Sunni troublemakers resulting in 14 mutilated bodies, including those of the bombers.

Omar whistles as he makes his way to the shop at the quiet corner of Iqbal road. He had spotted the perfect trinket for his three-year old girl - he picks up the silver anklets with its tiny bells chiming in his clasp. He looks up expectantly at the shopkeeper and declares the he wants two pairs - a child and an adult size. While he waits for the stalky owner to fish out the second pair, Omar contemplates the surprising turn of events, the new information he acquired from his grandmother. He pads his left breast pocket where his letter to Taara rests. He is happy. He is happy to find the connection between Taara's great-grandfather – Ram Lal, and his own grandfather – Halif and happy to learn of the loving relationship between the two families. He is happy to conclude that his own father, Haider Khan, will learn of the events leading to the murder of Taara's granduncle, Rajendra, and recognize his own folly. Omar is happy that Taara will finally be welcomed with respect into the Kakkar family, reuniting the two lines forever. Omar chimes the anklets in his hands absently.

Lost in blissful reverie, he does not hear the loud procession turning the corner onto his street. He misses the shopkeeper's shouts as he hands over the second pair of the *payal*. The loud and bloody procession moves behind Omar, separating him from the broken car. Before he can respond to the shopkeeper about the second set of anklets, the first pair still in his hand, Omar is greeted by a man. He knows this man - the taxi driver he met on his first day. A fleeting thought crosses Omar's mind, *this was no chance meeting*. Before the thought could take shape and Omar could excuse himself to the safety of his vehicle, he feels a hard knock on the back of his head. His last vision is of Taara's sad face and Payal's expectant eyes.

A few hours later, Omar opens his eyes, feeling a large bump on his nape, his head pounding. He feels weak but manages to sit up. Looking around his environs, he determines he is in a small warehouse. He can hear street sounds, the agonizing cries from procession participants as they self-inflict wounds on their persons. He struts toward the lone egress and peeks out from a small slit.

The rest of the room is engulfed in darkness, except for a hint of light permeating through the bottom of what must be a door. His kidnappers must have expected him to be knocked out for a long time for they did not bother to tie him up. Omar gropes for an opening, a way out, with no luck. He fumbles in his pockets in hope of an instrument to open the *roshan daan* egress. The opening is not wide enough for him. Omar finds the letter in his pocket, addressed and stamped. He scratches a quick note in the back, seals the envelope and drops it through the egress. If he is lucky, some kind-hearted soul will put it in the post. His only hope.

The taxi driver comes in first, followed by a large *pathan* looming over the tiny fellow. Blindfolding and tying up their captive, they drag him into a truck, where Omar is forgotten for hours. He feels the bumps, the twists, and turns. What must be partway through the journey, Omar is fed and offered water. In darkness and crisp air, the party arrives at a rundown shack. Omar can hear sheep and children. After several days of being locked up in the shack, Omar is dragged into the back of the truck again. His constant wiggling and fumbling has left his tied-up wrists bruised and bleeding. His aches from the rough handling and the bumpy rides are too numerous to count. He is weak from minimal food and water.

The second leg of the journey is jerkier. The kidnappers are speeding, venturing dangerous turns. Missing a narrow bend, the truck swerves out of control and rolls over down a cliff. Omar is thrown far off into a bushy area, and by now, his ties are looser. With free hands, unfolding the blind, he takes account of his surroundings. By the terrain and the mountains, he determines he could be in Afghanistan. Guided by the sun, Omar goes deeper into the country avoiding the mountains that lead back into Pakistan.

His journey to freedom is long and hard. Traveling by night in the chilly mountain winds, resting for days with do-gooders scattered in the countryside, Omar arrives in Kandhar.

His hope is the U.S. base. He must find the Americans and

convince them that he is an American citizen. This takes months while he scrounges to stay alive. Finally, after fingerprints are matched, a medical exam conducted and Omar has recuperated, an official airplane flies him back home - to the land of the free.

As long as he lives - for he will live long as his name Omar suggests - he will not forget the image of Taara on his homecoming. Amidst tears of joy and relief, they attempt an awkward embrace around her swollen belly with Payal squeezed somewhere between them.

BELA KAUL

ABOUT THE AUTHOR

Bela Kaul lived the first 10 years of her life in Dehra Dun, India surrounded by stories her grandmother weaved. She spent her teenage years in Hong Kong and has been living in USA for the past 29 years with her husband of 28 years. They have one daughter.

BELA KAUL

GLOSSARY

Aadhi ghar waali	half wife (jokingly)	Hindi
Aapa	older sister	Urdu
Abbu	father	Urdu
Abbujan	father (with love)	Urdu
Achar	pickle	Hindi
Amma	mother	Hindi
Ammaji	mother (with respect)	Hindi
Ammi	mother	Urdu
Angan	courtyard	Hindi
Angithi	coal burning food warmer	Hindi
Annar	pommegranate fruit	Hindi
Ashram	religious retreat	Hindi
Assallam-o-Aliakum	greeting	Urdu
Baaji	older sister	Urdu
Babu	sir	Hindi
Balti gosht	meat dish	Urdu
Baraat	groom's procession	Hindi
Basmati	rice	Hindi/Urdu
Bauji	Father (with respect)	Hindi
Begum	wife	Urdu
Beta	son	Hindi/Urdu
Beti	daughter	Hindi/Urdu
Bhabhi	sister in-law (brother's wife)	Hindi
Bhai	brother	Hindi/Urdu
Bhaijan	brother (with love)	Urdu
Bhainji	sister (with respect)	Hindi
Bibi	madam	Urdu
Bidai	bride's sendoff	Hindi
Boondiya	yoghurt snack	Hindi

Beyond Boundaries

Bollywood	Indian version of Hollywood	International
Chaarpayi	bed strung with ropes	Hindi
Chai walla	tea vendor	Hindi/Urdu
Chakki	stone grinder	Hindi
Chirag	light	Hindi
Choorra	special wedding bangles	Hindi
Chulla	stove	Punjabi
Chunni	scarf	Hindi
Cuchumber	mixed salad	Hindi
Daal	lentil	Hindi/Urdu
Dada	paternal grandfather	Hindi/Urdu
Dadi	maternal grandmother	Hindi/Urdu
Desi	people from Indian Sub-continent	Hindi/Urdu
Duphli	drum	Hindi
Didi	older sister	Hindi
Divan	day bed	Hindi/Urdu
Diwali	Hindu festival of lights	Hindi
Diya	clay lamp	Hindi
Dohli	bride's sendoff	Hindi
Dubba	box	Hindi
Dupatta	scarf	Urdu
Furlong	1/8 of a mile	Hindi
Ghaghra	long skirt	Hindi
Ghazals	songs of poetry	Urdu
Gitte	jacks	Hindi/Punjabi
Gobi	cauliflower	Hindi
Godd bharai	baby shower	Hindi
Gopians	maidens	Hindi
Gulegutch	white wash	Pashto
Gulli-danda	game with sticks	Hindi
Gurudwara	Sikh temple	Punjabi
Halwai	sweetmeat vendor	Hindi

Hijab	head scarf	Urdu
Holi	Hindu festival of colors	Hindi
Hooka	smoking pipe	Hindi/Urdu
Jalebi	dessert in sugar syrup	Hindi
Ji	yes with respect	Hindi/Urdu
Jijaji	brother-in-law (sister's husband)	Hindi
Jumna	great river in India	Hindi
Kabab	meat dish	Hindi/Urdu
Kaju	cashew nut	Hindi/Urdu
Kaka	father	Hindi/Urdu
Kameez	shirt	Urdu
Kandhari biradri	Hindu community in Kandhar	Hindi
Karai	deep fryer	Hindi/Urdu
Karakuli	Afghani cap	Pashto
Karvann	sweet Kandhari dish	Kandhari
Khaala	aunt (mother's sister)	Urdu
Khush	happy	Hindi/Urdu
Ki	what?	Punjabi
Kishmish	raisin	Hindi/Urdu
Kula	cap	Hindi/Urdu
Kundan	semi-precioud opaque crystal	Hindi
Kurti	ethnic shirt	Hindi/Urdu
Kuwatta	forth	Pashto
Ladke walle	groom's family	Hindi/Urdu
Landhi	whole lamb delicacy in Quetta	Pashto
Latthi	stick	Hindi
Laxmi	Hindu goddess of wealth	Hindi
Ma	mother	Hindi
Maati	mother	Punjabi
Maika	mother's home	Hindi
Mandir	Hindu temple	Hindi
Mangal sutr	Hindu wedding string	Hindi

Beyond Boundaries

Manji	bed strung with ropes	Punjabi
Masi	aunt (mother's sister)	Hindi
Mausaji	uncle (mother's sister's husband)	Hindi
Mehfil	gathering, party	Urdu
Mehndi	henna	Hindi/Urdu
Mela	carnival	Hindi/Urdu
Mithai	sweetmeat	Hindi
Mohalla	neighborhood	Hindi/Urdu
Moochh	moustache	Hindi/Urdu
Moodda	low stool	Hindi/Urdu
Muezzin	chosen person in mosque to lead call to prayer	Urdu
Mutton pulao	rice dish with goat meat	Hindi/Urdu
Naan	clay oven baked bread	Hindi/Urdu
Namaaz	Islamic prayer	Urdu
Namaste	greetings	Hindi
Nana	maternal grandfather	Hindi
Nani	maternal grandmother	Hindi
Nihari	Pakistani beef dish	Urdu
Oy	Heh!	Hindi/Urdu
Pahji	brother	Punjabi
Paisa	money, coins	Hindi
Pajeb	anklet	Hindi
Pakora	fritters	Hindi/Urdu
Pallu	end of a sari over the shoulder	Hindi
Pandit	Hindu priest	Hindi
Papad	Indian snack	Hindi
Parathas	stuffed flat bread	Hindi/Urdu
Pashmina	shawl made from pashmina wool	Hindi/Urdu
Pathani	Person from Pashtoon tribe	Hindi/Urdu
Pathani suit	ethnic shirt/pant attire of Pathans	Hindi/Urdu
Pattoo	oversize shawl for men	Kandhari

BELA KAUL

Payal	anklet	Urdu
Pitthu	stones and ball game	Hindi
Postman	mailman	Hindi/Urdu
Phabi	sister-in-law (brother's wife)	Punjabi
Praji	brother	Punjabi
Puttar	son, child	Punjabi
Razai	quilt	Hindi
Rishta	relation	Hindi/Urdu
Roghni naan	Afghani bread	Pashto
Roti	flat bread	Hindi/Urdu
Roshan daan	egress window	Hindi
Saab	sir	Hindi/Urdu
Saali	sister-in-law (wife's sister)	Hindi
Safedi	white wash	Hindi
Sajji	leg of lamb delicacy in Quetta	Pashto
Salwar	loose ethnic pants	Hindi/Urdu
Salwar-kameez	ethnic shirt & pants	Hindi/Urdu
Samosa	triangular snack	Hindi/Urdu
Sangali	coal burning heater/warmer	Urdu
Sangeet	song	Hindi
Sharara	divided long skirt	Urdu
Shehnai	wind instrument played at weddings	Hindi/Urdu
Sher	poem, couplets	Urdu
Shop-walla	shop vendor	Hindi/Urdu
Sindhur	vermilion	Hindi
Staapu	hop scotch	Hindi
Suit	ethnic shirt & pants	Hindi
Thaali	steel plate	Hindi
Tikka	jewel hanging in middle of the forehead	Hindi
Tillbare	sesame seed bridal ceremony	Punjabi
Tonga	horse drawn cart	Hindi/Urdu

Tongawalla	horse drawn cart vendor	Hindi/Urdu
Wallaikum-Assallam	return greeting	Urdu
Zanaana	women's room	Urdu
Zari	gold thread embroidery	Hindi/Urdu
Ziddi	stubborn	Hindi/Urdu

Made in the USA
San Bernardino, CA
01 April 2018